Abou[t]

Melanie Schuster st[arted] and believes that's wh[y] in love and romanc[e] fulfillment in writing stories about compelling couples who find true, lasting love in the face of all the obstacles out there. She hopes all of her readers find their true love. If they've already been lucky enough to find love, she hopes that they never forget what it felt like to fall in love.

Born and raised just outside of Toronto, Ontario, **Amy Ruttan** fled the big city to settle down with the country boy of her dreams. After the birth of her second child, Amy was lucky enough to realise her lifelong dream of becoming a romance author. When she's not furiously typing away at her computer, she's a mum to three wonderful children who use her as a personal taxi and chef.

Like any good Southern belle, **Kianna Alexander** wears many hats: doting mama, advice-dispensing sister, and gabbing girlfriend. She's a voracious reader, an amateur seamstress and occasional painter in oils. Chocolate, American history, sweet tea, and Idris Elba are a few of her favourite things. A native of the TarHeel state, Kianna still lives there with her husband, two kids, and a collection of well-loved vintage 80's Barbie dolls.

Summer of Love

Summer of Love: Taking a Chance on Forever

MELANIE SCHUSTER

AMY RUTTAN

KIANNA ALEXANDER

MILLS & BOON

First Published in Great Britain 2021
By Mills & Boon, an imprint of HarperCollins*Publishers* Ltd
1 London Bridge Street, London, SE1 9GF

www.harpercollins.co.uk

HarperCollins*Publishers*
1st Floor, Watermarque Building,
Ringsend Road, Dublin 4, Ireland

ISBN: 978-0-263-30024-6

MIX
Paper from
responsible sources
FSC™ C007454

A CASE FOR ROMANCE

MELANIE SCHUSTER

This one is for all my readers.
You have encouraged me in good times and lifted
me up during bad times and I appreciate every
one of you. Stay blessed and keep reading,
the best is yet to come.

Chapter 1

Pleasure swept over Ayanna like the warm water that was falling on her naked body. Standing under a waterfall in a secluded cove on a Hawaiian beach, her low moan was swallowed by her lover's mouth, the mouth that had taught her more about love and sensuality than she thought possible. A week ago she wouldn't have believed this kind of abandon was possible, but now she knew for a fact that it could happen. It had happened to her over and over again since their getaway had begun. Ramon had shown her passion beyond belief every day and night, and now he was giving it to her again.

"Ramon." She sighed as his hands tightened on her butt, pulling her closer to his rock-hard manhood. The sigh turned into a sudden gasp as he lifted her so she could straddle him. The powerful muscles of his thighs were braced to hold her as she clung to his broad shoulders. He looked into her eyes, and her already rapid heartbeat seemed to triple. The way he was filling her yearning body was enough to make her faint, but the look in his ebony eyes was drowning her in sensation. Her nipples were so huge and hard she thought they might explode, but Ramon took one in his mouth and sucked hard and fierce so that the only explosion possible was the one they shared as—

"Oh, crap!" Ayanna dropped the handheld shower attachment and groaned. Once again, the boys had used up the hot water before she'd gotten through with her shower. The now ice-cold water had jolted her out of her fantasy. It was her favorite one, too, the closest thing she had to any kind of sex life. *Goodbye, Hawaii; hello, Chicago*. She gritted her teeth resolutely and turned off the water before pulling back the shower curtain and reaching for her towel. As much as she didn't want to spend the money, she was going to have to get a new water heater. Her current one couldn't keep up with the demands of her two adolescent sons.

"When they were little, I practically had to stand over them with a stick to get them to bathe. Now they have to spend an hour apiece in the shower like they're mack daddies or something," she muttered. She wrapped herself in a fluffy pink bath sheet and laughed at her reflection in the mirror. "Well, at least they're clean. And who needs a sex life anyway? I've done without this long. I may as well go for the record."

She patted the excess moisture from her short curly hair and added some leave-in conditioner. With her usual efficiency, she dried her body quickly and put on her favorite scented lotion before getting dressed. It was Saturday morning, and she could have slept in a little longer, but she and the boys were going to a house-warming party that afternoon, and there was breakfast to be cooked and errands to be run before they left.

Ten minutes later she was dressed in jeans and a peach T-shirt and heading to the kitchen with a bag of laundry. Alec, the younger of her sons, appeared in the doorway. He took the laundry from her hands and stopped her from entering the sunny kitchen.

"Don't come in yet, Ma. We're making you a surprise," he said with his endearing smile.

"A surprise? For me? What's the occasion?" She returned the smile, flashing dimples that looked just like Alec's.

Cameron's voice answered. "We just wanted to do something nice for you. Okay, it's all done. You can let her in."

Alec stepped aside and bowed as he gestured Ayanna to the table, which was set for three. "Have a seat, Ma. We made breakfast."

"Aww, you guys are so sweet! What did I do to deserve this?" Ayanna had to blink away tears as she looked at the effort they had put forth. There were cloth napkins with napkin rings and even a bouquet of daisies in the middle of the table. And the food smelled and looked wonderful. "You made me waffles?"

"Yeah, Ma. Waffles and turkey bacon and grits and scrambled eggs. And it's all gonna get cold if you don't sit down and eat," he warned.

Ayanna beamed at the two loves of her life as they bowed their heads to say grace. They had always been sweet, cooperative children, and even now that Alec was fourteen and Cameron was sixteen, they were still good kids. The three of them shared a very strong resemblance, with the same rich brown skin and curly black hair. They all had the same big expressive eyes with long lashes, too; but that was all they shared. Her boys were now young men who towered over her. Ayanna was five-foot-six and slender, and she barely came to their shoulders these days.

Their hearty appetites were to blame for some of their growth. They loved to eat so much that they'd begun to learn how to cook so they could fend for themselves when they went off to college. "These are delicious," Ayanna praised. "And so are the grits and eggs. I can't believe you guys did this all by yourselves."

"I made the waffles and bacon, and Alec did the rest. And we're going to clean up the kitchen, too, as soon as you're done."

She obediently finished off her meal between compliments. "This was the best, guys. And to show you how much I appreciate it, we're going out to dinner after church tomorrow."

"Aww, Ma, you don't have to do that," Cameron protested.

"That's right," Alec added. "We didn't do this to get points or anything."

"That's why we're going to Dave & Buster's tomorrow. Just because you didn't expect a reward," Ayanna told them.

With big smiles on their faces, the brothers gave each other high fives. Dave & Buster's was one of their favorite places to go. They liked the games and excitement as much as the food, and since they didn't go out often, it would be a real treat for the family.

They made good on their promise to clean the kitchen, which they did loudly and cheerfully with Kanye's latest CD blasting as they put things back to rights.

Trying to ignore the loud music, Ayanna put a load of clothes in the washing machine. *Maybe I don't have a love life, but what I do have is wonderful,* she thought. *I have two beautiful boys, a nice home, a good job and a future. Life is good, and sex is probably overrated anyway. Can't miss what you haven't had, now can you?*

A few hours later, their weekly errands were done, and they were on their way to the party.

"So, Ma, did Miss Billie do all the work herself on this house?"

"Pretty much," Ayanna answered. "She designed all the changes and supervised everything, but a crew from

Hunter Construction did the actual work. She got her hands on a few things, though."

"Billie" was Billie Phillips Wainwright, one of her bosses at work and a very good friend. She'd been a top runway model until she quit modeling. Now her career was in home renovation with her brother-in-law Nick Hunter. When she married Jason Wainwright he'd surprised her with a big brick mansion, which she had remodeled and refurbished. The party was an open house for all her family and friends to see the end result of her hard work.

When they pulled up in the big circular driveway of Billie and Jason's house, there were several cars parked already. "Alec, will you get the cupcakes, and Cameron, please take that pan of bread pudding for me? Thanks, guys." The food was superfluous because all the women in Billie's family were there and they could all throw down in the kitchen. But Ayanna's Southern roots wouldn't let her go anywhere empty-handed, and her desserts were welcome everywhere because they were too good to be believed.

The recently wed Wainwrights came out of the side door of their new home to welcome Ayanna and the boys. Billie's eyes widened when she saw the packages being carried by Alec and Cameron. "Yummy! You shouldn't have, but I'm glad you did. Whatever it is I know it's good," she said. "Jason, look what Ayanna brought for the party."

Jason had his arm around Billie's slender waist and gave her a soft squeeze before greeting Ayanna with a hug. "I hope it's some German chocolate cake. That last one you made was the bomb. Here, guys, let me take those and you go hang in the back."

Since Jason had inherited some teenage nephews via marriage, Cameron and Alec were more than happy to comply. The backyard with its large patio and the tennis court beckoned, along with the prospect of an afternoon with friends near their age. Billie's big black dog, Sadie, was already in the yard and ran to greet them with her usual happy smile.

Billie held the door open for Jason, and she and Ayanna followed him into the big kitchen with all its new appliances. As Jason put the desserts on the counter, Ayanna grinned at him.

"You're in luck. I made cupcakes. Half are German chocolate and half are red velvet. And there's some pineapple bread pudding, too."

The swinging door between the dining room and the kitchen flew open and a loud voice boomed out. "Did somebody say red velvet? Who said red velvet? Is there seriously some red velvet cake on the premises?"

Ayanna burst into laughter with everyone else except the source of the voice, Billie's older brother, Johnny Phillips.

"Don't play with me. I just came back from the motherland. I've been delayed for hours in every major airport in the world, I may *never* see my other suitcase again and they were talkin' about strip-searching a brother at O'Hare just 'cause they could. So I'm not in the mood to kid around," he said sternly.

The afternoon sun streamed through the windows and glinted off his smooth shaven head. His slightly almond-shaped eyes were intense as his arms were crossed over his bare chest, and he towered over everyone as his expression demanded an immediate answer. Ayanna laughed again.

"Hello, Johnny. It's nice to see you, too," she said pointedly. "Yes, I believe the words *red* and *velvet* were used in the same sentence. Do they have special significance for you?"

Her last words were muffled because Johnny took a couple of steps toward her and gave her a big bear hug that lifted her off the floor. "I'm sorry, Ayanna. I didn't even speak to you, and I'm all over you for your cake. That was just wrong," he said contritely, kissing her on top of her head. "You smell good," he added as he set her down.

"So how was your trip? And how long are you going to be here?" She smiled up at him.

Johnny draped his arm around her shoulders. "I'm not saying another word until I get my fix." He was completely comfortable with his lack of attire, but his younger sister wasn't impressed with his rugged physique.

"Um, I hate to point out the obvious, but why are you in my kitchen half-naked? Where is your shirt?" Billie asked with a frown.

Johnny didn't look embarrassed in the least. He glanced down at his broad chest rippling with muscles and shrugged. "I was on my way to the car to get my stuff when I heard the magic words that made me lose all reason. Are you going to help a brother out or what?" His warm black eyes crinkled in a smile that made Ayanna's knees a little weak, but she ignored the sensation.

"If you put on a shirt, I might let you sample a little somethin'," she teased.

"Sounds like a plan," he agreed and went out the back door, jingling the keys he retrieved from the pocket of his jeans.

She washed her hands at the kitchen sink, and by the time she finished, Johnny was back with a garment bag. "Can I get a taste now? You're not going to make me wait until I go upstairs and put something on, are you?"

Glancing up at him with a grin, she daintily opened the white bakery box and took out a perfect cupcake with a thick, enticing swirl of cream cheese frosting on top.

"Here. Now you've got your fix so you can get dressed and tell me all about your trip to Africa."

"Not yet, woman! Let me savor this before my pop comes in here and we have to fight over it." Johnny had peeled off the cupcake paper and closed his eyes. His strong, even white teeth sank into the pastry, and he devoured it in two bites while moaning like he was in the throes of ecstasy. "Damn, that was good. That tastes like more, 'Yanna. Come on and hook a brother up," he pleaded. "Just one more?"

Ayanna was about to give in to his request when his other sister, Dakota Phillips Hunter, came into the kitchen with her new baby on her shoulder. "Johnny, leave this poor woman alone. What's he trying to get from you, Ayanna?"

By way of answer, Ayanna tipped the box so Dakota could see the cupcakes. "Oh, shoot. Well, you're on your own, girl. Nothing comes between a Phillips man and his need for high-quality sugar in the form of a delicious dessert. The groom's cake at my wedding was red velvet, and he ate the entire thing. I saw him do it. Go for it, brother."

The box had lost all interest for Ayanna. She was much more interested in getting her hands on Dakota's baby girl. "Knock yourself out, Johnny. I want to see this little cupcake right here," she cooed, holding her hands out.

The two women sat down in the dining room so Ayanna could dote on the baby. Johnny helped himself to two more cupcakes before joining them. "Ayanna, you're gorgeous, and you can cook. If I was a marrying man, I'd be chasing you down," he said sincerely.

Ayanna laughed softly and looked at little Bethany Anne Hunter, who was gurgling softly in her arms. "Sweetie pie, your uncle is nice, but he's crazy."

Johnny polished off the third cake with a deep sigh of enjoyment and licked a bit of frosting off his finger. "I might be crazy, but I know a good woman when I see one," he said with a wink.

The blush only showed on her cheeks, but Ayanna could feel it from the bottom of her feet all the way to the top of her head as she pretended that she wasn't listening to his joking. She cuddled Bethany to her shoulder and inhaled her sweet baby scent before stealing a look in Johnny's direction. Luckily, he was talking to Dakota, and she got a good look at his long, muscular frame and sexy rear end. Her face filled with heat again as he turned just in time to see her staring at him, and he winked at her again; but this time it was slow and sexy. She knew she looked like a critter caught in the high beams of a semi, but she couldn't look away to save herself.

She really didn't have a choice in the matter because someone came into the room to join them.

"Johnny, sweetheart, what is taking you so long? I've been waiting for you," a feminine voice purred.

Ayanna felt a weird sensation creep over her, but it wasn't the same pleasurable feeling she'd enjoyed earlier. This was dangerously close to jealousy, something she hadn't experienced in years. And she hadn't missed it one bit, either.

Chapter 2

Ayanna had to put on her best game face and act as though nothing were amiss, when in reality, she was a little unnerved to hear the dulcet tones of Dr. Davina Wainwright. She was Jason's sister, and she never let anyone forget that she was the most beautiful woman in the room as well as one of the top cosmetic surgeons on the East Coast. She was also one of the snottiest people Ayanna had ever met in her life. The only one who could top her was Cloris, the other Wainwright sister. She, too, was a plastic surgeon.

Both the sisters were tall and thin and quite pretty in a heavily painted sort of way. Since Billie had married into their family they had toned down a little bit of the diva behavior because they were never the prettiest anything when the Phillips sisters were in the room. They had refused Billie's invitation to be her bridesmaids, but once they found out that Billie's wedding was featured in every fashion publication in this country as well as the UK and France, they realized what a huge mistake they'd made in being rude and changed their tune.

When they saw all of Billie's A-list celebrity friends at the wedding and reception, they had done as Jason predicted and tried to join Billie at the hip. Luckily, Billie saw right through them like they were glass. Both of them lived in New York, but lately they'd spent a lot of weekends in Chicago. Ayanna had once suggested that they were trying to make amends, and Billie had just rolled her eyes.

"That's sweet, Ayanna, but their motives have nothing to do with being sisterly. It's all about meeting potential celebrity clients and maybe a man or two. Nip and Tuck don't fool me a bit," Billie had said with a sniff.

Ayanna wasn't about to let the presence of one of the snotty sisters ruin her day. She enjoyed being around Billie and Dakota too much to allow the woman to get on her nerves. She toured the house with Billie, who was as excited as a kid on Christmas morning to show off her dream house.

"The floors are bamboo, because it's a sustainable resource. And all the paint is environmentally friendly, too," she said as they looked in the second floor rooms. Billie put her arm around Ayanna's shoulders and gave her a sisterly hug. "I don't know why I'm telling you this. You were with me when I picked out a lot of this stuff. I'm just house-proud right now," she admitted.

"And you should be," Ayanna said. "This place is magnificent. One day I'm going to have a bigger place. I love my house, but the walls are going to close in on us in a little while. The boys are getting so big!"

"These walls are going to close in soon, to hear Jason tell it. He's decided he wants a bunch of kids and as soon as possible," she murmured with a blush.

"And somehow I think you're going to indulge him in this wish, aren't you?" Ayanna stopped peeking into the bedrooms and ceased walking so abruptly that Billie bumped into her. "You're pregnant already, aren't you?"

By way of answer, Billie just showed all her perfect teeth in a big grin. "That question will be answered this afternoon. But if you can keep a secret for a couple of hours, the answer is *yes*. Jason was determined I get pregnant on our honeymoon, but it took a little longer than that. But in about six months, there's going to be another baby around here."

Ayanna's face lit up. "First Toni and Zane with little Brandon, then Dakota and Nick with little Bethany and now you and Jason are getting ready to add to the mix. Y'all don't mess around when it comes to popping out those babies. Do any of you folks wait a year before reproducing?" she teased.

She was referring to Zane Beauchamp and his wife Toni. Zane owned the paper where Dakota worked.

Dakota and Toni were very close and their babies were a few months apart in age.

Billie laughed. "It was almost a year for me and Jason. Of the three couples, we showed the most restraint," she said airily.

"Y'all are gonna be *in* restraints when junior keeps you up all night." Johnny emerged from one of the guest rooms, this time fully dressed and looking good. "I don't know how people put up with all that racket. Ayanna, you have two boys, how did you handle the late-night feedings, the colic, walking them all night, potty training and all the other fun things nobody tells you about being a parent?"

He ducked when Billie aimed a punch at his shoulder. "Hey, I'm just trying to get somebody to talk sense into you people. There'll be babies all over this house in a few years if you don't cool your jets. Tell her about it, Ayanna."

Her face had changed into a rigid mask bearing a stiff and very phony smile. "I can't help you there. I didn't go through all of that with my boys. I adopted Alec when he was four and Cameron was six, so I got to miss all the fun of carrying a baby I loved from inception to delivery. I'm, um, going to go see what they're up to. See you later," she added hurriedly as she dashed down the stairs.

Johnny looked helplessly at Billie, who was staring at him with great exasperation. "You have a big mouth, you know that?" she said.

"How was I supposed to know I was saying something stupid? You never know when you've said something stupid until it's out there and you've made a daggone fool out of yourself," he said gruffly. "You could have given me a heads-up. You know I like her, and this is the first time we've had a chance to get together."

Billie didn't have time to ponder this revelation because Johnny was still talking. "Besides, those kids look just like her. How come they look like triplets if they're not hers?"

Billie sighed and put her hand on her brother's arm. "Because they're related by blood. Those boys are her sister's children. She died when the boys were quite young, and Ayanna was their guardian. She adopted them and has done her best to raise them to be the delightful young men they are today." Billie looked reflective for a moment. "She's sacrificed a lot for Alec and Cameron, although she doesn't consider it to be any kind of burden. They're her whole life, and she loves them devotedly.

"Now what's this about you liking Ayanna?" she asked with a frown. "Your track record with the ladies isn't one I want to wish upon my best friend. If you want to play, stay away from my girl. She's isn't your normal disposable party favor, so don't even think about it."

The warm clasp on his arm was replaced by a sharp pinch. He jerked away from her looking stunned. "That was just wrong, Billie. In the first place, you make me sound like some ol' cheap playa, and in the second place, I think you left a mark, you wildcat. Does Jason know about this side of you?"

"I don't think you're cheap," she said earnestly. "I think you're a very high-priced playa, top-shelf, in fact." She turned to run down the stairs and looked at him over her shoulder. "And Jason knows all about my wild side, and he loves it. He encourages it," she added, wiggling her hips as Johnny covered his ears and made a horrible face.

"Oversharing, little sister. That's called oversharing."

Ayanna felt like a nitwit for her reaction to Johnny's innocent remarks. After she reached the first floor, she got a glimpse of Davina regaling Toni and Zane Beauchamp with a story about her illustrious medical practice, and Ayanna quickly slipped out of the French doors that led to the big terrazzo patio. It was a soothing place with comfortable chairs and big potted plants surrounded by a low brick wall. Taking a deep breath, she watched her boys playing a noisy game of basketball with Nick's nephews. Sadie was also playing, running back and forth and barking with gusto.

Why did I act like that? It's not the first time the subject has come up, she thought. *So why did I act like I was running from the law or something?*

Just then she felt two strong hands on her shoulders. Johnny turned her around to face him. "I didn't mean to say anything out of line, Ayanna. Are we still friends?"

She looked up at his handsome face, which was completely serious for the first time she could remember. Johnny was always laughing and making jokes, so this was quite a change. "We're fine. You didn't know my boys are adopted, and there's no real reason that you should've known. But it's not like it's a secret," she told him.

He nodded and continued to look at her like he was trying to memorize her face. "I just realized that I don't know very much about you," he said thoughtfully.

Ayanna was looking at him with the same kind of intensity. "No, I guess you don't. I met you at Billie's wedding, and I've seen you a few times since then. It's not like you live here in Chicago or anything."

Johnny didn't seem to be listening to her. His big palms were making circles on her shoulders, and he showed no interest in removing his hands from her body. But he was paying attention, as his next words demonstrated. "Well, I think we should start remedying that. I'm moving here, and I think getting to know you better is going to be a priority."

"You're moving here? Permanently?" Ayanna sounded slightly breathless.

"Yes, I am. Didn't Billie tell you? Let's get something to eat and talk about it some more."

"Is food all you think about?"

"Pretty much. Food and sex. What else is there, besides football?" Johnny's face resumed its normal, humorous expression as he smiled down at her.

Ayanna's eyes widened. "You need Jesus, Johnny Phillips. You need help."

"So are you gonna help a brother out or what?" His hands flew off her shoulders as he heard Davina's voice float out through the French doors. "Billie, where's that brother of yours? He just disappeared."

"Help me get away from that succubus," Johnny said urgently. "She's been on me like a duck on a june bug, and I'm trying not to hurt her feelings. Come on. Let's go in the side door."

"Johnny, you're crazy!" Ayanna's dimples wreathed her smile as she allowed him to hustle her away from the sound of Davina's voice.

"No, I'm not. I need help, just like you said. Help me stay away from the man-eater and I'll give you anything you want."

A warm pleasant feeling settled over her at his teasing words. "Don't make promises you can't keep. You have no idea what I might want," she warned.

They had reached the door that led to the kitchen. He squeezed her hand, which he'd taken when he led her off the patio. "That's true, I don't. But whatever it is, I'll give it to you gladly. Count on that," he replied with his devastating grin.

They went into the big kitchen, and he stared at the table loaded with all kinds of good things to eat.

"Dang, that looks good. Fix me a plate, and we'll get started on your list." Johnny went to the sink and washed his hands while Ayanna stared at his beautiful butt and his long legs that were slightly bowed.

"I'll fix you a plate, but what list are you talking about?"

He turned around, wiping his hands on a dish towel. "Your desires, Ayanna. I told you I'd give you anything you want."

She couldn't move for a moment, and then she laughed at his foolishness. "Move out of the way so I can wash my hands. Your blood sugar must be low."

Chapter 3

After the party ended and everyone went home, Johnny was still thinking about Ayanna. He'd insisted on following her home to make sure she got there safely, even though it was kind of superfluous seeing as how it was barely dark and she had Alec and Cameron for protection. He did it anyway and pulled up in the driveway behind them. He watched until they were all in the house safely, and then he punched in her number on his cell phone.

"I told you I was going to call you," he'd reminded her. She had laughed, the tinkling little giggle that reminded him of spring rain.

"Yes, but I didn't think you'd be calling from the driveway. You want to come in and have a cup of coffee?"

He had done so at once because it gave him a chance to see her again, even for a little while. He had admired her house and got to observe her easy relationship with the boys up close. Actually, he'd spent more time talking with Alec and Cameron than he had with Ayanna, but it was cool because he liked them. She had raised some fine young men. She'd finally called the evening to a halt because they had to get up early for church the next day. He would see her there since she and Billie and Dakota attended the same church, and he always went with them when he was in town.

Now Johnny was in the media room of Billie's house, stretched out on one of the big leather sofas. The plasma TV was on ESPN, but he wasn't watching it. He was thinking about Ayanna's smile. She'd made an impression on him the first moment he'd seen her at Billie's wedding. He'd gotten into Chicago the morning of the ceremony, and he'd missed all the festivities leading up to it, so he hadn't seen the bridesmaids until they were walking down the aisle. Her huge black eyes, the big dimples and her perfect golden brown complexion were all adorable, but he'd thought she was about nineteen or twenty, way too young for him.

After the ceremony he'd found out that Alec and Cameron, who'd played the violin and piano during the ceremony, were her sons. This made him think she was married. By the time he realized she was single, the reception was almost over and he'd hooked up with some tall leggy woman who was into a good time for one night only, which was his style. He remembered, though, watching Ayanna dance the night away with what seemed like every man there. She could dance her butt off, he recalled, in a sexy and alluring but not sleazy way. She was graceful and moved like she'd been doing it all her life.

Billie entered the room and interrupted his thoughts. "Who won the game?"

"Huh?" He turned to look at her. "Who won what?"

She pushed his feet aside and sat down on the end of the couch. "Were you asleep? I asked who won. Aren't you watching the scores?" she asked as she pointed to the TV.

"No, I was thinking about Ayanna. She's beautiful, isn't she?"

Billie tilted her head as she looked him over. "If you were any other man on the planet, I'd say you were smitten, but we know that's not true, don't we?"

"You don't know anything, little sister. Where did she learn how to dance like that?"

"She used to be on a dance squad when she was in high school, I think, and she took dance when she was little. She teaches a dance class at a community center near her house. That girl can get down like a pro," she said. "Wait, I have a DVD from the hospital benefit. Todd asked her to be his partner in this ballroom dance thing. Hold on, let me get it." Todd Wainwright, Jason's younger brother, had missed the party because he was at work.

She rose gracefully and went to the wall where the DVDs were stored. "Let's see…" she murmured. "Oh, here it is. I'll put it in for you."

Jason appeared in the doorway as she slipped the disc into the player. "Baby, isn't it time for you to go to bed? You did a lot today, and I don't want you to tire yourself out," he said.

Billie went to him and nuzzled the base of his throat as he wrapped her in his arms. "I was just getting ready to come upstairs. I'm a little tired, but not because I did too much. You did everything for me, as usual."

Johnny sat up and waved the couple off. "Take your lovey-dovey newlywed expectant-parent selves out of here before I get sick from watching you," he said.

"Aw, man, don't hate, participate," Jason drawled. "This is what you get when you turn in your playa card and start being a real man." He stopped talking and kissed Billie deeply.

"I'm blind, I'm blind," Johnny moaned. "Stop doing that, man, that's my baby sister."

Billie and Jason shouted with laughter. "I might be your sister, but I'm his wife. This is what married life is like."

"Yeah, well I may never know. Good *night*. *Please,* good night, sleep well, etcetera. By the way, speaking of sisters, where is yours?" He pointed at Jason as he spoke.

"She hooked up with some quarterback or whatever. We might not see her until tomorrow," Jason answered. "See ya."

Johnny pumped his fist in the air as the couple left. "Thank you! Now I can have some peace." He pushed play on the DVD player and was immediately transfixed by what he saw on the high definition screen. "Oh damn, I could be in serious trouble," he murmured as he watched Ayanna come into view. "But it's just the kind of trouble I like."

Ayanna was thinking about the events of the day as she got ready for bed. The party was wonderful, just like any gathering with Billie's family. They had to be the sweetest people she'd ever met. Dakota's in-laws and Billie and Dakota's parents were just delightful. And what could you say about Johnny Phillips? He was every woman's dream—tall, intelligent, funny and kind and his looks were off the chart. Too bad he was way out of her league. Men like Johnny ended up with women like his sisters: Billie, the former supermodel who was now making her mark in the construction business, and Dakota, the Pulitzer prize-winning author who'd also won an Oscar for screenwriting. Yes, with sisters like that, he'd look for a doctor, a CEO or even a lawyer, since that was his profession. Standards had been set pretty high in the Phillips family.

She was in her bedroom, taking a last look in the mirror before getting in the shower. A pleasant face looked back at her. Her skin was good; her hair was passable, although it wasn't long and cascading like the Phillips women. *I guess I could get a fifteen-hundred-dollar weave like Davina,* she thought. She made a face at her reflection. *No need to take a swallow of haterade. You are what you are.*

She took off the cute celery-green cotton sweater

she'd worn with a pair of light-colored jeans and a pair of stylish little yellow flats from Payless. She laughed as she took off the shoes to put them in the closet. She couldn't see Johnny Phillips with a woman who scouted for clothes on clearance at Target and shoes from the Payless buy one, get one sales. She wasn't a high-powered executive or someone of national prominence. She was a single mother with an office job who had to pinch pennies hard to make sure her sons were well-fed, nicely clothed, safe and secure. And that her bills were paid on time. She didn't drive a luxury car, unless a five-year-old PT Cruiser was in that category. Her house was sparkling clean and charming, but almost everything had been done by her two hands, assisted by the boys. Nope, she was not his glass of champagne, not by a long shot.

She finished undressing and took a long shower. It was the only way she could be sure to get some hot water because the boys would monopolize it the next morning before church. Sighing as the sweet scent of her bath gel filled her nostrils, she thought again about how much fun she'd had with Johnny. She loved his irreverent humor and outrageous flirting; she was so busy being a mom she'd forgotten how much fun it could be. Ayanna could be shy with people she didn't know, but her acquaintance with Johnny and his family made him feel safe and familiar. For a brief moment she wished with all her heart that she was more than what she was. She wished she was the kind of woman who could attract a man like Johnny for real.

* * *

Ayanna couldn't wait to get to church the next morning to pray for forgiveness. The dreams she'd had the night before were so vivid and explicit that she'd awakened sweaty, trembling and moist in places that should have been bone dry. And "Ramon" was not the star attraction that night. He'd been replaced by someone taller, broader of shoulder and chocolate brown with a clean shaven head. She didn't need an advanced degree in psychology to know what that was about. She kicked the covers off and glanced at the clock on the bedside table. It was 5:00 a.m. She sat up groggily and tossed aside the wrinkled bedclothes. She needed another shower to wash away all traces of her drastically misplaced erotic desires.

She scrubbed herself from head to toe, using her nylon bath puff like a weapon. When she washed her small, firm breasts and the sensitive area between her legs, she was dismayed to find them tender and responsive to her touch, as though the wild sex of her dream was real. To shake off all vestiges of her nocturnal fantasies, she lowered the temperature of the shower until it was quite cool. She had to stifle a scream, but she ran the cold water over her body resolutely and thoroughly. If anyone knew what she'd been thinking, she'd die of shame.

Okay, that's a little dramatic, she admitted as she toweled herself dry. But the things they had done to each other in that dream were so vivid and so wild! *I've got to leave those romance novels alone.* No more

Brenda Jackson, Maureen Smith or Altonya Washing-
ton for her. And definitely no more Adrianne Byrd! The
books she read were well-written, delightfully sensual
and they'd been her obsession ever since she discovered African-American romance. She had so many of
the books that she had to catalog them.

The newest ones were in her to-be-read pile next to
the bed. Her favorites took a place of honor in her
bedroom bookcase. The older books were in boxes
under her bed, each box labeled with a sheet that told
the name and author of each book. She sighed heavily
as she made her bed, still wrapped in her towel. It was
pathetic enough that her sex life was confined to reading
the delicious love scenes the authors so generously
provided her in their fascinating books, but when her
loneliness—and yes, her unfulfilled desires—made her
include a real live man in her dreams, well, it was time
for a change.

I'm the one who needs help, she thought. *Maybe
there's some kind of herbal thing I can get at the health
food store to cool my jets.* She had to laugh out loud at
that thought. It wasn't that serious. She just needed to
exercise more. That would work out those urges quite
nicely. She could teach another dance class; it would
give the boys more time at the rec center, which they
would enjoy. Problem solved. No more crazy dreams
about having wild sex in the middle of a bed with red
satin sheets with a chocolate hunk of man for her. She
would exercise that man right out of her thighs, that's
what she would do.

She looked around, realized that she'd made the bed, rearranged her dresser and organized her closet. And she still had over thirty minutes before the boys' alarm would go off. Okay, she'd put on her underwear and a robe and go make some cinnamon rolls for a surprise. Keeping busy was the answer. If she just kept busy and kept her mind focused on productive things, she had no doubt that her current state of constant longing would dissipate. It was a good plan that only took a few hours to blow up in her face.

Chapter 4

Johnny slept a lot better than Ayanna, and the dreams he had about being with her weren't a cause for angst. On the contrary, he was looking forward to seeing her that morning. He'd watched the DVD of her dancing three times before he went to bed, after making a point of taking it out of the player and taking it to the guest room with him. He had every intention of keeping it, and Billie could just get over it until he could copy it. *If* he copied it. For some reason, he didn't really want anyone else looking at it. The way Ayanna looked was amazing, but the way she was dancing was too sexy to be believed.

He was still in bed, wearing the sheet that was covering him and nothing else. He smiled lazily as he recalled with total clarity every act of consensual loving he'd shared with Ayanna during the night. It was the costume she'd worn in the DVD that had done it. It was some kind of gold getup with those sparkly things on it. It had a top part with one shoulder strap and a skirt thing that bared her navel and was split on the side to show off her long, shapely legs. Ayanna might be slender, but every inch of her was bangin' as his early-morning tent pole testified.

He chuckled as he enjoyed the sensation of his erection. Some men got bothered by the early-morning wake-up call by their nether regions, but Johnny liked it. It let him know that he was still in business, and after the night of fantasies he'd had courtesy of the captivating Ayanna, he couldn't blame his body for reacting. The way she had worked her body around that stage was so blazing hot it had seared his eyeballs. She moved like she didn't have any bones in her hips, especially when she was doing the Latin dances. She had such control of her beautiful body that all he could think was what she would feel like in his arms.

The only hitch was Todd Wainwright. Were they involved or something? Todd hadn't made it to the open house because he was head of the trauma unit at John Stroger Hospital, and he'd been on call yesterday. They seemed to move as one person on the DVD, and the way he touched her and looked into her eyes during the dance was more intimate than Johnny liked. Was it part of the show, or was there something going on? He'd already made two wrong assumptions about

Ayanna that had put him off the trail, and he wasn't going to make a third. First he assumed she was too young, and then he assumed she had a husband because she had two sons. "Yeah, well, they say assumptions are the mothers of all screwups. I'm getting to the bottom of this ASAP," he said aloud.

He tossed back the covers and got out of the bed, stretching as he did so. First a long hot shower, then a little grooming of his goatee and a shave of his cheeks. Then he'd get dressed for church before going downstairs to grill his sister about her brother-in-law's intentions toward the delightful Ayanna. This time he was going to get it right.

Johnny came into the kitchen to find Billie and his mother at the table. He kissed them both, and after exchanging greetings, he got right down to business. "Billie, what's the deal with Todd and Ayanna? Are they kickin' it or what?"

Lee Phillips looked at her oldest child with equal parts amusement and amazement. "You sound rather territorial, dear. What's going on? Are you interested in Ayanna?"

Johnny didn't hesitate. "Yeah, I sure am. Why shouldn't I be interested? She's smart, she's a great mother, her boys are well-mannered, well-behaved and intelligent and she's gorgeous. Why are you asking if I'm interested? Don't you like her? You think there's something wrong with her?" He had a very defined scowl on his face, which neither woman had ever seen on behalf of a woman.

Lee and Billie exchanged glances before bursting into laughter.

"I think he's serious, Mama," Billie said. "I'm going to finish cooking breakfast before Daddy comes down here growling like a bear."

"Come sit down, dear." Lee invited him. "Have some coffee."

"I'm not sitting down until you tell me why you don't like Ayanna," he said defensively. "She's a lovely woman. What's not to like about her?"

"Ooh, you're really going off the deep end, aren't you?" Lee's eyes twinkled with affection for her son. "Now sit your lanky butt down, and let me drop some knowledge on you."

Johnny sat down at the pub table in the spacious kitchen and crossed his arms on the table. Lee took a sip of coffee before speaking.

"Ayanna Porter is an outstanding young woman, and your father and I adore her. But she's not like those gangly airheads you normally spend two or three weeks wining, dining, bedding and forgetting. She's not for you, son. All you want is a good time, and she's not a good time gal. So unless you're willing to go the distance, you need to go away." Her words were kind but firm.

"Don't hold back, Mama. How do you really feel about it?" he said dryly.

Billie's giggles could be heard as she took a tray of maple crisped turkey bacon out of the oven. "I guess she told you, big brother. But she's right. I told you,

Ayanna ain't anybody's play toy. If you're looking for a playmate, I think I heard Davina in the shower. She got in late, but she should be rarin' to go."

"Well, thanks for the gratifying assessment of my personality," Johnny said curtly. "I think I'll just meet you at church," he added.

"Oh, don't get mad. I made stuffed French toast," Billie wheedled. "It's Ayanna's recipe. We're not trying to say that you're a hound, but you haven't had any long, sustaining relationships. Unless that's what you're looking for, Ayanna's not the one for you. She deserves someone who's going to love her unconditionally and permanently and that hasn't been your pattern, you have to admit."

Jason came into the room and kissed his wife before going to his mother-in-law and giving her a good morning kiss on the cheek. "I heard you all when I was coming through the dining room. Ease up off Johnny. I was a coast-to-coast hound before I met Billie. When a man meets the right woman, he becomes the right man for her. Am I right, baby?" he asked, looking at Billie.

"Yes, you are," she answered. "Johnny, there may be hope for you yet."

Johnny didn't respond to her encouraging words. "Jason, maybe I can get a straight answer from you. Are Todd and Ayanna involved?"

Jason looked surprised. "No, not at all. They're friends and occasional dance partners, but Todd is too wrapped up in his work to get into a relationship. If he was, I'd know because his mouth runs like water. They're totally friends," he assured Johnny.

Johnny's face relaxed into its normal smile. "That's good to know."

The outside door opened, and Johnny's father, Boyd, walked in with Sadie, who was glad to see everyone. "What's good to know? Where's my breakfast? My grand-dog and I are ready to eat."

Johnny was fondling Sadie's ears and didn't answer. Lee was more than happy to fill in the details, though.

"Your son was finding out whether or not the adorable Ayanna Porter was involved. He's happy that's she's available," she said archly.

Boyd shrugged his broad shoulders as he went to inspect the spread Billie was preparing. "I'm glad to know that, too. It's about time you settled down, son."

Everyone waited for Johnny's usual declaration that he was going to stay single forever, but it wasn't forthcoming. "You could be right, Pop," was all he said. "You want me to set the table, little sister?"

Lee and Billie were shocked by his laconic response, but Boyd and Jason acted as though nothing was amiss. Mother and daughter exchanged a look that said they'd be talking about this at great length once they were alone.

Ayanna's peace was invaded once again when she saw Johnny at church. She had been enveloped in the serenity that always surrounded her every Sunday, when she got a tap on the shoulder. Turning around to

find the source of the tap, she saw Johnny looking
even better than usual in a fabulous gray suit. His shirt
was pale blue and his silk tie had a rep pattern in shades
of blue and gray and to make matters worse, he smelled
terrific. He was smiling at her, too, which made her
heart give a few extra beats. Great, fine, swell. Here she
had just prayed the man out of her mind and here he
was in the flesh, temptation personified. She mustered
a smile and a greeting.

"I didn't see you earlier. Where were you sitting?"
she asked politely.

"We were sitting about two rows behind you. I saw
you," he said with that darned sexy smile. "You look
good from the back, but even better from the front."

Ayanna felt a bit of heat from his words. She always
liked getting dressed up for church, and she'd worn a
pink linen Ralph Lauren suit she'd gotten from the con-
signment shop. It was brand new, too; the tags were still
on it. It was her favorite spring outfit, and hearing his
compliment was nice but unsettling considering the
blazing hot dream she was trying to delete from her
mental hard drive.

He took her arm like they'd been walking together
for years, and before she knew it, they were outside the
church with his family. She greeted everyone and looked
around for Alec and Cameron. The sooner they got out
of there, the better it would be for her peace of mind.

Cameron came out of nowhere, and she breathed a
sigh of relief. "Where's your brother?" she asked, after
he exchanged polite greetings with everyone.

"He's headed to the car, I think. He said he was starving." Cameron grinned.

"Well, why don't you all come on over to the house? We've got tons of leftovers, so we thought we'd just have a second-day party," Billie said.

"Thanks, but I told the boys I'd take them to Dave & Buster's," Ayanna said.

"One of my favorite restaurants," Johnny said. "Mind if I tag along?"

"No, that would be great," Cameron assured him. "I wanted to ask you some more questions about your foundation, if that's okay, Mr. Phillips."

Ayanna looked down at the peep toes of her Payless wedge-heeled beige sandals. Why did her children have to have such good manners? She looked up to see Johnny pointing at his father.

"That's Mr. Phillips over there. Just call me John," he said. "Why don't we go in my car?"

Ayanna finally found her voice and said something about changing clothes. That's how they wound up in a mini-caravan, with Johnny following her to the small brick home she shared with the boys. Cameron and Alec rode with Johnny, and she led the way, giving herself a pep talk as she drove.

"Quit being a drama queen. It's just an afternoon with the boys and Johnny. It's not like it's a date. He has no idea that you have a dirty little mind, and there's no reason for him to find out. Just chill, and try to act like a grown woman instead of a schoolgirl," she mumbled.

She pulled into the driveway and was already at the back door when Johnny and the boys arrived. Alec and Cameron bounded out of the SUV with Johnny following at a more sedate pace.

"Mom, we got an idea on the way over here. Guess what John's favorite meal is?" Cameron asked.

"I couldn't possibly. What is it?" she asked faintly.

"Lasagna! We told him what a good cook you are and how good your lasagna is, and I know there's some in the freezer, so why don't we all have dinner here?"

Alec joined in the plea, double-teaming her. "Yeah, Ma, that would be fun. Can we stay here, please?"

Ayanna looked at their pleading faces helplessly. They were so hard to resist when they asked for something—and they asked for so little. She bought some time by opening the back door and entering the kitchen. She put her purse and keys on the table and turned to face the three of them. "But this was supposed to be a treat for you guys," she said. "I'm sure Johnny would rather go to the restaurant than eat here. Besides, I don't have any Italian bread and, umm…" She vainly tried to think of other reasons why this was a bad idea.

"I can't think of anything I'd like more than eating here with you and the guys. And if you need anything from the store, we'd be happy to go get it for you. We'll clean up afterward, too. And," Johnny added persuasively, "I'll take you all out to Dave & Buster's later in the week or on the weekend or whenever you like. How's that for a deal?"

Ayanna looked at the three pairs of eyes that were

all beseeching her to agree, and she caved. "Fine. I'll get the lasagna out while you guys change clothes, and then you can go pick up a few things for me. And that kitchen had better be spotless," she said playfully.

"Cool!" Alec and Cameron slapped each other five while Johnny gave her a satisfied smile. She wondered what she had just gotten herself into.

Chapter 5

Dinner was actually a lot more fun than Ayanna expected. After the boys went to change out of their church clothes, Johnny surprised her by going out to his SUV and coming back in the house with a garment bag. He explained that he was in the process of moving.

"I just got in yesterday morning, and most of my things are still in the car. I'm going to stay at Nick's old apartment until I get a house. So if you don't mind, I'm going to get into something more casual so I don't get sauce on my good suit."

"Of course you can," Ayanna said. "Come on, I'll take you to the spare room, and you can change there."

She led him down the hall to a small room that she had set up as a place where the boys could do their homework and she could work from home. It had a chaise lounge, a comfortable chair and a computer desk. Like all the rooms in her house, it was neat as a pin as well as attractive. Warm cocoa walls, bamboo blinds and several colorful prints made it warm and welcoming. There were green plants hanging in the two windows and an African-inspired print rug on the hardwood floor.

"Here you go. You can hang your garment bag on the back of the door or in the closet," she said, ignoring the warmth that invaded her as he stood close to her body. He took her hand and gave her a look that could have melted a glacier.

"Thanks, Ayanna. I really appreciate you doing this. I don't want to put you to any trouble, but I don't get home-cooked food for months at a time, so I really look forward to it when I can get some," he told her.

The feel of his big hand wrapped around hers was intoxicating, but she forced herself to speak in a normal voice and act casual. "It's no bother at all, don't be silly. I'm going to make a list while you change."

Johnny's compelling eyes continued to lock with hers. "Is this your grocery list or the list of the desires I'm going to fulfill?"

"Groceries! I'll need my computer to list everything I want from you," she said without thinking. She was glad he took it as a joke, and the sound of his laughter followed her down the hall. Her hands were trembling while she jotted down a few things to round out their meal. She went to the refrigerator and poured a big glass of ice-cold water, which she drank rapidly in an effort to cool off the fire that he ignited in her. *It's just dinner. Just one dinner, and then things will be back to normal. Try to act like you got some sense,* she chided herself.

In a few minutes Alec, Cameron and Johnny presented themselves in jeans and T-shirts and announced that they were ready to do her bidding.

"Here you go. They boys can tell you where the store is, and they know what brands I like. I think they do, don't they?" She glanced at her sons, who looked amused.

"Of course we do, Ma. Give us some credit," Cameron said. "We know everything you like."

Johnny looked mischievous and said, "Good, you can give me some pointers on how to get on her good side." They went out the door like they'd been hanging out for years, and Ayanna stared after them until she reminded herself that she had work to do.

She went to the side-by-side refrigerator and pulled open the freezer door. Ayanna liked to power cook, as she called it. If she made spaghetti or chili or macaroni and cheese, things her sons really liked, she would double or triple the recipe so that there were always two or three casseroles in the freezer to be popped in the oven at a moment's notice. She took out the lasagna and put it on a cookie sheet before sliding it into the oven. She would make garlic bread and stuff some mushrooms with pesto to round out the meal along with a big green salad.

By the time the guys came back from the store, she had changed into some nice fitting jeans and a violet scoop-necked T-shirt that showed off her figure without being too provocative. She was also wearing lavender flip-flops, and her toenails were polished in a pretty shade of pink. "Thank you, gentlemen. Now if you go play some ball or watch the game or something, dinner will be ready in about forty-five minutes."

Alec stayed to set the dining room table for her while she made the garlic bread and the stuffed mushrooms. The salad took no time, since she used a pre-bagged mixture of romaine lettuce.

"I can do that for you, Ma," Alec offered.

"Thanks, sweetie. You're too good to me," she said.

"Aww, Ma, cut it out. I'm supposed to be good to you because you're so sweet and nice and you do everything for us. We're lucky to have you for a mother," he said.

Her eyes filled with tears, and she started to hug him but he held up the oversized salad forks like a cross. "No mushy stuff, Ma! Step away, or I'll put something weird in the salad."

"Like what?" Ayanna smiled. Like typical adolescents, both Alec and Cameron had moments when the "mushy stuff" was just too much for them to handle.

"Grub worms, locusts, lizards, stuff like that. John said people in Africa eat them. They're a delicacy in some places."

"Ewwww! My palate isn't that sophisticated, thank you."

"John is a really cool guy, isn't he? He's really smart,

and he's done a lot of traveling. He's the kind of guy you should date," he added innocently.

"Okay, thanks for your help. Tell Cameron and Johnny to wash up and dinner will be on the table in about fifteen minutes," she said hurriedly. When he left the room, she leaned against the counter and sighed deeply. What next?

Ayanna was used to getting compliments on her cooking, but Johnny looked and acted as though he'd been transported to some idyllic land when he tasted her meal. He praised the garlic bread and the mushrooms, but he declared his love for the main course.

"This is the most magnificent meal I've had in a long time. I don't know how to thank you for allowing me to disrupt your family time," he said.

"Oh, that's easy. You guys are cleaning up the kitchen, remember?"

Alec and Cameron were already clearing the table and bringing in dessert, which was raspberry sorbet and some of her homemade brownies, which had been known to make people swoon when they tasted them. Johnny was in that category. His eyes lit up when he saw them, and when he swallowed his first bite, he closed his eyes in bliss.

"Alec, Cameron, I know we don't know each other too well, but once I marry your mother, we're going to be good friends. Sound okay to you?"

Suddenly the tension that had been building in Ayanna dissipated, and she started laughing. This was the Johnny she'd been getting to know, and this was his usual exaggerated sense of humor. So what if he'd visited her dreams? Stuff happened, and you got over it. "Johnny, you really do need Jesus," she said.

"Ma, why do you call him Johnny? He told us to call him John," Cameron pointed out.

"I can help you with that. My dad named us all after singers. I was named after Johnny Hartman, this amazing jazz singer. So Johnny is my given name, but I usually tell people to call me John because it just sounds more adult, more businesslike," he admitted.

Alec, ever-curious, had to ask another question. "So why don't you tell Ma to call you John?"

Johnny looked directly into Ayanna's eyes. "Because I like the way she says my name."

"You did an excellent job on the kitchen," Ayanna said. Dinner was over, and the promise to clean up was fulfilled. Alec and Cameron were at a friend's house, and it was just Ayanna and Johnny, sitting on the sofa listening to music and talking.

"You did a superlative job on everything else," Johnny said. "You're an amazing woman, Ayanna. Besides being beautiful and a perfect mother, you cook like a Cordon Bleu graduate, and you dance like a professional. How did you learn to dance like that?"

"Like what? Oh no, did Billie show you that DVD?" She covered her face and groaned.

Johnny pulled her hands away from her face. "Don't

go getting all shy with me. You could be headlining in Vegas or Miami with those moves."

"I didn't think she was going to show it to anyone."

"She won't be showing it to anyone else. I stole it from her just so I could keep it to myself," he said.

"Are you kidding me? You actually took it? Why?"

"Because it turned me on." He leaned toward her. "You were too hot for anyone else to see. You kept me up all night thinking about the way you moved, the way you looked. You were blazin' hot, Ayanna. Do you still have that little outfit you wore?"

"That's for me to know and you to find out, if you can," she said sassily.

"Don't dare me," Johnny warned. "I've been known to play dirty to get what I want."

"Don't threaten me," she said. "I'm the one with the brownies, remember?"

Johnny held his hands up in supplication. "You win."

Ayanna turned her head toward the stereo and then looked back at Johnny. "What is that playing? It's beautiful."

"That is John Coltrane. The singer is Johnny Hartman. He's the only vocalist Coltrane ever recorded with. That's the man I was named for. You like him?"

"I love his voice. It's like velvet."

"You can keep that one. I just happened to have it in the car stereo, and I thought you might like it."

"You're very thoughtful. Would you like some coffee?"

"Only if I can have another brownie."

"It's yours. Come with me."

Soon they were seated in the kitchen while Ayanna poured cups of fragrant coffee. She was adding cream to hers when Johnny asked her a question.

"Why aren't you married?"

"You don't hold back, do you? Whatever comes up comes out with you." Ayanna picked up her cup to take a sip.

"You're right. I'm very direct. I don't know any other way to be. When I want to know something I ask, and I want to know why a gorgeous, talented, kind woman like you is still single." Johnny tasted his own coffee and made a deep sound of satisfaction. "Let's add 'making coffee' to your list of accomplishments."

"I was engaged once," Ayanna said. "I was engaged my senior year of college, and we were going to get married after I finished at the Cordon Bleu." At his look of surprise, she nodded. "You weren't so far off when you said I cooked like a pro. I majored in business and minored in culinary arts. I got accepted at the Cordon Bleu in Paris, and I would have gone, but my sister died, and I was guardian to my nephews, so my life went down a different path. You know they say if you want to make God laugh, make plans."

Johnny sipped his coffee before asking her another question.

"What happened to your sister, that is, if you don't mind talking about it?"

She met Johnny's concerned gaze with a steady one of her own. "I can tell you about it because it happened ten years ago. My sister had been in a very unhappy relationship for a long time. She had finally had enough, and she was in the process of leaving him. He followed her into the parking structure at her job and killed her, and then he blew his own brains out. He did it," she said bitterly, "because he loved her so much."

"I'm so sorry for your loss," Johnny said as he put his hand over hers. "Do the boys know how their parents died?"

"No, they don't. I can't bring myself to tell them yet. If ever. They think it was a car accident. That's why I moved here, so we could have a fresh start. My sister was living in Atlanta, and even though they had their school and their friends, I didn't want them to hear the news on TV or hear local gossip. I had a friend who was going to grad school here, and she helped me find a job. I put the insurance money into a trust fund for their educations, and here we are. I never did go to cooking school, but what I did do was a lot better, I think."

They sat in silence for a moment, and then Johnny asked her another candid question. "What happened to your fiancé? I'm assuming you never got married."

"No, we didn't. After my sister died, he announced that he didn't intend to raise somebody else's kids, and it was them or him. So I passed on him."

"It was his loss," Johnny said.

"And my narrow escape."

Alec and Cameron came in the back door, talking some trash about their favorite athletes. "Hey, Ma. Is there anything to eat?"

"You know what's in there. Help yourself, and leave the kitchen clean," she said fondly. "It's getting to be about that time, isn't it?" she said, looking meaningfully at the clock. She insisted that they go to bed at a decent hour for school.

"Not too much longer, Ma," Cameron answered. "Can we get you something, John?"

"Not a thing. Thanks for your hospitality, guys. Don't forget Dave & Buster's this week. Can I persuade you to walk me to the door?" Johnny stood up and held his hand out to Ayanna.

"I think I have just about enough strength in my frail little body to do that."

When they reached the front door, Johnny took both her hands and looked down at her. "Ayanna, this was one of the best days I've had in a long time. And being the greedy person we both know I am, I want more days just like this one. I want to spend more time with you and Alec and Cameron. I want to get to know you better so I can start checking off that list," he said grinning. "Can we do that?"

Ayanna cleared her throat before answering, trying to think of something to say that would be lighthearted and noncommittal. "Sure, that sounds like fun. Just give me a call sometime, okay?"

Johnny pulled her closer to his body as he placed her hands on his shoulders. He leaned in to give her a kiss, and she automatically turned her head to accept a brotherly peck on the cheek. He turned her face so he could touch his lips to hers and brought her even closer so that they were body to body, separated only by the clothes they wore. He covered her mouth with his own and teased her lips apart with his tongue. In seconds the kiss deepened and sweetened into something that Ayanna had never experienced before.

She was blazing hot from the soles of her feet to the top of her head, and her arms were locked around his neck. He was holding her as tightly as he could without hurting her, but even in her hazy state Ayanna didn't care about anything but being closer to him. He lifted her off the floor, and she fit against him even better. His lips were as tasty as dark chocolate and just as sweet. His tongue was doing things to hers that was making her body hungry for more. He nibbled at her full, pouty mouth and suckled the sharp sensation away while drinking her in so deeply that her flip-flops fell off her feet, and she didn't realize it until he gently lowered her to the floor, giving her little kisses as they pulled apart with great reluctance.

"I wanted to make sure there were no misunderstandings, Ayanna. I don't want to be your big brother, your play cousin, your pal or your buddy. I want to be your man."

Ayanna's face reflected her utter surprise, and Johnny had to tease her a little.

"You called it, baby. I don't hold back. Can you handle that?"

Before she could answer him, he was kissing her again, and the need for conversation vanished for the moment.

Chapter 6

Johnny knew he'd behaved brashly, but there was no going back. And he wasn't about to let her hide from him. After he kissed her totally senseless, he called her. He didn't wait until he got to Billie and Jason's house; he called from his cell phone.

He smiled when he heard her voice. "Are you scared of me now?" he teased.

"Yes!"

He laughed at her gently. "You have no reason to be. I meant every word I said, Ayanna. I want you."

"Oh...."

Johnny tried hard not to laugh again. "Look, I know this seems a little hasty—"

"Ya think?"

"Okay, I'll grant you that my behavior may seem a bit precipitous, but I don't believe in wasting time. Do you like me?"

He could hear a little sigh from her end. "Of course I do. You're a very nice man."

"Ouch. If you still think I'm nice after the way I kissed you, I wasn't doing it right."

There it was; the little giggle he loved to hear. "It's been awhile, but you did it just right."

He was immediately intrigued. "How long is 'a while'?"

"Almost ten years," she answered.

"Not since your fiancé?" He tried not to sound incredulous, but it was impossible to keep the shock to himself.

"That's right."

He didn't respond right away, and it was her turn to tease him. "Are you scared of me now?"

"Not in the least, baby. I was just thinking about what fools men can be, that's all. Do you date much?"

"I have two growing sons, a full-time job and I do volunteer work. I don't have time to date."

"I see. Well, get a new planner or PDA or whatever because that's about to change."

When he reached the house, he wasn't surprised to find Billie and his mother waiting for him. He entered the dining room to find them sitting next to each other looking over some catalogs of what seemed to be baby things. They looked at him expectantly, and he crossed his arms and looked back.

"Go ahead, get it over with."

"What are you talking about, Son?"

"That innocent voice doesn't fool me. You're dying to know what happened with Ayanna today, and I'm not going to tell you."

Lee sniffed and went back to her catalog. "He was always a difficult child."

Billie just smirked at him. "I'll see her at work tomorrow, and I'll find out," she said cheerfully.

"You do that. Let me know what she says." He left the room and grinned when he heard her go "Humph."

His father, Boyd, and Jason were watching CNN in the media room, and he sat down to join them. Boyd waited a few minutes before turning to Johnny.

"You had a good time with that young lady, didn't you?"

"The best."

"Good. She's a keeper."

"I agree."

"That's because I'm always right."

Johnny decided to let that one pass. "Pop, how did you know you were going to marry Mama?"

"That's easy. I knew when she told me."

He and Jason slapped hands while Johnny just shook his head.

"I'm going to bed. It's been a long day, and I've got to get ready for the new office," Johnny said as he rose to leave the room.

He detoured through the dining room and whispered to Billie, "Where's the piranha?"

"Davina took an early flight back to New York. You're safe."

"Thank you, Jesus."

As soon as Ayanna got to work, she found Billie waiting for her with a big cup of herbal tea and a cheesy grin on her face. "Here you go," she said sweetly. "It's herbal and decaf because that's all I can have, but it should work."

"Work for what?"

"I'm hoping it'll lubricate your jaws because you know how nosy I am! Did you have fun with Johnny?"

Ayanna put her canvas briefcase on her desk, followed by her purse. She sat down and took the steaming cup from Billie. "You are nosy. Johnny warned me that you were going to snoop," she said, enjoying the look of surprise on Billie's face.

"He told you? When did he tell you?"

"This morning. He called me to say good morning, and he warned me to expect an inquisition."

Billie's eyes widened with admiration. "He never calls women in the morning. Ever. That's definitely a first. So did y'all have a good time or what?"

Ayanna put her cup down and held out her hand to Billie. "Give me your little finger," she demanded.

Billie complied, hooking her pinkie with Ayanna's in the time-honored girlfriend's vow.

"Okay, you can't lie to me. Is your brother crazy?"

"Nope. He's one of the most levelheaded, responsible, caring people in the world. In the universe, really."

"I was afraid of that," Ayanna said glumly. She let go of Billie's finger.

"I'm lost. You find out he's sane, and that scares you?"

"Yes, it does. I haven't been out with a man or been with a man since I broke up with my fiancé. Johnny is a wonderful person. He's very sweet and kind and handsome and he likes my boys and it's just too much for me to take in."

Billie's eyes softened, and she took Ayanna's hand. "I have a question for you. How do you eat an elephant?"

"What?" Ayanna looked and sounded bewildered.

"It's a riddle," Billie explained. "How do you eat an elephant?"

"I have no idea," Ayanna replied.

"One bite at a time. Don't try and figure everything out all at once. I tease my brother a lot because he's always been a ladies' man, but he's a *good* man. Just enjoy yourself."

Enjoying herself proved to be easier than she anticipated, because Johnny made it so. He called her often, and they had long talks that were both funny and sexy. He took her out several times, always including Alec and Cameron. They went to restaurants and movies and to a baseball game and every outing was more fun than the last. In addition to getting to know him better, Ayanna got a fabulous dessert every time in the form of his divine kisses. On the one hand, she wasn't dreaming about the imaginary Ramon anymore, but her days and nights were full of fantasies about a real man—Johnny.

They were going on a date that night, just the two of them. Alec and Cameron were going to their best friend's house for an end-of-school cookout, and Johnny was taking her for an early dinner.

"Ma, are you ready? John is here to pick you up." Cameron's voice floated up the stairs.

"Tell him he's early! I'll be down in a minute." She wasn't dressed up, but she looked nice. She was wearing jeans and a red halter top in a lustrous rayon knit with a matching shrug to cover her shoulders. Her hair was blown straight, and she had curled it with a one-inch iron for a different look. She had on little makeup, just a powder foundation, mascara and lip gloss. She picked up her clutch bag from the bed and slid her feet into a pair of sexy sandals with three-inch heels. She put another dab of lotion on her hands and her neck so the scent would last, and she was ready to go.

"You look beautiful, as always."

They were seated in a secluded booth in a bistro with a nice atmosphere and a great jazz trio. Ayanna propped her chin in her hand and looked at Johnny. "Thank you. And you look very handsome. Are you still sure you want to make that twelve-hour drive with us?"

"I wouldn't have it any other way." Johnny crossed his arms on the table and gave her one of his long, searching looks.

"It's really nice of you. I've driven it lots of times, though, and we do just fine."

The drive was the distance between Chicago and Columbia, South Carolina, where her mother lived. Alec and Cameron were going to spend the summer with their grandmother and their aunt, and Johnny volunteered to drive down with them.

"I'm sure you do, but you don't have to do things like that by yourself anymore. I wouldn't feel comfortable with you driving by yourself with the boys. People are too crazy these days. It's not like back in the day when it was safe to go on the road. Gas prices have people freaked out; people are scared about losing their jobs…" He stopped talking when Ayanna put her hand over his mouth.

"Wow. Don't hold back. Tell me how you really feel," she said lightly. A soft sound escaped her lips when his tongue stroked her palm. She felt the sensation radiating up her arm and down through her chest right to her nipples. She pulled her hand back and picked up her glass of water.

"I apologize for sounding like your father, but I can't apologize for being concerned about you. Besides, a road trip can be a lot of fun. It'll give us time to work on your list."

"Will you stop with that list? I haven't given you a list of my desires." She made a little face at him.

"I'm going to make one for you. Are you a virgin?"

Ayanna rolled her eyes. "Nice segue, chief. No, I'm not a virgin. I haven't had a lot of experience, but I've had some."

"But not since your engagement," he said.

"That's a big assumption. Who says it's been that long?"

"You did," he reminded her.

Ayanna bit her lower lip. "Okay, you got me."

"How have you gone so long without intimacy? People need that closeness, that contact. It's part of what makes us human." Johnny took one of her hands and started rubbing his thumb on the back of it, stroking it softly but firmly.

"Really? Well, not everybody thinks that sex is the be-all and end-all. I didn't think it was all that great."

The soft stroking of her hand continued. "That's because he didn't do it right. What was his name, anyway?"

Ayanna's palm was moist and warm, and she was feeling that same heady damp heat in other parts of her body as she looked into his hypnotic eyes. "His name was, umm, Percy."

"Well, Percy didn't know what the hell he was doing. You're a very sensual woman, and you need a man who appreciates every inch of you and knows how to bring you the kind of pleasure you were meant to feel."

She pulled her hand away quickly and used it to fan her face. "Whoa. Does that line usually work for you?"

"I can't say, I've never said those words to a woman before. But I have to say I've never met a woman who needed to hear them more than you."

His words rang in her ears all the way back to her

house. They barely spoke on the way, and she was still distracted when they reached her door. She tried twice to insert the key in the lock and failed.

"Let me do that for you." He took the keys from her and opened the door. After they were inside, he looked around the house to make sure everything was secure. Ayanna followed him down the hall to the spare room and watched as he checked the windows.

He turned to see her standing in the doorway and held out his hand.

She walked to him slowly and took his hand. He sat down on the chaise and pulled her into his lap. "Did I embarrass you at the restaurant?"

"A little. I was more excited than embarrassed," she mumbled into his shoulder.

"That's good." He kissed her hair, her forehead and tilted her chin up so he could kiss her mouth. It was slow and tender at first, his tongue teasing the edge of her lips. He sucked gently until her mouth opened to receive him. Her hands moved to his shoulders, and she held on tight as a strange sensation took over her body. She felt an urgency building between her legs, and she wanted to get closer to Johnny, wanted to feel him on her and in her. Suddenly everything came to a head, and she tensed, moaning his name out loud as she felt a convulsive shock of pure bliss.

Only when their lips came apart did she realize that he'd somehow freed her breasts from her strapless bra and was stroking them, his thumbs circling her nipples and making her crazy with desire.

"He never did that to you, did he?"

Ayanna couldn't speak; she was too amazed by what had just happened. He moved so that she was straddling him on the chaise while he took off her shrug and slid the top and bra down to free her breasts. He bent his head to her nipples and stroked one with his hot tongue before taking it in his mouth like a piece of his favorite candy. He sucked and licked one, then the other until that amazing feeling took over again, and she was rocking her hips against his massive erection and stifling a scream.

All too soon, he released her and pulled her top back up. He was still holding her and his lips were still warming her throat and her collarbone, but now the quivering and throbbing were going on deep in her womanly recesses, and she didn't want them to stop.

"Shh, it's okay, baby. I shouldn't have done that, but I wanted you to see that it can be that good. I'm not going to have the boys come home and find me pawing you so we have to stop, even though it's the last thing I want to do. But when we're on our way back from South Carolina, you're all mine, every sweet inch of you. And I'm going to show you what loving is all about."

Her eyes were glazed as she continued to gently rock against his manhood. "You mean there's more?"

He kissed her hard, cupping her face in his hands. "There's a whole lot more, and we're going to love every minute of it."

Chapter 7

When they pulled up in the driveway of the beautiful two-story home of Lucie Porter, Johnny felt right at home. The house was as gracious and warm as Ayanna's mother, who made him feel welcome as soon as she greeted her doting grandsons.

"Cameron and Alec! I thought you'd never get here," she exclaimed. "Come give me some sugar, you two." The boys ran to her open arms and embraced her willingly.

"I practically have to sit on them to get that much love," Ayanna said laughingly. "Hey, Mommy, I'm here, too, or did you not see me?"

Lucie came down the porch steps with a big smile. "Of course I see you, sweetie. How could I not see my baby?" She threw her arms open for a big hug, and Ayanna took it gratefully. They hugged tightly and Lucie said, "You look beautiful, honey, just gorgeous. Have a real glow about you."

Finally it was Johnny's turn. "Johnny, this is my mother, Lucie Porter. Mommy, this is Johnny," Ayanna said shyly.

Johnny took the hand Lucie extended to him and kissed it. "Mrs. Porter, it's an absolute privilege to meet you," he said.

"The pleasure is all mine. And call me Lucie," she said, taking his arm. "I have a feeling we're going to be very good friends. You all can get the luggage later. I've fixed you a little something to eat, and we can get acquainted."

The interior of the house was mid-century modern but uniquely Lucie with pops of color against the neutral palette. The furniture was oyster-white, but there were bright pillows and paintings and healthy green plants everywhere. It reminded Johnny of Ayanna's home, very feminine and warm. Lucie was almost as good a cook as Ayanna, and she'd made a feast of braised short ribs, macaroni and cheese, hot homemade rolls, fresh okra and tomatoes and green beans. The boys ate like they hadn't seen food in weeks, and Johnny wasn't far behind.

"Lucie, this was delicious," he said. "I can see where Ayanna got her skill."

"Oh, honey, that's sweet of you, but Ayanna actually taught me a few things. She really learned to cook from her great-grandmother and my mother. She used to love to be in the kitchen with Nonnie, my grandmother.

She would sit on a big stool and watch everything she did, and by the time she was five or six, she was helping her bake cookies and make piecrust. She was fascinated by everything that went on in the kitchen. I knew she'd be a chef one day," Lucie said fondly.

They were sitting in the dining room sipping Lucie's delicious sweet tea and letting their meal digest. The boys had gallantly cleared the table and started the dishwasher before taking off to explore the yard and shoot some hoops.

"Johnny, I can't thank you enough for bringing my family home safely. That was so kind of you," Lucie said. She seemed to be taking his measure as she spoke, and she liked what she saw.

"It wasn't kind at all," Johnny said, caressing Ayanna with his eyes. "I didn't want her driving that far by herself. I wanted to make sure she and the boys got here okay. There're a lot of loony tunes out there these days."

"Very gallant," Lucie murmured.

Johnny had a question that surprised Ayanna. "So why did you always think she'd be a chef and not a dancer? Where did she learn to dance like she does?"

Ayanna groaned. "So, the garden looks really nice," she said loudly, hoping to change the subject, but it was too late.

"Honey, my baby started dancing in the womb," Lucie said. "If there was music on, she'd start kicking and jumping until it went off! When she was a baby she danced before she could walk. Come on in the living room, and let me show you some pictures."

"I'm going to call Emily. Johnny, don't let her start showing movies or we're leaving tonight," she threatened.

Johnny was enthralled by the pictures of Ayanna as an adorable dimpled baby, a charming toddler and the prettiest little girl he'd ever seen. Most of the pictures showed her with long curly hair, and she looked like a doll. All her dance recital pictures were there, and they were so unbearably cute he couldn't stand it. Ayanna came into the living room to report that her sister Emily hadn't answered her phone.

"I left her a message. Mommy, don't show him those," she protested.

"Too late," Johnny said. "You were a beautiful baby, and you're an even more beautiful woman. Don't be embarrassed."

She went to the sofa where he was sitting with Lucie and sat down next to him. He put his arm around her and kissed her on the cheek. "You could have been a professional dancer, you know."

"It was fun, but it was never my passion," she said simply. "I like feeding people more."

He whispered in her ear, "You can feed me anytime you want."

Lucie smiled and pretended that she didn't notice a thing.

"Why do all men think they have to do the grilling?" Ayanna was smiling as she looked out her mother's kitchen window. Johnny was explaining to Alec and

Cameron all the finer points of turning out perfectly done barbecue.

"Honey, it's a man thing, that's all I can tell you. They might not be able to boil water, but hand them a slab of raw meat and an open flame and they go right back to being cavemen. Can you do me a favor and put some eggs on for the potato salad?"

"Hmm? Oh, I made it already. It's in the refrigerator," Ayanna said absentmindedly.

"Oh, thank you, honey. You're still Mama's sweetie pie. Now, do you think you can tear yourself away from the window before you wear your eyes out looking at that big hunk of man?"

Ayanna turned to give her mother a big cheese-eating grin. The resemblance between the two was evident in the color of their skin and their big dimples, as well as their long curly eyelashes. Lucie Porter was a little shorter than Ayanna, and her layered hair was shoulder-length. It was streaked with rich chestnut-brown, and she had the same slender build as her daughter.

"I'm trying to, but I can't seem to stop."

Lucie laughed. "He is awfully pretty. I'd look at him, too, if he was mine. Tell me again, what does he do for a living?"

Tearing her eyes away at last, Ayanna went to the freezer to take out some of the peaches her mother put up every summer. "I think I'll make a cobbler." While she was getting the flour and butter and sugar, she reminded her mother about Johnny's occupation.

"He's a lawyer. He used to be in labor law, but he left that to head up an international relief foundation that does work all over the world. He travels to Africa a lot and to other places, too. He's very compassionate, and the boys are so taken with him! He likes to spend time with them."

"I can tell. It's about time you—" Lucie's words were cut off by the banging of the back door.

"About time she got a man, Mother?"

Ayanna and Lucie exchanged a look as the youngest member of the Porter family, Emily, came in the kitchen wearing her customary deadpan expression. She continued talking in a sneering tone. "Ooh, let's have a parade because Ayanna done found her a man! 'Cause Lawd knows that's all a woman is good for. Got to get her a good man and settle down to start pumpin' out babies."

Emily bore little resemblance to her mother or sister. She was five-foot-eight and a good bit heavier than either woman. She would have been attractive, but she made no effort with her appearance or her attitude. It was a hot, sunny day, and she was wearing denim overalls and a long-sleeved henley shirt with thick-soled boots. Her hair was thick and long, but it was dry and unruly, and the way she had it pulled back into a sloppy ponytail did nothing to emphasize her features. All it did was give her an angry look because she had a rather low hairline.

"Hello, Emily. It's nice to see you. Thanks again for inviting the boys to your science camp." Ayanna did what she almost always had to do with Emily, which was change the subject and act as though she hadn't heard any rudeness.

Emily gave her a mean little grin. "Oh no, you're not going to go all passive-aggressive on me. I did my thesis on that crap."

"Which one of the three?" Ayanna murmured as she washed her hands. Emily had so many degrees Ayanna had lost count. She was a college professor and apparently a good one because her students loved her and she enjoyed the respect of her peers. Ayanna was quite proud of her younger sister, but they weren't very close. Emily's prickly personality made it impossible for anyone to get close to her.

"So who's the loser you've hooked yourself up with?"

"I don't know any losers," Ayanna said. "But that's my friend John Phillips at the grill, and if you'd like to meet him, the boys will be happy to do the honors." She began measuring the ingredients for her pastry crust to show Emily that this particular conversation was over. She was in too good a mood to let her sister upset her. But Emily got the last word.

"I would like to meet him. I'd love to see what all the fuss is about." She turned around and headed for the back door.

The two days they spent in Columbia went quickly. Johnny thoroughly enjoyed meeting Ayanna's family, especially her mother, who was as charming and per-

sonable as Ayanna. He glanced over to the passenger
seat where Ayanna had her nose buried in a book. She
was wearing red shorts with a white blouse, and her
little black flats with the red bow on the toes were, even
to his male eye, too cute. The best part of her ensemble
was the shorts, however. He could look at her fantastic legs as much as he wanted, and even better, he could
touch them, which he did. He reached over and stroked
the warm silky skin of her thigh, waiting for her
response.

She didn't let him down; she went "ooh" before the
adorable little giggle followed.

"Are you trying to give me a heart attack? I'll give
you exactly fifteen minutes to stop that."

He stroked her again and kept his hand on her leg.
"Did you have a good time, baby?"

"I always do. My mom and I are very close, so it's
always good to see her. She thinks you're a magnificent
specimen of man, by the way. That's a direct quote."

"Aw, you're gonna make me blush. The feeling is
mutual, though. Your mother is a goddess," he said.
"She reminds me of my mother. They're even in the
same profession."

Like Lee Phillips, Lucie Porter had started as an RN
but kept taking classes until she got two masters
degrees and started teaching nursing. Now both of them
were college department heads: Johnny had a feeling
the two women would really hit it off, although he
knew no such thing would happen with sister Emily.
With his usual frankness, he asked Ayanna a question.

"About Emily. Does she hate all men, or is it just me?"

A long sigh came from Ayanna. "Look, don't take it personally. There aren't too many people she likes, regardless of gender. She's an equal-opportunity hater. She dislikes men, women, cats, children, old people, young people, rainy days, sunny days, vegetarians, meat eaters, whatevers. She's just not real sociable," she said. "I don't know how she got to be so crabby at such a young age. She was really close to Daddy, and when he died it was very hard on her. It was hard on all of us, but she was the worst."

Johnny continued stroking her thigh, because he loved the feel of her and because he wanted to impart some comfort to her.

"Sometimes I think that's why Mommy never dated again. There are any number of men who've wanted to get closer to her, but she keeps them all at arm's length. I think it's because of Emily. She would pitch such an unholy fit whenever a man would come around that Mommy just quit trying to have a normal life. Even now that Emily lives on her own and has a career, Mommy is still single and unattached. But I think she'd really like to have a man in her life."

Her paperback book slid to the floor, and she dove after it.

"What the heck are you reading? I'm taking you to one of the most romantic cities in the South for some alone time, and you're reading a book on the way?" He shook his head.

"Aw, now don't get pouty. I'm very excited about going to Charleston. It's a beautiful place, and it was very thoughtful of you to think of it. But I'm not really reading, I'm studying."

On the night of their date, before Johnny left to pick up the boys from their friend's party, he'd announced that he was kidnapping her. "Since we're going all the way to South Carolina, I'm taking you to Charleston for a couple of days. Do you like Charleston?"

"I love it, but—"

"Take that word out of your vocabulary, Ayanna. I want us to be someplace unique, beautiful and private when we make love for the first time. You deserve the best, and I'm going to give it to you, always."

Two days later they left for South Carolina, and now they were on their way for the first vacation Ayanna had ever taken with a man. And she called herself studying?

"What in the world could be so important that you have to bone up on it now?"

Ayanna showed him the cover of the book, which depicted a handsome man and a very sexy-looking woman locked in a passionate embrace. "I'm brushing up on my technique," she said mischievously.

"You read those things? Is that porn or something?"

Ayanna shook her head vigorously. "No, this is not porn. I love romance novels, I always have. Mommy used to read them, and I used to steal hers. These are regular novels, but they're just really sexy and exciting."

"Baby, you are looking at all the excitement you need right here," Johnny said.

"I'm sure I am, darlin'. But I'm the neophyte, remember?"

"Read it to me. I want to see what some writer thinks passes for real grown and sexy romance."

"Okay."

She began reading in the voice that drove him crazy. She had a low, sexy way of speaking that made him melt inside, and when she got to the love scenes he almost drove off the expressway.

"What's up, chief? You want me to stop reading?"

"Hell, no. Keep going, baby. This is hot."

"Just remember, you asked for this." She kept reading until he finally said enough.

"All right, Ayanna, that's enough. That's like audio erotica. I had no idea that's what those books were like. It's got a good plot, the characters were real and the sex was, well, let's just say it was inspiring."

"Do you mean that, or are you just trying to humor me?"

He took her hand in his and placed it over his thigh so she could feel his erection. It was rock-hard and ready for business.

"I'm not trying to humor anybody. I'm trying to get to the hotel before I pull off the road and do something real crazy."

Ayanna's eyes got big as she realized the length and width of him. "Um, Johnny? Hurry up, please."

He gave a harsh, short laugh and glanced at the dashboard clock. "We'll be there in about twenty minutes. Ten if you don't move your hand."

He laughed again as she snatched her hand back like his pants had burst into flames.

"Johnny, this isn't what I expected at all."

"Don't you like it here?" He sounded a little bit apprehensive, and she quickly assured him that she loved it.

"Oh, I love it, but I thought we'd be going to a hotel. This place is like something out of a movie. It's amazing." She was standing in the living room of their villa at the Wild Dunes Resort on the Isle of Palms. It was about a half hour from Charleston, and it was magnificent. The living room had a modern yet tropical feel with warm earth colors and every possible creature comfort. A small kitchen and two bedrooms with baths completed the cottage.

Johnny crossed the room and put his hands on her hips. "Did you think I was going to take you to some no-tell motel? You should know me better than that. You only get the best, baby. And I didn't want to keep our neighbors up since I think you're gonna be loud."

She opened her mouth for an indignant retort and got a mouthful of joy for her efforts. He covered her lips with his and kissed her until she was breathless. "I'm not loud," she whispered.

"Yes, but you will be." Still holding her hips, he pulled her closer, stroking and squeezing her butt. "Did I ever tell you what a cute bottom you have?"

"Actually, no, you've never mentioned it." She put her hands on his behind and moved them up and down.

"Are you hungry?" He lifted her up, and she had to put her arms on his shoulders for balance.

"No, I'm not."

"Tired?"

"Not at all."

"Want to take a shower?"

Ayanna nodded her head before putting one hand on each side of his face. "Yes, I do. With you," she said before kissing him gently. He lifted her higher, and she wrapped her legs around his waist and kept kissing him until they were in the bedroom.

Somehow he managed to get her on the bed and lay down on top of her without breaking the kiss. She loved feeling his weight and his warmth so close to her, but it didn't last long because he rolled over on his back, taking her with him. Now she was on his chest, looking down at him.

"You're really strong, aren't you?"

"You don't weigh that much. I could carry you all day. But right now, I want to get you out of these clothes." He was trying to unbutton the small buttons on her blouse.

She rose to her knees and took over, undoing one button at a time until the blouse was undone, and she removed it.

"You can unhook my bra," she offered.

"Thank you," he said. He sat up and kissed her flat, toned stomach, licking her navel while he tried to unhook the bra from the back. "How do you undo this thing?"

"See this little flower in front? That's the hook."

The words were barely out of her mouth before he'd released it and her breasts were bared to his welcoming eyes. "Those are the prettiest... Mmm," he took one in his mouth while he slid the bra off her body.

"Your turn. We're supposed to be taking a shower, remember?" She wasn't aware that her voice was shaking a little, but Johnny heard it.

He pulled away from her long enough to stand up and take off his shirt while he kicked off his loafers, and then he unbuckled his belt and unzipped his jeans. Ayanna felt a warmth building between her thighs, and her nipples were already engorged from his brief play. He was beautiful, in every sense of the word. His dark skin gleamed in the afternoon sunlight, and when he pulled down his briefs and jeans in one motion, she could see the full length of his arousal. Her eyes widened and her mouth formed an O of awe.

"I'm not going to hurt you, baby. It's not as big as it looks."

Ayanna looked at him with a sexy smile. "Oh yes it is. And I want it," she murmured.

She unfastened her shorts and took them off with Johnny's help. Her thong followed, and before she knew it, he was carrying her to the shower.

Chapter 8

The warm water felt wonderful but not as good as it felt to be in Johnny's arms. His strong, muscular arms were locked around her waist, and she stood on tiptoe to get closer to him. He lifted her so that she was resting on his erection, and the heavy thickness of it made her tremble. "Johnny," she moaned.

"I'm right here, baby." He gently slid her down so she was facing him. He reached for a bottle of bath gel and put some in his palm. He poured out some of the lightly scented liquid and rubbed it on her breasts. "You are so pretty. These are perfect," he told her. "Everything about you is perfect." She was holding his waist while he rubbed her body in circles, making a soft lather that felt heavenly. "Turn around," he said.

She did, holding her arms up so he could lather every inch of her body, making a soft sound of pleasure when he started palming her buttocks. He knelt down and kissed each one, lavishing her tender skin with his tongue. This time he didn't say anything, but he turned her to face him.

He applied more gel to her body, this time concentrating on the silky triangle that covered her womanhood.

One of the two handheld showerheads was on the floor of the tub next to him, and he picked it up, using it to rinse away the foam. It was a wonderful sensation, but not as good as what came next. He gripped her hips and positioned his head so that he could kiss the inside of her thighs, licking his way to the treasure. His tongue was deep between her legs, stroking her femininity and caressing the throbbing pearl, sucking and licking until the pleasure got to be too much to hold in. She cried out but he didn't relent; he kept going while she climaxed again and again.

He gradually slowed down, finishing in one long, passionate caress that left tears rolling down her face. She collapsed onto him, and he held her tightly. He lifted the lever that stopped the tub and it began to fill with warm foamy water. "Happy?"

He was leaning back against the high, broad tub, and she was lying on his chest. Small aftershocks rippled through her, and she felt amazing, lighter-than-air, dreamy and satisfied. "Yes, I am. Are you?"

"Better than that." He put his lips to her ear and whispered, "You were so worth the wait."

Ayanna was looking around for the bath gel, and

when she found it, it was her turn to bathe him. She straddled his long legs and started rubbing his broad chest with the foaming gel. She loved touching him, loved the feel of his skin. She leaned forward to lick the base of his throat, and it tasted so good she kept doing it, stroking and licking until she got to his nipples. She treated them just like he'd treated hers, kissing and sucking until she heard a long groan.

Looking really pleased with herself she sat up and said, "Don't you like that?"

"Don't play with me," he said sternly. "You know I like that."

"How about this?" She moved so that she was sitting down in the tub facing him, and she took his manhood in both hands. "You might have to teach me how to do this," she confessed as she stroked it gently, moving her hands up and down the hard shaft. "I'm not very good at this kind of thing," she added.

"You're doing just fine," he assured her.

He was caught off guard when she lowered her head and covered the tip with her mouth. Her tongue circled it gently and tentatively at first, but she parted her lips wider and increased the pressure as she continued to stroke the shaft.

"Ayanna, oh damn, Ayanna." His voice was hoarse, and his breathing had quickened. "Slow down, baby. Come up here. Stop, stop," he groaned.

She allowed him to gather her into his arms although she protested. "Was I doing it wrong?"

"You were doing it way too well. I'm trying to make

this all about you, and I want it to last all night, so we just need to slow down or… Well, never mind. So is that what you've learned from those novels of yours?"

"Yep. I'm a quick study."

He stood up, taking her with him. He wrapped a towel around her before putting one on himself. "Sweetness, you're the valedictorian of your class. Get me that author's address, I want to send her some orchids," he said as he carried her into their bedroom.

He set her on the bed like she was a precious work of very fragile art. Her hair was wet from the shower, and it was already forming curls around her face. Her makeup, what little she wore, was gone. Her skin was dewy and moist and he wanted to lick all the droplets of water from every bit of her body. He spread a dry towel over the bedspread, and then he pulled the pillows out. He lay down and smiled when Ayanna joined him. She leaned over to kiss him.

"My hair is wet," she murmured.

"So? You're still gorgeous," he replied as he undid the towel to reveal her body.

She returned the favor, undoing the thick terry cloth to reveal his thickening desire for her.

"I thought you'd be shy," he said, smiling as she wrapped her small hand around his tumescence.

"I thought I would be, too. Maybe I'm a hoochie at heart and never knew it." She was stroking him up and down, slowly and deliberately. Her arousal was evident in the way her nipples were beginning to harden and grow larger. He leaned over to take one in his mouth and sucked hard, making her moan softly. Her free hand began rubbing the back of his head, spreading a soft fire down his back. He pulled harder, making her arch her back and whisper his name. He wanted her to feel even more, and using his long fingers, he found the source of her pleasure and began to stroke until she felt wet and hot, ready for more.

He used his thumb to stroke her pulsing clitoris, moving in circles to increase the sensation while he moved his mouth to her other breast, applying the same strong suction. Her hand trembled then tightened on his fully engorged penis, and he could feel the beginning of her climax. Her hips were moving, and her breaths were coming rapidly. He kissed his way up her chest to her neck, then to her lips. He kissed her open mouth and looked at her face as her eyes fluttered closed and her body responded to his touch. When her release came, it was long and gratifying, and the sounds of satisfaction were music to his ears.

He was going to ease her down on the bed to rest, but she surprised him again. "I want to make love to you, Johnny. I want to make you feel what you do to me," she whispered. "Kiss me, please."

He did so at once, tasting her, sucking and licking her lips until he had to stop to get the condoms or risk putting his baby into her. He retrieved them quickly, and she insisted that he let her do it. He lay back and watched her apply it, slowly and carefully. He loved looking at her, especially now with her legs spread over him and her body moist and ready.

"Have you ever done it like this?"

Her eyes widened. "On top?"

"Yes. You're going to get on top of me, and we're going to take it slow and easy until you're ready for more." He slid his hands up her thighs and held her hips, helping her balance as he entered her. She closed her eyes and sighed as he began to push slowly, trying to establish an easy rhythm. She moved with him, rocking back and forth, rising and falling with his every thrust. She was tight, hot and wet, and when he felt her muscles clench and flex on his manhood, it was his turn to call her name. He let go of her hips to hold her hands, and with their fingers clasped, they rode out the passionate storm together. He was watching her face again, and when she threw her head back and a low, musical sound came from her throat he let go of her hands and grasped her hips again, holding her tightly as he let out his own release, thrusting up sharply as a sharp cry was torn from his throat.

She fell onto his chest, and he held her close. His heart was pounding as hard as hers, and they were both sweaty and very satisfied. He kissed her every so often and rubbed her back gently. If it had meant his life he couldn't have let her go. He held her until her soft, regular breathing told him she'd fallen asleep, and only then did he close his own eyes.

When Ayanna finally awoke, she was groggy and disoriented. She reached over to touch Johnny, but the bed was empty. She sat up, clutching the sheet to her naked body. *Was I dreaming? Did it really happen or have I finally gone over the edge?* As she started to get out of bed, she felt the pleasant aftermath of their fierce lovemaking, and she knew it wasn't a fantasy. But where was Johnny? The phone on the bedside table rang, and she got her answer.

"Hello, sweetness. I let you sleep, and I went to get us something to eat. I'll be back in about a half hour if you want to take a shower."

"That sounds nice. I'll get up now," she said, covering a dainty yawn.

"How do you feel?" he asked.

"Wonderful. Fabulous. Hungry."

His deep laugh warmed her heart. "I'll see you soon, baby."

She stood up and found that last night she'd used some muscles that hadn't been active for some time, so she decided to take a bath and get rid of the slight soreness. She found her small bag with her cosmetics and took out the rose-scented bubble bath and creamy body wash. Soon the bathroom was filled with the heady scent of roses, and she was soaking in a tub full of bubbles. She amused herself by playing with the jets in the whirlpool tub, and in a short time she felt relaxed and ready for more of Johnny's passionate loving.

He was unlike anyone she'd ever met in her life. And he made her feel like she'd never felt before. He made her feel like a real woman. *What did I do to deserve this?* They always say to be careful what you wish for, and she understood the meaning of the phrase fully, now that

all her wishes had come true. For years she'd wished for
a prince and now she had a king. Of course, she only had
him for a short time, but every minute they were together
would be worth the pain she'd endure when their fling
was over. He wasn't the marrying kind, and she wasn't
the type he'd ever marry. The thought made her catch
her breath and massage the area right over her heart. It
would kill her to have to give him up when the time
came.

"Where are you, baby?"

Hastily wiping her eyes, she cleared her throat. "I'm
still in the bathroom."

He opened the door asking if she was decent.

"Not anymore. Come on in," she invited.

"It smells good in here. Here, let me do your back,"
he offered. He had changed shirts and was wearing a
linen one with the sleeves rolled up. He knelt next to
the tub and kissed her, then took the bath puff from her
hand and put some more body wash on it. He began
washing her back as if they were a real couple and he'd
done it for years. She stretched like a cat as he soaped
her from the nape of her neck down to her rounded
derriere.

"Did you sleep well?" he asked.

"Absolutely. When I woke up and you weren't here,
I thought it had all been a dream until I realized I wasn't
at home," she admitted.

"I should have left you a note. I'm sorry. Next time
I will. I just didn't want to wake you because you looked
so sweet." He leaned in for another kiss.

"You're sweet," she murmured. "What did you get to eat?"

He was still rubbing her back with one hand, but the other one was making a voyage of its own beneath the suds. "Something that will keep for a while. Want some company?"

"How fast can you get in?"

In less than a minute, he was rid of his clothes and they were entwined in the tub, kissing madly. It was a huge circular tub that could easily hold four adults, making it the perfect size for Johnny's long legs. She made him lie against the bath pillow and began rubbing his chest with her soapy hands.

"I know you're already clean, but I just like the way you feel. I like the way you look, too. You're probably the handsomest man I've ever seen. Better than Ramon." She giggled.

"Who the hell is Ramon?" he demanded.

She laughed at his reaction and at what she was about to reveal to him.

"Ramon was my imaginary lover. I used to dream about him and make up these elaborate fantasies. Isn't that pathetic?"

"What did he look like, this Ramon?" His voice sounded slightly gruff.

"Oh, he was the generic type, typical tall, dark and handsome. I think he had long hair," she said thoughtfully. "To be honest, he was like a composite of all the heroes from my novels. He was just there when I needed him."

She was still massaging him, kneading his firm flesh and reveling in his sheer maleness. He guided her in the water so that she was sitting in his lap. "You're not going to need him anymore," he said firmly. "You got that?"

"I might need some convincing," she teased as her thumbs played with his nipples.

His fingers immediately found her most sensitive spot, and he manipulated it with loving skill until she was throbbing and begging for more.

He relented but only long enough to reach out of the tub to get a condom out of the pocket of the jeans he'd discarded. "Now that I know what a hot little thing you are, I'm always going to be prepared." He quickly sheathed himself, rising to his knees to do so. "Get in front of me, Ayanna. Just like that, but bend over," he urged.

He helped her get into a kneeling position, running his palms up and down her sides and palming her round brown globes. "Hold on to the tub, baby." She put her hands on the rim and had to stifle a scream as she felt him enter her body from behind. Once he was fully inside, he began to pump slowly, in and out. As she got used to the pace, she began to respond and he took her on a ride to paradise. He squeezed her breasts and whispered loving words to her as he thrust his hardness into her softness.

He held her hips and she was spiraling out of control while he continued the ride. When his thumb began to caress her jewel her moans turned to a long cry of passion fulfilled, and his voice joined hers as he stopped pumping and ground his hips into her. She thought it was over but he gently helped her turn to face him. He kissed her rough and hard, then soft and sweet. "I have to see your face, Ayanna. When you come it's the sexiest thing in the world. Come for me now, baby. Let me see it on your face," he coaxed.

Incredibly, he was still hard and she was still yearning for him. He continued to pump and thrust, and she met him stroke for stroke. She held on to his shoulders, and their eyes were linked by the intensity of their desire until the world turned over and she came apart yet again. "That's it, Ayanna, that look on your face. Ayanna…" His words turned to moans, and he roared like a lion as he joined her in ecstasy.

It was much later, after they rinsed off the bubbles and dressed quickly, that Johnny told her something she didn't know. He was wearing another towel, and she had on one of his shirts and nothing else. They were sitting on the sofa in the living room sipping champagne. Johnny had bought a roast chicken, a loaf of French bread, wine, cheese and fruit for dinner. She had just fed him a strawberry, and he'd finished his glass of Cristal champagne. He stretched out on the sofa and put his head in her lap. After they kissed, he gave her a really sweet smile and asked if she knew his middle name.

"No, I don't actually. What is it?"

Grinning like a Cheshire cat he said, "It's Raymond."

"Oh, snap," she said, and they both laughed until the kissing began again.

Chapter 9

The smell of coffee roused Ayanna from sleep. And this time she wasn't alone. Johnny's arm was around her waist, and he was kissing the back of her neck.

"Good morning."

"Good morning to you," she said with a smile. She could feel him cuddled up to her body, but when she put her arm on his she could feel clothes. "Why are you dressed?"

"Because I got up early, took a shower and went to get breakfast. And because I have no intention of wearing you out. We clocked a lot of loving hours yesterday, and I don't want to break you," he said. "I could hurt a little thing like you."

She hurriedly sat up and wished she hadn't. "Ouch."

She looked over her shoulder at Johnny, who was lying on his side, propped up on his elbow. "See? I told you we overdid it yesterday. So today, we're taking it slow and easy. I ran a bath for you, and I brought you breakfast and then you're going to the spa."

"Spa? Really? I've never actually been to one," she said. "That's very thoughtful of you, Johnny." She was looking around for something to cover herself and didn't see a thing.

"Looking for this?" Johnny was holding her silky pink kimono on his index finger.

"Yes, as a matter of fact, I am." She reached for it only to have him pull it away.

"Where's my good morning kiss?"

She covered her mouth with one hand and held out the other. "In the bathroom with my toothpaste and mouthwash, and you should be real happy about that. Gimme."

She slipped on the robe after flashing her perky breasts at him. She stood up and had to stifle a groan. She was feeling pain in body parts she didn't know she had. How could she have felt so wonderful last night and so miserable this morning? She took one small step and then another.

"Aw, baby, let me carry you." Johnny was beside her before she knew it.

"Absolutely not. I'm going to walk into the bathroom with what's left of my dignity, and you are not going to say another word about it," she said. "Not a word."

She did her best to take slow, normal steps, but it was hard. She tightened the robe around her body and bit her lower lip as she hobbled to the door where a hot, scented oasis awaited her. Sighing with relief when she reached the doorway she tossed the robe aside and put one foot in the tub.

"You sure look good from the back, baby." Johnny gave a low whistle.

Ayanna sank into the piles of bubbles and prepared to let the hot water do its work. The bath pillow cradled her neck, and she closed her eyes to relax. She might be stiff as a board today but every minute she and Johnny spent making love was worth it. If she never in her life experienced anything like it again, it was worth it.

She was about to drift off to sleep when Johnny's voice roused her. "You have twenty more minutes, and then I'm coming to get you. If you drown in there, your mother will never forgive me."

"I wouldn't be too happy, either. I'd haunt you for the rest of your days," she said with a laugh. *Just like you're going to stay in my heart forever.*

The spa treatments she received were absolutely wonderful. She got a facial, a mud bath and a wonderful massage that made her feel and look like a new woman. Her hair was shampooed, blown dry and curled, and the makeup artist accentuated her features with a light application of color.

"You have fabulous skin," the woman, whose name

was Candice, praised. "You really don't need much of anything to look good because you have those nice black eyebrows and long eyelashes. I'm just going to put a little highlight under your brows and a gold shadow before I put on the mascara," she murmured. "Then I'm going to give you some bronze blush and a rose-gold lip gloss." She touched Ayanna's face lightly and thoroughly and in a few minutes, she was finished. "There, what do you think?" She turned the chair around so Ayanna could look in the mirror.

Ayanna was pleased with what she saw. She looked good, even to her own eyes. So good, in fact, that she decided to buy a new dress. She went into the boutique next to the spa and found a summery-looking dress of sheer fabric that was patterned with flowers. It had a low back and spaghetti straps, and the skirt flowed out from the flattering empire waist. She was so taken with it that she bought it at once. She was still feeling guilty about it when she got back to the villa, but she put it out of her mind. It was by far the most expensive dress she'd ever purchased, but she wanted to look good for Johnny. They were going to a nice restaurant that night, and she wanted to dazzle him.

Her ploy worked because when she came out of the bedroom dressed for dinner, he had to take a deep breath.

"Every time I think I know exactly what you look like, you surprise me. I thought I knew what beauty was, but you surpass everything I've ever seen," he said.

The look in his eyes made Ayanna want to cry, but

she swallowed hard and tried to give him a lighthearted response. "If you're trying to get out of feeding me, you can forget it," she said.

He ignored her quip and leaned down to kiss her gently on the lips. "Just beautiful."

The restaurant he'd chosen was called Middleton Place. It was a historic landmark that boasted gardens, a stable and museum. They arrived early so they could walk through the gardens before their meal. Ayanna loved the feel of the warm air on her bare shoulders as they roamed through the exquisite gardens. They walked hand in hand looking at the carefully cultivated flowers. To be more accurate, Ayanna looked at the flowers while Johnny looked at her. That was why they didn't see the guided missile headed their way.

"John Phillips! What are you doing in Charleston?"

The high-pitched female voice pierced the restful aura of their solitude. Ayanna saw a tall, thin woman with enormous breasts heading their way and she froze. She was pushed to the side like a swinging door as the woman latched on to Johnny. She was babbling a mile a minute, completely ignoring Ayanna's presence.

"It's been so long," she gushed. "I haven't seen you since that weekend in Capetown! How have you been, you handsome thing?"

Johnny took his time in answering. He took his hand-kerchief out of his jacket and wiped her bright lipstick off his face like it was snail slime. "Hello, Peyton." Putting his arm around Ayanna's waist, he anchored her next to his body. "Ayanna, this is Peyton Smith. Peyton, this," he said, looking down at Ayanna, "is Ayanna Porter."

Ayanna returned the woman's phony smile with one of her own. She could feel the woman assessing her, and she sensed the exact moment the other woman decided she was no competition.

"So nice to meet you, Alana." She turned the full power of her silicone chest on Johnny and started to ask him about some conference, but Johnny cut her off.

"If you'll excuse us, our table is ready. Nice seeing you," he said as they walked away.

Despite that interlude, the evening was lovely. She appreciated the fact that Johnny cleared up any potential misunderstanding about Peyton. "You'll have to excuse her. She's obviously full of herself, which is why she deliberately mispronounced your name. She's the president of a pharmaceutical company, and I met her a couple of years ago. That weekend in Capetown she was referring to was just two people at a conference who went their separate ways afterward. Period. This is the first time I've seen her since then."

"I believe you. You didn't have to explain, but I'm glad you did," she replied.

"How did you know? Have you got some psychic abilities you haven't told me about?" Johnny looked at her over the rim of his glass.

"All women are psychic. It's part of our charm. But if you must know, I didn't even have to use my superpowers for this one. She called you John, not Johnny, so I knew she was a business acquaintance. And she looked at me like she wanted to slap my eyeballs out of my head and feed them to me. That's how I knew she'd slept with you."

She lifted her glass in a little salute to him and grinned at his expression. "You grew up with three women, and you didn't realize how astute we are?"

"You're right on that count. How was your dinner?"

"Fabulous. And yours?"

"Delicious, but not as good as your cooking."

Ayanna beamed and excused herself to go freshen up. He rose from the table as she left. After attending to the necessities, she washed her hands and was checking her makeup when the door to the ladies' room opened and in walked Peyton Smith.

"I thought that was you," the other woman said. "I had to see for myself who that drab little thing was with John."

Ayanna sighed deeply. The woman might be a corporate giant, but when it came to common sense, she demonstrated very little. Ayanna obligingly put out her arms and executed a perfect runway spin.

"There you go. If you want to look any closer we'd have to start dating, and you aren't my type." She walked a few steps toward the door and turned back to Peyton with a look of concern on her face. "Look, it's not my business, but you might want to line up the girls because lefty looks like she's about to head for the border."

Peyton turned to the mirror and gasped. Before Ayanna left, she could see her frantically trying to push and shove the unruly blobs back into their corral. She was wearing a true Mona Lisa smile when she reached the lobby where Johnny was waiting.

"Where to now? Dancing, a drive by the river, live music or what? Anything you want, it's yours."

"Then I want a nice drive by the river on our way back to the villa. Then I want to…" She stood on her toes to whisper in his ear.

"We can be there in ten minutes." He grinned as they waited for the valet to bring the car around.

It was more like an hour before they got back to the villa. Despite his teasing, Johnny did take them the long way home. It was the perfect ending to a perfect day. When they got back to the suite, Johnny told her he had a surprise for her.

"It's in the other bedroom. Go in there and see how you like it."

She went into the bedroom and found a short silk nightgown with thin ribbon ties and a matching robe. Both of them were so sheer she could see straight through them, and she couldn't wait to put them on. She took off her clothes and freshened up before donning the ensemble. It was an amazing shade of red, and it looked daring but feminine. She went into the living room expecting to see Johnny waiting for her. There was a trail of rose petals instead. She followed them across the living room and into the other bedroom. The door was open and the petals led into the room, right up to the bed. The covers were turned back, and there were scented candles burning all around.

Johnny was in the bed wearing a smile and red silk boxers. Seductive music was playing and there was a bottle of champagne nestled in a silver ice bucket. A crystal bowl of fresh fruit and a bowl of whipped cream were next to it. She was so surprised that she didn't know what to say.

"Johnny, this is… Wow, you weren't kidding when you said you had a surprise," she murmured.

He was looking at her with deep appreciation. "Stop talking and come here, woman. Walk slowly so I can get a good look at you."

Ayanna blew him a kiss and turned like a model. She held the robe open so he could see what awaited him under its sheer cover, then turned around and slipped it off her shoulders. She looked back at him before letting it flutter to the floor. Executing another slow turn, she finally started walking to the bed with slow, measured steps. She put one knee on the bed and leaned in for a kiss. She licked his lips and gently sucked the tip of his tongue.

"How was that?"

By way of answer, he simply scooped her up and put her on the cushiony softness of the bed. "I don't have any words to describe it. This is going to have to be show-and-tell."

She put her head on the pile of pillows, and he kissed her, slow and deep, while his hands touched her all over. He stroked her sides, her stomach and hips and somehow managed to untie the ribbon straps and take the nightie off her so fast she forgot she'd had it on. He didn't even break the kiss when he took off his boxers. Lying naked next to him was amazing. His skin was hot and smooth, and the feel of his body on hers set her on fire. Her hands stroked his smooth shaven head as he kissed down her chest to her already engorged nipples.

By now his touch was so familiar that her body reacted at once, and she was arching her back as he gently nibbled the ultra-sensitive tips. The nibbling turned into the hard suction she loved, and she could feel an orgasm mounting. He knew she was about to come, and his clever fingers plunged into her so he could bring her closer to the brink. Just when she was about to explode, his tongue replaced his fingers. It was like fireworks bursting all over.

He placed her long legs over his shoulders and continued to lavish her with his lips and tongue until she came again. He wouldn't relent until she had a third soul-shattering climax and her voice was raspy from moaning and calling his name. He finally slowed down and began to lick his way up her body until they were face-to-face. He kissed her, and she sighed with bliss as she tasted herself on his lips and his tongue. She sucked his lower lip and caressed his face with both her hands.

She was trembling, but it wasn't from being cold; it was because of the way he made her feel. He held her tight while she came back to herself. Once her breathing had slowed down he asked if she was thirsty. When she nodded, he gently let her go so he could pour the champagne.

"Told you you'd be loud."

Ayanna pouted and sipped her icy cold drink. "It wasn't my fault. You made me," she said.

"I made you what? Say the words, Ayanna."

She wanted to tell him the truth, which was that he'd made her fall in love with him. Next to her sons and her family, she'd never known love like this, and she didn't know how she was going to do without it. But she took the coward's way out and played along.

"You made me lose my mind along with every inhibition I've ever had. How's that?"

Johnny looked satisfied. "It's a start."

"I've got your start right here, darling. Hand me that bowl of whipped cream," she said.

"Okay, here's the cream. What else?" he asked, looking at the fruit.

"Lie down."

He did so, but with a dubious look on his face. "Don't get scared. This isn't going to hurt a bit. Do you like whipped cream?"

"Yeah, sure, who doesn't like whipped cream?"

Ayanna held the bowl in one hand and dipped her finger into the cream. She licked it off and smiled. "I love whipped cream." She dipped her finger again and held it to his lips. His long tongue licked it off and he ended by sucking her finger, which made a chill go over her, but she ignored it.

"I'll eat anything with whipped cream on it," she

purred. "I'd happily eat mud if it was covered with whipped cream."

She moved closer to Johnny and spooned the cool fluffy cream onto his manhood, which was already hard and ready. She used her fingers to make sure it was evenly distributed. He was watching her with lowered lids, his eyes heavy with desire. She leaned down and began to lick the cream off while her hands were busy stroking him and holding him in place. She could hear him moaning her name over and over, and the moans turned to long groans of extreme pleasure. He had clearly reached a point of no return at the very moment she finished divesting him of all the cream.

She had barely raised her head when he rolled over and grabbed her so fast she couldn't blink. He entered her fast and hard and filled her to the brim with every thrust. Their mouths joined in a long hot kiss that ended only because Johnny had to look into her eyes. This was different than any of the times they'd made love. It was hot, urgent and even more fulfilling than before. Ayanna moved her hips instinctively, and her walls tightened on him. His eyes closed and he thrust once more, even harder, while she used her hips to pump with him until he exploded on a long hoarse cry that was pure passion, but something else, too.

Minutes later they were still tightly wrapped in each other and still locked together because neither one of them wanted to end the embrace. When he was finally able to speak again, Johnny said, "I didn't mean for that to happen. I was going to give you pleasure all night because I didn't want you to be uncomfortable. That was my plan, but it failed miserably."

Ayanna kissed him and rubbed her nose in his goatee. "You gave me more than mere pleasure, darling. That was…" She paused while she tried to think of the right word.

"Yes, it was," he agreed. "It was very, very special. Almost as special as you are."

He kissed her forehead and rolled over so that she was resting on his chest. While she drifted off to sleep, he stared at the box of condoms on the bedside table and wondered what they'd just done. Ayanna moved closer to him and drowsily said his name. He pulled her closer, and he knew it didn't matter. He was in love for the first time in his life, and if he'd just planted his seed in her lovely garden, so much the better.

Chapter 10

Ayanna had three more days of her vacation left. Johnny was pleased to find out that she didn't have to return to work right away because, as he told her, he wanted to monopolize her time. She was a revelation for him; she was gorgeous, no question, but her beauty wasn't her only attraction. He enjoyed her company because she was a good conversationalist and a good listener. She was the sexiest woman he'd ever met, and she did nothing to emphasize it other than be herself.

She didn't load herself up with heavy perfumes, she didn't drape herself in gaudy jewelry and she didn't dress like a hooker. But she always looked perfect to him, whether she was dressed for church or a night on the town. Even in jeans, like she was now, she was the cutest thing he'd ever seen. They were on their way back to Illinois from Charleston and she was reading aloud from one of her romance novels, but it wasn't holding his attention. Now that he knew the kind of heat she was packing in her slender body, other people's sex lives were of no interest to him, especially the lives that were only on paper.

He reached over and took the book from her fingertips, smiling when she laughed.

"Getting bored or heated up?" she asked playfully.

"Neither one," he said. "I'm thinking about what we're going to do for the next five days. You have three more days of vacation plus a weekend. What would you like to do?"

"Laundry, for sure. Sort the boys' clothes so I can figure out what they'll need for school this fall. Maybe paint the kitchen."

"You are the most conscientious woman I've ever met, but you need to learn how to play," Johnny chided her.

"I do know how to play," Ayanna protested.

"No, you don't. We're talking about five days where you don't have to go into the office and all you can think of to fill the time is more work. Loosen up, Ayanna! You're too young to be so serious."

"It's easy to be carefree when you don't have kids," Ayanna pointed out. "I have a lot of responsibilities. How are things going to get done if I don't do them?"

She sounded defensive and a little hurt, which were the last things Johnny wanted to make her feel. He took her hand and kissed the back of it.

"I'm sorry, sweetheart, I wasn't trying to make fun of you, and I certainly didn't want to belittle you in any way. You're an amazing person, and you have all my respect. But," he said, kissing her hand again, "I want you to have more relaxation in your life. From what I can see, you work hard, and I just want you to play a little, too."

He smiled when she returned the kiss. Her soft lips felt wonderful on his hand. "So you think I need a little more playtime, hmm?"

"Yep. And I'll be more than willing to be your playdate. Starting tonight," he said with a grin.

"I hate it when you smile like that," Ayanna said. "When you do that you look so darned good I can't refuse you anything."

Johnny laughed so hard he almost missed their exit. "Does that mean I get my way?"

"Yes, it does. You win," she said with a sigh.

"Oh no, angel, we win. Both of us," he reminded her.

Ayanna couldn't believe her audacious idea even while she was conceiving it. A few weeks ago this would have been completely out of the question, but through Johnny, she'd discovered a new side of her womanhood. She'd finally gotten in touch with her inner diva, the femme fatale sexy siren that she'd ignored for years. Now that Johnny had let the genie out of the bottle she wasn't trying to put it back in. She was, in fact, trying to find more and better ways of expressing herself, and tonight she was going to show

Johnny that not only did she know how to have fun, but she knew how to play, too.

He'd gone into his office in the morning, and she'd talked to him a couple of times on the phone. She'd invited him over for dinner, asking him what his favorite dish was.

"Whatever you cook. I'm not picky, and whatever you make tastes good," he'd said.

Since it was a really warm day and she didn't want to heat up the house, she decided to grill a chicken and rosemary skewered potatoes and keep them warm in the oven. With the chicken she would serve ratatouille, a green salad and her homemade lemon squares for dessert. She had to time everything perfectly so that the meal would be ready when Johnny got there and that she would be ready, too.

She took a long hot shower and scrubbed away every trace of charcoal smoke from grilling the chicken. She shampooed her hair three times to make sure that its only scent would be sweet and floral, not smoky. She used her precious stash of Chanel No. 5 body cream from head to toe, and then applied her makeup. It was a little heavier than she usually wore it; she actually hadn't worn makeup as heavy since the last time she'd danced in public with Todd. But she still knew how to work it.

Foundation, blush a shade darker than usual and charcoal eye shadow that deepened and lengthened her eyes. Gold highlighter and inky-black liquid liner made her look much more glam than usual. Several coats of black mascara made her lashes look so long and lush they appeared to be false, and she was satisfied that she looked nothing like her normal self. She combed setting gel through her hair and parted it on one side, slicking it back. Adding a little gold highlight powder to her collarbone and her cleavage, she added a mist of Chanel eau de parfum and began to get dressed. Johnny was due in fifteen minutes, and she knew he'd be prompt.

Sure enough, he arrived right on time, and he'd brought her flowers, a beautiful bouquet of irises, freesia, calla lilies and roses. And in the other hand he had a giant houseplant. "Johnny, you're so thoughtful. Why two?"

"Because I know you like flowers. And I know you like plants, so why shouldn't you have both?" He put the plant on the coffee table and handed her the flowers. He leaned in for a kiss, and she turned her cheek. He kissed it, and then stood back and looked at her.

"Are we going out tonight? You look way better than I do," he said.

It was true; he was wearing a short-sleeved print rayon shirt and jeans, and Ayanna was wearing a black pinstriped three-piece pant suit. The vest was buttoned up, and she had on a white blouse with the collar turned up. Her lips were sexy but looked unfamiliar with the shiny deep red gloss she had on.

She put the flowers on the dining room table and walked toward Johnny with a look that meant business on her pretty face. When she reached him, she pulled his head down to hers, and instead of kissing him, she ran her mint-tasting tongue over his lips. "Sit down," she whispered in his ear.

He held up both hands and did exactly as she asked, backing up until he was on the sofa. He crossed his legs and spread his arms out across the back of the couch. He watched wordlessly as Ayanna put on a black fedora and turned her back to him. She used the remote control to start the music. A long blues riff filled the room as "Loan Me a Dime" by the legendary Boz Scaggs came on. Ayanna dropped the remote like it was red-hot, sliding her legs apart and bending her knees until her butt touched the floor before taking a stance that showed off her long legs, made even longer by the four-inch stiletto pumps she was wearing.

The song was slow and lush, and Ayanna matched her movements to every beat. First her jacket came off, slowly, but with such deliberate finesse that it was like an act of foreplay. She slowly turned to face Johnny and began to unbutton her vest with excruciating precision until it was finally open. She slid it off and tossed it across the room to Johnny, who caught it with one hand.

The dance went on, a slow, sensual exhibition that was both erotic and artistic. She could hear Johnny groan as her wide-leg pants were eased down her legs revealing lace-topped hose attached to black garters. She stepped out of the pants without missing a beat and finally started taking off her blouse. It had French cuffs, and she prolonged her striptease by taking off the cuff links one at a time before beginning on the buttons. When they were all undone, she pulled the blouse open to reveal a black-lace merry widow that made the most of her small rounded breasts and made her waist look incredibly tiny.

She tossed the blouse into the air, and as it fluttered down, she executed some moves with her hips that could have caused a riot in a gentleman's ballet. All that was missing was a pole, but Johnny didn't seem to mind.

The song was thirteen minutes and three seconds long, but Johnny didn't seem terribly interested in hearing the end of it. Before she could finish the dance and toss her fedora at him, he had left the sofa and picked her up as he kissed every bit of the shiny black cherry gloss off her mouth. She had to wrap her arms around his neck and her legs around his waist to steady them.

"I wasn't finished," she murmured.

"We can finish in the bedroom," he groaned.

"But the chicken will dry out," she whispered.

"That's why God made gravy," he informed her as he took her to the only place he wanted her right then—the bed.

They finally managed to eat dinner after their appetite for each other was satisfied. The chicken and potatoes weren't dried out, as Ayanna feared. Johnny was wearing a towel and nothing else, and Ayanna had on a little Japanese kimono with nothing underneath. She sat in his lap, and they fed each other with their fingers and talked. "Ayanna, you're full of surprises. I love that in you," he said as he nuzzled her neck.

"I told you I could play," she murmured.

"You're right. I'm never going to challenge you again."

He ate another bite from her fingers and sighed in repletion. "You should be running a five-star restaurant," he said. "Why aren't you doing that instead of working for a construction company?"

Ayanna shrugged. "I never went to the Cordon Bleu like I'd planned. I needed to work, and I needed a stable job with benefits that would give me time with the boys. Restaurant work is long and hard and you work crazy hours. The benefits suck if there are any at all. So I started teaching. I loved it, but it's not the best money in the world. Why do they pay professional athletes so much and teachers so little?" she mused.

"I have no idea. It's a screwed up system, I'll grant you. So why did you quit teaching?"

"Two reasons. It was too hard to make a nine-month income stretch to twelve months for one thing. For another, there were going to be layoffs in my district. Since I didn't have as much seniority as some of the other teachers, I knew my head would be on the block. Then I heard about the job with Hunter Construction. Nick was paying more than I was making, the hours were about the same and I'd have weekends and holidays off. I don't get the summers off anymore, but the money makes it easier for us," she said.

"But what about when the boys go to college? Cameron will be gone in a couple of years, and Alec will be right behind him because he's in that accelerated program. What about picking up your dream where you left off?"

Ayanna looked at him in surprise. "How did you know Alec was in an accelerated program?"

Johnny gave her a smug smile. "I know because he told me. Alec and Cameron and I have gotten to be quite close, thank you. I know more than you think. You've raised a couple of really wonderful young men, Ayanna."

"I think we raised each other," she confessed. "They're really good kids, and they haven't given me any grief. They're pretty well-behaved and cooperative. I keep waiting for horns to sprout and police to show up at my door, but praise God, nothing like that has happened. I tried to raise them like my parents raised us, and so far it's worked. I'm waiting for those teenage hormones to kick in, though. I've heard some horror stories from my friends about adolescence."

"If they haven't started acting out yet, maybe they won't. I was a hellion when I was little, but I was real mellow as a teenager. I was too scared of my dad to act out," he said, and laughed.

"Yes, but they don't have a dad," Ayanna said and could have cheerfully bitten her tongue off for saying it. It sounded like she was asking for something from Johnny that she knew she wasn't going to get. Her phone rang, and she flew off his lap to answer it.

"Cameron! I was just talking about you and Alec. How are you guys?" She had to turn away from Johnny because the sight of him nude from the waist up sitting at the kitchen table was just too much for her to take. There was only so much heat one woman could handle.

Chapter 11

Ayanna had such a good time with Johnny that she didn't even mind the inquisition when her vacation was officially over. She knew that Billie and Dakota would want all the dish, and she wasn't about to begrudge them. A week after they returned to Chicago, she went over to Dakota's house for a girls' night. Along with Toni Beauchamp, Dakota's best friend, they were gathered in Dakota's kitchen around the table. They had coffee and peach ice cream with Billie's delicious peach cobbler. Ayanna was praising it when Billie held up her hand.

"Okay, you can stop with the false modesty. I've always been known as the baker in the family but my big brother let me know that mine doesn't hold a candle to yours. I swear, every bite he puts in his mouth these days is followed by him saying 'Ayanna's is better,' or 'Ayanna does hers different.' You've got him spoiled rotten already," she said.

Ayanna blushed pink, but the other women wouldn't let her get away with it. Dakota and Toni laughed at Billie's statement, but they assured Ayanna that it was a good thing.

"Honey, if that man thinks you can do something in the kitchen no other woman can, let him!" Dakota said.

Toni agreed wholeheartedly. "I don't do a lot of cooking, but I am like the sandwich queen. I can make sandwiches that will make you cry, they're so good. Zane won't eat anyone else's now," she said. "Of course, that means I have to pack him a gourmet lunch to take to work every day, but it's a small price to pay."

Ayanna looked around the table at the three women, all of whom had been married less than two years. They were acting like she would soon be joining their ranks, and she felt like a faker. And a failure. It wasn't going to happen for her.

"So, you and Johnny went to Columbia to drop off the boys, and you stayed two days." Dakota, the investigative reporter, always liked to get her facts lined up. "What was your favorite part of your visit home?"

Ayanna's eyes crinkled in a smile. "Going to the drugstore!" They all looked puzzled until she explained. "My ex-fiancé was going to medical school, but he ended up being a pharmacist because he's terrified of the sight of blood. Anyway, I had to get Alec's allergy prescription filled, and we went to pick it up," she began. The story was short but hilarious.

They went to the Walgreens drugstore that was closest to her mother's house in the University Hill section of town. While they were there, Ayanna started walking the aisles to see if there was anything she needed. She loved drugstores and was always inspecting the end caps where the clearance items were displayed. Johnny was walking behind her when she stopped, her eyes caught by something on the shelf.

"Johnny, what is that?"

He'd picked up the item and told her it was a personal lubricant. "I don't think you need that, but if you want to try some, go ahead."

Ayanna had blushed bright red, and Johnny's arms had gone around her at once. "Look, sweetness, I can promise you that we're not going to need anything but each other. But there's nothing wrong with using creams and oils or gels or whatever turns you on."

He had rubbed his cheek against her hair while she stared at the amazing array of goods. "Cherry-flavored, raspberry-chocolate, mint… My goodness there's a lot of stuff here." She leaned against Johnny and smiled. "But all I want is you. There can't be anything on those shelves that could make me feel better than you do."

He answered her with a lingering kiss. "There is one thing I need, though." He reached for two boxes of condoms. The PA announced that her prescription was ready, and they went to the back of the store to claim it. Johnny put the two boxes of condoms on the counter and pulled out his credit card to pay for everything. Ayanna was looking at the store's weekly circular when she heard her name.

"Ayanna? Ayanna Porter?"

She turned to see Percy Stubbins behind the pharmacist's counter. "Percy! Fancy meeting you here."

"It's been a long time, Ayanna. Are you moving back here or something?"

"No, I just brought my sons to spend the summer with my mom." Percy was staring at her so hard she thought he'd developed X-ray vision along with the receded hairline, jowls and paunch he was sporting.

"Do we need anything else, or is this it, sweetness?"

Percy had looked from Ayanna to Johnny and back again. There was Johnny, all six foot four inches of him in a short-sleeved polo shirt that showed off his magnificent biceps and jeans that made his long, hard legs look even better than usual. He'd put his hand on Ayanna's back, which was bared in a sexy little sundress, and the gesture wasn't missed by anyone within ten feet of the couple. It was a simple gesture that signified affection and possession in equal parts.

Ayanna looked up at Johnny with a secret smile that made Percy drop his ink pen. "I think that's all."

Percy's glasses actually fogged up when Johnny kissed Ayanna like there was no one else around. He cleared his throat loudly and began to ring up the prescription, and when he saw the two boxes of condoms, his light brown face reddened, and his grandpa-looking eyeglasses slipped.

"Magnums!" The word was out before he realized he'd spoken aloud.

While he was fumbling to put their purchases in a bag, Ayanna asked about his wife.

"She's fat, um, fine," Percy said. "So is this your, um…"

"My manners, what must you think of me? Percy Stubbins, this is John Phillips. John, this is Percy."

Percy nodded and tried to say something suave. "So are you two, um, ah, married?"

Johnny bent down for another kiss. "Not yet. Nice meeting you."

When she finished telling the story, minus the condom part and the marriage comment, Toni was laughing so hard that tears were running down her face, and Dakota was looking at Ayanna with new respect. Billie was, too. Ayanna looked from one sister to the other.

"What?"

"This is a first, honey. Johnny doesn't do the domestic thing at all. I can't ever remember him doing normal, mundane things with a woman. Certainly not driving fourteen hours with her and her kids, not meeting her family and going to the neighborhood drugstore. Never!" Billie shook her head in amazement while she drank a glass of milk, her new favorite beverage since becoming pregnant.

"Yes, but—"

"Take that word out of your vocabulary, honey. Your life is getting ready to change, big time," Dakota said wisely. A soft cry from the baby monitor caused her to excuse herself and go see about little Bethany.

Dakota had sounded so much like Johnny when she said that. "Take that word out of your vocabulary." They'd said the same thing to tell her to stop saying "but". In the world of these women, there were no buts. Nothing stood in their way, nothing was impossible for them. A chirp from the baby monitor made Toni get to her feet.

"I'd better go see about the big guy," she said with a smile. Her baby was a few months older than Bethany, and he was asleep in the nursery with her—or at least he had been.

Billie waited until she and Ayanna were alone. "What's on your mind, girl? I can tell something is bothering you. Has Johnny done his famous disappearing act?"

"Oh no," Ayanna said. "I talk to him every day. Twice a day, usually. And we had dinner last night. He wanted to have dinner tonight, but I had plans. He's cooking dinner for me tomorrow night at his place."

"Nick's old apartment? Have you seen it yet?" When Ayanna said no, Billie grinned. "Wait until you check the place out! Dakota called it a pimp's pleasure palace, but I loved it. It's wild." She finished her milk and went to the sink to rinse out the glass.

"But so much for Nick's old place, you'll see it tomorrow. What's up, Ayanna?"

Ayanna knew Billie too well to try and bluff her, but she didn't want to put all her business out in the street, either. "Pre-period blues is all. You know how I am. I walk around sniveling for a few days every month."

"Dakota was the same way. I think having the baby mellowed out her hormones, though. She doesn't seem to have that problem anymore."

The conversation switched easily to other topics, and when Dakota and Toni returned with the babies on their shoulders, Ayanna felt like she'd dodged a high-caliber bullet. There were a few more questions about her vacation, but luckily Nick walked into the house followed by Jason and then Toni's husband Zane and all personal inquiries ceased.

Ayanna felt oddly lonely as she drove home. There was so much love and caring among the three couples she'd just left that she felt left out. She'd cared strongly for Percy at one time. She certainly thought she loved him enough to marry him. But when her sister was killed, the bottom dropped out of her world. She didn't even consider not taking Alec and Cameron, because she loved them dearly and because it was her sister's wish. The guardianship had been in place for years, even though she never thought she'd be called upon to follow through with it.

Percy wanted nothing to do with Alec and Cameron and made her choose between him and her nephews. Without a second's hesitation, she told him to take a flying leap. Her mother told her then that he was all wrong for her.

"Ayanna, any man who could impose a condition like that on you isn't worth your time or your tears.

There's someone waiting for you, and when you meet him, you'll know. He'll treat you like a queen, and those boys will be his princes. Just give it time, and he'll find you."

Ayanna parked in the garage and went into the house, dutifully turning off the alarm before checking all the windows and doors. It was still early, barely nine, and it was still light out. She looked around for something to do, but the house was spotless, and there wasn't even a load of laundry waiting its turn. She decided to take a shower and go to bed early, with her latest romance. She wanted to call Johnny, but she wasn't going to wear out his number. They had talked earlier, and he knew she was doing girls' night with his sisters and Toni. It was good to have space, she mused. There was nothing worse than being a clingy woman who couldn't spend a night alone.

When she got out of the shower, her phone was ringing. The caller ID showed her mother's number, and she answered at once. "Hello?"

"Hi, Ma! How was your girls' night?"

"It was fun, Cameron. And how did you know what my plans were for the evening?"

Alec's voice answered her. "John told us."

Her eyebrows went up in surprise. "You talked to John?"

"Sure, we talk every day. He e-mails us, and we e-mail him back. We send him cartoons."

Ayanna rallied from her shock ,and they enjoyed a nice conversation. She was still amazed after she hung up the phone. She talked to the boys every day and to John every day and she just found out that they had been communicating with each other all along. She knew they had a mutual admiration society going on, but this was really touching.

She was putting on lotion when the phone rang again. This time it was John.

"Wanna go to the movies?"

"Hello to you, too. It's kind of late for the movies, isn't it?"

"Yes, if we were going to a theater. But if I brought the popcorn and the movie, we could watch one at home. Is it too late for that?"

"That sounds nice."

"See you in thirty minutes."

Johnny was prompt, as always. Ayanna couldn't really decide if she liked him better in casual clothes or dress clothes, because he looked so good in both styles. He was very casual tonight in a football jersey and jeans with athletic shoes. She wasn't dressed up, either, in a red tank top, denim shorts and bare feet.

After a brief kiss, they went into the living room, and he showed her the bag from the rental store. "No, just surprise me," she said. "You get it queued up, and I'll pop the popcorn."

She came back into the living room with a big bowl and a stack of napkins. "I have to go get the sodas, and I'll be right back."

Johnny insisted on getting the drinks. He brought

them in, sat next to her on the sofa and put his arm around her shoulders. "Ready?"

He pressed the play button and Tyler Perry's *Why Did I Get Married?* came on.

"That's a surprising choice," she said.

"You don't like Tyler Perry?"

"I love him, but this is dangerously close to a chick flick," she warned.

"I'll take my chances." He kissed her again. "No talking."

She curled up next to him and settled back to watch the movie. Somewhere between the opening credits and the end of the movie, she drifted off to sleep. She woke up from the kisses he was planting all over her face.

"Wake up, sweetness. You need to go to bed because tomorrow morning is going to come all too early."

She smiled sleepily. "Why don't you spend the night?"

"Because neither one of us will get any sleep. Tomorrow is Friday, you're coming over and I get to show off my skills and have my way with you. Plus, nobody has to get up early on Saturday. That's a better plan for us both. Come walk me to the door, and turn on the alarm."

Protesting, she yawned her way off the sofa and automatically reached for the popcorn bowl and glasses, which were gone.

"My mama raised me right," he said. "I took care of them."

Their good-night kiss was sweet but much too short for Ayanna. Johnny was adamant that she get her rest, though, and he left, but she suddenly didn't feel alone. She felt cherished, which was ridiculous. She touched her lips and thought about him calling her boys every day. Maybe theirs was just a friendship with summer benefits, but it was wonderful while it lasted.

Chapter 12

Ayanna looked over the art deco style apartment building. It looked pretty normal to her eyes. Billie had told her that the place was something else, but she couldn't see it. The lobby was stylish and understated and the workmanship was outstanding. She took the elevator up to Johnny's floor and looked down the hallway. He was standing in the doorway waiting for her, which was endearing for some reason.

"Welcome to my crib," he said in a gangsta voice. He ushered her in the door and waited for her reaction.

"Oh my. This is something, isn't it?"

It was wild, just like Billie said. There was the longest couch she'd ever seen, done in camel-colored leather with cheetah spots hand-painted on it. The chairs were obnoxious but entertaining. They were gold velvet high heels. There were many cheap versions of the chair available at any bargain furniture mart, but these were the original art-gallery versions. The floors were beautiful hardwood, but there was a horrible area rug in bright peacock-blue with faux zebra stripes. Ayanna was stunned.

"Well, at least the rug matches the walls," she said lamely. It was true; the walls were covered in the same shade of blue. Raw silk, the carpet was obviously expensive, but the color was blinding. The lights were blinding, too. They were big pillars of rough cut glass that were way too bright. "The Flintstones called. They want their lamps back."

She stared at the huge heavy glass dining-room table and the hideous chairs. They were made out of cowhide or pony skin or something. They were hairy, and each one was painted to resemble some poor wild animal. Just awful. She glanced at the huge light fixture over the table and groaned. "I always thought Nick had such good taste," she murmured.

Johnny laughed. "He does now. Dakota got him on the right path. He was with this woman who called herself a decorator, and he just let her have at it. We like to tease him about this place. Come on in the kitchen, it's safe. You look great, by the way. And you smell fantastic."

She was wearing a black wrap dress with big red flowers on it that came from the clearance rack at T.J. Maxx. This was the first time she'd worn it since last summer, and she was glad it still looked good. She was also wearing red sandals from the same place. She smelled wonderful, too, because she'd found a bottle of Safari in the bath and body department. She denied herself perfume and jewelry because she watched her budget so carefully. Her mother always hooked her up on her birthday and Christmas, but she used the fragrances very sparingly to make them last. She was pleased that Johnny noticed because she had done it for him.

She smiled to herself as she followed him into the surprisingly nice kitchen. There was nothing weird in here; it was super clean with gleaming appliances and a marble-topped work island in the middle of the room.

"This is much better. What smells so good?"

"Another surprise," he said mysteriously. "It'll be ready in a few if you want to do whatever it is you women do before you eat."

"I do this," she said, pulling him down for a kiss. "Now, where's the bathroom so I can perform my secret lady ritual?"

He showed her the bathroom, and once again she was impressed. "This I like." It was a soft buff color, all marble with gold fixtures. The tub was almost as big as the one at the Wild Dunes Resort and was outfitted with whirlpool jets and dual faucets with handheld showerheads. The tub was enclosed in glass, and there were glass shelves that held some really luxurious-looking towels.

"Yeah, that gives me some ideas. I've got to start

looking for a house next week. Good thing I've got a brother-in-law in the business."

He left to check on dinner, and she washed her hands while admiring the pedestal sink. She wondered what kind of house he'd want. Jason was the leading real-estate mogul in the city, so he'd certainly have the inside track on the best property available. What would his bachelor pad look like? *Probably not like this one, except for the bathroom.* She was still smiling when she went back to the kitchen.

"What can I do to help?"

Johnny was doing something mysterious at the stove. "Not a thing except go into the living room and sit down on the sofa. We're eating in there tonight."

She went down the hall and did as he asked. Now that the initial shock of the decor had worn off, she noticed two low tables next to the sofa. There was a tablecloth on one table with big cloth napkins, but no silverware. There were big thick goblets and a flat bowl with a single flower floating in water over some glass pebbles. Johnny came in the room with a huge covered tray, which he put on the other table.

The music was already playing, and it was perfect for the occasion, low and sultry jazz. Johnny grinned at her. "I've really got you thinking now, don't I? We're going to sit on the floor," he said, indicating four big silk-covered cushions. "I want you to sit here, and I'll sit here." Once she was comfortably ensconced on her cushions, he told her there was one last thing he had to do. "Don't get nervous," he added.

He turned off the lights, and the room was completely dark. So dark that she couldn't see a thing, not even the streetlights, because he'd closed the blinds and drawn the curtains. "What happened?"

She was relieved to feel his hand on her arm. "I said don't get nervous," he reminded her. "I heard about this restaurant where they turn off the lights completely and all the servers are blind. It's supposed to really enhance the dining experience. Are you game?"

Ayanna nodded her head and then laughed because she realized in a split second that he couldn't see her. "Yes, let's go for it. What happens now?"

"First I want you to take a deep breath and tell me what you smell," he said.

He was holding her hand, and the warmth was comforting and stimulating at the same time. Coming out of the pitch black of the room, his voice sounded even deeper and sexier than it normally did.

"I smell that flower, the one on the table. It smells like spring, sweet and light. I smell basil, rosemary and pepper," she told him.

"Very good. I'm going to let go of your hand for a moment, okay?"

In seconds he was pressing a goblet into her hands. "Okay, smell that. What does it smell like?"

She inhaled the contents of the glass and smiled. "It's wine. I smell raspberries and black cherries and, mmm, lavender, I think."

"Very good. Taste it," he said.

She took a sip and the flavors rolled across her

tongue and warmed the back of her throat. "This is very good," she praised. "I really like it." She took another sip, and he reached over to take the goblet from her hands.

"Everything we're eating is finger food," he said. He reached over and somehow found her face with no effort. "Open your mouth, baby."

She did and was rewarded with a bite of the tenderest filet she'd ever tasted. It was marinated in the herbs she'd named as well as the wine she'd just tasted. It was just the beginning of a wonderful meal. He'd made steamed snow peas, marinated cucumbers, the filet mignon and bacon-wrapped bites of chicken. It was a long and sensual meal and her senses were so heightened by everything that she thought she could hear their hearts beating. She felt so close to him she could have sworn they were breathing in unison.

Dessert was being served in the bedroom. He wouldn't tell her what it was, and he made her close her eyes while he led her to the room so the spell of darkness wouldn't be broken. Once they were in the bedroom, he undressed her and put her in the middle of the bed. "Don't move," he cautioned. "This bed is kind of different."

When he was naked and sitting behind her, she relaxed into his arms. He kissed the back of her neck and she shivered in anticipation. "What are we having?"

"You're having chocolate-covered strawberries. And I'm having you with whipped cream," he said while he caressed her breasts.

"I told you I love whipped cream," she reminded him.

"I know you do, and so do I. And I'm going to enjoy every bit of you."

He lay her back on the bed and parted her legs gently, helped her bend her knees. When she was positioned to his liking, she had to bite her lips to stifle a gasp when she felt the cool cream between her legs.

"What goes around comes around, sweetness. Open wide," he growled.

The next morning Ayanna drifted slowly into wakefulness. She didn't want to move because she felt so relaxed and well-loved. The things Johnny had done to her last night belonged in the pages of a book of erotica. She laughed to herself as she remembered every single moment of their lovemaking. Everything had been done in the pitch blackness of the apartment, which made everything seem so much more intense. They even took a shower in the dark, and she knew she'd never look at a handheld showerhead the same way again.

She rolled over on the silky sheets and found Johnny's warm body next to hers. This time he hadn't gone out for food and coffee or anything; he was right next to her where she wanted him to be. His arms went around her automatically, and he held her tight. She'd gotten so used to doing things by touch and not sight that she was reluctant to open her eyes. She had to force them open slowly, and when she did, she was stunned to see red satin sheets. And they were on a round bed, no less. *This is just like my dream,* she thought. *The hot dream I had the night of Billie's house-warming when I dreamed about a beautiful bald man and some red sheets. Snap!*

Determined not to let him catch her with morning mouth, she slipped out of bed and looked in her big purse for her toothbrush. After brushing her teeth thoroughly and doing a few other necessary morning things, she went into the kitchen to see what she could make for breakfast. The calendar on the refrigerator door caught her eye. She kept staring at the date, trying to make it register. Something was supposed to happen on the fifteenth. What was it?

Shrugging, she opened the refrigerator and took out a carton of eggs. Her hands started shaking as it came to her in a rush. Her period should have started three days ago. Where was it?

Chapter 13

Ayanna was trying her best not to dissolve into a pool of panic. It was a week since the erotically sexy dinner at Johnny's, and her period was still nowhere to be found. They had gone without a condom only once—that night in Isle of Palms. Surely one little slip couldn't have left her with child. She wasn't going to give energy to the thought. It wasn't unheard of for her to skip a period. They would come like clockwork every single month on the same day. Then the cycle would change by about five days, and it would start coming on *that* day for about a year before skipping to another day. That had to be it; her body was changing its date cycle for reasons known only to it.

She did her best to hide any sign of angst from

Johnny. They were too busy having a good time for her to derail their train with a late period. It would turn out to be nothing so there was no reason for her to rock the boat. In the meantime, she was enjoying every moment she was with him. He could always think of something exciting to do, and even when they weren't out and about, he was the best company she could imagine.

They went to the legendary Taste of Chicago and walked around sampling so many different restaurant offerings that even Johnny got full. They went to two Cubs games, to the movies and they did things with his sisters and their husbands. They went out dancing often because he said he loved to see her move. He was by far the most thoughtful man she'd ever known, and her love for him grew every day.

One evening she finally talked to him about his relationship with Alec and Cameron. They were sitting on the small screened porch she had added to the house when she bought it.

"By the way, the boys told me that you talk to them and e-mail them," she said. "I was surprised to hear that."

"Why? Do you not want me to? I apologize if I overstepped my bounds or something, but they're such great kids I wanted to make sure they were having a good time. And I won't lie to you. I'm trying to make a good impression on their mother. I want her to know that I'll be good to her kids because I like them, not just because I'm crazy about her," he said.

Her eyes filled with tears, and her chin trembled

with the effort not to cry. He was alarmed by her reaction. He took her hands and led her into the house. "I don't want your neighbors to think I'm beating you or something. What's wrong, baby?"

"Nothing's wrong, nothing, nothing. You're just so sweet and kind and wonderful. I don't know what I've done to deserve you."

He took her into the living room and sat down on the sofa with her in his lap. Kissing her teary eyes, he assured her that she was the wonderful one. "In my entire life, I've never done anything to deserve you, Ayanna. You are the most giving, the most incredible person I know. You give so much and expect so little," he said, kissing her again.

"In fact, I have something for you. I bought it in Charleston and was keeping it for a surprise. I hope you like it," he said, pulling a small box out of his pocket.

"It" was the most stunning piece of jewelry she'd ever seen. A pair of diamond and pearl earrings set in yellow gold. The iridescent pearls dangled from a ball of sparkling brown stones, and they were by far the most incredible things she'd ever seen. "Johnny, these are amazing," she whispered.

He kissed her before responding. "I'm glad you like them. Those are chocolate pearls and chocolate diamonds. Try them on. I want to see them against your skin."

"Diamonds and pearls? You mean they're real?"

"Of course they're real. Do you think I'd give you fake jewelry? Put them on, Ayanna. I want you to see how gorgeous they'll look on you."

But she snapped the box shut and handed it back to him. "I can't take these, Johnny. This is way too much. I can't let you spend that kind of money on me."

Johnny sat back and looked at her incredulously. "What do you mean you can't take them? It's just a little gift. It's not like I'm trying to give you the Hope Diamond or something. Can't I show you how I feel about you with a present?"

She was feeling distinctly uncomfortable and got up from his lap. He was so confused by her attitude that he let her. She walked away from him and turned her back, trying to control her hands, which were shaking. Turning to face him she said, "Look, Johnny, if this was a real relationship, sure. But this is a summer fling for us, and we both know it. It's not right for you to spend so much money on me when we're going to go our separate ways in a few weeks."

Johnny rose to his full height. "Summer fling? Who's having a summer fling? I sure as hell am not. All I think about is you, Ayanna, you and Alec and Cameron. All I want is you. I never said anything, but when we made love without the condom I was happy because I thought you might get pregnant and nothing would have made me happier than giving you my child. Does that sound like a summer affair to you?"

"No, it sounds like selfishness," she said with her hands on her hips. "If that's what you wanted, you should be thrilled because my period is over two weeks late! I have two sons, Johnny, two impressionable boys! It's hard enough being a single mother to two boys.

How the hell am I supposed to take care of a third? We barely make ends meet as it is. And you'd be glad to plant another one in me? Thanks a lot!"

Johnny was pacing around her like an angry panther. Her words didn't seem to register with him. He was too furious for that. "So this has been all about sex with you? You were trying to make up for eleven years of celibacy with the first man who came along, is that it? Damn, Ayanna, I thought I was the master of the game, but you got me beat for sure. And I was fool enough to fall in love with you." He stopped pacing and laughed, a harsh bark that held no amusement whatsoever.

"Thanks for a good time. And let me know if you're pregnant. That's all I want to hear from you from now on. E-mail me because I don't want to hear your voice again."

Without another word, he turned and left the house. Ayanna sank into the sofa that still bore his scent and wept. She hadn't cried like this since her sister died, which seemed appropriate because a part of her had just stopped living.

Ayanna spent the next two weeks in total misery. She tried to disguise her feelings, but it was difficult. No, it was impossible, because Billie knew without being told that something was wrong. She came into the office the morning after the horrible argument, and when she saw Ayanna's face, she could tell something disastrous had happened.

"Whatever you're working on can wait. Come on in my office, and tell me what's wrong."

Ayanna turned to her computer and brought up a posting for a property the firm had just acquired. "It's nothing, Billie. I'm just not feeling too well. I miss Alec and Cameron," she said lamely.

"Ayanna, you don't want to cross a cranky pregnant woman. Come with me and unburden yourself or I'll make a huge ugly scene right here in reception," Billie vowed.

Ayanna had to laugh, seeing as how Nick and everyone else was out in the field and there was no one in the office but the two of them. She allowed Billie to usher her into her private office, and the two women sat on the small sofa.

"I know I'm nosy, but you already knew that. You and Johnny were getting along so well. What happened? This is about Johnny, isn't it?" Her eyes were warm with concern.

"We had an argument. A big nasty one," Ayanna admitted. "He thinks I'm only interested in the, um, physical aspects of our relationship, and he says he wants more."

Billie's mouth dropped open. "He asked you to *marry* him?"

"No, no, no! But he said he wanted me to have his child, and he said he loves me," she murmured, unable to meet Billie's eyes.

Billie wasn't looking at Ayanna at the moment; she was digging through her tote bag for something to eat. "That's not like the Johnny I know and love. He's always been a playa," she said between bites of a banana. "I've never known him to stay in a relationship long enough to get really attached. I've never known him to have a relationship, really. You were the first real girlfriend I can ever recall," she said.

"I mean, babies and love are words that are just not in his vocabulary. He must have some really deep feelings for you to even let the words out of his mouth."

"Is this supposed to be making me feel better? Because it's not," Ayanna said sadly.

"I'm sorry, sweetie, I'm just having a hard time getting my head around this. You two were doing so well. What started the argument?"

Ayanna tried to explain and ended up making a muddle out of it. "Billie, he gave me these really expensive earrings, and I told him I couldn't accept them and then things just went all crazy."

"Why couldn't you take them? What's wrong with him giving you a gift?" Billie looked baffled.

"Billie, these earrings were real diamonds and pearls! How could I take something like that from someone who was just having a summer thing with me? I *couldn't,*" she answered her own question. "I couldn't let him spend that kind of money on me. It's not like we were really involved," she added.

Billie's expression changed. "You thought he wasn't really interested in something long-lasting and permanent, and you were guarding your heart. Oh, sweetie, I wished I'd known. I could have told you that he was really serious about you. Why wouldn't he be?"

"Why *would* he be? I'm not like you and Dakota and Toni or even your sisters-in-law," she began.

"Thank God you're not like Nip and Tuck." Billie shuddered. "Why on earth would you want to be?"

"Because they're doctors," Ayanna said. "From what I can see, Johnny is used to high-profile career women with titles and degrees and credentials. I'm your basic soccer mom. I have a bachelor's degree and a culinary certificate and two growing boys who can eat me out of house and home. I'm not the type he'd go for long-term so I took what I could get."

Billie put down her banana and stared at Ayanna. "Girl, if you weren't my best friend I'd smack you. Now I'll admit that Johnny has had a tendency to be as shallow as a puddle on a hot day when it comes to women, but I think—no, I *know*—that he was serious about you. He's a good man, despite his playboy ways. One thing I know for sure is that someone's profession or education is the last thing he'd be worried about if he loved the woman. And my question to you is why would you settle for sex anyway? Don't you want to have real love with marriage and babies and all the rest of it? Why the hell are you selling yourself short?"

"Because my first obligation is to my sons," Ayanna said hotly. "They're my true loves and my respon-sibility for life. I'm not going to choose between my boys and a man. They deserve the best mother they can have, and I intend to be that person for them. I'm not going to choose, Billie."

"Question: who asked you to? That jerk of an ex-fiancé told you to choose, and you made the right choice. But has Johnny ever acted as though Alec and Cameron were in the way, or were an inconvenience or a potential burden?"

"No, he didn't," Ayanna said softly.

"No, he didn't, because he's crazy about those boys. And you waited until they were gone for the summer and decided to have a good time with Johnny because it was convenient. Is that what I'm hearing? If that's the case, I can't really blame Johnny for being angry. He thought you felt the same way he did, and finding out that he was just your release from tension probably crushed him."

Ayanna couldn't answer. Billie hit the nail squarely on the head, and hearing it like that made Ayanna feel small and dirty. Billie's private line started ringing and she rose to take the call. Ayanna escaped the office like the sniveling coward she'd turned out to be. Just when she'd thought she couldn't feel any worse, she'd found out how wrong she was.

Chapter 14

The next three weeks were sheer hell. She and Billie eventually made up, but the first few days of working together were rough. Billie had apparently filled Dakota and Toni in on the breakup because they discreetly didn't mention it. Not that Ayanna saw them much; she made excuses to miss any suggested outings with her friends, and they always seemed to work, for which she was grateful. The hard part was to turn off the waterworks because for some reason crying relieved the pain, even though it was only a temporary respite. She forced herself to stay dry-eyed and stoic. It was sometimes impossible, especially when she was around Billie, and since they saw each other five days a week, it was doubly tough. They were over their tense discussion, but Ayanna still felt uneasy. She was sad that her friend was having morning sickness, but it did serve as a distraction, like today.

Billie came out of the office bathroom looking pale. She was wiping her face with paper towels and moaning. "If I read one more interview with some damned actress talking about how she never had morning sickness even though she was carrying sextuplets, I'ma go to Hollywood and beat the bitch *down*," she said savagely. "Being pregnant is hard. Nobody tells you how miserable it is. They just tell you how wonderful it is to have a beautiful baby," she sniffed.

Ayanna sympathized. "Did Dakota have morning sickness?"

Billie brightened. "Yes, she did. She felt like hell for three months. She's a good sister," Billie said as she reached for the saltines that were never far away.

"Let me get you some ginger ale," Ayanna said solicitously.

"Lots of ice, please, and a little water." Even the soothing ginger ale could cause a riot in tummy town for Billie, so she usually watered it down a little.

Ayanna came back from the break room with the ice-filled glass and a paper-wrapped straw. "Here you go, Billie."

Billie brightened and took the glass. "You're a lifesaver," she sighed. "So when are you going to pick up the boys?"

"Next week. School doesn't start for three weeks, but Cameron has preseason practice with the football team. And we have school shopping to do." She shuddered. Back-to-school shopping was expensive and tedious. She thought about the crowds of harried mothers all searching for the best items at the best prices, hordes of pouting children who wanted something way outside the family budget that would also flout the school dress code. Not to mention the long lines of shoppers at the cash register. She wished with all her heart she could have done it earlier, but with growing boys, there was no point in trying to buy their clothes ahead of time.

"It's too bad Johnny won't be here to help you drive," Billie said.

Ayanna was jerked out of her negative thoughts by Billie's words.

"What do you mean?"

"Oh, you didn't know, I guess. Sorry. Anyway, Johnny's going to Africa next week, and then he has to go to Switzerland and England after that. This is the longest trip he's made in a while. We won't see him until Halloween, probably, if then. I think he has something going on in New York when he gets back from the U.K." She belched loudly and begged Ayanna's pardon. "I'm so sorry, honey. I'm not trying to be rude, but this baby must be a soccer player. It just kicks the gas out of me. I'm going to my office to rattle the walls in private."

Ayanna was glad of the privacy because she wasn't sure she could hold back the tears. He was going away without a word to her. After the way she'd behaved, she couldn't blame him. She'd made such a mess of things, and she had no idea how to get things back together. The only good thing was that she wasn't pregnant. Her period had finally come. Just as she'd hoped, it was a cycle change that caused her to be so late. It had taken her three days to finally e-mail him, as he requested. He didn't even bother to answer, which was to be expected.

The really sad thing was that she was still madly in love with him. She still believed she wasn't the right woman for him, no matter what he said in a moment of passion. She just couldn't settle for an affair, and he couldn't commit to marriage. She'd heard him say so too many times, and she'd heard it from his sisters, too. Even when Billie was dressing her down about the way things had ended, she never said that Johnny wanted to marry her. So she'd had a little taste of love and she'd savor it for the rest of her life because she knew she'd never feel anything like it again.

Anyone who knew him well would know that Johnny was in a foul mood. His sisters, praise Jesus, were busy with their own lives, and he'd managed to duck and dodge them for the last couple of weeks. Dakota was busy with the baby, and Billie was deep in the throes of constant morning sickness so he was able to successfully claim that he was busy at work, which was true. He welcomed the travel that lay ahead of him because he wanted out of Chicago with a vengeance.

Why the hell had he taken a job that would put him in the same city as that deceitful little wench?

He was in a place he despised—O'Hare Airport— while he mulled this over. True, he hadn't known that he was going to get involved with Ayanna. And he hadn't known that all his faculties would desert him once he did. The bitterness boiled up in him again as he thought about how she'd fooled him completely. The first time he really fell in love and all she wanted was a good time. The irony made him smile grimly, an expression that frightened the hell out of two little old ladies who were approaching the area where he was sitting. They turned around and went the other way, but he didn't notice them.

His flight was finally called, and he went to the gate with all his boarding papers in one hand and his new laptop over his shoulder in its leather carrying case. He'd had to purchase it when the other one broke. "Broke" wasn't the right description; when he'd gotten the one-line e-mail from Ayanna that read "not pregnant," he'd smashed the expensive computer into pieces.

He stowed his carry-on under his seat and hung his sport coat in the first class locker area before sitting down. He always paid the difference between business class and first class because of his long legs. He had a lot of flying to do, and he wasn't in the mood for a stiff back and cramped legs. He had fastened his seat belt and closed his eyes to await take off, when he could recline his seat and go to sleep. He was hoping he could get some sleep on the plane because he wasn't doing much of it in Nick's garish apartment. He despised that horrible bed and everything it represented, since it made him think of Ayanna. She was the last person he wanted to think about in this life.

A sultry voice roused him. "I think this is my seat. Would you prefer the aisle? We can switch if you like."

He opened his eyes to see a statuesque woman with a thick head of long hair standing next to the aisle seat. "Sure. That's very thoughtful of you," he said as he undid his seat belt and stood up.

They switched places, and he felt the warmth from her curvy body and smelled her perfume. He gave her a quick glance before sitting down. If this was his companion all the way to London where he would change planes, life had just gotten a lot more pleasant.

"I'm Celeste Brown," she said, offering him a hand.

"John Phillips." Her hand was soft and warm, and she looked like an intelligent, charming seatmate. Yes, things were looking better already.

Chapter 15

Ayanna had always enjoyed driving long distances, but not this trip. She drove steadily, listening to NPR all the way down to South Carolina because music of all kinds just served to remind her of Johnny and the love she still had for him. Even though it meant she would probably never see him again, she was happy he was out of the country because it would make it easier to transition the boys out of the relationship. With him out of the country for a few months, they would gradually get used to his absence and the fact that he was no longer a part of their lives.

She was hoping that the excitement of school, with football practice for Cameron and band practice for Alec, would keep them from noticing how bad she looked. She was losing weight, and it showed. She looked anorexic, and to an extent she was, because she just couldn't bear eating. She made herself eat because she had to, but it was as pleasurable as eating gravel. She just hoped her mother wouldn't notice how haggard she was. Nothing much got past Lucie Porter.

The drive wasn't horrible, although the gas prices were astronomical. She had already set money aside for the trip, and it was a good thing that she always budgeted on the high side or she might have been stranded on the side of the road. She made the trip in thirteen hours, stopping only to fill up the tank and her thermos cup with coffee. Her mouth was puckered and bitter from all the brew she'd consumed, but it would all be over soon. She'd already passed the sign that indicated the exit for Columbia was coming up. She popped a few Altoids in her mouth and tried to school her face into a pleasant expression, a lighthearted look of carefree happiness. When she pulled into her mother's driveway she could feel what a failure the effort was. Her sunken cheeks actually hurt from the effort of trying to smile, but she did her best.

"Hi, Ma!" Cameron and Alec leaped off the porch and grabbed her.

"Let me look at you," she exclaimed. "Good heavens, I think you grew three inches, Alec!"

"Two and a half, Ma," he said proudly. "Cameron only grew two inches."

"Yeah, but my feet got a size bigger," Cameron boasted.

With her arms around her boys' waists, she went up the stairs to greet her mother. "Hi, Mommy!" she said in a too-cheery voice.

Lucie just raised an eyebrow. "We'll talk later. Boys, get your mother's things out of the car, please."

She hugged Ayanna tightly, making a face when she felt how thin she was. "I made you your favorite rhubarb pie," she said comfortingly. "You're a little thin, aren't you, dear?"

The tears started running before Ayanna could stop them.

"Go on upstairs. I'll get the boys to set the table or something," Lucie said.

Ayanna gladly went upstairs to her mother's bedroom. She threw herself across the bed and waited for Lucie to come talk to her. The faint scent of Giorgio was in the room, as always. In a couple of minutes, Lucie was in the doorway with a bowl of rhubarb pie topped with ice cream in one hand and a glass of iced tea in the other hand.

"Life is short, honey. Eat dessert first," she quipped.

Ayanna sat up and crossed her legs like she'd done when she was little, and her mother handed her the bowl of pie.

"Tell me what happened, Ayanna. I could tell something was bothering you from your phone calls, but I was going to wait until I saw you to dig it out of you. Now I can see with my own eyes that something's wrong, and if I'm not mistaken, it has something to do with that magnificent specimen, doesn't it?"

"Yes, it does." Ayanna swallowed hard to get rid of the lump in her throat. She told Lucie all about her fight with Johnny and how he'd reacted. Lucie listened closely, and when Ayanna wound down, she reached out to take Ayanna's hand.

"Sweetie pie, you know I love you to pieces, but I'm afraid this is more about you than it is about him." She held a hand up to stop the indignant response Ayanna was about to deliver. "Ayanna, you're my daughter, and I know you better than anyone, so I have to ask, what in the world made you think you weren't good enough for that man? You got stuck on stupid, honey. You planted this seed of doubt in your head, and you let it flourish into a big plant instead of plucking that lie out of your head and tossing it aside.

"Who on earth told you that the only women he gets involved with are the doctors and lawyers and Indian chiefs? Sounds to me like they're the ones he goes though like a box of tissues. How did you get to have such a poor self-image that you think you can't be the answer to somebody's prayer?" Lucie was really wound up now, and she started walking around the room, the way she always did when she was excited.

"I'm going to tell you something I thought you already knew. Men don't know who they're going to marry until the woman lets them know. They can't make up their minds about what they want for breakfast much less who they're going to spend the rest of their lives with. Now this man has spent his whole life running from fast women, and when he meets you, he knows you're the one because that's the message you sent out there to the universe. He just knew in his heart that you were the right one." She stopped pacing long enough to stroke Ayanna's face and then pat her head.

"When a man like Johnny loves, he loves hard. He puts everything into making you happy. Couldn't you tell how he felt about you? I could, but that's not the issue." She started winding down at last and sat down on the bed again.

"Well, you're just going to have to get him back," Lucie said firmly. She held up her hand again to cut Ayanna off. "I don't know how you're going to do it. You're a smart woman. You'll figure it out. But you're just going to have to get him back. That's my son-in-law," she said. "I want him in my family."

Ayanna almost choked on the sweet sassafras tea. "But, Mommy, he's gone to Africa. He might not come back, ever."

Lucie stood up grandly and gave Ayanna the look that said "don't be ridiculous." "Honey, everything and everyone comes back. Besides, Africa is just a plane ride away. When you finish your pie, come on down for dinner. I made smothered chicken and succotash with angel biscuits."

As improbable as it seemed, after fifteen minutes in her mother's house, Ayanna felt better. What her mother said made a lot of sense, as usual. She had been stuck on stupid. She had planted the seed of unworthiness in her head and let the resulting poisoned vine choke off all her common sense. Nobody could have treated her like Johnny had unless he loved her the same way she loved him. And he had to know she loved him.... Or maybe not. She had been screaming at him like an idiot the last time she'd seen him.

She polished off the last of the delicious tart pie and gulped the iced tea. Suddenly she realized she was still hungry. Smothered chicken and angel biscuits sounded like the perfect thing to her. She was going to get her appetite back. And maybe, if her mother had anything to say about it, she would get her man back, too.

She pattered down the stairs and went into the kitchen. "Everything smells so good! Do you need help with anything?"

Lucie smiled and patted her cheek. "Not a thing, Ayanna. Just sit down and eat. Eat a *lot.*"

Johnny looked at his seatmate for the tenth time. She had been pleasant but quiet, and she'd been typing steadily on a thing that was the size of a laptop but it looked like a weird typewriter of sorts. He finally had to ask what it was.

"This? It's my AlphaSmart," she said and laughed. "All I can do is type on it so I stay focused on my manuscript. I can't be trusted with my laptop because I'll start reading e-mail or checking out things on the Internet, and before I realize it, I'm staring down my deadline like a deer caught in the headlights. This way all I can do is write."

"So you're a writer. What do you write?"

She gave him a sexy, playful smile. "I write

romance. I also write murder mysteries. I'll bet you don't read much romance."

"Actually, I've read a few. I thought I knew your name from somewhere. My lady loves romance novels, and you're one of her favorite authors." He paused and his expression changed. "My former lady, I should say."

"You just broke up, didn't you?"

Johnny gave her a half smile that couldn't have fooled anyone. "Are you psychic, or does it show?"

"Well, my husband thinks I'm psychic because he says I can read his mind, but really the look is all too familiar. That's how I looked before I got married. We had a terrible falling out, and we called off the wedding."

Johnny grimaced again. "Well, I don't have to worry about that because I never got around to proposing. This was a clean break."

Celeste gave him a good once over. "I don't think so. I think this really hurt you, and if she has half the feelings you have, she's probably just as miserable."

"I doubt that. She was interested in one thing only—sex. She wasn't into having a relationship or anything close to it. She'd been cooling her heels for eleven years, and I was her summer stud. She sent her boys off to her mom's for vacation, and then she and I got busy. When I called her on it, it blew up in her face, and it was over."

Celeste looked concerned and caring. "This is going to be a long flight. Why don't you start at the beginning, and tell me all about it. I think you might be missing a few elements in your assessment of the situation," she said.

"There's really nothing to tell," Johnny said, and for the next four hours, he told her the long version of "nothing."

Celeste waved to the attendant who was serving first class. "I'm getting a glass of wine, and I think you should, too," she said to Johnny. "You could really use one."

Johnny gave a rough laugh that didn't sound amused. "This must be your worst nightmare," he said. "To be trapped on a crazy-long flight with a lovesick fool."

Celeste patted his hand. "Let me tell you something. There's nothing wrong with being lovesick. It's better than being heartless. And whether you realize it or not, your lady's heart is broken, too. I don't know how you leapt to the conclusion that she was just using that big fine body of yours for sex, but I can tell you with all the authority vested in me by the Romance Writers of America that it's just not so. Your Ayanna loves you with all her heart." She smiled as their server brought her a chilled glass of chardonnay and insisted that he take a sip of his merlot.

"You need to mellow out a little. Now then, let's go over what you just told me. Remember, I love mysteries and romance, and this is a little of both," she told him. "First of all, she's a good woman. She gave up her career dreams to raise her sister's kids without complaint. She lost a fiancé in the process, although personally, I think she didn't lose much.

"She works hard, her life revolves around her kids, she's helpful and kind and she was celibate. In no court of law would she be found to be anything but a good woman, John. And from the pictures you showed me on your BlackBerry, she's lovely. She could have had plenty of sex if she wanted to. Why do you think she waited for you?"

Johnny thought about it and before he could come up with an answer, Celeste was talking again. "This lady loves romance. She loves to dance. She loves to cook for people she loves. She put her dreams on hold and her life, too. She could have had a very different life, but it wasn't in the cards, so she did the best with what she could. And then comes you."

Their server brought their meal, and as they began to eat the surprisingly well-cooked prime rib, Celeste continued to educate him. "John, I'm not ashamed to tell you that if I wasn't about to celebrate my silver anniversary with the man I've adored since I was nineteen, you'd tempt even me. So poor Ayanna had to have been swept off her feet.

"But she's so humble and down-to-earth it never occurred to her that an international lover like you would be interested in settling down with a homebody like her. She was taking what she could get, John, because she thought that's all there was."

"But she should have known how I felt, Celeste. I never held anything back from her."

"Did you tell her you loved her? Aside from the night you were fighting, that is."

"Well, no," Johnny admitted.

"Did you discuss the future, marriage, what your role as stepfather to her sons would be? Where you would live, what her role would be as your wife, what your hopes and expectations were about a life with her?"

"Well, no, I didn't," he said slowly.

"So exactly how was she supposed to know how you felt? You're talking about a woman with relatively little experience in dating. The experience she had was ten years out of date, and you expected her to be some kind of love psychic because you had good sex? Does that make sense to you?"

The things Celeste was saying in her friendly, down-to-earth way were so simple that he felt like a jackass for not thinking of them himself.

He asked the flight attendant for another glass of wine. He had a feeling he might have yet another before the flight was over.

"And remember, John. This all blew up because you gave her an impulsive gift that she thought was too expensive. A skank would've taken the bling and run with it, but she really cared about you spending money frivolously. She loved you too much for that."

"Celeste, you really are special. I can see why you've had a romance that's lasted so long. Your husband is a lucky man."

"We're a lucky couple. But don't get it twisted.

We've had our share of ups and downs over the years. I told you we'd broken off the engagement at one point."

"Yeah, but you didn't say what happened. Tell me about it." Johnny invited.

And for the next couple of hours, she did.

Chapter 16

Ayanna was so happy to see her boys that it took the edge off her misery. She'd missed Alec and Cameron terribly, and they'd missed her, although they'd had a wonderful summer. Lucie, bless her heart, had a surprise for her. She was deeply grateful to her mother for doing their school shopping before she came to get them. The time it was going to save her was worth gold, in her estimation. Plus, her mother refused to accept payment for the clothes and shoes. She had fussed at Ayanna in her loving way.

"Ayanna, don't be ridiculous! You never did know how to take things from anyone. You're so independent it borders on fanaticism. When your father died, he didn't leave me destitute. I've always worked and had my own money, my own savings. And he left us money as well. Since you were smart enough to get full scholarships, your college money has just been gaining interest. It was supposed to support you while you were in Paris at the Cordon Bleu, but you didn't go, and the money's just sitting around," Lucie said.

They were on the back porch sipping coffee after breakfast the day after Ayanna arrived. "Why didn't you tell me this before?" she asked her mother.

"I did tell you, but I think you were too distraught to take it in. I just held on to it because it would be there for you when you needed it for something. I figured the insurance money from Attiya was tiding you over."

Attiya was her sister, Alec and Cameron's birth mother. "Mommy, I put that money in trust for Alec and Cameron. I've never touched it. It's just sitting there gaining interest," she said. "And before you say anything, I did tell you I was going to do that. I told Daddy, and that was just like telling you."

They looked at each other and laughed. Lucie had to get in the last word, though. "The point is you deserve to have a little relief in your life. You have worked like a Hebrew slave to take care of my grandsons, and I couldn't be more proud of the job you've done. But at some point you've got to take some time for yourself. Buy an outfit that isn't on clearance and some shoes that aren't from Payless. Let your hair grow out. I know you keep it short so you can do it yourself to save money, but you deserve to pamper yourself a little. I'm going to give you some of that inheritance so that you can have a little more wiggle room in your budget." Lucie stood and poured her now cold coffee on the flowers that surrounded the porch. "Besides, you might need to go to Africa one of these days."

Ayanna shook her head as she followed her mother into the house to begin packing the boys for the trip home. She could appreciate her mother's optimism; she just needed a dose of her vision. Right now, she just couldn't see how a reunion with Johnny was going to happen.

It was wonderful having her boys back home. She was so busy she didn't have time to mope. She was back to the usual routine of taking them to school, packing lunches, attending parent-teacher conferences and the like that her days were too full to think about Johnny. The nights were a different situation, because he haunted her dreams in ways that she desired to be rid of, but there was nothing she could do about that.

She was leaving work early today for Cameron's first official game of the season. Preseason was over, and there'd been a couple of nonconference games, but this was the first one that would count. She'd been a little concerned about him lately because he seemed to be somewhat listless and tired, but he assured her he was fine.

"I have some tough classes this semester, and between studying and football practice, I've just been kinda tired. I'll start taking vitamins. That should do it."

She looked into his eyes and felt his forehead that

very morning. "You seem a little warm to me," she said. "I'm making an appointment for you with Dr. Brady."

"Aw, Ma," he said, scratching the back of his neck.

"Why do you have that bandage on? Did you hurt your arm?"

"This? No, it's just a spider bite. It's been itching a lot, though, so I put some Neosporin on it and covered it up so it wouldn't get dirty."

"Let me see." she reached for his arm but he pulled away.

"Ma, look at it when I get home. C'mon, we're gonna be late, and I need to talk to my chemistry teacher before class."

She let him get away with it and promised herself that she'd look at it carefully that evening. After a busy day of work, she picked up Alec from school, and they had the rare treat of burgers and fries at their favorite greasy spoon before the game. She was really touched to see Nick and Jason in the stands. "I'm so glad to see you," she said. "How are Bethany and Dakota?"

"They're fine," Nick said. "Dakota was just saying that it's been too long since she's seen you. She wants you to come for dinner soon."

She promised that she would, and she and Alec sat down to cheer Cameron on. The game went well; their team won and Cameron made a touchdown, which thrilled Alec to no end. After the game, though, Cameron still seemed listless and didn't want to go to a party, nor did he want something to eat.

"I'm just gonna crash, Ma. See you in the morning."

It was too late to check his arm, but Ayanna vowed she was going to corral him first thing in the morning.

This time she didn't forget. She practically pounced on him before he got out of bed, and she took off the bandage. She tried not to let her panic show, but she didn't like the looks of it at all. His arm was swollen and red, and there was a nasty ooze of pus that looked terribly infected. *Spider bite, my foot. This looks like a tarantula chomped him.*

Suddenly she didn't want to wait for her appointment with the doctor; she wanted him seen that day. "Why don't you get up and take a shower, sweetie? I'm going to have that arm looked at today. No arguments, Cameron. Shower now, please."

She went right to the phone and called Todd Wainwright. Besides being Billie's brother-in-law and head of the emergency room at John Stroger Hospital, he was a good friend of Ayanna's. He would tell her what to do for Cameron.

She was pleased when she got him on the phone right away, and she explained his symptoms. God bless him, he was a comfort to her right away. "It's probably nothing, but go ahead and bring him in, Ayanna. I'll meet you in the emergency room. Just ask for me at the desk, and I'll let them know you're coming in."

Ayanna made sure that Alec bathed and dressed, too. "I'd rather you come with me than stay here by yourself. It's not going to take long, and we can go get something to eat afterward," she said.

"Sounds good to me, Ma." Alec was always ready to eat.

When they got to the emergency room, it wasn't too crowded. Ayanna went to the admitting desk and said her name, adding that Dr. Todd Wainwright was expecting her. The person at the desk told her to have a seat and someone would be with her shortly. Sure enough, Todd came to get her in a few minutes. He was tall, dark and handsome and the object of many a woman's desire, but he was too busy working to settle down in a relationship. He was dedicated to his profession.

"Hello, Ayanna, Cameron, Alec. Cameron, I understand you're not feeling too well. Come with me, and let me take a look."

He took Cameron into an examining room and Ayanna followed. Cameron sat on the edge of the uncomfortable cot and rolled up his sleeve when Todd asked him to. Todd held his arm and examined it closely, then he put his arm down and looked in his eyes, his ears and down his throat, asking him questions the whole time. "Are you tired more than usual? How's your appetite? Playing sports this year? Oh yeah, which one? Good for you, that's great. Lie down, and let me listen to your heart," he said. He listened in several places and had Cameron take deep breaths, cough and pant rapidly.

"Cameron, somebody's going to come in and take some blood from you in a few minutes. Your mom and I will be right back, okay?"

Todd took her elbow and led her out into the hallway. "Ayanna, I'm going to cut to the chase. Cameron has MRSA."

Ayanna thought she might faint. She could literally feel the blood draining from her face. "That super-bug staph infection? Are you sure, Todd?" She'd read several tragic stories about children Cameron's age who'd died from the disease. It had been referred to as a pandemic in the media, and all the news she'd heard about it was bad.

"I'm as sure as I can be without the lab work. We'll know for sure shortly. But the spider bite on his arm is definitely a staph infection. The infection mimics other things like a boil or pimple or insect bite, and it often doesn't get diagnosed until it's had a chance to really infect the patient."

"But how could he get this thing?" Ayanna was trying hard to hold it together, but she was terrified by what she was hearing.

"Staph infections are fairly common. Even MRSA is fairly common, but it used to be confined to hospitals, nursing homes, places where people are exposed to bacteria and viruses on a daily basis. This new strain can be found in schools, Ayanna, especially in locker rooms. We don't know why, but the bacteria flourish there. A person could get a little scratch during football practice, and then the person could touch someone who may be a host or some piece of equipment that the host has handled and the person could get the infection. The problem is that this strain is resistant to antibiotics."

Ayanna looked like she was about to pass out, and Todd put his arm around her shoulder to support her. "I'm going to admit Cameron to the hospital because he definitely has pneumonia, which is an escalating symptom of MRSA. What we want to do is start treatment as quickly as possible to increase the odds that he'll be back playing ball in a week or two. Okay?"

Ayanna nodded her head. "Just get him well, Todd. Just get him well."

"And you know this," Todd said. "He's young and healthy, and he's going to fight this thing. What I need you to do now is go to Admissions and get the paperwork going. When you're done, I'll come and get you and bring you to Cameron."

"Okay. I need to get Alec, I don't want him to be in the waiting room by himself," she murmured.

"Is there anyone I can call for you, Ayanna? I don't want you to be here alone, either."

"Oh no, there's no one here but me and the boys. I mean, my family is in South Carolina. I'm fine, really. Where is the admitting office?"

She went to collect Alec, and they made the trip to the office. She was trying to hold it together for the sake of her sons, but it was hard. She caught a glimpse of Alec's face and forced herself to smile. "This won't take too long, and then we can go see Cameron," she said.

"Is he really sick? I mean really, really sick, Ma?" He sounded so young and frightened that Ayanna found the strength to reassure him.

"He has an infection, and Todd is going to do his

best to get it cleared up. He's in good hands, Alec. He's going to be fine." As they approached the office, she prayed with all her heart that her words were true.

Chapter 17

Despite Todd's optimistic and comforting words, Cameron's lab results not only confirmed the diagnosis of MRSA, but it showed that the disease was affecting his internal organs. Within twenty-four hours, he was moved into intensive care, and Ayanna had a glimpse of what hell must be like. Todd had wisely informed Billie and Jason that Cameron had been hospitalized, and Jason showed up at the hospital with Nick shortly after his initial admission.

They hugged Ayanna, who was trying to stay as calm as possible. "Look, I'm not going to tell you what Billie said, but the gist of it was that she's a little peeved that you didn't let her know. She's still battling the morning sickness or she'd be here herself," Jason told her.

"Dakota didn't want to bring Bethany out in the rain, or she'd be here, too," Nick said. His green eyes were warm with concern. "She says we're family, and she doesn't appreciate you treating us like strangers." He hugged her again as her eyes filled with tears. "Look, I'm going to take Alec with me. He doesn't need to be here for all this. We'll get him fed and get clothes from your house and all that. You look like you could use some food, too."

Ayanna shook her head and said she was fine. "To be honest, I don't think I could keep anything down. But thank you for asking," she murmured. "Alec, why don't you get your jacket and go with Nick. I know you must be starving, and you look like you could use some rest."

"But what about you, Ma? You need some rest, too," he protested.

"Sweetie, I'm fine. I'm a superwoman. Don't worry about me. I need to stay here with Cameron to make sure he's all right. I'll call you as soon as I know something."

She hugged him tightly and found it difficult to let go. With an effort that was truly superhuman, she smiled at him and said she'd see him soon. She watched him walk away with Nick and started trembling. Jason put his arm around her waist and hugged her to his side. "Hang in there, kid. Come on and sit down. I'm going to go get you something to eat, and you're going to eat it, too."

Jason stayed with her until she insisted that he go

home and see about Billie. "Tell her I'm sorry I didn't call. It's just that things were happening so fast, I didn't think about it."

"Have you called your mother? She's not going to be any happier than Billie or Dakota if she finds out about this later," he pointed out.

"You're right, I should call her. But I have to go downstairs to use my cell phone, and I just don't want to leave him in case the doctors have something to tell me or he gets worse…" Her voice trailed off.

"You go downstairs and make the call. I'll stay right here, and if we need you, I'll call you," Jason said firmly.

"Okay, I will. Thanks, Jason. Thank you so much."

She went down to the lobby and out the front doors. She needed some fresh air desperately. It was raining, like Nick had said. She had lost all track of the time or the day. She tried to think and realized it had been over twenty-four hours since she'd brought Cameron to the hospital. She was holding her cell phone so tightly it hurt her hand. She moved it from one hand to the other and flexed her cramped fingers. She pushed a few buttons and was soon listening to her mother's voice.

"Mommy, I've got some bad news. Cameron is in the hospital. He has MRSA, and it has invaded his, um, his internal organs."

She didn't start crying until Lucie said, "I'll be there on the next plane. Hang on, honey, I'm coming."

When Ayanna went back to the waiting area, she was stunned to find Cameron's football coach, his school principal and his closest friends in the waiting area talking to Jason. The coach's name was Nathan Bridges and he was a tall, handsome fellow whose concern was plain to see.

"Ms. Porter, I heard that Cameron was sick, and I wanted to let you know how sorry we were to hear about it. He's a great young man, and if there's anything I can do to help, I'll be more than happy to do it. His teammates are really concerned about him, in fact the whole school is," he told her.

The principal, Mrs. Carter, agreed. "Cameron is such a lovely young man. He has a brilliant future ahead of him, and we're praying that he gets well soon."

His friends, Zack and Anthony, weren't as polished as the adults, but they hugged Ayanna and asked if they could do anything to help.

"Just pray for him. If you all would just keep praying," she said, "I think God will hear all our prayers and answer them."

To her surprise, the coach took her hand and held out his other one, and Anthony took it without hesitation. They formed a circle with Jason, and he said a simple but well-worded prayer that was so comforting to Ayanna that for the first time she didn't feel like crying. She felt something that she really needed, which was hope.

Lucie looked around the waiting area, which was full of flowers and teddy bears and school mascots and get-well cards, and pressed her hand to her cheek. One of the chairs was completely taken over with the bounty of tributes that Cameron's teachers, classmates and teammates had brought, and it was clear that Ayanna had been in the same position for the seventy-two hours that had passed since Cameron's admittance to the intensive care unit.

"Ayanna, honey, you've got to go home," Lucie pleaded. "You need a hot bath and some real sleep. You can't keep hovering around here napping in these waiting room chairs. And you've got to get the flowers and things out of here. It's too hard for the nurses to deal with all this. It needs to be at your house. That's why I'm here, sweetie pie, to handle things so you can get some rest. Go home for just a few hours, and come back later. You're not alone anymore. Mommy is here, honey."

Ayanna knew what her mother was saying made sense, but she couldn't bring herself to do as she suggested. She was so riddled with guilt and anxiety that she couldn't think straight. When her mother had come into the waiting area she'd finally broken down in her arms. After a brief cry, she resumed her stoic posture, but Lucie had seen right through it. It was time for tough love.

Billie, Dakota, Toni and their husbands had all come up to sit with Ayanna, fetch her food and just support her. She was never alone now, but she couldn't bring herself to leave. Lucie had to turn into a drill sergeant to get her out of there.

"Ayanna Demetria Porter, you are going to listen to me and do what I say. Billie is going to take you home, and you are going to take a hot shower. Dakota has made you a meal, and you are going to sit down and eat it. And then you are going to sleep in your own bed," she said in her sternest department-head voice.

"But, Mommy," she began.

Lucie almost stamped her foot in frustration. "Baby girl, take that word out of your vocabulary. There is no 'but' around here except the one you sit on. Alec is worried half to death because he hasn't seen you, and you have to remember that if you fall, the whole family falls. You must keep up your strength."

Lucie took her by the hand and led her over to Billie. "Please take her home, Billie. Sit on her if you have to, but keep her there, please. And can Jason or somebody please put all this stuff in your car and take it to the house later?"

Billie set her jaw and assured Lucie that she would do whatever it took to get Ayanna to cooperate. "She'll do it or else. Come on, sister girl. Enough with the dumb stuff, I'm taking you home right now. Jason will get all the flowers and things."

Ayanna just nodded her head numbly and went along.

She didn't think it was possible, but she really did feel better after a few hours. The shower felt wonderful. She scrubbed herself over and over with her bath puff and copious amounts of bath gel. Afterward, she applied lotion and body butter because her skin felt so dry and neglected. She didn't have enough energy to get dressed, but it didn't matter because Dakota brought her a tray.

"Here you go, Ayanna. I know it's the middle of the afternoon, but if you're like me you can eat breakfast any time of the day or night. It's just so comforting."

"You're so right, Dakota. This looks delicious," she said with a smile. It wasn't her usual big dimpled smile, but it was a start.

Dakota had made her scrambled eggs with toast, creamy grits, bacon and sausage and fried apples. There was a big glass of orange juice and a cup of tea. Ayanna suddenly realized she was starving and started eating everything on the tray.

"This is so good," she said. "I can't thank you enough."

"You don't have to thank me, girl! It was my pleasure. I would have made you some biscuits, but that is not one of my skills," she added dryly. They talked until Ayanna had finished every bite. Dakota took the tray and told her to sleep for a while.

"You really need this rest. Your mom is there, and Cameron is getting the best possible treatment. Sleep while you can."

And to her surprise, Ayanna was able to drift off for a much-needed nap. When she woke up, Alec was sitting in the chair looking lost. There was a book in his lap, but he hadn't been reading it.

"Hey, sweetie. Come give me a kiss," she said.

She sat up, and he came over to give her a big hug and a kiss on the cheek.

"How are you feeling, Ma?"

"I'm better now that I see you." She smiled and gave him another squeeze. For once he didn't back away and protest the mushy stuff; he let her hold him.

"Ma, is Cameron going to die?" His voice broke as he asked the question.

"No, he's not," she said fiercely. "He's not going to die. We're going to pray about it right now, okay?"

They held hands tightly and prayed for God's healing protection for Cameron.

Lucie didn't really want her to go back to the hospital, but Ayanna couldn't stay away. She'd showered, changed clothes, eaten and rested and she was back. They let her put on a paper gown, gloves and mask to go into intensive care to see him, but she could only go in for fifteen minutes at a time. It didn't matter, though. Fifteen minutes was better than nothing. Cameron looked so young and helpless as he slept. He was basically unconscious most of the time. The medication wasn't working yet, and Todd had told her that he might have to undergo surgery to clear the infection from his internal organs, especially his lungs.

She was frightened beyond reason, but she controlled her fear. Todd introduced her to the surgeon who would be operating on Cameron, if necessary, and to the infectious disease specialist. Everyone was very kind and professional, but it didn't ease her mind as much as her continual prayers. Lucie had reminded her that He was still in the miracle business and that it was only His word that mattered.

Ayanna was alone now. She didn't really mind because she needed to be near Cameron, and she needed the solitude to pray. The lights in the waiting area were dimmed because it was so late. She wasn't sure but she thought it was midnight or close to it. She wasn't completely sure what day it was. Lucie was at home with Alec, and Billie and Dakota were at home with their husbands. It was quiet and almost peaceful, even though she was trying to curl up in a decidedly hard chair.

She was cold and uncomfortable and wished she had a pillow or something. She could ask the nurses, but she didn't want to bother them. They had enough to do. She wrapped her arms around herself and rocked back and forth. She was thinking about the possibility that her baby would have to undergo major surgery, and she clasped her hands and put them to her mouth. Her thoughts became overwhelming, and she stood up and started to pace. She thought she heard someone say her name, but she figured she was hearing things.

She heard it again and turned around to see Johnny walking toward her. She stood still, not believing her eyes until he reached her and put his arms around her, holding her tight.

"Baby, I'm so sorry. I'm so sorry," he whispered.

She didn't hear his words. She was too caught up in the fact that he was there and he was holding her. She looked at him with dazed eyes. "I'm not dreaming, am I? You're really here, aren't you?" she said shakily.

"I'm right here, sweetness. I'll always be here for you."

Ayanna buried her head in his comforting shoulder and held on for dear life.

Chapter 18

"How did you know?" Ayanna asked when she was finally able to stop holding him. He walked her over to the unyielding sofa and sat down, keeping one arm around her and holding her hand. "Billie called me. Then Dakota called me. My mother called me. Jason called me. I was already on my way to the airport by the time my mother got on the phone," he said.

"I can't believe you're really here," she said softly. "I'm so scared, Johnny."

"I know you are, sweetheart, but this isn't in our hands anymore. It's all up to God, and He's going to take care of our boy." She nodded and looked at him with absolute trust in her eyes. He kissed her on each cheek and on her lips, very gently. "Tell me what happened, Ayanna."

She told him about Cameron's listlessness and his lack of appetite and about the day she'd noticed the bandage. "When he was little he'd run to me with every scratch," she said sadly. "I was too busy and too caught up in my own misery to even notice that my child had a staph infection," she said brokenly. "By the time I actually saw it, I knew something was wrong, and I brought him to the E.R. so Todd could take a look, and he's been here ever since. The infection has spread to his internal organs, and they're probably going to operate on him tomorrow because he's not responding to any of the medications. MRSA is resistant to antibiotics," she said, and then she looked embarrassed. "Why am I telling you this? You probably know more about it than some of the doctors around here."

He stroked the side of her face and kissed her again. He did know more than the average person about a lot of infectious diseases because of the nature of his work, but he'd hardly consider himself to be an expert.

"Will they let me see him?"

"Yes, but not yet. Visiting hours don't start until nine, and you can only go in fifteen minutes at a time. You'll have to say you're family, though. Only family members can visit."

"I am family," he said. "You're my family, you and Alec and Cameron. You're the woman I love, Ayanna. I know we made a mess of things, but that's the past and from here on out, we're only concerned with the future. No more misunderstandings, no more screwups. I love you."

"I love you, too. I love you so much, and I thought— Never mind what I thought. I love you, Johnny. It was never just sex for me."

"I know that, baby." He stole another kiss and then gave her the devilish grin. "But the sex was good, wasn't it?"

"You are a sick, sick man."

"That may be true, but I'm *your* man, and don't you ever forget it."

Nick arrived to spell Ayanna for a while so she could stretch her legs and get some coffee. While he knew she probably wouldn't do either, he wanted to check on her. When he came around the corner and saw her holding hands with Johnny, he frowned.

"It's about time you got here. Your mama and daddy are here. I just picked them up at the airport, and since I was already up, I came on over here to see about my girl. You better call your folks because they're about to disown you," he said dryly.

"Good to see you, too, bro. Aren't you glad you married my sister? See what a fun family we are?" Johnny shook his brother-in-law's hand and smiled.

Nick grinned back. "You got the best family in the world, and I'm a part of it so show some love. Take this poor woman out of here for a while, and I'll hold it down here."

"I have something for you."

Ayanna was across from Johnny in a big booth at an all-night diner near the hospital. Her face turned red and she looked panicked. Johnny reached into the pocket of his sport coat and pulled out a paperback book. "Don't get scared, it's just a book."

He slid it across the table, and she picked it up with curious hands. "This is a Celeste Brown book. It's not due out for two months. How did you get it?"

"I met her on a flight to London on my way to Africa. She sat next to me on the plane, and we talked about you for seven hours."

"You didn't!" Ayanna was really blushing now. Her face looked as hot as fire.

"Yes, we did, sweetness. I told her all about you and how I messed everything up between us. I owe you a big apology, Ayanna. I want you to know how sorry I am that I hurt you. It's the last thing I ever wanted to do in this life."

Ayanna stared at him, and there was no mistaking his sincerity. "But, Johnny, you didn't mess anything up. I did. I thought so little of myself that it just didn't occur to me that you really cared about me. I couldn't see that you couldn't have treated me the way you did unless you had real feelings for me. I just took your love and tossed it in your face," she said sadly. "I'm the one who should be begging your pardon. I couldn't see clearly what I had done until my mother and Billie got me straight," she said. "I hope you can forgive me."

Johnny came over to her side of the booth and kissed her. "Ayanna, angel, don't ever apologize to me again. We both made mistakes. We both acted hastily, and we won't ever do it again. I promise you that from my heart," he said.

They were deep into a long, soul-healing kiss when a voice brought them back to the present.

"Y'all don't really want this, do you? I can bring it back, 'cause y'all look a little busy." It was their server, a gangly college kid named Keyshawn. He was holding a tray of cheeseburgers, onion rings and two cherry colas, and he looked vastly amused.

Ayanna giggled and put her head in the crook of Johnny's neck.

"Hey, I'm starving, and she needs to eat, so put it right here, partner. Sorry for the show," Johnny said, but he didn't sound sorry in the least.

"Hey, no problem. Now I know I have something to look forward to when I get…um, out of school," Keyshawn said as he unloaded the tray. "Enjoy your meal," he added.

"Was he about to call me old? I know he wasn't going to call me old, fine as I am," Johnny mumbled.

"You're gorgeous. Now eat. I can hear your stomach growling from here," Ayanna said.

"By the way, Celeste signed that book for you."

Ayanna eagerly looked for the inscription that read, "This book was handed to you by the man who will love you the rest of your lives. Be good to him and to yourself. Hugs, Celeste."

They went back to the hospital and held hands and talked all night, until all the pain was a thing of the past.

When the time for visiting hours arrived, Johnny was allowed to go in to see Cameron. Ayanna was touched to her heart to see tears in his eyes when he came out.

"He's going to be fine, Ayanna. God's not going to take him from us, I promise you." He held her tight and they prayed together.

"It's about time you got here." The voice was Lucie's. She held out her arms for a hug, which Johnny gladly gave her.

"Sorry it took so long, but I was in England," he said.

"You're here now, that's all that matters. How is my grandson this morning?"

Ayanna said sadly, "There doesn't seem to be any change, Mommy."

Lucie took her hand and held her tightly. "Don't sound so sad, honey. When there seems to be no change it isn't a bad thing, Ayanna. He's stable, which is better than him taking a sharp turn for the worse. I'm going to talk to the nurse, I'll be right back."

While Lucie went to pry information out of the charge nurse, Lee and Boyd Phillips showed up. Lee went to Ayanna and held her tight. "Ayanna, darling girl, we've been praying for you and the boys. I'm not going to get in the way, but I had to be here with you. How are you holding up?"

"I'm fine now," Ayanna said. "I can't believe you came all the way from Pittsburgh just to see about us," she said tearfully.

"You're family," Boyd said gruffly. "Now don't start crying again. I had three women in my house that would cry at the drop of a hat. Please don't start," he pleaded.

"I'll try," she promised. Turning to Johnny, she said, "Johnny, I'm going to be here the rest of the day, so you might want to get some rest." Lucie came back in time to hear her.

"No, you're not going to stay here. Johnny, please take her home. She left here yesterday for the first time since Cameron was admitted, and she was right back here six hours later. She's been here over twelve hours now, and she needs some rest." She looked at Lee and Boyd and said, "You must be Johnny's parents. I'm sorry to sound like a shrew, but my daughter doesn't like taking my advice. She really does need some rest."

Lee agreed. "Johnny, get our girl out of here, and don't let her come back for a good long time. We can hold down the fort here."

Johnny agreed with her. "Come on, sweetness. I'm taking you home."

In a couple of hours, Ayanna was in bed in a way she thought was a thing of the past. She was curled up next to Johnny, feeling the warmth of his embrace. When they got to her house, they took a shower and went to bed. Even without making love, the contact was intimate and reassuring.

"I thought you hated me," she whispered.

"I could never, ever hate you. You're too precious to me. You are the other half of my heart," he said with a huge yawn.

"That was romantic," she giggled. "Can you show a little more interest, please?"

"Just as soon as I wake up, I'll show you all the interest you can handle," he promised.

He went to sleep almost immediately, but Ayanna stayed awake for a while. Despite her joy at being reunited with Johnny, she couldn't close her eyes. She was too consumed with Cameron's condition. She finally drifted off and slept surprisingly well in Johnny's arms.

A phone call woke them, and Ayanna's heart leapt into her throat. "Johnny, we have to get to the hospital. There's been a change."

Ayanna wasn't sure her legs would support her as they rounded the corner to the intensive care unit. Lucie, Lee and Boyd were waiting for her, and so was the doctor.

"There has been a profound change in his condition," the doctor said. "The medication is taking hold and the infection is clearing up. It looks like he won't need surgery after all."

Tears of joy ran down her face as Johnny wrapped his arms around her. "Can I see him, please?"

When she went into the unit, she felt a thrill like no other as Cameron looked at her sleepily. "Ma, I'm hungry. What do I have to do to get some real food?"

This time her tears were from nothing but joy and gratitude.

Chapter 19

"John, I'm ready to go home. When can I get out of here?"

Cameron was out of intensive care, and Todd and his other doctors had assured Ayanna that his release was imminent. Johnny smiled at his eagerness.

"Cam, you're going home tomorrow if all your tests come back clean. Just chill and enjoy taking it easy for one more day."

"I'll chill when I get home. I miss being at home with Ma and Alec," Cameron countered. "Being stuck here is not 'taking it easy.' I have a lot of homework to make up, and besides, Ma's been missing work, and she's had a whole bunch to deal with me being sick and all. When

I'm home she'll know I'm well, and she can relax for a change."

Johnny was surprised to hear Cameron speak with such maturity. He knew more about Ayanna than she realized, he thought. He was shocked at Cameron's next words.

"She doesn't know this, but I know what happened to my mother and father. I heard Aunt Emily talking about it to one of her friends. My dad wasn't such a good man. I can remember him yelling and screaming at my mother a lot," Cameron said solemnly. "He used to hit her, and when he started hitting us, she said she was leaving and going back to Grandma. And then one night neither one of them came home. Ma and Grandma came to get us and told us there had been a car accident. But I heard what Aunt Emily said about what Dad did."

Johnny prayed for guidance and moved his chair closer to Cameron's bed. "Cam, your dad wasn't well," he began.

"I know that," Cameron said. "He had to be sick in the head to do what he did. But I don't want to be like him, so I try to do what Ma tells me to do and to be a good man." He was silent for a moment, and then looked Johnny in the eye, man-to-man.

"You know, she never went out before she met you. Alec and I think you're a good man, John. You're the kind of guy she should be with."

"I try to be a good man, Cameron. And I can promise you that I would never mistreat your mother in any way.

I've never gotten physical with a woman in my life, and I never would. Especially not your mom. She's very special to me."

Cameron was fiddling with his PSP as they talked. His thumbs stopped moving, and he raised an eyebrow. "You love her, don't you?"

"Yes, I do. I love her with all my heart."

"Good. You made a good choice, John. She can cook, she's very tidy and she can refinish furniture. And she's very thrifty, too. She won't waste your money, that's for sure. My mom is tight with a buck," he said ruefully.

Ayanna came into the hospital room looking more rested and less harried. Alec was with her, carrying one of her bakery-style boxes. Johnny stood up when she entered and kissed her on the cheek. "What are you guys talking about?" She kissed her son on the forehead.

"Man stuff, Ma. What did you bring me to eat?"

"You act like they're starving you, sweetie."

"They may as well," he said mournfully. "The food here sucks."

"It really does. The cafeteria food even sucks," Alec agreed.

"Cameron and Alec, what have I told you about that word?" Ayanna sounded amused and exasperated at the same time.

"Sorry, Ma." Cameron grinned. "The food here isn't as palatable as your cuisine. How's that?"

"Better. You can have your chocolate chip and peanut butter cookies now."

"Cool beans!" He gleefully took the box from Alec. Johnny put his arms around Ayanna and hugged her. Everything was getting back to normal, but if he had his way, everything would change again—this time for the better. At least he hoped it would.

In a couple of weeks it was just like nothing had happened. Cameron had spent some time at home before he was considered well enough to go back to school. The school had been completely sanitized after the officials realized there was a MRSA infection. Lucie had taken vacation time so she was able to stay with Ayanna and the boys. As Johnny suspected, Lucie and his mother, Lee, got along like long-lost sisters, and they thoroughly enjoyed each other's company.

Ayanna went back to work and promised Nick that she'd make up the time she'd taken off for Cameron's illness. Nick had looked at her like she was crazy.

"Ayanna, don't even try it. You're family, girl. Call it sick leave, compassionate leave, FMLA or whatever you want, but don't try and make it up. Your child was sick. What were you supposed to do but take care of him?" He walked off muttering, and that was the end of it. Ayanna already knew she was blessed, but his response made her realize how lucky she was. A lot of employers would have fired her for missing so much time, but he wouldn't even let her try to make up the time off.

She was too blessed to be stressed, as the saying went. One of the best things was having Johnny back in her life. When he had come to her in the hospital, it was like waking up from a coma. He had dropped everything and flown home from another country to be with her in her time of need. She didn't need any more proof than that to know he really cared about her and about her boys and that was all that mattered.

They didn't have a lot of time together, what with her mother and his parents in town and Cameron coming home, but the time they did have was precious to her. But it was wonderful having everyone around, too. She felt like part of a really big happy family. For so long it had been just her mother, her sister and the boys, and now she felt like she was part of a loving community. Johnny surprised her one day by asking how she felt about families.

"Do you ever want to get married and have more children?"

They were on the screened porch of her house, stealing a minute to say good-night before he went to his borrowed apartment. It caught her off guard but she answered him honestly.

"Yes, Johnny, I do. I want to get married and have some babies. At least two," she said firmly.

"So you like big families? All the commotion and racket and people getting in each other's business, that doesn't bother you?" he asked curiously.

"Not at all," she replied. "I love it, in fact. You seem to thrive on it, why wouldn't I?"

"Some people prefer their privacy," he said mildly.

"'The grave's a fine and private place,'" she quoted.

"Life is for the living, and after what I've been through I'll take as much as I can get."

"I see," he said thoughtfully. He cupped his hands around her face. "I love this face. It's beautiful," he whispered.

"I love you," she said softly.

"I have to go back to the brothel," he said. That was the name he'd given the apartment. "You know, if you'd help me find a house I wouldn't have to stay there," he reminded her.

"Well, if I had a better idea of what you wanted, I could," she retorted.

"That's easy. A big brick house with enough room for four or five kids and a wife." He watched her face change as she digested this information.

"Sounds like you're a man with a plan," she said slowly.

"I am," he agreed.

"It's about time," she said saucily and moaned as Johnny kissed the smile right off her face.

That Friday Cameron begged for a special dinner. He wanted a lasagna dinner, and he wanted everyone to come. "Please, Ma? This way I can say thank you to Miss Billie and Miss Dakota and Mr. Hunter and everybody. Everybody was so nice when I was sick, and now I can thank everyone personally," he explained.

Ayanna was so touched that she agreed at once. Lucie thought it was a brilliant, wonderful idea, and the two of them started cooking. It was a big party and required a big menu. They decided on antipasto and bruschetta for appetizers, lasagna, spaghetti and eggplant parmigiana for the main courses and a huge green salad. There would be lots of garlic bread, wine for the adults and juice for the children and gelato, tiramisu and cannoli for dessert. Billie and Dakota insisted on contributing, even though Lucie and Ayanna said it wasn't necessary.

It was a casual affair, so Ayanna didn't understand Lucie's insistence that she look her best, but she did take special care in her attire. She wore a pretty summer dress with a gold shimmer and cap sleeves to show off her arms and a wide gold belt to show off her waist. The skirt of the dress was wide and flared out around her knees so her legs were on display, too. She applied makeup like she was going out on the town, just to appease Lucie.

"Oh, you look so pretty, sweetie pie," Lucie said.

"Mommy, I wish Emily had come," Ayanna said. "We used to be so tight, but now she acts like we're strangers."

Lucie nodded. "She'll come around eventually, I'm sure. But let's worry about the ones who are here, not the ones who couldn't make it, okay?"

Ayanna saw the wisdom of her mother's words as their guests arrived. Nick and Dakota and Bethany, Toni and Zane and little Brandon, Lee and Boyd Phillips, Billie and Jason, Todd, Cameron's friends Zack and Anthony and their parents and more filled the house. The food was superb, the company was joyful and the evening was so much fun that Ayanna wasn't surprised when Johnny proposed a toast.

"To our lovely hostesses, thanks for an amazing feast. To Cameron, who came up with the brilliant idea of bringing everyone together tonight. And to my parents, who raised me right," he said.

Ayanna tilted her head slightly when she heard that. He was standing behind her with his arm around her waist, so she couldn't see his expression, but she thought it was an odd direction for the toast to take.

"I'm really happy that all our friends and family were able to be here for this occasion," he said. "Those of you who know me well know that it sometimes takes me a long time to decide what's best for me, but once I make that decision, nothing changes my mind. It didn't take me long to realize that Ayanna is the best thing that ever happened to me, but I took my own stupid time to let her know that."

Ayanna's mouth opened, and she covered it with her hand. Johnny turned her to face him and spoke directly to her. "I love you with all my heart, and I want to ask you if you'll be kind enough to marry me so I can spend the rest of my life taking care of you and Alec and Cameron and all the beautiful babies I hope we have in the future. Will you please say yes?"

Without hesitation, she said, "Absolutely. I love you." They kissed to a chorus of cheers and applause. Alec and Cameron were smiling from ear to ear as he slipped a three-carat diamond solitaire on her ring finger.

"This is some serious mushy stuff," Alec said.

"Yeah, but it's way cool, too," Cameron replied.

Chapter 20

The next logical step in the process of becoming a family was finding a house and planning a wedding. Ayanna was stunned to find out that Jason had the perfect property, located about three blocks from where he and Billie lived.

"I've had my eye on it, and I figured it would be perfect once you guys got your stuff in order," he said. "It has six bedrooms, three and a half baths, a study, a media room, a four-car garage and a laundry room on the second floor. Plus," he added, smiling at Ayanna, "the previous owner was a gourmet chef. The kitchen is stupendous. Wait until you see it," he assured her. "You'll love it."

It was indeed an amazing house. Lucie, Alec and

Cameron loved it immediately, and Johnny was ready to close the deal as soon as he saw it. Lee and Boyd had already seen it and thought it was perfect. Ayanna went from room to room in awe, trying to calculate the monthly upkeep and the mortgage on a house of that size. She was almost completely silent on the way home, something that Johnny noticed at once. After Alec and Cameron went to bed and Lucie went to the study for her nightly CNN fix, he talked to her about the house.

"Didn't you like it?" he asked.

"I thought it was wonderful, Johnny, but it's so expensive! Can we afford it?"

"Absolutely," he assured her. "First of all, it's not as pricey as you might think. The previous owner moved to California to open a restaurant, and he wants to sell fast because he needs the money. In the second place, I never intended to live in a condo or an apartment the rest of my life. I have money put aside for a home. In the third place, I may not be as frugal as you, but I don't waste money, either. I have some good investments. My mom's hobby is investing. She started a club about ten years ago with a few of her friends, and those women know the market better than a lot of brokers. We'll never be broke."

They were on her sofa with her in his lap while he kissed her neck and reassured her. "By the way, you never did put these on," he reminded her. He pulled the pearl and diamond earrings out of his pants pocket and presented them to her again.

"You're so sweet to me. What am I going to do with you?"

"Let me kidnap you," he replied.

"Kidnap me? Are you serious?"

"I am. Before Lucie and my folks go home, I want to take you away for the weekend. Have you ever heard of French Lick?"

Ayanna gave him a seductive smile. "Didn't you do that to me a few times?" She collapsed in laughter while he tickled her.

"Yes, yes, I've heard of French Lick, Indiana. There's a resort and a casino there," she gasped. "Did I ever tell you how ticklish I am?"

"That's good to know," he answered. "But yeah, there's a really nice resort and spa and casino and stuff, and I want to take you there for the weekend. It'll be the last time we have any time together before the wedding, so let's take advantage of it. Please say you'll be my willing hostage," he whispered as he rimmed her ear with his tongue.

"Keep doing that, and I'll agree to anything."

French Lick was everything Johnny said it was and more. They arrived on Saturday morning, and Ayanna was awed by everything she saw. The French Lick Springs Hotel was an amazing place, built in the 1800s and recently restored to its original grandeur. The grounds were magnificent, as well as the lavishly ornate lobby. Their room was so sinfully comfortable that Ayanna didn't want to budge, but Johnny reminded her of the spa experience that awaited her.

"They have this special mineral water that's supposed to make you feel fantastic."

"I read about it. It's called Pluto water, and it used to be sold as a laxative," she said.

"Okay, that's just nasty."

"If you really needed one, you wouldn't think so," she said cheerily. She was across the bed, still fully dressed.

He pounced on her, and they wrestled playfully. "The purpose of this weekend is not to talk about digestive problems. We're supposed to be relaxing, rejuvenating and releasing, or did you forget?"

"You're right. Lead me to the spa."

Four hours later, she came back to the room in a state of bliss. Her skin looked and felt like silk, and she felt like a million dollars. There was a note on the pillow that read "Take a nap, sweetheart. I decided to get a massage, too. See you soon. Love you."

Ayanna got undressed and slipped into the soft comfortable bed, falling into a deep sleep almost instantly. She slept for three hours, until she was wakened by the warmth of Johnny's hand stroking her back. Smiling sleepily, she turned in his direction and invited him to join her.

"Nope. If I get in there with you I'm not getting out until an hour before we leave to go home. We're going to have a really nice dinner, and then I'm going to do something I've never done with you before."

She propped herself up on one elbow. "What's that?"

"We've never danced together, and I'm going to remedy that tonight."

It was the sweetest thing she'd ever heard. "What in the world am I going to wear?"

Johnny gave her his familiar, endearing smile. "How about this?" he asked, holding up a garment bag.

It was an ivory dress in silk, cut on the bias so it would cling to her body. It had wide-set straps that crossed in the back and a skirt that would swirl around her knees when she moved. It was truly the sexiest dress she could ever remember owning. There was also sheer underwear to go with it, a bustier and thong in a café-au-lait shade that matched her skin. She was enchanted with what she saw.

"Did you pick this out all by yourself?"

"I did," he said proudly. "Lucie gave me the sizes, and I went for it."

"I can't wait to put them on," she said. "You have good taste. Excellent taste, really."

"I sure do. I picked you, didn't I?"

Ayanna looked fabulous in the dress. The bodice of the dress dipped low with a sexy drape that showed an enticing bit of cleavage. She was shimmering from an artful application of gold powder here and there, and she smelled of her usual Chanel No. 5. Even her feet looked sexy in gold sandals. She touched her earlobe and smiled. The chocolate diamonds sparkled, and the pearls seemed to make her face glow. Her hair was blown out and curled, and it was evident that it was growing out because it touched the back of her neck. It was very becoming in a tousled, sexy style. She turned around to see if Johnny approved of her ensemble, and her breath caught in her throat. He looked so handsome she couldn't say a word.

He was wearing a custom-tailored suit in a heavenly shade of brown with an ivory shirt and matching silk tie. His dark chiseled features stood out against the ivory, and his meticulously barbered mustache and goatee were impeccable. She was staring at him so intensely he thought something was amiss.

"Is my tie crooked?"

"No, it's perfect. My goodness, we're going to have the most amazing sons," she said in a hushed voice.

"I already have two amazing sons. I want a couple of sweet little girls," he said. "Stay right there, I have to do something."

Ayanna stood patiently while Johnny's masculine scent wafted over her. She was acutely aware of his nearness, so much so that she didn't feel the necklace until he fastened the clasp. She touched it before looking at it in the mirror. "Oh, Johnny, it's beautiful! It matches my earrings."

The delicate gold chain with the large chocolate pearl and the sparkling chocolate diamonds made her want to cry, but she held it in. "This is the most beautiful thing I've ever seen."

"Then I did really good because it's on the most beautiful woman in the world. Let's get out of here before I lose my mind."

Ayanna was reluctant to leave because the only thing she was hungry for was Johnny, but she went with him to the restaurant. She was glad they did because the food was lovely. It was well-prepared and a treat for the eye as well as the palate. She had a petite filet that was pink in the middle—just the way she liked it. It was served with a little cup of sorbet to refresh the palate between bites so that each bite would taste like the first. It was served with wild rice pilaf and *haricots verts,* the slender French green beans that were so tender they melted in the mouth. Johnny had chosen an excellent wine, and she was having such a wonderful time that she never wanted the evening to end.

But Johnny was serious about dancing. "Did you enjoy your meal?"

"Did you see me try to lick the plate? Yes, I did, it was delicious. How was yours?"

"Not as good as your cooking, but it was tasty. Now then, my lady, I think you owe me a dance."

They went to the casino, which was as lively as Vegas, but classier. The neoclassical style of the architecture and the extraordinary high ceilings gave it a certain elegance and grandeur. The jazz band was playing a Latin number when they entered, and Johnny took Ayanna out on the dance floor. She was by far the best partner he'd ever danced with. He'd known a lot of women who thought they could dance, but Ayanna could burn up the floor.

At one point they literally cleared the floor, and people stood and watched them execute their moves like they'd been dancing together forever. They had to take a bow because everyone applauded like mad.

"I'm ready for a breather if you are," Ayanna told Johnny.

"Of course, sweetness." They went to a table and Johnny ordered Perrier water for both of them. "There's some champagne on ice in the room, but if you want something stronger now, go ahead."

"This is wonderful. You've been holding out on me. You're a wonderful dancer," she told him.

"I get around on the floor, but damn, Ayanna, you float. We're going to throw down at our wedding."

Ayanna looked at her sparkling ring, loving the weight of it on her delicate finger. "Johnny, this wedding is going to break us," she said worriedly. "Even a small wedding with about seventy-five people can cost about twenty thousand dollars when you factor in food and drinks and flowers and invitations and favors."

Johnny laughed at her softly. He leaned over to kiss her. "Sweetness, when are you going to realize that I got this? Your job from now on is not to worry about anything. And you can forget about eloping. Your family, my family, our extended family and our boys all want a celebration."

Ayanna smiled and kissed him. "Okay, okay, okay. But I want everything pink, and I want you to wear a white tux and a pink ruffled shirt."

The look on his face was without a doubt the funniest thing she'd ever seen, and they were still laughing when they strolled through the casino on their way back to their room. "Wait a minute, Johnny. I've always wanted to play one of these."

They stopped next to a ten-dollar slot machine, and she pulled out a crisp new bill. She kissed it for luck and fed it into the one-armed bandit. She pulled the long shiny metal arm and watched the cylinders spin around and around. "I should have kept my ten bucks," she murmured.

Suddenly buzzers and lights started going off and the noise seemed deafening. "What happened?" she asked Johnny.

"You just won the jackpot, baby, that's what happened."

"Wow. Cool beans," she said with a grin just like Cameron's.

Chapter 21

The jackpot was almost two hundred thousand dollars. Ayanna was giddy but contained it when they got back to their room. "You're going to have to remind me tomorrow that this happened," she said. "I don't think it's really real."

Johnny laughed as he took off his tie. "It's real, baby. You are now a moderately comfortable woman," he teased her.

"We are a fortunate family," she corrected him. "What's mine is yours. And what's yours is mine, and I want to see it," she said seductively.

"See what?"

"Skin. Take off your jacket, please."

"If you take off your shoes," he countered. "I love your little feet."

She took off one shoe and dangled it from her little finger. "Your turn."

He obligingly removed the jacket. "Other shoe, please."

She took the other one off, and then she tucked her feet under her skirt. "Shirt, please."

He pulled it out of his waistband and unbuttoned it.

"All the way off," Ayanna insisted.

He removed it, and she sighed when she saw his rippling muscles. "You're way too sexy."

"No, that's you, baby. Take off that pretty dress for me."

"This isn't coming out right. You have on more clothes than me. Take off those shoes and socks," she demanded.

"If it'll make you happy," he said as he kicked off his expensive Italian shoes and sat down to remove his socks.

"I need help," Ayanna purred. She rose to her knees and turned so he could unfasten her dress. Once the straps were undone he slid the zipper down, blowing softly on her back as he did so.

She was now wearing nothing but the seductive lingerie and her jewelry. She didn't have to say anything about his pants because he took them off with a quickness, along with his briefs. "Oh, now I'm over-dressed," Ayanna said.

"Leave that on," Johnny said. "You look amazing."

In seconds they were under the covers, kissing like they'd been apart for a year. They were hungry for each other, starving for the sensations they could only get in each other's arms. Their lips caressed, and their tongues met and mated over and over again while their hands explored passion-heated skin.

"Johnny, take it off. I need you to touch me," she whispered.

He was already rubbing her breasts but she wanted more. He unhooked the front clasp and freed her so he could do what she wanted him to do. He licked the tender spot between her breasts and started massaging one erect nipple with his fingers while he sucked the other.

"Mmm, Johnny," she moaned.

His other hand was palming her behind, squeezing and rubbing until the flesh was dampened with perspiration. He moved his mouth to her other breast and his hand to the juncture of her thighs, which was already wet from her desire. She climaxed almost immediately, and he could feel the tremors rippling through her body. He kept kissing her, going down her torso until his mouth could bestow the most intimate kiss possible. She tasted so good he could have stayed there forever drinking in her sweetness. The way she moved her hips when she came, the sounds she uttered were so arousing that he didn't want to stop, but she pleaded with him.

"I need you inside me right now, Johnny, right now," she moaned.

He didn't hesitate to give her just what she wanted. He joined their bodies in a smooth, easy motion that turned into a wild coupling that brought her over the brink again and again. He wanted to make sure she was satisfied before he let the silky heat of her body take him away. When she tightened on him and said his name with so much tenderness, he fell in love with her all over again and finally let go. He moaned out her name as his orgasm took over his body. He thrust his manhood into her sweetness one last time, holding her so tight their hearts beat as one.

They drove back to Chicago with dreamy smiles on their faces. "We were supposed to go horseback riding, you know."

Ayanna looked over at Johnny and rubbed her free hand on his muscular forearm. Her other hand was holding his. "I didn't want to ride a horse," she said.

"We could have gone on a tour," he pointed out.

"I saw everything I wanted to see," she answered.

They looked at each other and smiled again.

"You'd better wipe that smile off your face before Lucie sees you or she's going to know what we've been up to," he cautioned her.

"Honey, once we tell her about that jackpot she won't give a rip. We could tell her we robbed a bank and she wouldn't care. Our moms can plan the wedding of the century for all I care. And we can get the house and lots of furniture, too."

"And you can quit your job. If you want to," he said.

"I can what?"

"You don't have to work anymore, if you don't want

to. I make enough to support us all. You can go to culinary school and open those restaurants the way you planned. How does that sound?"

"It sounds like something I never thought about," she admitted.

"Start thinking about it, Ayanna. I want you to be happy. From now on, you and Alec and Cameron are my priority, my only priority. I want you to be happy and safe and protected, and that also goes for all those little girls we're going to have."

"You really want little girls? Most men want boys."

"I told you, I have two fine sons already. If we have more, that's fine. But you've seen how cute Bethany is. Just imagine what our baby will look like. Sweet and pretty and adorable, just like her cousin. You must admit that seeing Nick with Bethany is something else."

"She has him wrapped around her tiny little finger, that's for sure. And you want that, too, don't you?"

"Absolutely. She'll look just like you, and she'll be smart like Cameron and Alec and funny like me."

"Johnny, you've given this an amazing amount of thought," she said.

"Just since I met you. When I was a litigator in labor law, I used to spend a lot of time thinking about my clients and preparing a case. I guess the habit carried over," he admitted.

"So you've been preparing for a case, is that it?"

"The biggest one of my life. This was a case for love, baby. I had to win."

"You did, on all counts."

* * *

Ayanna gave in to her mother and future mother-in-law and let them plan the wedding of their dreams. Money was literally no object, and they went nuts, but she was too happy to care. Johnny had no preferences except for the theme. He surprised them all when he said he wanted it to be "Diamonds and Pearls." "Because my wife is a true diamond and her skin is as smooth as a perfect pearl. Because that's the first real gift I gave her and because that's going to be the song we dance to at the reception," he explained. The women were in the living room of the new house, arranging furniture and making plans.

"You can do whatever else you want as long as it's diamonds and pearls. You can have dancing monkeys, singing frogs and a marching band if you want. Oh, and the groom's cake must be red velvet." He left the room singing the Prince tune and looking perfectly happy.

"That's an amazing young man," Lucie said.

Lee smiled at her. "He's my son, and I love him, but he's a crazy young man. Well, 'Diamonds and Pearls' it is then."

They worked like crazy to create a beautiful day for Johnny and Ayanna, who really appreciated everything they were doing. They kept her in the loop and consulted with her on various things, but for the most part, they had carte blanche. It was going to be a Christmas wedding, and Ayanna was sure it would be beautiful. Her main concern was getting the house ready for them to move into.

Johnny was supportive and surprisingly helpful. He patiently went over color charts with her; he went furniture shopping and let her know what he liked. With Billie and Dakota and Toni helping her, she was really pleased with her choices, especially in the master bedroom.

The walls were a soothing shade of robin's-egg blue and with ivory crown molding and the silk bedding was chocolate-brown and pale blue. The bed was so big she needed a set of steps to get in and out, but it was the right size for a big man like Johnny. The furniture wasn't too masculine or feminine, and the teak stain went beautifully with the colors she'd chosen.

The boys selected their own colors for their bedrooms. They were bouncing off the walls with excitement, even when Lucie told them they were going to be in the wedding. Johnny had asked if they could be part of the ceremony as he committed himself to their mother. "I wanted them to be a part of it, because this is going to make us a family," he said. The formal adoption would be after New Year's, but he wanted them to feel included from the very beginning.

By Thanksgiving everything was set except for the maid of honor. Emily had been acting as though she didn't care whether or not she participated, and Ayanna couldn't stand it anymore. She called Emily the week before Thanksgiving and told her point-blank that if she didn't come to Chicago with Lucie for Thanksgiving she would assume that Emily had better things to do than be her maid of honor.

"You're my baby sister, and I've loved you since the day you were born. I've always tried to be there for you even when you've made it plain that you don't want to be bothered with me. But this is it, Emmie. I'm through begging you to be a part of my life. It's time to fish or cut bait. If you're not here for Thanksgiving, I'll know your answer," Ayanna said.

After the call, she fretted, thinking that she'd pushed too hard. But when Lucie arrived for the holiday, Emily came, too. Ayanna was overcome with joy and hugged her sister tightly.

"Just don't put me in something frilly and stupid," she muttered. "I'd look like a lumberjack in drag."

She had no worries on that score. Toni had found a shop with an amazing array of styles. Ayanna had chosen a simple, elegant dress for the bridesmaids. The dresses were café au lait with ivory sashes, except for Emily's—she would be wearing the colors in reverse. She annoyed everyone by not letting anyone see her dress until the wedding day. Even Lucie hadn't seen it.

"I know my daughter has good taste, but this is killing me," she confided to Lee. "She picked the darndest time to start being mysterious."

Lee commiserated with her. "At least she let us put on a big wedding. Nick and Dakota had that little ceremony at their house! It was wonderful, but she was my oldest daughter, and I wanted something big and lavish like Billie's wedding, doggone it."

"Well, she made up for it, Lee. You have the prettiest little grandbaby in the world. And pretty soon, we'll have some more. I have a feeling that Ayanna and Johnny are going to make some beauties."

"And you know this, girl!" Lee held up her hand for a high five.

The wedding took place the day after Christmas. It snowed during the night, and everything looked like a beautiful Christmas card. The trees and shrubs were coated with sparkling white, and everything looked pure and pristine. The limousines hired for the wedding party were white, too, and they made a very elegant appearance as they pulled up to the church. The bridesmaids were all dressed before they arrived at church. Ayanna was already there, getting dressed with only Toni to assist her.

Toni's blue eyes filled with tears as she looked at Ayanna. "Thank goodness for waterproof mascara. You look amazing, girl."

"Thank you, Toni. And thank you for helping pick out the dress and keeping it a secret. I just want to wow everybody. I have no idea why," she murmured.

"Because you can. You're the bride, it's your day. Knock 'em dead, toots! I've got to go get in the line. See you soon!"

Toni went to join the other bridesmaids, and Ayanna said a silent prayer. Taking a deep breath, she opened the dressing room door. When her maid of honor, Emily, entered the church, it was Ayanna's cue. She went into the hallway and waited until the wedding coordinator opened the door, and she began her walk down the aisle to Johnny.

She had debated about having her mother escort her, or Jason or even Todd, but in the end she decided to go it alone. No one was giving her away to Johnny; she was giving herself, freely and lovingly. Her friends and family all rose to watch her walk down the aisle, but she couldn't really see them. Her eyes were fixed firmly on Johnny, on her future.

A collective "ooh" rose as she walked gracefully down the aisle. Her dress looked like it was made of diamonds and pearls. It was a creamy white with a halter neck and a fitted bodice to show off her curves. The bottom of the dress was a column with a split in the front and a train in the back. It was made entirely of lace with hundreds of pearls and crystals that caught the light like little twinkling stars. She carried a bouquet of creamy white and green orchids, and she had smaller orchids in her hair.

Johnny looked like a prince in his elegant black suit. He wore an ivory shirt and ivory silk tie, as did his best man, his father, and all the groomsmen. Alec and Cameron looked so grown up she wanted to cry. But there were no tears during the ceremony, at least not from Johnny and Ayanna. Their smiles were constant and full of the joy they felt. Ayanna had to dab her eyes with her grandmother's lace hanky when the minister asked Alec and Cameron to come forward and Johnny said the words that bound them as family. He gave them each a gold bracelet to wear and they gave him one. Ayanna wanted to weep, but from what she could hear, Lee and Lucie were doing enough of that for the whole family.

When the minister pronounced them man and wife they kissed each other, briefly and sweetly. When he pronounced them a family, they all hugged. It was a moment she'd never forget as long as she lived.

The reception was held at a big hotel in downtown Chicago, and it was the best party she'd ever attended, bar none. The ballroom looked like a fantasy come to life. There were tall crystal vases with orchids and calla lilies submerged in water supporting branches of crystals and white roses. The table settings looked like they belonged in a palace, and the cakes were amazing. The wedding cake was covered with edible pearls and sugar crystals, and it looked like some royal baker had done it for a king and queen.

When she and Johnny took the dance floor for their first dance she looked up at him with her heart in her eyes. "I'm not going to wake up, am I? We're really truly man and wife, aren't we?"

"Oh yes, sweetness. For the rest of out lives, we're together." He looked over at Alec and Cameron, who were dancing on the sidelines. "All of us."

Epilogue

"I hope you're happy," Ayanna said sleepily.

"I'm ecstatic," Johnny told her.

"Next time I tell you I'm in labor, I'll bet you'll believe me, won't you?" They had barely made it to the hospital before she delivered.

Johnny laughed softly and kissed his beautiful wife.

"Sweetheart, I'll never doubt you again." He was sitting on the side of their bed, holding a tiny beauty with a head of thick black curls.

"Which one do you have?"

"I have Madison. Your mother has Lindsey," he told her.

"No, your mother has Lindsey, and I've come for Madison," Lucie informed them. "Come see Grandma, sweetie," she cooed as she took the sleeping infant. She hummed happily as she left the room.

"Come lie down with me," Ayanna said softly. "I want my husband."

"You've got me, sweetness." He put his arms around her and held her close to his heart. "How did you manage to have twins nine months to the day after we got married and still be the sexiest woman I've ever known?"

She cuddled closer to him. "You need glasses."

He stroked her hair, which was much longer and thicker. "You're my beauty and always will be."

Ayanna's eyes were closed, and he knew she'd be asleep in a minute. She was so amazing. Billie, Dakota and Toni were all appalled when she never had a day of morning sickness. She didn't even get fat; she just got really big breasts and a huge belly, which he found incredibly sexy. Every day and every way she was a total source of joy and happiness for him.

He'd had to change jobs and found a better-paying position with a firm based in Chicago because he couldn't handle being away from her and their sons. She was worth any change he'd made, any sacrifice at all because in her arms he was whole. She made his life complete. And now she'd given him not one but two little girls. She was going to flip out when she saw the diamond earrings he'd bought her and the babies, but she'd get over it.

He kissed her forehead and listened to her peaceful, even breathing before joining her in sleep.

HIS SHOCK VALENTINE'S PROPOSAL

AMY RUTTAN

This book is dedicated to Montana. Your beauty, even four years after I visited you, still haunts me and makes me long to spend endless summers wandering through your mountains, your plains and your badlands.

This book is also for James, who spent his third birthday in Montana on our cross-country trek and loved every second of it. Love you, buddy.

CHAPTER ONE

"WHAT DOES SHE think she's doing?" Carson grumbled to himself.

"Looks like she's planting flowers in a pot," Nurse Adams remarked.

Carson turned and glanced at his father's nurse, who had worked in the practice longer than Carson had. Actually, she was technically his nurse now. He hadn't realized she'd snuck up behind him. Like a ninja.

"I didn't ask for your opinion."

She looked down her nose at him in that way she always did when he was little and causing mischief in his father's office. A look that still sent shivers of dread down his spine and he realized he'd taken it a step too far.

"If you didn't want my opinion, Dr. Ralston, you shouldn't be talking out loud in *my* waiting room."

"Sorry, Louise." He rubbed the back of his neck. "Just hate seeing all these changes going on in Crater Lake."

Her expression softened. "There's a building boom. It was inevitable that another doctor would come into town and set up shop."

Carson frowned and jammed his hands in his trouser pockets as he watched the new, attractive doctor in town planting flowers outside the office across the street. Crater Lake was changing and he wasn't sure he liked it too much.

His father had been the lone physician in Crater Lake for over forty years, long before Carson was born. It was a practice he'd taken over from his grandfather; now Carson had taken over the practice since his parents retired and moved south to warmer climates.

There had always been a Ralston as the town's sole practitioner since Crater Lake was founded in 1908. Something his father liked to remind him of constantly.

The only other time there had been a notion of two town doctors was when Danielle had lived with him for a time after medical school, but that had been different. They were supposed to work together, get married and raise a family. It hadn't lasted. She hadn't liked the slow existence or the winters of living in northwest Montana.

Luke is a doctor.

Carson snorted as he thought of his older brother, who was indeed a licensed practitioner, but Luke didn't like the confines of an office and preferred to be out in the woods tracking bears or whatever he did up on the mountains. Luke didn't have the same passion of upholding the family tradition of having a Ralston as the family practitioner in Crater Lake. That job fell on Carson.

The new doctor in town, Dr. Petersen, stood up, arching her back, stretching. Her blond hair shining in the early summer sunlight. He didn't know much about the newest resident of Crater Lake. Not many people did. She'd moved in and kept to herself. Her practice hadn't even opened yet and though Carson shouldn't care he couldn't help but wonder about her, who she was.

The door jingled and he glanced at the door as his brother came striding in, in his heavy denim and leather, a hank of rope slung around his shoulder.

Louise huffed under her breath as his brother dragged in dirt with his arrival.

"Slow day?" Luke asked as he set the rope down on a chair.

"Yeah. I have the Johnstone twins coming in about an hour for vaccinations."

Luke winced. "I'll be gone before then."

Louise stood up, hands on her ample hips. "Would you pick up that filthy rope? My waiting room was clean until you showed up! Honestly, if your parents were still here…"

Luke chuckled. "You make it sound like they're dead, Louise. They're in Naples, Florida. They live on the edge of a golf course."

Carson chuckled. "Come on, let's retreat to my office. Sorry, Louise."

Carson glanced back one more time, but Dr. Petersen had gone back inside. His brother followed his gaze out the window and then looked at him, confused.

When they were in his office, Luke sat down on one of the chairs. "What was so interesting outside?"

"There's a new doctor in town," Carson said off-handedly.

Luke grinned, leaning back in his chair. "Oh, I see."

"What do you see?"

"I've seen her. I'm not blind."

Carson snorted. "That's not it at all."

Luke cocked an eyebrow. "Then what is it?"

"It's a new doctor in town. It's threatening our family practice."

Luke shrugged. "It's your practice, not mine."

So like his brother. Not caring much about the family practice. Not caring about generations of Ralstons who'd sweated to build this practice and this town up. Well, at least he cared.

Do you?

Carson pinched the bridge of his nose. "I thought you were against the town expansion and the building of that ski-resort community."

"I am. Well…I was, but really there was no stopping it."

"You could've attended a few town meetings," Carson said.

When had Luke stopped caring so much?

It wasn't his concern and by the way Luke was glaring at him Carson was crossing a line. His brother quickly changed the subject. "I guess my point was that it didn't look like you were checking out the competition the way you want me to think you were."

"I'll work that out later." Carson moved around and sat down on the other side of his desk. "What brings you down off the mountain and what in heaven's name are you going to tie up with that rope?"

Luke grinned in the devilish way that used to cause their mother to worry. It usually meant that Luke was about to get into some serious trouble.

"Nothing much. I actually just came for some medical supplies. I'm taking some surveyors deep into the woods."

"And the rope is to tie them to the nearest tree and use them as bear bait?"

"The thought had crossed my mind, but like you,

little brother, I took the Hippocratic Oath. I swore to do no harm."

"Hmm."

"You need to liven up a bit, little brother. You're too tense."

Carson snorted. "Look who's talking. You know the local kids refer to you as the Grinch in the winter. One of the Johnstone twins thought you were going to come down and steal Christmas last year."

"Because I told her that. She spooked my horse."

"You're terrible with kids and have a horrible bed-side manner," Carson said.

"I'm great with kids. Dad just knew you were more of the office type of person and I like to run wild."

Must be nice.

The thought surprised him, because he should be used to Luke's lifestyle after all this time. Luke always got to run free, do what he wanted. Carson was the re-liable one.

Dependable.

Never took risks.

Carson shook his head. "As long as you're not naked while running wild then I don't care."

Luke grinned. "I didn't know how much you cared."

Carson couldn't help but chuckle. "You need to get your butt out of my clean office before you give Louise a heart attack and get yourself back up that mountain. I have patients coming in soon. Patients who think you're going to steal their Christmas."

"Right. So, do I get the medical supplies? I may not have regular office time but I technically have part ownership."

"You know where they are. I don't have to tell you."

"Thanks." Luke got up.

"Take your rope, too."

Luke winked and disappeared into the stockroom while Carson leaned back in his father's chair and scrubbed a hand over his face.

Luke had one thing right. He was tense. He worked too much.

You're wasting your surgical talent here. Why didn't you take that internship at Mayo? Why are you giving up a prestigious surgical residency to become a general practitioner?

Danielle's words haunted him.

Lately, they had been bothering him more. Ever since the old office building across the road had been bought and he'd got wind that a new doctor from Los Angeles was moving into town. There weren't many full-timers in Crater Lake. The ageing population was a threat to the small town and now with this resort community going in, it would bring more people, but not people who would be here all the time and Carson couldn't help but wonder if the time of the small-town doctor was gone.

Perhaps he had wasted his life? Maybe he should've cared less about the practice like Luke. Maybe he would've become a great surgeon.

More and more lately it seemed he was thinking these thoughts. He didn't take risks, but he was happy with the choices he made.

This was the path he chose and he was happy.

He was happy.

Who are you trying to convince?

He groaned inwardly. He didn't have to let the ghosts of his past haunt him.

Get a grip on yourself.

Carson shook those thoughts away.

No, he was doing what he'd always wanted to do. Sure, he'd been offered several amazing residencies, but surgery was not what he wanted to do.

He liked the small-town life; he liked the connection he had with the people in Crater Lake. He would be stifled in a big city; he'd be trapped in a busy hospital in the OR for countless hours. This he preferred. *Still...*

It irked him that another doctor had moved into town, but he couldn't stop it and frankly he hoped she was up to the challenge. She was from California. He doubted it very much that she would be able to survive her first winter here and that thought secretly pleased him.

Louise knocked and then opened his door. She looked worried. "Dr. Ralston, Mrs. Johnstone is in the waiting room. She needs to speak with you."

"Is everything okay? I thought the twins' appointment was later?"

Louise's lips pursed together. "She's here to cancel her appointment and take their chart."

"Hold on!" Esme called out. She had no idea who was banging on the front door of her office. She wasn't open yet. The big day was at the end of the week. If it was a delivery they could've read the sign and come along to the back alleyway.

Only the banging was insistent. It sounded almost angry, which made her pause. Perhaps she should take a peek out the window. The last thing she wanted was it to be the tabloids outside pounding on her door. Not that they'd bothered with her for the past three months.

She'd dealt with enough press in LA before she'd

hightailed it to the solitude of the mountains. Of course, when she'd chosen Crater Lake as her new home, she'd known that there was going to be a resort community, but she hadn't realized another high-end spa and hotel was going up.

Esme could handle a small ski-resort community, but a huge high-end spa and hotel? That was not what she wanted. Small. Sleepy and in need of a friendly and eager town physician. Of course, once she'd spent all her money on buying her practice she really hadn't been able to change her mind. The building she had bought had been on the market for five years.

She knew there was an *old* family practice in town. Dr. Ralston had been practicing medicine in Crater Lake his whole career and his father before that and his father before that. It was time to breathe some new life into Crater Lake.

The pounding reminded her why her inventory of medical supplies was being interrupted and she glanced out of the window of her primary exam room.

"Whoa."

The handsome man standing in front of her office was definitely not paparazzi or press. He didn't have a camera or a recorder, or even a smartphone on him. He was well dressed in casual business attire. His brown hair combed neatly, clean shaven, but definitely an outdoorsy type of guy, because she could see his forearms where he'd rolled up the sleeves of his crisp white shirt were tanned and muscular.

He was a well-dressed country boy and Esme had a thing for country boys. Always had, but that was a hard thing to find in Los Angeles.

Unless you counted the country singers she'd treated,

and she didn't. Of course, when she'd thought she'd found the perfect guy it had turned out she hadn't and she was terrified by who she'd become and about what he wanted from her.

Don't think about Shane.

Well, whoever this guy was, he was off-limits. She wasn't here to get involved with anyone. Besides, he was probably married or taken. One thing Esme had discovered about her new place of residence was that Crater Lake was mostly filled with older people and young families. It wasn't a happening place for singles and that was fine by her.

She was here to hide, not find happiness. She didn't deserve that. Not after what she'd done to Shane.

Not after what happened in the OR with her last surgery. It was too painful. Love and friendship, they were not what she was here for. She was here to be a doctor. She was here to blend in, to hide so no one could find her.

He banged on the door again.

She ran her hand through her hair, hoping she didn't smell of sweat too much. Even though she had no interest in impressing him, she didn't want to scare off any potential patients because she gave off the impression of being smelly.

"Just a minute!" Esme called out as she undid the chain and bolt on her office door. She opened it. "Hey, look, I'm not open today."

"I'm aware," he said tersely. "Can I come in?"

"I don't even know you."

"Is that how you plan to treat residents of Crater Lake?" he asked.

What's this guy's deal?

"Okay, how about we start with introductions? I'm Dr. Petersen." She held out her hand, but he just glanced at it, ignoring her proffering.

"I know who you are, Dr. Petersen." His blue eyes were dark, his brow furrowed.

Oh, crap.

"You do? You know who I am? I'm sorry I can't say the same."

He was clearly annoyed and she didn't have time for this. "Look, I'm kind of busy today. Why don't you call my office and my nurse will call you about an appointment time? I'm pretty open for appointments as I'm not open for business just yet."

"You have a nurse?" he asked.

"Well, not yet, but I've interviewed some interesting candidates."

"I bet."

Esme frowned. "Have I offended you some way? If I have, I'm really sorry, but again I haven't opened yet."

"I'm aware you're not open yet. Of course, that really doesn't stop you from poaching patients."

Esme was stunned. "Who are you?"

"I'm Dr. Ralston. I was the Johnstone family's practitioner up until about two hours ago."

Okay, now she was really surprised. "You're Dr. Ralston?"

"Yes."

"Dr. C. Ralston?"

"Yes."

"I don't get it." Esme stepped aside to invite him in, but didn't even get the words out as he wandered inside and then sat on the edge of the waiting-room desk, his arms crossed.

"What don't you get? I can show you my ID."

"Dr. Charles Ralston has been practicing medicine in Crater Lake for forty years." She shut the door, but didn't lock it just in case this guy was crazy or something. "You guys either have the fountain of youth up here in Crater Lake or someone's records are incorrect."

A small smile played on his face, some of that fury fading. "Dr. Charles Ralston is my father. I'm Dr. Carson Ralston. I took over my father's practice when he retired five years ago."

"Oh, and I'm the fool who just poached some of your patients. Gotcha."

"Essentially."

Esme crossed her arms, too. "So how can I help you?"

"Stop poaching my patients." There was now a slight twinkle in his blue, blue eyes and he didn't seem as angry anymore.

"I'm really sorry, but your patient wanted to change. I couldn't turn them away," she stated.

"Look, you have to know when you come to a small town you don't go around stealing the patients of a practitioner who has been here for quite some time."

Esme raised an eyebrow. "Is that some kind of doctor rule? If so, I'm not aware of it."

"It's common courtesy." He didn't seem as though he was going to budge until she handed over the files to him. Although, she hadn't been given the files yet.

"I'm sorry to disappoint you, Dr. Ralston, but when I bumped into Mrs. Johnstone at the general store her twins took a shine to me and she wanted me to be her physician."

"What do you mean the twins took a shine to you?"

She grinned. "I mean I didn't scare them like the old, grumpy Dr. Ralston."

His mouth fell open in surprise for a moment and then he snapped it shut. "Okay, then. I won't bother you about it anymore."

"That's quite the defeatist attitude."

He shrugged and headed to the door. "If I'm old and grumpy then there is nothing more I can do."

A sense of dread niggled at her. "What do you know about them you're not sharing?"

Now it was his turn to grin with pleasure. "Nothing. Just good luck with the twins, but I will tell you that if you take any more of my patients it'll be war."

Esme couldn't help but laugh. "Are you declaring war on me, Dr. Ralston?"

"I believe I am, Dr. Petersen." He winked, chuckling to himself as he shut the door behind him and Esme couldn't help but wonder what she'd gotten herself into. She would have to keep her distance from Carson, though in a small town that was going to be hard to do, but she was going to try.

CHAPTER TWO

CARSON WAS GLAD that summer was coming, the days were longer, but then he really couldn't enjoy the extra daylight when he stayed late and he usually stayed late because he didn't have anything to go home to.

He had a big empty house that he used for sleeping. That was it. He'd built it for Danielle and him. Of course Danielle hadn't stayed long enough to live in it.

The sun was just beginning to set behind the mountains, giving a pink tinge to the glacier on Mount Jackson. He never got tired of it. He loved Montana and if he did have regrets about his past, staying in Montana wasn't one of them.

Still, the mountains, the scenery weren't any kind of companion, but at least the mountains would never betray him and wouldn't break his heart the way Danielle had done.

As he locked up the clinic he couldn't help but glance across the street at Dr. Petersen's clinic. The lights were still blazing. She'd opened at the end of last week, but Carson hadn't lost any more patients. Most of her patients seemed to be coming down from the resort community and with that new high-end hotel and spa going in there would be even more people coming.

There were a few timeshares that were in operation, but he knew the main lodge was still under construction, as his brother was still taking surveyors and construction workers out on the trails.

Once the main spa hotel lodge opened and the community got its own full-time doctor, a job he'd turned down, then Dr. Petersen might feel a bit of pain financially.

A twinge of guilt ate at him and he felt bad for declaring war on her.

"You declared war on her? How does that even happen?" Luke had had a good laugh over that.

Of course, the last time Carson had declared war on someone was when Luke and he had been kids. Carson had declared war on Luke when he was ten and Luke had been fifteen. Carson had gone about booby-trapping parts of the house. The ceasefire had come when Luke had set a snare and Carson had ended up dangling upside down in a tree with a sign that said bear food.

Their father had put a stop to all present and future wars.

Carson sighed. He hadn't been thinking that day in her surgery. She got on his nerves a bit and he had been put out that the Johnstone twins had thought he was grumpy and old. He honestly was glad to be rid of the little hellions.

It was the principle of the matter.

In all the years his father had practiced he'd never been called grumpy or old. He'd never lost a patient to another doctor.

There never was another doctor in Crater Lake.

A lot of new families had come into town over the past couple of years. Dr. Petersen was advertising. He'd heard her ad on the local radio station. Perhaps he needed to advertise. Maybe he was a bit too comfortable in his position and he was in a rut.

Carson rubbed the back of his neck.

He should go make amends with her.

He crossed the street and peered inside the clinic window to see if he could catch sight of her, get her attention, then maybe he could talk to her.

Before he knew what was happening there was a shout, his wrist was grabbed and he was on the ground staring at the pavement.

"What in the heck?" Carson shouted as a pain shot up his arm. He craned his neck to see Esme Petersen, sitting on his back, holding his left wrist, which was wrenched in an awkward position behind him. "Um, you can let go of me. I kind of need my arm."

"Oh, my gosh. Dr. Ralston, I'm so sorry." She let go of his wrist and got off his back. "I thought you were a burglar."

Carson groaned and heaved himself up off the pavement. "There aren't many burglars around Crater Lake. It's a pretty safe town."

"I'm really sorry for attacking you like that, but you scared me. Why the heck were you skulking around the outside of my office?"

"How the heck did you do that?" Carson asked, smoothing out his shirt.

"Do what?" Esme asked.

"Take me down?"

Esme grinned. "Krav Maga."

Carson frowned. "Never heard of it. What is it?"

Esme shook her head. "You still haven't answered my question. Why were you peering through the windows and generally acting suspicious? This doesn't have to do with the *war*, does it?"

"Kind of." Carson touched his forehead and winced. "I think I'm bleeding."

"Oh, my God. You are." Esme took his hand and led him to the open door. "Come inside and I'll clean that up. It's the least I can do."

"No, thank you," Carson murmured, trying to take his hand back. "I think you've done enough damage."

"No way. You owe me this." She dragged him into her very bright and yellow clinic waiting room. It was cheery and it made him wince. "You can head into the exam room and I'll take a look at the damage."

Carson snorted. "Are you going to charge me a fee?"

Esme rolled her eyes. "So petulant. I just may, since you were creeping around in the shadows trying to scare me."

Carson sat on the exam table as she came bustling into the room and then washed her hands in the sink, her small delicate hands. They looked soft, warm, and he wondered how they would feel in his. He couldn't think that way.

"I wasn't trying to scare you," he said.

"You said it was about the war you declared on me. Doesn't that usually involve trickery and scaring tactics?" Esme stood on her tiptoes and tried to get a box from a high shelf. She started cursing and mumbling under her breath as she couldn't quite reach it.

Carson stood and reached up, getting the box of gauze for her, his fingers brushing hers as she still tried to reach for it.

So soft.

His heart raced, he was standing so close to her,

and he looked down at her and she stared up at him in shock that he'd done that for her. He hadn't realized how blue her eyes were or how red her lips were and the color was accentuated by the white-blond of her hair. She kind of reminded him of a short, feisty Marilyn Monroe.

Focus.

Carson moved his hand away and tossed her the box of gauze. "If you can't reach it, you shouldn't put it up so high."

"I didn't. My nurse did. He is a bit taller than me."

"He?" Carson asked, teasing her.

"Sexist, too, are we?"

"Please."

"Sit down. You're such a whiner, Dr. Ralston."

Carson sat back on the table; his head was throbbing now. "Dang, you did a number on me. What did you call that again?"

"Krav Maga." Esme pulled on gloves. "Sorry."

"No, it's fine. You're right. I shouldn't have been… what did you call it?"

"Skulking." She smiled, her eyes twinkling as she parted his hair to look at his injury.

Carson winced again, ignoring the sting. It wasn't the sting that bothered him, it was her touch. Just the sudden contact sent a zing through him. It surprised him. It was unwelcome. He wanted to move away from her, so he wasn't so close, but that was hard to do when she was cleaning up his wound. "Right. Skulking. I shouldn't have been doing that outside your office."

She nodded and began to clean the wound. "So why were you?"

"I came to apologize."

Her eyes widened. "Oh, really?"

"Yeah. I shouldn't have come barging over here and accusing you of stealing my patients."

"So are you calling a truce?"

"I am. Ow."

Esme *tsked* under her breath. "It's just a scrape. Don't be such a baby."

"Do you talk to all your patients this way?"

"Only ones who whine so much." She smiled and continued to dab at his scrape. "There. I'll just put some ointment on it. Do you want a bandage?"

"No, thanks."

Esme shrugged and then rubbed some antiseptic ointment on the scrape.

"Ow."

"Doctors are the worst patients," she muttered.

"For a reason." Carson chuckled.

"I've never really understood that reason." She pulled off her gloves and tossed them in the medical-waste receptacle. "There. All done."

"Thanks."

"Are you sure you don't want a bandage? Maybe a pressure dressing." She was chuckling to herself and he rolled his eyes.

"Pretty sure." Carson sighed. He had to get out of the clinic before something else happened. Such as him doing something irrational. Only he couldn't move. "I better be going. Again, I'm really sorry for being such an idiot before."

She grinned. "Apology accepted."

Esme didn't really know what else to say. She felt very uncomfortable around Carson, but not in a bad way. In a very good way and that was dangerous. When their hands had barely touched a few moments ago, it had sent a zing through her. One that wasn't all that unpleasant. Actually, it had been some time since she'd felt that spark with someone. Of course, relationships never worked out for her. Men couldn't handle her drive and focus to commit to surgery and she had liked her independence and career too much. No one messed with her career.

Well, not anymore. She couldn't forget why she was a surgeon.

Hold on, Avery. Please.

Let me go, little sister. It hurts so much...let me go.

She'd dedicated her life to surgery. To save lives.

And until Shane, surgery had been her life. Her father had been so proud and she'd been training under Dr. Eli Draven, the best cardio-thoracic surgeon on the West Coast.

She'd thrown herself into her work. So much so, that she hadn't had time to date, until Eli had introduced her to his son.

She'd met Shane and surgery had become second, because he had always been taking her somewhere. Esme had been swept off her feet and, being the protégée of Dr. Eli Draven, she'd become too cocky. Too sure of herself. She'd thought she'd had it all.

Then in a routine procedure, she'd frozen. A resident had jumped in, knocking sense back into her and they'd worked hard to save the patient's life. But in the end they'd lost the fight.

Esme hadn't been able to go on, because in that moment—in that failure—she'd realized that she didn't know who she was anymore. She didn't know who she'd become, but it wasn't her.

Pulled back from her memories, Esme stared down at her hands, watching how they shook.

You're not a surgeon anymore, she reminded herself.

She'd come here to rebuild her life and right now she should be focusing on building her practice up, because every last dime of her savings had been sunk into this building. She'd bought the clinic, the license and the apartment upstairs.

This was her life now. She didn't have a retired parent to hand off a practice to her. Her stepmother had been a teacher and her father a cop.

They'd scrimped and saved to send her to the best medical school. Scholarships only went so far and she owed it to them to pay them back, since she could no longer be the surgeon they expected her to be.

She'd lost herself.

And she'd lost Shane. If only she'd come to the realization that he wasn't the man for her *before* she was in her wedding dress and halfway down the aisle on Valentine's Day. It was something she had to live with for the rest of her life.

Her father had made that clear to her. He'd been so disappointed. She'd let him down.

I don't know who you are anymore, Esme.

She didn't deserve any kind of happiness, or friendship. All she deserved was living with herself. Living with the stranger she'd become.

"Well, I have a bit of work to do tomorrow. I better

hit the hay," she said awkwardly, rubbing the back of her neck and trying not to look at him.

"Yeah, of course. I…" Carson said, trying to excuse himself when there was banging on her front door. Incessant and urgent.

"Who in the world?"

"Just stay here." Carson pushed her down into her chair, letting her know that he wanted her to stay put, before he headed out to the front door.

"As if," she mumbled, following him.

"I told you to stay in the exam room," he whispered as he stood in front of the door.

She crossed her arms. "You don't know Krav Maga. I do."

He rolled his eyes. "Fine."

Esme stood on her tiptoes and peered around him. When he opened the door a man let out a sigh of relief.

"Thank God I found you, Doc Ralston."

"Harry, what's wrong?" Carson asked, stepping aside to let the man in.

The man, Harry, was sweating and dirty, dressed in heavy denim, with thick work boots and leaving a trail of wood chips on her floor. He nodded to her. "Dr. Petersen."

"How can we help you…Harry, is it?"

"Yes, ma'am." He was twisting a ball cap in his hands and it looked as if he was in shock. "There's been an accident at Bartholomew's Mill."

"An accident?" Carson asked. "What kind?"

"Jenkins had a nasty incident with a saw, but there's bad smoke from a remote forest fire and we can't get a chopper in to airlift him to a hospital and paramedics are still two hours away."

Esme reeled at that information. She knew they were far off the beaten path, but medical help was two hours away? Why wasn't there a hospital closer?

"Let's go. I'll go grab my emergency medical kit." Carson slapped Harry on the shoulder. "I hope you don't mind driving, Harry. You know those logging roads better than me in the dark."

"No problem, Dr. Ralston."

"Can I help?" Esme asked.

Carson nodded. "Grab as many suture kits as you can."

Esme panicked. "Hospitals take care of suturing. We're not surgeons."

Carson shook his head. "Not around here. I hope you have some surgical skills. We're going to need them."

Harry and Carson disappeared into the night. Esme's stomach twisted in a knot. Suturing? Surgery? This wasn't what she'd signed up for.

When she'd moved here she'd put that all behind her. She wasn't a surgeon.

No.

Then she thought of Avery. Her brother bleeding out under her hands. She was being foolish. They needed her help. Someone was in pain. This wasn't an OR. She would make sure she wouldn't freeze up. She wouldn't. She couldn't. This was about sustaining a man's life until paramedics arrived. Esme rushed into her supply room, grabbed a rucksack and began to pack it full of equipment. Her hands shaking as she grabbed the suture kit.

I can do this.

Besides, she might not even have to stitch him.

Carson could handle it and nothing was going to happen.

This man wouldn't die.

This wasn't a surgery case. At least she hoped it wasn't.

CHAPTER THREE

ESME BIT HER lip in worry as they slowly traversed some windy hills up into the mountains. At least that was what she assumed by the bumps and the climbs that tried the engine of Harry's truck. She couldn't see anything.

She'd thought she knew what pitch-black was.

The sky was full of clouds and smoke from a forest fire, which Carson had assured her wasn't any threat to them. California had wild fires, but not really in Los Angeles, at least not when she was there. Then again, she wasn't a native Californian.

Fire, wilderness, bears, this existence was all new to her, but then this was what she wanted after all. This was a big wide place she could easily blend in. She was small here. A place she could hide, because who in their right mind would come looking for her here?

A large bump made her grip the dashboard tighter. She was wedged between Harry and Carson as they took the logging road deep into the camp.

Another bump made her hiss and curse under her breath.

Carson glanced at her. "You're mighty tense."

"Just hoping we don't die."

Harry chuckled. "We're not on the edge of a cliff. Our only threat is maybe a rock slide or a logging truck careening down the road, but since there are no trucks running we're pretty safe."

"I'll keep telling myself that we're safe, Harry."

He shook his head, probably at the folly of a city girl. Only it was a dark night like this when Avery had died. She'd only been ten years old, but the memory of her brother's gaping chest wound was still fresh. The feel of his exposed heart under her small hands, the warmth of his blood felt fresh. It was why she'd wanted to be a cardio-thoracic surgeon.

Why she'd worked so hard to be the best, because Avery had been a constant in her parents' strained marriage. Even though he'd been twelve years older than her.

He'd been her best friend and when he'd died, her world had been shattered. So she'd dedicated her life to surgery.

The nightmares of his death faded away but nights like this made it all rush back.

Carson slipped an arm around her shoulders and then leaned over. "Relax. You're okay."

She glanced at his arm around hers and she wanted to shrug it off, but it felt good there. Reassuring. It made her feel safe and she wished she could snuggle in. Esme let out the breath she hadn't realized she'd been holding in trepidation and leaned back against the seat, shrugging off Carson's arm. She could handle this. Alone.

"So what happened again, Harry?" Carson asked.

"Jenkins was overtired and nervous. Our new client, Mr. Draven, was headed out our way tomorrow. One wrong move and..." Harry trailed off.

Esme froze at the mention of the name Draven.
Dammit.

Though it couldn't be Dr. Draven, her former mentor. Eli was a cardio-thoracic surgeon. Still the name sent dread down her spine.

Draven was a common name. So there was no way it would be Eli or Shane. Dr. Draven had money, but he invested it in medicine and science. All of Shane's money was tied up in his company. She doubted he would invest in lumber or a hotel in Montana.

Harry slowed the truck down and she could see light through the trees as the forest thinned out. There were floodlights everywhere and people milling around one of the buildings, which looked like an administrative building. Harry pulled up right in front of it.

Carson opened the door and jumped out, reaching into the back to grab their supplies. Esme followed suit, trying to ignore all the eyes on them as they made their way into the building. The moment the door opened they could hear a man screaming in pain.

Esme forgot all the trepidation about anyone recognizing her. That all melted away. Adrenaline fueled her now as she headed toward the man in pain. There was blood, but it wasn't the damage done by the saw that caught her attention. It was his neck, and as she bent over the man she could see the patient's neck veins were bulging as he struggled, or rather as his heart struggled to beat. Only it was drowning.

She'd seen it countless times when she was a resident surgeon, before she'd chosen her specialty. Before she'd become a surgeon to the stars. First she had to confirm the rest of Beck's Triad, before she even thought about trying to right it.

She didn't want to freeze up. Not here. Not in her new start.

"Dave, you're going to be fine," Carson said, trying to soothe the patient. Only Dave Jenkins couldn't hear him. "It doesn't look like he's lost a lot of blood."

"He's lost blood," she said, trying not to let her voice shake.

Just not externally.

Carson took off his jacket, rolling up his sleeves to inspect the gash on Dave's right arm. "It's deep, but hasn't severed any arteries."

The wound had been put in a tourniquet, standard first aid from those trained at the mill. It wasn't bleeding profusely. It would need cleaning and a few stitches to set it right.

"That's not the problem." Esme pulled out her stethoscope.

Carson cocked an eyebrow. "Really?"

"Really." She peered down at Dave. His faceplate, his eyes rolling back into his head. He was in obstructive shock. "Who saw what happened? There's more than a gash to the arm going on here."

"A piece of timber snapped back and hit Dave here." Esme glanced up as the man pointed to his sternum.

"The gash came after?" she asked.

"No, before, but Dave didn't get out of the way and he didn't shut off the machine after the first malfunction. He was overtired—"

"Got it." Esme cut him off. She bent over and listened. The muffled heart sounds were evident. A wall of blood drowning out the rhythmic diastole and systole of the heart. Drowning it. Cursing under her breath, she quickly took his blood pressure, but she knew when the man pointed to his sternum what was wrong.

Cardiac tamponade.

Dave wouldn't survive the helicopter coming. He probably wouldn't have survived the trip to the hospital.

"What's his blood pressure?" Carson asked.

"Ninety over seventy. He's showing signs of Beck's Triad."

"Cardiac tamponade?"

Esme nodded and rifled through her rucksack, finding the syringe she needed and alcohol to sterilize. "I have to aspirate the fluid from around his heart."

"Without an ultrasound?" Carson asked. "How can...? Only trained trauma surgeons can do that."

Esme didn't say anything. She wasn't a trauma surgeon, though she worked in an ER during her residency. She'd done this procedure countless times. She was, after all, the cardio God. She knew the heart. It was her passion, her reason for living. She loved everything about the heart. She loved its complexities, its mysteries.

She knew the heart. She loved the heart.

Or at least she had.

"It's okay. I've done this before. Once."

She was lying. She'd done this countless times. She'd learned the procedure from Dr. Draven. It was a signature move of his that he taught only a select few, but they didn't need to know that. How many general practitioners performed this procedure multiple times? Not many.

"Once?"

"I really don't have time to explain. It's preferable to have an ultrasound, but we don't have one. I need to do this or he'll die. Open his shirt."

Carson cut the shirt open, exposing Dave's chest where a bruise was forming on the sternum.

You can do this.

"I need two men to hold him in case he jerks, and he can't. Not when I'm guiding a needle into the sac around his heart."

There were a couple of gasps, but men stepped forward, holding the unconscious Dave down.

Esme took a deep breath, swabbed the skin and then guided the needle into his chest. She visualized the pericardial sac in her head, remembering from the countless times she'd done this every nuance of the heart and knowing when to stop so she didn't penetrate the heart muscle. She pulled back on the syringe and it filled with blood, the blood that was crushing the man's heart. The blood that the heart should've been pumping through with ease, but instead was working against him, to kill him.

Carson watched Esme in amazement. He'd never encountered Beck's Triad before. Well, not since his fleeting days as an intern. It was just something he didn't look for as a family practitioner. Cardiac tamponade was usually something a trauma surgeon saw because a cardiac tamponade was usually caused by an injury to the heart, by blunt force, gunshot or stab wound.

Those critical cases in Crater Lake, not that there were many, were flown out to the hospital. How did Esme know how to do that? It became clear to Carson that she hadn't been a family practitioner for very long. She was a surgeon before, but why was she hiding it?

Why would she hide such a talent?

It baffled him.

Because as he watched her work, that was what he saw. Utter talent as she drained the pericardial sac with ease. She then smiled as she listened with her stethoscope.

"Well?" Carson asked, feeling absolutely useless.

"He'll make it to the hospital, but he'll need a CT and possibly surgery depending on the extent of his injuries."

There was a whir of helicopter blades outside and Harry came running in. "The medics are here to fly him to the hospital."

Esme nodded. "I'll go talk to them. Pack the wound on his arm."

Carson just nodded and watched her as she disappeared outside with Harry. She was so confident and sure of herself. She had been when he'd first met her, but this was something different. It reminded him of Danielle. Whenever she was on the surgical floor Danielle was a totally different person.

Actually, Carson found most surgeons to be arrogant and so sure of everything they did, but then they'd have to be. Lives were in their hands. Not that lives weren't in his hands, but it was a different scale.

Carson rarely dealt with the traumatic.

He turned to Dave's wound and cleansed it, packing it with gauze to protect it on his journey to the nearest hospital.

Esme rounded the corner and behind her were two paramedics. He could still hear the chopper blades rotating; they were going to pack him and get out fast, before smoke from the forest fires blew back in this direction and inhibited their takeoff.

Esme was still firing off instructions as they carefully loaded Dave onto their stretcher and began to hook up an IV and monitors to him. Carson helped slip on the oxygen mask. They moved quick, and he followed them outside as they ran with the gurney to the waiting chopper.

Esme stood back beside him, her arm protecting her face from the dust kicking up. There was no room on the chopper for them and they weren't needed anymore. The paramedics could handle Dave and he'd soon be in the capable hands of the surgeons at the hospital.

As the door to the chopper slammed it began to lift above the mill, above the thinned forest and south toward the city. Once the helicopter was out of sight, Esme sighed.

"Well, that was more excitement than I was preparing for tonight."

"You were amazing in there," Carson stated. "Was your previous general practice in a large city? I rarely see cardiac tamponades in my clinic. Or did you work at a hospital under a cardio-thoracic surgeon? The way you handled that I'm surprised you didn't become a cardio-thoracic surgeon. You had the steady hand of an experienced surgeon."

Esme's eyes widened and she bit her lip, before shrugging. "Sure, yeah, a cardio-thoracic surgeon mentor. So where's Harry gone? I really want to get back home. It's getting late. I better get my things."

She turned and headed back into the building, her arms wrapped tight around her lithe body.

Carson sighed and followed her and helped her clean up. She didn't engage him in any further discussion about the matter. They just disposed of soiled material and bagged up the rest of their stuff.

"Docs, I have the truck ready. I can take you back to town now," Harry said as he wandered into the room.

"Thanks, Harry." Carson glanced at Esme, who seemed to have relaxed and returned to herself. "You ready to go, Dr. Petersen?"

"Yes. I'm exhausted!" She smiled. "Thanks for taking us back to town, Harry."

Harry shrugged. "It's no problem. I don't stay up here at the camp. I'm local."

"Oh, you're local, all right, Harry," Carson teased as he picked up his bag. Harry just chuckled and they followed him out of the admin building to his pickup truck.

Now that the excitement had died down, workers were headed back to their bunks or back to the mill to work. He could hear the saws starting up again.

Esme climbed into the middle and Carson slid in beside her.

Harry turned the ignition and then rolled down his window, to lean his elbow out the side. "Yeah, the guys are a bit stressed around here. Mr. Draven is coming here tomorrow morning to inspect the mill. It's got the boss Bartholomew on edge. With the Draven contract for his resort that will mean a lot of work. A lot of money."

"What's Mr. Draven's first name?" There was an edge to Esme's voice.

"Silas. He's a big hotel mogul from out east," Harry said.

"East?" There was a bit of relief in her voice.

"Do you know Mr. Draven?" Carson asked.

"N-no. Just heard of him. The name sounded familiar, but I don't know Silas Draven."

Somehow Carson knew that was a lie, just by the nervous tone to Esme's voice and the way she'd sounded so relieved.

"He's never come to the mill before," Harry remarked. "I mean, he's a big rich investor. Doesn't know much about lumber mills other than what his advisors tell him, but I suspect it has something to do with competing. There's untapped tourist resources."

"Another hotel?" Carson asked.

Great.

It was supposed to be a simple resort community. Small and unique. Every time he heard something new about it, it was spiraling out of control. Perhaps it was the competitors that Luke had been taking up into the mountains to do surveying. More change.

Change can be good.

Only he didn't believe that. Change only brought heartache, disaster.

Temptation.

And he glanced over at Esme, sitting beside him in the dark. She was definitely a temptation.

"You okay?" she asked.

"Fine."

"You're scowling."

"I'm not. Besides, how can you tell? It's pitch-black out there."

"There's a moon and the dashboard light."

Indeed, in the flicker of light he could see her smiling at him, her eyes twinkling in the dark, and he couldn't help but smile, even though he didn't feel like it at the moment. Even though he knew nothing about her, being around her tonight had been a bit magical. It had been exciting and he couldn't remember the last time he'd felt such a rush.

Don't think about her like that.

"Do you think Dave will make it?" Harry asked, breaking through his thoughts.

"He should. Once he's in the hands of a capable cardio-thoracic surgeon." Esme leaned against the seat. "Which I'm not."

"You said that with such force," Carson said. "You really want to be clear that you're not a cardio-thoracic surgeon."

Her smile disappeared. "Because I'm not. I'm just lucky enough to have had the chance to perform that a couple of times."

"I thought it was only once?"

Esme stiffened. "Once was an understatement."

"Clearly, because the way you executed that procedure was superb. In fact, it looked like you'd been doing that for quite some time. Especially since you executed it without the use of an ultrasound."

Esme snorted. "I'm just a general practitioner and I did what I had to do to save a man's life. Can we drop the interrogation?"

"I'm not interrogating you."

She shrugged. "I've told you I've done it a couple of times. I guess I was lucky—really there was no other choice. Dave would've died had I not performed it then and there."

"You're right. Let's drop it."

"Good."

Carson turned and looked out the window, not that there was anything to see in the dark, on a logging road, in the middle of the forest, but he didn't feel like engaging in small talk with Esme. She was maddening.

It was clear to Carson by the way she wasn't looking at him and the way her body became tense that she wasn't too keen on discussing the matter further. What was she hiding?

Why do you care?

Perhaps because he'd been duped by a female before.

Working at your dad's practice sounds great! I would love to.

Then of course Danielle's tune had changed.

This is never what I wanted. You didn't give me much of a choice.

Not that he should care if Esme was lying to him. Let her have her secrets. It didn't matter. They weren't involved, they weren't colleagues and they certainly weren't friends. They were just two doctors in the same, sleepy small town.

That was it.

CHAPTER FOUR

ESME MANAGED TO avoid Carson for two weeks after working up on the mountain. She just decided it was in everyone's best interest if she laid low. Less questions to be asked that way. She knew Carson didn't believe her lies.

Great.

Why did that accident have to happen in front of Carson? She was here to be a simple physician. Not a surgeon, but then if she hadn't been there, Dave would've died. He wouldn't have made it to the hospital.

So she'd done the right thing, even if it had meant she'd had to perform a surgical procedure in front of Carson. Something she'd sworn she wasn't going to do when she got to Crater Lake.

The best solution was to avoid Carson for a while.

Which was why Esme was standing in the produce section of a big chain grocery store two towns away, staring at a pile of cantaloupes.

Run.

That was what she was telling herself, or at least the cowardly voice in her head was telling her.

Where?

That she didn't know. She couldn't go home to her

father. He'd made it clear that her running away was not the answer. That was what her mother had done. After Avery's death, she'd packed up and run away.

I've been a wife and mother. It's time for me. I gave up my life for you.

It had broken her father's heart. He'd lost a son and wife in the same year.

Now a daughter.

Ever since she'd left Los Angeles her father had made it clear how disappointed he was in her, so she was the last person her father wanted to see. She was just a big failure.

"Nice melons."

Esme shook her head and looked up to see Carson standing on the other side of the counter of cantaloupes.

"What?" she asked in disbelief.

He grinned and then rubbed the back of his neck. "Sorry, it was just a joke. You were staring so intently at the produce I thought you were trying to see through it."

Esme chuckled when she realized she had been staring at the cantaloupes for a long time. "Sorry, lost in thought. What're you doing here? I thought you went to the co-op in Crater Lake?"

"I usually do, but I was in town visiting a friend and remembered I needed a few things." He walked around the produce counter to stand beside her. "I thought you usually shopped locally? I didn't even know you had a car."

"I don't. I took the bus down here." She picked up a melon and sniffed it, hoping this would be the end of the conversation, that he would get the hint to walk away. Instead he lingered.

Damn. Take a hint.

Carson whistled. "That's a pricey ticket to go grocery shopping."

Esme shrugged. "Didn't have a choice."

"The local co-op is a choice."

"The prices here are better?"

Carson smiled. "Why did you pose that in the form of a question? I doubt they're low enough to justify the price of a bus ticket."

"Are you really going to sit here and lecture me about my shopping habits?"

"No, but I can offer you a ride back to Crater Lake at the very least."

Say no.

Only she couldn't, because she really didn't want to lug all her groceries on the passenger bus back up to Crater Lake. And after this one excursion she knew she'd either have to invest in a car or just pluck up the courage to shop at the co-op, because she obviously couldn't avoid Carson even two towns away.

"Thanks. I appreciate that." She pushed her shopping cart away from the melons and Carson fell into step beside her.

"I haven't seen you around much," Carson remarked.

"I've been busy."

"I saw that Mrs. Fenolio is now one of your patients."

Esme sighed. "Are you going to start on me about stealing your patients again?"

"No. I'm not. Honestly, I'm glad that she's headed over to you. You seem to have more of a grasp of cardiothoracic care."

Her heart skipped a beat.

Oh, God. Had he found out?

"Who told you that?"

"I saw it with my own eyes, Esme. Only someone with cardio-thoracic knowledge would be able to perform that procedure in that kind of situation. I think you've done that more than once or even a couple of times."

He was really persisting about the procedure. He was digging for information, information she didn't want to share. Information she wasn't going to share. It was in her past. She was here to start a new life. She wasn't that person any longer.

"I must have really impressed you."

"Well…yes." And he looked away quickly, rubbing the back of his neck again, as if he was embarrassed. As if he didn't want to give her a compliment.

"It was nothing. Now, about Mrs. Fenolio…"

"She's your patient now and you're the expert."

"I'm not. Not really."

Liar.

"Besides, she's only moved over her cardio care to me. How long has she had that murmur?"

"Do you really want to talk about this in a grocery store?" Carson asked as he picked up a loaf of bread and plunked it into her cart.

"Since when am I buying you groceries?" Esme teased.

"It's my fee for taking you back to Crater Lake. You can buy me my sandwiches for a week."

Esme chuckled. "I'm so disappointed."

"Why?"

"You're a sandwich man."

"What's wrong with liking sandwiches?" he asked.

"Nothing per se, but I'm a bit of a foodie."

Carson snorted. "Right, I forgot you're from Los Angeles."

"You don't have to be from LA to be a foodie. You can be from small towns, too. Not that I expect many people from Crater Lake to have many options."

"What're you talking about?" he asked.

"Oh, come on. Ray's is a fantastic Mom and Pop shop, but it's hardly gourmet."

"We have gourmet in Crater Lake," he said, sounding mildly insulted.

Esme looked skeptical. "Do you?"

"We do, but it's a bit of a secret."

"A secret?"

"Would you be interested in sampling a dinner there? I mean, since you're such a gourmand."

A zing traveled down her spine. Was he asking her out on a date? No. He couldn't be. She should say no, just on the off chance, but then again she couldn't resist a chance at a gourmet experience in Crater Lake.

It was better than sitting at home alone.

Don't do it.

"Okay…but as long as it's not up at the lodge." She didn't want too many people to see her with Carson. She wanted a low profile in town.

"No, it's not up at the lodge. It's been around longer than the lodge."

"Sure, then. Sounds intriguing."

"Good. So perhaps tonight?"

"Tonight?" she asked, trying not to let her voice hitch in her throat. "So soon?"

She thought maybe a day or two so she could get used to the idea.

"Is there something wrong with tonight? Do you have plans?"

Lie. Tell him you're busy.

Of course, if it was tonight she could get it done and out of the way.

"No. Tonight is fine. That's if you can get reservations to such an exclusive posh restaurant."

"Trust me. I can."

"Okay, then, it's a..." She paused because she was going to say *date*, but that was not what it was. At least she wasn't going to admit that was what it was. If she said it was a date, then it was and she couldn't have that. It was like eating a whole cake when no one saw you—the calories didn't count.

You know better than that. The calories do count.

And she might've just bitten off a little bit more than she could chew at the moment.

Carson couldn't believe what he'd just done, but before he could even think logically about what he was doing he was asking her out to a nonexistent restaurant. He was asking her over to his place, for dinner tonight. Carson couldn't help but think that he'd set himself up for failure and he didn't know why he'd asked her out.

Carson hadn't asked out anyone since Danielle.

He'd sworn off women when Danielle left and broke his heart.

He didn't want to get hurt again. It should be a simple matter staying away from Esme, but he couldn't.

He was drawn to her like a moth to a flame and he knew if he kept up this way he was going to get burnt.

Bad.

He was a masochist.

Perhaps she'd only said yes because she wanted to discover this great new restaurant in a very small town. Some hidden gem. Foodies liked to find hidden and new restaurants, especially places that were off the beaten trail, so to speak, and it was all innocent.

Yet the things she stirred deep down inside him were hardly innocent. And it scared him that she stirred desires that he'd buried long ago.

How would she feel when he picked her up and took her to his place, out in the woods? Not that he was that far out in the woods. He had an acre of wood lot and a nice cabin, which Luke had helped him build years ago, when Carson had thought he was building a home for him and Danielle.

There were neighbours within sight, but how would a city girl feel being brought out into the woods by a man she barely knew? He could be a serial killer for all she knew.

You're overthinking things again.

"You've gone positively pale," Esme remarked as they walked side by side through the store.

"What?" he asked.

"Are you okay?"

"I'm fine."

She frowned. "I don't think you are. You totally drifted off there. If it's about tonight, we can make it for another night."

"No, no, it's not that."

Yes, it is. You're setting yourself up for hurt.

"Are you sure?"

"Positive. I was just thinking about one of my files."

"Mrs. Fenolio?"

"Uh, yeah, sure."

Esme bit her lip. "We can talk about it tonight. I get that she's been at your family practice for some time. I understand it's hard to let go of some patients. Boy, do I ever." She mumbled the *Boy, do I ever* and he couldn't help but wonder why. Did she lose a patient that it still affected her so profoundly?

The loss of a patient was something that never sat right with Carson, but then, working in his father's practice, the patients they would lose were elderly. He wasn't a surgeon. Patients rarely died on his table.

When he thought about heading down that path to become a surgeon, he quickly changed his mind because he didn't want to just stitch them up and send them on their way. He wanted a connection with them. He wanted to be their primary caregiver.

It hurt when one of his patients died or became ill, but it wasn't the same as being responsible for someone's death and he couldn't help but wonder if Esme had experienced that.

"You lost a patient in LA?" he asked as they walked slowly down an aisle.

"Why would you ask me that?" She didn't look at him; she pretended to be studying the cans on the shelves.

"Because you're avoiding eye contact with me."

She shrugged and briefly glanced in his direction. "I'm not avoiding eye contact with you."

"You are too. I can tell when patients are lying to me."

She frowned. "I'm not your patient."

"Semantics."

Esme sighed. "I did lose a patient. It was hard, but

I moved on. You can't tell me that when you lost your first patient in your first year it didn't affect you?"

Esme was twisting the subject around back to him. It was a good evasive maneuver that he'd used many times to avoid uncomfortable questions.

Impressive.

"Well?" There was a small smile tugging at the corners of her lips.

"Okay, it affected me. Of course it would affect me. Anyone with any sense of compassion would feel that loss keenly."

"Exactly."

Carson decided he would drop the subject. For now, but he was still going to dig into her cardio-thoracic past. He was convinced that a family physician, just a family physician, wouldn't be able to perform such a procedure with such skill and precision.

She'd been so sure of herself.

So confident.

In that moment Esme had reminded him of a surgeon. A bit of her reminded him of Danielle. The drive, the ambition, and someone with that kind of passion wouldn't want to stay in such a place as Crater Lake.

They didn't talk much about anything else. They finished their grocery shopping and he drove the hour back to Crater Lake. Just chatting politely about nothing really. It was the most uncomfortable car ride Carson had ever taken in his life.

The whole way back to town he tried not to think about Danielle and how her leaving had left a hole in his heart. It had hurt, but he'd moved on. He'd built a solid practice with his father. He was safe and secure.

At least he'd thought his existence was safe and secure. He was comfortable. That was until Esme Petersen had set up shop in town and that had totally rocked the foundation of his safety net. He wasn't sure if he liked it.

Don't you?

He shook his head as he pulled up in front of her clinic.

"So what time will you be picking me up?" Esme asked.

"About seven?"

"Sure. That sounds great." She smiled; it was bright and cheerful. It warmed his heart, made him feel things he hadn't felt in a long time and that scared him.

Back out of the date.

He knew he was playing with fire, but he couldn't help himself. It was just an innocent dinner. He wanted to find out more about her, about her practice and maybe discuss some cases. Things that Luke never wanted to do, things he used to discuss with his father before his parents had upped and moved to Naples, Florida.

"Is there a dress code at this restaurant?" Esme asked, still not getting out of his car.

"No."

She glanced at him. "A gourmet restaurant and no dress code. I think I'm liking this place already."

Carson chuckled. "You'll like it. Trust me."

"And if I don't?" she asked.

"Then I owe you one."

Esme just grinned, but didn't say anything more as she opened the car door. "Pop the trunk for me and I'll see you at seven."

"Seven. I'll be waiting."

Esme climbed out and shut the door, collecting her groceries from the trunk and shutting it. She waved and then headed down the alley toward the back of her clinic.

Carson gripped the steering wheel and sat there for a few moments. What was he doing? He didn't really know. When Danielle had left him, when she'd crushed his heart, his hopes and dreams, he'd sworn he wouldn't let someone in again.

No dating, no nothing.

He was comfortable in his existence.

There were no surprises.

It was nice.

And it was also absolutely and utterly boring.

CHAPTER FIVE

ESME WANTED TO call and cancel the dinner date about three times before seven o'clock. The only problem was she didn't know Carson's phone number. She knew his office number, but the clinic was closed, so she was kind of stuck.

It's just as friends. Colleagues. Nothing more.

That was what she kept telling herself over and over again. The problem was, she wasn't sure if she was able to convince herself of that fact.

This was how it had started with Shane. A dinner with her mentor's son. As a favor to Eli, who hadn't been able to take his son out that night. It had been just a friendly dinner and then it had escalated from there. There was only one difference between Carson and Shane.

The simple fact was Carson Ralston made her nervous and no one made her nervous. Not Shane, not a difficult surgery. Just Carson.

Not even Eli Draven, the surgeon she idolized, made her nervous. He'd yelled and screamed at her before and she didn't care. The only reason she avoided Shane's father was because it reminded her of how she'd hurt Shane.

She was made of stronger mettle than to fold under the pressure of someone like Eli. Of course, Eli was someone else she'd disappointed.

Her father had always taught her to be strong. To stand up for herself and not let anyone walk all over her. Not that Carson was walking all over her. It was just that being around him made her nervous. He made her blood rush, her stomach zing and her body heat.

Carson made her weak in the knees. He made her think of romance and she wasn't a romance type of girl. Love only led to heartache. The only time she'd come close to anything romantic was when she'd almost married Shane on Valentine's Day, and look where that had got her.

Yet, being around Carson made her nervous, made her irrational.

There were times she could feel the heat in her cheeks from blushing and Esme had never blushed in someone's presence before.

Not since she was in the seventh grade and had that crush on Matthew Fenwick.

You do not have a crush on Dr. Ralston.

That was what she kept trying to tell herself over and over again. She didn't have a crush on Carson. She couldn't have a crush on him, she just couldn't, because she didn't deserve it. Men like Carson needed a wife and Esme wasn't wife material. Something that had become quite clear to her when she'd picked up the voluminous skirt of her designer wedding dress and climbed out of the bathroom window of the church, running in the opposite direction to Shane.

He'd demanded so much of her. He'd wanted her by his side constantly, which had taken her away from surgery. She'd forgotten about why she'd become a surgeon. She'd realized all of this when she'd frozen during surgery. How dating Shane had made her off her game.

How could she be the best cardio-thoracic surgeon if she was a society wife and mother? With Shane she couldn't. She couldn't be herself. So Esme had run. *I don't know who you are anymore. I didn't raise a daughter who runs.*

Her father's voice was still so clear in her mind.

She didn't know who she was. Not anymore.

A textbook procedure on a patient and she'd frozen. Not knowing what to do next.

Lost.

And then it had all come back in a rush and despite her best efforts she hadn't been able to save the patient. It hadn't mattered that it hadn't been her fault, that she had done everything she could. All she'd been able to see was her failure in that moment.

That was when she'd walked away from surgery. She was done. Broken. From there things had spiraled and it had led to the collapse of her plans for happy ever after with Shane. If only she could have known her own heart sooner.

That was why she had left Los Angeles. To find herself again. Though that was easier said than done, because her guilty conscience was attacking her at every angle.

She'd run away.

She'd disappointed her father.

Still, there had been no choice in the matter. Here she could live in peace. Here she didn't have to run.

When it came to matters of the heart though, that

was where she was weak. Maybe she should run now? Go somewhere else until Carson left. Then she wouldn't have to go out to dinner with him and then she wouldn't have to feel so nervous around him.

Carson's SUV pulled up in front of her building. He honked the horn a couple of times. Esme sighed and grabbed her purse.

No turning back now. She just hoped she was dressed okay. She didn't want to stick out like a sore thumb. She'd opted for casual classy. A nice pair of jeans, boots and a black sweater that was off the shoulders. Also accessories.

So no matter where he took her, she'd blend in and that was what it was all about. She just wanted to blend in. She didn't want to stand out.

She didn't want to be extraordinary, because she wasn't. Not anymore anyway.

When she walked over to the car Carson got out and held open the door for her.

"You didn't have to get out," she said.

"My mother taught me good manners." Once she was in the car he shut the door and then slid back into the driver's seat, buckling up before he pulled away. "So this place we're going, it's out in the country. I didn't want to freak you out or anything."

"Why would I freak out?" she asked.

"You know, a man you barely know is taking you out into the wilderness."

Esme chuckled. "I assumed it was out of town."

"You did?"

"Main Street, or rather the town of Crater Lake, isn't that huge. The only eating establishments within the major downtown core are Ray's, Little Mamma's Bakery and Main Street Deli...which has been closed for repairs for a seemingly long time."

"Twenty years," Carson responded.

"That's a shame. I enjoy a good sandwich." She tried not to laugh. It was so easy to tease him. All the trepidation she'd been feeling seemed to melt away and that was what scared her. It was so easy to be around him.

"What? I thought you had an issue with sandwiches. I mean, that's why I'm taking you to this exclusive spot. You seemed to have a problem with my sandwiches when we were shopping today."

"I like traditional deli sandwiches within moderation. Somehow, though, I think that you're taking bologna sandwiches to work. Two pieces of white bread, mustard, an imitation cheese slice and a piece of bologna. Just like Mom used to pack in school lunches."

"All smooshed down and everything?" Carson asked.

Esme smiled. "Yes, with the crusts cut off."

He shook his head. "You think you know me so well. I'll have you know it's not just bologna in my repertoire. I also enjoy a good salami."

She couldn't help but break out laughing at that and when he realized what he'd said a blush crept up his cheeks and he shot her an exasperated look.

"That's not what I meant at all and you know it."

"Do I? I barely know you," she said. "You could be an axe murderer or something. A doctor who injects his patients with a live virus just so he can test his maniacal cures on them."

"Hardly."

"Whatever you say, Dr. Moreau." Then she laughed.

"Fine, then. Believe what you want." He winked and turned down a gravel drive. She glanced out the window as she saw a beautiful log home in a clearing, built into the side of a foothill.

"What is this place?" she asked.

"The exclusive restaurant. Also known as my house."

Her heart beat a bit faster. *His house?* This was dangerous.

"Your house?" she asked, the words barely getting out.

"I'm sorry for tricking you. I guess I should've explained that it was my place I was taking you to."

"Yeah, you should've."

"Would you have come?"

"No," she said. "I don't think so." And it was true. She wouldn't have. Having dinner with him was temptation enough. She'd thought at least other people would be around. Now they'd be alone, out in the woods in his gorgeous cabin. Suddenly, she was very nervous again. *Dammit.*

It was all too seductive for her liking.

"Sorry, but I wanted to prove to you that I'm not just a sandwich guy. Even though I'm not from LA and I don't have exposure to some of the best restaurants in America, I do have experience of some gastronomical delights."

"That remains to be seen."

"You don't believe me?" he asked in mild outrage.

"My expectations were set high," she teased. "You have a lot to live up to, Dr. Ralston."

Carson parked his car. "You can call me Carson. We're not on duty."

Blood rushed to her cheeks and she turned her head away briefly, hoping he wouldn't notice how he was affecting her physically.

Think about something else.

"Okay. You can call me Esme. I mean, no one else is around so no one has to know we've formed this sort of ceasefire."

"Right."

They got out of the car and she followed him up the steps to the front porch. She stopped to take in the breathtaking sight. From the front porch she could see Crater Lake, nestled in the foothills, like in a little valley. The mountains in Glacier National Park rising up to protect the town, as if it were this little sheltered place. Untouched and hidden.

"Wow," she whispered.

"I know. When I have time I like to sit out here at night. It's also beautiful in the morning with the sun rising."

Lucky.

If this was her place she'd do the exact same thing.

Esme walked over to the railing and leaned over, taking in her surroundings. She spotted another house, down the hill in the trees. It looked dark, but lived in. "Whose house is that?"

Carson came up beside her and she was suddenly aware of how close he actually was. His hand so close to her on the wooden railing, they were almost touching. She could smell his cologne. It was subtle, masculine and very woodsy. It made her tremble. It made her weak in the knees.

It turned her on.

So she moved an inch away, trying to put distance between them.

"That's my childhood home. Or rather my parents' house. They come back and visit from time to time. That's where they stay. This land is my family's land. With me nearby I can keep an eye on my parents' house."

"Where are they now?"

"Naples, Florida. They have a condo that backs out onto a golf course. They love it there."

"And I hear you have a brother, right?"

Carson nodded. "Yes. I do."

"Does he live there or here with you?"

"No, he lives up the mountain in a shack."

Esme rolled her eyes. "Are you having me on? He doesn't live in a shack."

"Yes, he does."

"I thought you said he was a doctor."

"He is, but he lives in a shack up the mountain. He's a bit of a mountain man. He doesn't practice traditional medicine. He was an army medic for years in Special Ops and then after he was discharged he liked living in the rough so much he built a shanty out in the woods. He takes surveyors out; he's a first responder. He teaches people how to survive in the hostile environment of a mountain. He will do emergency surgery."

"Emergency surgery in the woods?"

"Sometimes there's no choice."

Esme cringed inwardly at the thought of emergency surgery out in the forest. Hardly ideal, but if you were an ex-army man living rough in a remote community, then it made sense.

"Wow. All the power to him." She moved away from

him. "So are you going to let me inside or are we going to stand here all night?"

Carson grinned and unlocked the front door, stepping aside. "After you."

She tried not to gasp when she stepped inside his house. She was expecting rustic, but on a smaller scale. She was not prepared for the high roof, exposed wooden beams and the massive stone fireplace that dominated the northern wall. All around them were windows, which offered a three-sixty view of the mountains, the town and a lake that seemed to be sunk in, like a hollow. Even in the evening sunlight, you could see its brilliant coral and aquamarine colors. In the center the blue darkened, like a deep hole.

She'd seen the Great Blue Hole in Belize; this wasn't as big, but it was still impressive given the setting. She moved toward the far window to get a better look at the lake. There was no wind outside so the mountains were perfectly reflected in the water. Like a mirror. It was the most beautiful thing she'd ever seen.

Carson came up behind her; she could feel the heat of his body against her back. It made her uncomfortable and she remembered his arm around her when he'd tried to comfort her on the trip up the mountain to the mill. She shifted away, trying to put some distance between the two of them.

Distance was safe.

"What's the name of the lake?"

"That's Crater Lake, what the town was named after."

"I expected something different for Crater Lake."

"Different?"

"Something bigger perhaps." He smiled at her, that smile that made her melt just a little bit. This was why Carson was dangerous.

"I think it's pretty substantial." Carson raked his hand through his hair and then crossed his arms. When he had the blinds in his office windows open, she watched him dictating charts, just like that. His arms crossed, head bent and usually pacing back and forth.

There was something calming about it. Soothing. It made her feel at ease.

She couldn't think about him like that.

"Why is it so blue?" Esme asked, trying not to think about the fact she was standing in Carson's home, that he made her calm and yet nervous at the same time. She couldn't think about him this way. She didn't want to.

This was not what she was here for.

"Mineral water off the glacier in the mountains. When the water is blue like that, it's from the glaciers. If it's more clear, more like a normal lake, it's spring fed." He moved past her to the south end of the house and pointed. "That's Mitchum Lake—see the difference. It's spring fed."

"I think these are better views than where that new resort community was built on the other side of town. I'm surprised that no one made you an offer on this land."

"Who says they didn't?" Carson grinned. "Would you like some wine?"

Esme nodded as he moved past her to the kitchen.

"I'm sure it was a lot of money they must've offered. Most people wouldn't turn that down."

"I'm not most people." He winked and set down two wine glasses on the counter. "Red okay?"

"Perfect." She dropped her purse on an end table. "So what do you plan to cook for me tonight?"

"Bison."

What? "Did I just hear you correctly? Did you say bison?"

"I could cook you elk if you'd prefer?"

"Bison is fine. I have to say I'm disappointed."

Carson cocked an eyebrow and then started to get food ready for dinner. "Why?"

"Isn't Montana famous for beefsteak?"

He flexed and made pointed glances at his biceps, which made her laugh out loud. She couldn't remember the last time she'd laughed like that. It was so easy to laugh with Carson. When the giggles stopped she followed him out onto his deck, which overlooked the lake. He had a stainless-steel barbecue there, where he was grilling the bison steaks.

Esme wandered over to the side and leaned over the railing. She could see the construction off in the distance where the new Draven resort and spa were going to go up. They were going to be an eyesore.

At least that was Esme's opinion.

"What're you thinking about?" Carson asked.

"Pardon?"

Carson glanced over his shoulder at her. "I asked you what you were thinking about. You were staring off into space. You do that a lot."

She couldn't tell him why she had been doing that a lot lately and he was right, she had been drifting off. It was nice and quiet. It was easy enough to do around here.

"I was relaxing and enjoying the view."

"Easy to do," Carson said as he turned back to the

grill and flipped the meat. "I've thought about putting a hot tub out here."

"That would be nice. Especially in the winter, I bet."

"Have you ever experienced winter?" Carson asked.

"Yes, I wasn't born and raised in California. I'm from Ohio."

"So you're used to bitter winters."

Esme nodded. "Yeah, but it's been a long time since I experienced one. I'm honestly not looking forward to it."

He laughed. "I don't doubt it."

"Can I help?"

"You can grab the cobs of corn in the fridge, then I can grill them here on the barbecue."

"Sure thing." Esme set her wine glass down on the patio table and headed inside. She found the shucked corn in the fridge and brought it back to Carson, who threw it on the grill. "Why don't we eat outside?"

"Sure. We can do that."

Esme headed back inside and found plates and cutlery. She brought everything outside and set it all out. Just in time for the meat and corn to be done.

They sat down together.

"I hope you like it. My brother says I'm the best at grilling bison."

"Well, since I have nothing to compare it to." Esme took a bite. It was so tender and absolutely delicious. She'd tried lots of different food before, but never bison.

"What do you think?" Carson asked.

"It's fantastic."

"See, I told you it was the best place in town."

"You were right. Great view, too."

"I always thought so. It's why I built my house here."

Esme was stunned. "You built this house?"

"I did. I like working with my hands. I like building things. I didn't draw up the plans, but I did a lot of the work myself. Luke and my father helped, too."

"That's amazing. Most doctors I know just participate in golf or attend parties at their club."

"Those are surgeons. I can't see a surgeon risking injuring their hands by doing work like this. Well, at least not any surgeons I know."

"I thought you didn't know any surgeons?"

Carson sighed. "Well, I do have to refer my patients who need work to surgeons. Thankfully, most of those surgeons are in Missoula."

"You don't like surgeons very much, do you?"

"Who said that? I have no problems with surgeons. There are some general practitioners I know who are just as goofy as the ones in Missoula."

Esme laughed. "So I take it you don't have many friends?"

"I'm a bit of a loner. I prefer it that way."

"Me, too." And she did, to some extent, but suddenly the idea of going back to her apartment above her clinic made her sad. She had a hard time falling asleep in the quiet.

She wanted to be alone, she didn't deserve happiness, but still. It sucked. And sitting here with Carson made her forget for just a moment that she was lonely. It was amazing being here with him and just talking.

Which was a dangerous thing indeed.

Carson smiled at her; when he smiled like that there was a dimple in his cheek. It was so sexy. She was a sucker for dimples on a man. There were a lot of enticing qualities about Carson. He was so different from

Shane. So down to earth, but she could tell he wasn't the type of guy to be pushed around by anyone.

She was definitely treading on dangerous ground here.

"So Mrs. Fenolio is quite stubborn."

Carson chuckled under his breath. "I thought you didn't want to talk about Mrs. Fenolio?"

"I didn't want to talk about her in the store, but I'm willing to discuss her file with her former physician in this private setting."

She was trying in vain to turn the conversation around. If they talked about work she wouldn't think about how good he looked in the button-down flannel shirt he was wearing, the tight starched jeans and the cowboy boots. Or the fact that he was a fantastic cook.

If they talked about the patient, she wouldn't stare at his slim hips or those muscular forearms or his smiling face with the devious sparkle in his eyes. A sparkle that was promising lots of very bad things that she really wanted to indulge in.

Damn.

He nodded and poured the wine. "You have knowledge in cardio-thoracic surgery."

"A bit."

He looked at her. "Oh, we're going to play this game again."

"I'm not playing any games, Dr. Ralston."

"Carson."

She glared at him. "Carson, then."

"Better."

She sighed. "Okay, I spent some time in a hospital before I decided to open a family practice and that's all you need to know about the matter."

* * *

Carson wanted to press her further, because he felt as if here she was opening up more, but then he didn't want to scare her away either. She might be the competition, but maybe, just maybe, if they were on good terms they could work together and do something more. The town was expanding and it might be nice to have a larger practice. Something his father had never dreamed of.

If it's not broken you don't fix it. That was his father's mantra when it came to business. Thankfully not when it came to medicine.

The Ralston family practice had been the way it was since the town was founded. It was sufficient and efficient.

If a patient required any other kind of care that the practice didn't offer, the hospital was only an hour away. That was the reason why they had air ambulance up in this part of Montana.

The family practice was solid.

It didn't need to be changed and just thinking about that change scared him. He shouldn't be thinking about changing it. What would change do? It could potentially destroy everything his family had built. Did he really want to cause the demise of the Ralston family practice?

He wasn't the one who was going to end that legacy.

Carson wasn't that person. Even if he wanted more, he wasn't going to change a thing.

He turned around and put a stopper in the wine, setting it on the far counter, his back to Esme so she couldn't see him. He didn't want to be thinking about Danielle. Not here, not now. Also it got his mind off the fact Esme was in his home and that his bedroom was just ten feet away. She was so damn sexy and he had to keep reminding himself she was off-limits. He refused to get hurt again.

He had to stop staring at the curve of her neck, her red lips and her bare shoulders.

"I spent some time as a surgical intern, as well," Carson said casually as he handed her the glass of wine.

"Did you?"

"I did. For about three months and I realized that surgery is not my thing."

"Not your thing?" she asked. "Why?"

"I want to save lives."

Her brow furrowed. "You don't think surgeons save lives? They're all about saving lives. They endure grueling training, long hours and sometimes life-threatening situations so they *can* save a life."

There was a fire in her eyes as she passionately defended surgery.

Not a surgeon, my foot.

"How long were you a surgical intern?"

"Ah, a year, and then I decided to open a practice in Los Angeles."

"Huh, I thought you might've gone all the way."

Esme shot him that flinty glare again, the one he was quickly learning to fear. It was the look she seemed to give when someone had pushed her too far. "Why would you assume that?"

"Because you talked so passionately about surgery. Only surgeons talk with such passion and fire about surgery, because those who are meant to be surgeons are married to it. It's their first love."

The glare softened and she smiled. "I just respect them. That's all."

He nodded. "I respect them, too, and I quickly learned in my few months that I was not a surgeon and that was probably for the best for all patients."

She laughed at his joke, the tension melting away. "Well, I tried a new prescription regimen on Mrs. Fenolio, but darned if I can get her to take it."

Carson frowned. "A new prescription regimen? Why?"

"What she was taking for her condition was not working anymore."

"Digoxin wasn't working anymore? Physicians have been using digoxin since the pioneer days."

"Yes, and it did work fine. In Mrs. Fenolio's case it doesn't apply any longer. She's suffering from ventricular tachycardia. In Mrs. Fenolio's case amiodarone works substantially better."

He frowned again. "That's horrible. I'm sorry she's deteriorated. My father was treating her for a decade."

"And he did fantastic. Mrs. Fenolio's disease is progressing rapidly. I've actually added her to the transplant list."

"You...you did what?" Carson was baffled. For a decade his father had treated Mrs. Fenolio and there had been no issues. She had survived and now suddenly Esme was standing here in his kitchen saying that Mrs. Fenolio required a heart transplant. He was having a hard time believing it. Probably because Mrs. Fenolio used to babysit him and Luke. Especially given the fact Esme had only completed her intern year, something she'd just told him. He could believe that a physician who had one year of surgical training could complete the procedure she'd performed up at the mill, but changing Mrs. Fenolio's treatment plan completely and telling the woman she needed a heart transplant? That wasn't someone who did just a year as an intern. It firmed his belief Esme was a surgeon.

"What're you basing your opinion on?" he asked.

"On the tests I ran in my clinic and the fact she wore a Holter monitor for twenty-four hours."

"You admitted yourself that you're not a cardio-thoracic specialist. How can you diagnose someone? How can you make that call to put her on the transplant list? You can't. Only a surgeon can do that."

Her eyes widened for a moment as if he'd caught her in a lie and she was trying to think up an excuse.

"Well?" Carson asked impatiently. "Someone who only completed one year of internship of surgery can't diagnose that condition. They wouldn't know and a general practitioner can't put a patient on the transplant waiting list without a surgeon's assessment. Admit you're a surgeon, Dr. Petersen."

"You've lost your mind." She put down her wine glass and grabbed her purse. "I think I'm going to head for home."

Carson stood in front of her, blocking her path. "You're a surgeon, Esme. You have an incredible talent. I've never seen anyone drain a cardiac tamponade or recognize a Beck's Triad that quickly in that kind of situation. I just don't know why you're trying to hide it from me."

She stared up at him. Those blue eyes, so wide. She was afraid to admit it, but why? Why should she be so afraid to admit that she had a gift? Yeah, maybe he didn't want the life of a surgeon. Maybe he'd left something he'd always dreamed about to uphold a family tradition, but why would she throw something extraordinary away?

"I...I don't know what to…"

He gripped her shoulders. "You can tell me. You have skill, Esme. Amazing talent."

"Carson, I don't know you and you don't know me. I shouldn't be having this conversation with you."

"You can trust me."

"Can I?"

"Yes," he whispered as he reached out and brushed back her hair. It was so soft and he fought the urge to kiss her, because that was what he wanted to do. He wanted to kiss her. Badly. "Tell me. You can tell me."

"You might think less of me."

"Doubtful."

Esme smiled, but in a sad way that made his soul ache a bit. "So sure of yourself. I had confidence like that once."

"You still do."

"No, I don't."

"Yes, you do. That was a confident doctor I saw up on that mountain."

She was going to say something else when his door opened and Luke came barging in.

"Carson, I've been looking all over for you." Then he saw Esme. "Sorry, I didn't realize you had company."

Esme pushed out of his embrace. "I was just heading back to town."

"Good, you both need to head back to town," Luke

said. He sounded a bit winded. "I thought you two would be down at the clinic."

"What's going on, Luke?" Carson asked.

"I brought a surveyor down off the mountain. His appendix is going to blow. There's no time to take him to the hospital."

CHAPTER SIX

EVEN IF SHE wanted to hide the fact that she was a surgeon from Carson now, there was no way she could. Not when there was a life on the line.

With this surveyor who was in Carson's exam room in agony, she wasn't going to let the man die from a ruptured appendix because she had something to hide.

Because she was scared.

She was going to operate on him. She might not practice as a surgeon now, but she was a surgeon. Lives were in her hands.

This man's life was in her hands. Luke was examining the surveyor while Carson began to strip off his clothes in the other room. She knew she shouldn't watch, but she couldn't help it. He saw her watching him and her cheeks bloomed with heat as his intense gaze burned into her soul. He pulled out a pair of scrubs and tossed them to her.

"You're not going to want to get your clothes dirty," Carson said. "They look too...nice to get ruined."

"Thanks."

He nodded and turned his back to her as he finished changing. Esme snuck into his office and quickly peeled off her clothes and pulled on the men's scrubs, pulling the drawstring as tight as she could, but they were still large.

As she pulled on her shirt Carson came bursting in, pausing in the doorway. He looked away quickly, rubbing the back of his neck in that awkward way he always did.

"I'm sorry. I thought you were finished."

"It's okay. I'm done. I'm impressed you keep scrubs on hand."

"My father always insisted. I guess in case of emergencies like this."

"I thought he wasn't a surgeon," Esme teased.

Carson smiled. "I never said that. You look nervous. You okay?"

"I'm okay. It's just…"

"It's nothing. You can do this."

"It's a simple surgery."

"Exactly. It'll be easy."

Easy. Right. Though she wasn't sure. The last surgery she'd done was routine. It had been easy and she'd frozen.

"I'll see you in there. Have you performed an appendectomy before?" she asked.

"Once, in the few months I was an intern."

"How about your brother?" she asked.

"He's performed several emergency procedures in extreme situations. He was an army medic. He's a surgeon, but he's not staying. He left the rest of the surveyors up on the mountain."

Esme nodded. "Oh. Well, you'll have to handle the anesthesia."

"Of course."

Esme let him change and entered the exam room

where Luke was pulling down supplies to perform the surgery in this place. The patient had been given morphine and was basically in and out of consciousness.

"Have you performed surgery before, Dr. Petersen?" Luke asked.

"Yes. Many times."

Luke nodded. "Good, I need to get back up the mountain. Carson said you were a surgeon."

"I was. I am." She cursed under her breath as she stumbled over her words. "I've performed more appendectomies than I care to admit."

Luke grinned and nodded. "Fair enough, Dr. Petersen."

She made her way over to the sink and scrubbed the best she could given the situation. Four-minute scrub. Could she even remember the words to the song she sang when she scrubbed? And then it came back to her. She scrubbed and it felt weird to be scrubbing for surgery again, but also it felt good. "Has he been given any antibiotic?"

"Doing that now, Dr. Petersen," Carson said as he was setting up an IV. Carson's brother had left. It was just the two of them here. Alone.

She might have done a ton of appendectomies and emergency appendectomies, but she'd never done one outside of the OR and not in these conditions. Though she was pretty positive if Luke Ralston was a former army medic, he'd probably seen worse. And right now she really didn't need to see worse.

There were no scrub nurses so Esme scurried to lay out the surgical instruments and the supplies she'd need.

"He's under," Carson said over his shoulder as he intubated the man. "I can assist you if you need."

"No, just manage his airway."

Carson nodded. "I'm here if you need me, but you got this."

Esme took a deep breath and palpated the patient's abdomen.

You can do it. You're a surgeon. This guy won't die.

This was just an appendectomy. This was not an open heart. Appendectomies were routine. She could do this.

You used to be able to do open hearts, too.

She *had* to do this. Help was too far away for this man. He wouldn't survive unless she did this. Esme took another deep calming breath, took the ten blade in hand and made the incision over McBurney's point. Once she was cutting down through the layers, everything fell into place. She remembered everything. It was routine. It was easy.

Her hands didn't shake.

Carson watched and then began to assist her while managing the man's airway. As if reading her thoughts he knew what instruments to hand her. The only sound was the rhythmic beat of the manual ventilator.

She found her rhythm as a surgeon again, even though it had been months since she held a scalpel. She'd forgotten what a high it was. How much she loved it. Not that she deserved to love something so much.

Still, it was a thrill. It was amazing.

All too soon she was pulling on the purse strings and inverting the stump into the cecum and closing him up.

"Excellent work, Dr. Petersen," Carson remarked.

"Thank you, Dr. Ralston." She glanced up at him while he continued to manually ventilate the patient. "Has an ambulance been called to take him to the hospital? You may be set up to do emergency surgery, but you're not set up for post-op care. He's going to need a course of antibiotics."

"Yes," Carson said. "I called from my office before we started."

Esme finished stitching and heard the sirens coming closer toward them.

"Speak of the devil," Carson muttered. "Dr. Petersen, can you take over the ventilation and I'll let the paramedics in as I know the surveyor and can give them the information they need."

"Of course." Esme pulled off her gloves, throwing them into the receptacle and putting on a fresh pair. She took over the manual ventilation since she was finished stitching, cleaned the wound and applied the pressure dressing. Carson returned quickly.

"I didn't expect to be doing that again," Esme said.

"You did an amazing job." Then he smiled at her in a way that made her heart melt. "I knew you could."

Why did he have so much faith in her?

She cleared her throat and looked away. "Your clinic was very well prepared for surgery."

"My father and Luke were always insistent on being prepared for any situation. Especially up here in the mountains," Carson said. "First time it has happened under my watch, though."

"Smart move, given the hospital is more than an hour away. This man didn't have an hour in him."

"Accidents and emergencies up here can happen when you least expect it," Carson said, peeling off his gloves. "You did well."

"Thank you." And she blushed again, their gazes locked across the room. She wanted to say more, but couldn't. She just couldn't. She had to keep her distance from Carson.

"There's no need to thank me," Carson said. "I'm just speaking the truth."

"Well, you don't need to say I did well. There's no need. I wasn't going to let him die. I did what needed to be done."

"I know that, but—"

Their conversation ended abruptly as the paramedics entered the exam room. Esme let them take over as they brought in their equipment. In a matter of minutes the paramedics had the surveyor loaded up, leaving Carson and Esme to clean up the clinic. She didn't know what Carson was going to say to her there, but it didn't matter.

Whatever it was, she didn't need to hear it.

They worked side by side in silence. She knew she couldn't really hide who she was. Not after this moment. She admitted it, but she didn't want to tell him why. She didn't want to get into it and she hated that her past was sneaking into her present life.

"So..." He trailed off.

"I was a surgeon in Los Angeles. More than an intern."

Carson smiled. "I figured that."

She laughed uneasily. "I'm not a surgeon anymore."

He stopped his cleaning. "Why?"

Because I froze during a procedure and a patient died on my table. I lost my confidence. I lost myself.

"I wanted a quiet life." Then she laughed at the absurdity of that and he joined in. "I thought Crater Lake would be quiet."

"Well, it usually is. Come to think of it, it was until you came to town."

"Thanks for that." She grinned.

He winked. "Any time."

"I hope it calms down," she said offhandedly.

"With all these new people coming to town I doubt that very much. In fact I can see a hospital being built here."

"You say that like it's a bad thing."

Carson sighed. "No, it's not a bad thing. It's just... change."

"You don't like change, do you?" Esme asked.

"No, I don't. Not really."

"Why?"

Carson didn't say anything. He didn't even look at her and she realized that she must have touched a nerve. Something he was obviously not comfortable talking about. Why didn't he like change? Something had hurt him.

It's not your business.

And it wasn't. Yet he had pushed and pressed her about being a surgeon. Maybe it was tit for tat.

"Change can be good. I mean, I changed..." She trailed off. A lot had changed in her life, but then again maybe it hadn't. She had run away from her career and when she was holding that scalpel it felt so damn good. She felt as if she was at home and for that one brief moment she regretted the fact that she'd left the hospital. That she'd left surgery.

Esme zoned out and Carson couldn't help but wonder what she was thinking. He'd known she was a surgeon, even though she'd denied it. He'd known it the moment she'd stuck that needle into that patient's chest and drained fluid.

She had a gift. Such a tremendous gift.

And he couldn't help but wonder why she would want to give that up.

What is it to you?

It really wasn't his business at all. They were just neighbors, both doctors. Heck, they weren't even friends and even if they were friends it still wouldn't be his business. So why did he care so much?

"Did the change make a difference?" he asked.

"What change?"

"Moving here from LA. You said you changed."

She shrugged. "I think it did…"

"You don't sound certain."

"I haven't been here long enough, but, as they say, a change will do you good." She continued to clean up his exam room as he mulled over her words.

A change will do you good?

He wasn't sure he believed that. Why change something that worked? It was a dangerous thing to do, to ruin one's safety net. He'd tried to once. Tried to make a change in his life and look how that had turned out.

It had left him with a shattered heart, but he'd put away all those feelings in a box. Locked them away because taking over his father's practice had been the right thing to do. It was safe and comfortable. Packing up and moving out of state. Changing professions.

Throwing away a career. One that Carson knew she would've studied long and hard for. Surgeons competed. It was a shark tank and only the fittest survived.

Why would she give that up?

It's not your concern.

Then he realized it wasn't so much that he cared, but he was angry that such a talented surgeon was throwing away her gift. She could be using that education to save lives.

You save lives.

Only not in the same way. He saved people's lives, but not in the same way that she could save lives.

It was a waste and he wanted to tell her that. Berate her. Only he couldn't. That wasn't his place, but he just didn't understand how someone could walk away from talent like that.

One day soon she'd decide that a general practice in a small town in Montana wasn't surgery. She'd close her practice, his former patients would come back and she would go back to the exciting life of a surgical practice.

Just as Danielle had left.

Surgeons wanted more. They needed more.

More than he could offer and he had to distance himself now. He could handle this.

He didn't want to handle this.

He didn't want to be her friend.

He didn't want to be... Carson couldn't even finish that thought, because that thought was dangerous and out of the question.

"Are you okay?" she asked as she tossed the rest of the drapes into the receptacle.

"Fine," he snapped and then he cursed under his breath. "Just tired."

"It's been a long day."

"It has." He couldn't even look at her. Carson just had to get away from her. "Why don't you head home for the night? Like you said, it's been a long day."

"Are you sure you don't want me to stay and help you clean up?"

"Yeah, I'm sure. Just…go."

"Okay." Esme walked out of the room. "Should I leave the scrubs in your office?"

"Yeah, that's fine." Carson could barely look at her, because if he looked at her he might start lecturing her that she was throwing away all that talent that could be used for saving lives.

She nodded. "Okay. Good night, Dr. Ralston."

Carson just nodded as she left the exam room.

He had to keep away from Esme.

If he kept away from her his heart would be safe. If he kept away from her, maybe, just maybe, she'd realize the folly of her mistake and return to surgery where she belonged.

CHAPTER SEVEN

ESME SAW CARSON across the street, walking to his clinic with a cup of coffee, from where she was outside picking up the papers off the front step of her clinic. She hadn't seen him since the night of the emergency appendectomy three weeks ago.

If she saw him, he seemed to turn in the other direction and it was clear that he was avoiding her, which shouldn't bother her, but it did and she was mad at herself that his avoidance bothered her.

This was what she wanted. She wanted to keep her distance from him. She wasn't here to make friends. She wasn't here to find love. She was here to practice medicine.

When she first came to Crater Lake all she wanted was solitude. She wanted her practice and to be alone. She didn't need anyone. She didn't want anyone. That was why she'd left Shane, right, because she didn't want to be tied down to anyone.

She didn't want to chip away pieces of herself to suit someone else. Romance and love weren't for her. She'd proven that to the universe many times. Love only brought pain. Love made her forget who she was. It changed her.

And then she laughed at that thought. Three weeks ago she was telling Carson that change could be good. Yet she was not willing to change herself.

You've done that before, remember?

That was why it was good that he was avoiding her. It was good, so why did it tick her off so much?

Probably because his change after the emergency appendectomy didn't make sense. One moment they were becoming friends. One minute his arms were on her and he was telling her that it was okay if she told him that she was a surgeon, asking her to open up, and now he'd closed her out.

She'd caught him watching her a few times during the surgery and she thought he'd looked impressed or awed. Maybe almost validated in his assessment of her.

Then when they'd been cleaning up, when she'd admitted that she was a surgeon, things had changed. Carson hadn't even been able to look her in the eye. As if he was disgusted with her, as if she was the worst person ever.

So what was his problem? He'd told her it would be okay if she divulged her secret. He'd lied to her. It clearly wasn't okay with him, but he was avoiding her now. She was tired of being ostracized. He had no right to judge her.

Doesn't he?

Esme ignored the voice in her head. Her grip around the flyers tightened and she marched across the road and blocked Carson's path to his clinic.

Carson stopped in midstep, surprised to see her standing there, and she knew by the way his eyes started darting around he was looking for a way to escape, but there was no way to escape. She had him trapped.

"Dr. Petersen," he said.

"Morning, Dr. Ralston. Long time no see."

He rubbed the back of his neck, in that way that he always seemed to do when he seemed to be uncomfortable. She usually found it sexy, but today it annoyed her.

"How can I help you today?"

You could tell me why you're being such a jerk. Only she didn't say out loud what she wanted to say.

Instead she asked, "How is the surveyor? You never updated me after the surgery. I was just wondering how he was doing."

"Mr. Tyner, the surveyor, he's fine. He spent a week in the hospital on IV antibiotics, but other than that he made it through fine. Once he recovers fully in about three more weeks he'll be back to work."

"And the others? Did Luke get them down off the mountain?"

"Yes. He did."

Esme nodded. "Thank you. I was…concerned. I figured the way you were avoiding me that perhaps he didn't make it. That you blamed me for his death, but he made it so…why are you avoiding me?"

"I'm not avoiding you, Esme. I've been busy."

"Busy."

"Yeah."

Awkward tension fell between them. He couldn't look her in the eyes. Something she was used to after she'd frozen during that surgery. Other surgeons had avoided her. They'd avoided working with her; her name had disappeared from the OR board numerous times. It was the same look on her father's face when she'd run out on Shane.

No one trusted her. She didn't trust herself either.

She was used to it, but she was getting tired of it.

Just turn around and walk away. Let him ignore you. It doesn't matter.

Only it did matter. It annoyed her. She didn't deserve this.

Don't you?

"Well, I'll let you get back to your busy day." Esme turned around to head back to her clinic, dumping the flyers into a recycling bin.

"Esme, wait up."

She glanced round to see Carson heading toward her.

Just ignore him.

Only she couldn't. Even though she kept reminding herself over and over again that she didn't need anyone. That she was here in Crater Lake to just find herself again. She was lonely. She hadn't realized how much she enjoyed Carson's company until he was no longer talking to her.

So she waited for Carson, because, even though she didn't deserve to have friendship or companionship, she was lonely and she couldn't help herself. She couldn't help herself and that made her weak.

She was so weak. Especially when it came to him.

"I'm...not ignoring you. I mean I was, but...I'm sorry," Carson said. "It got intense in there and...look, I'm not used to intense situations."

"Fair enough."

"I should've told you about Mr. Tyner's recovery earlier. For that I'm sorry." And he smiled at her, those blue eyes of his twinkling.

Esme nodded. "Yeah, you should've. I mean, I may have been a surgeon and done quite a few appendectomies in my past, but that was the first time in a long time I've performed one in that kind of situation and not known the outcome. I was worried."

"I bet you were. I'm sorry."

"Thanks for telling me. I'm sorry if I attacked you there. Especially on a Sunday morning."

"You had every right to. I should've known better, but…well, it was my first time ever. I did a few months of a surgical internship, but I never did perform an appendectomy on my own."

"You never did a solo surgery?"

Carson shrugged. "What can I say? I wasn't a surgeon. I'm not a surgeon."

"I would ask you if you were fired, but that's a bit too much information for a street conversation." They both laughed.

"Yeah, I haven't told anyone beyond my family that I was an intern."

Esme winked. "Got it. I'll leave you to your clinic." She turned to leave again, at least satisfied with the answers he'd given her. At least knowing she wasn't totally being ostracized in this town. She remembered when she'd left Shane standing at the altar on Valentine's Day when she'd played runaway bride. How most of her so-called friends had dumped her.

When the press had been hounding the hospital, when she'd been called into the board meeting in front of Dr. Eli Draven to be questioned about how she'd frozen during surgery and her resident had thrown her under the bus because that resident had wanted to take her place as Dr. Draven's new protégé.

That was when she'd noticed the pointed stares, the whispers and seeing her name disappear from the OR boards. When patients she'd been treating for months had moved to other doctors and hadn't even been able to tell her why other than it "fit their schedule better" or "they wanted a second opinion" because maybe she was a bit emotionally scarred.

It was cutthroat. All of it, and once she'd been like that and that thought made her sick.

She'd deserved that punishment. She deserved to be alone.

But then Carson had reached out to her, handing her an olive branch. Even though it was dangerous to accept it, she hadn't been able to help herself. Loneliness had made her weak.

Ever since she'd started interacting with Carson she'd done two surgical procedures in her short time in Crater Lake. Something she had promised herself she wouldn't do. Yet she had.

He brought out something in her. Something she'd thought was long gone. Something that scared her.

It didn't have to mean anything. She could be his friend, even if she did want a bit more, but that bit more was out of the question. She didn't deserve that bit more.

She didn't deserve any of it.

"Esme, wait."

She turned around again. "Dr. Ralston?"

"It's Sunday. I just have to fax off a referral and then I was planning to take a hike around Crater Lake later. Would you like to come? You seemed to enjoy the view from my place. I thought you might want to check it out firsthand."

Say no. Say no.

But another part of her said, *You can be his friend.*

And she did want to see around the area. It was Sunday, the clinic was closed and her plans for the day involved cleaning and possibly binge-watching some reality shows she'd been recording. Nothing that exciting.

Do it.

"I'd like that. What do you think, an hour?"

"Two. Wear a good pair of shoes and pants…there's ticks in the woods." He winked and grinned, before turning and heading back toward his clinic.

"Ticks?" Esme called out, but he just waved and disappeared into his clinic.

She chuckled and headed back to her own clinic. Apparently she had to find a clean pair of yoga pants and socks that went up to her waist, maybe a turtleneck, too, and she shuddered at the thought of ticks.

There were a couple of times that Carson seriously thought about calling Esme up and canceling the hike. After he wrote up and faxed in his referral, he just sat there letting it all sink in that he'd actually asked Esme to go on a hike with him today.

He hadn't planned on going on a hike today. He hadn't planned on seeing her. Yeah, he had been avoiding her, which was a hard thing to do when she lived and worked across the street from where he worked. Even though he hadn't spoken to her, he'd seen her and it had killed him just a bit not to go out and talk to her. To kiss her.

Kissing would lead to more and he wasn't sure he could give more. He was whole again and he couldn't risk his heart again.

So Carson had kept his distance.

Then he'd seen her, blocking the way to his clinic, and all those reasons for avoiding her had melted away. He'd missed her. Missed her feistiness. Missed her smile, her laugh. He hadn't realize how lonely he'd been without her around to annoy him.

The invitation for the hike had not been on the agenda at all. It just had been a spur-of-the-moment decision really. Everything was spur-of-the-moment when it came to her. He planned things. He liked the familiarity of it. Being around Esme changed all that. He didn't plan or prepare, he just did and that was far out of his comfort zone.

Why he'd chosen a hike today, he had no idea. He didn't particularly like hiking around in the woods. He liked living in the woods, he liked working with his hands and working on his house, but he didn't like traipsing around in bear country. He liked the comforts of home. His brother and he were totally opposite in that way. His brother liked living in a shanty up the mountain and using an outhouse. Carson liked plumbing.

Live a little.

Instead of canceling on her, he pulled his hiking gear out of his office closet and got changed. If only Luke could see him now.

Luke would probably laugh over the predicament he'd got himself into.

And as he stood out in front of her clinic, waiting for her to come down, he was really fighting the urge to turn around and head back to his office, call her up and cancel.

Avoiding her was better for him. Inviting her to join him in the woods was not avoiding her. It was the complete opposite. And that was dangerous.

If he didn't see her, he wouldn't be tempted by her,

but he was made of stronger stuff than that. He could be her friend. Couldn't he?

Carson could be around her, he just had to keep his distance when he was in her presence. He had to resist the urge to touch her or get too close and be caught up in the scent of her hair, her skin and he definitely had to fight the urge to reach out and kiss her.

Turn around. Just turn around and run. Don't go on a hike with her. Don't be alone in the woods with her.

He shook his head and stood his ground. He had to do this. He was the one who had invited her and he wanted to be on good terms with the only other doctor with a clinic in town. He wanted to be on good terms with the competition, even if he wasn't really even thinking of her as competition at the moment.

Esme walked out of her clinic, locking the door behind her. She'd changed and was wearing what looked like yoga attire.

"I'm ready. I think." She spun around, waiting for his approval on her outfit. At least that was what he assumed she was doing. He tried not to stare at her. It looked okay.

Actually it looked better than okay. She looked damn good.

Carson looked her up and down. The yoga pants and jacket hugged her curves and made his blood heat.

She looked so good.

Think about something else. Don't think about how tight her clothes are. Don't think about pulling her into your arms and squeezing her butt.

He was doomed.

"Well? What do you think? Is it okay for the hike today? You kind of freaked me out about the ticks."

"Well, it's an interesting choice for a hike in the mountains."

"Yoga is all I had. Sorry, I'm not really outfitted for mountain living." Esme's eyes sparkled.

"Not kitted for mountain living? Aren't there mountains in California? Isn't Mammoth Mountain in California?"

"Yes, it is, but I've never been to it."

"Doesn't Hollywood have hills as in Beverly Hills?" He winked at her.

"You're teasing me now, Carson. Los Angeles mountains hardly compare with Montana mountains. Besides, there's more comfortable amenities in Beverly Hills."

"You're right on that," he said. "Okay, I'm sure it's fine. To be honest, I really am not the mountain man I make myself out to be."

"What? Don't you live up in that cabin in the woods? I thought you were a regular Davy Crockett. King-of-the-wild-frontier type of guy."

Carson chuckled as he headed toward his SUV. "That would be Luke."

"So you're more refined?" she asked, falling into step behind him.

"Most certainly. He's a Neanderthal."

Esme laughed. "Here I thought you two had a loving relationship."

"We do most definitely, but like all brothers we have our differences, as well. I still haven't forgiven him for scaring me numerous times when we were playing in the woods. To tell you the truth Luke was a bit of a butt head when we were growing up."

Esme laughed again and he held open the door, closing it once she'd climbed up into the SUV. When he slid into the driver's side she was still laughing.

"It must've been nice growing up with a brother," she said wistfully, but there was a touch of sadness to her voice.

"I take it you don't have any siblings?"

"I did, but he died." There was hesitation.

"I'm sorry," he said.

She shrugged. "It was a long time ago. I was raised by my father and stepmother."

"What happened to your mother?" Carson asked.

Her smile disappeared. In the short time he'd known her he'd discovered when she didn't want to talk about something she clammed up and avoided the topic.

So he was bracing himself for the fact she was going to go silent again.

Instead she sighed. "My mom left me and my dad when I was little. It's no big deal—she just didn't want to be a wife and mother."

"I'm sorry." Carson couldn't imagine not having his mom around. He'd had a good childhood, a stable childhood. His dad had worked late a lot of the time, but it had never been detrimental to him or his brother.

His father had still been there taking them fishing and camping.

He'd been there to play baseball with them and teach them how to build things.

Carson's dad was dedicated and had had a sense of pride in his work. He was a good father.

As a child he'd felt safe, secure.

"There's nothing to be sorry about. I saw my mother from time to time when she came through town. My father remarried and I had an awesome stepmother. So don't feel sorry for me. I had a great childhood." Only the hint of sadness remained as she stared out the window, as if she had gone far away.

"Sorry. Are you okay?"

Esme smiled. "I'm okay. When I say my mom left me I know the look it gets. I see the sad, forlorn look thinking that I had this horrible childhood and that's why I became a cold-hearted surgeon."

"Well, isn't that the reason?"

They both laughed at that. Then silence fell between them as they headed out of town. Only it wasn't an awkward silence. It was companionable. It was nice. As he glanced over a few times to look at her, she was looking out the window with a smile on her face as she took in the scenery around her. She was seeing it through new eyes and he envied her, but he also enjoyed it.

The look of wonder at the place where he grew up.

He never got over its sense of beauty and majesty.

Yeah, he liked the modern conveniences like plumbing, but he was glad he wasn't living in a city surrounded by concrete and fumes.

He turned into the gravel parking lot that was at the head of about three different hikes that you could take around Crater Lake. Carson parked the car. There was only one other car in the lot and he recognized it as Mrs. Murphy's. She was a seventy-year-old voracious hiker and dog walker. Her St. Bernard, Tiny, was a slobber hound and he really hoped they didn't run into them.

"Wow, three paths to choose from!" Esme slung her knapsack over her shoulder.

"I think we'll stick with the easiest one for your first time out."

"Are you afraid I can't handle the challenge?" she teased.

"No. See that truck there?" he said, pointing toward Mrs. Murphy's orange truck.

"Yeah, what of it?"

"That's Mrs. Murphy's truck."

"So?" Esme was looking at him as if he were a crazy person.

"She has a very large dog that is overly friendly and overly smelly."

Esme laughed. "Are you serious?"

"Very."

Her eyes widened. "Okay then, we'll take the path you suggested."

Carson chuckled. "Good choice."

"Lead the way, Macduff."

"Mac…what?"

"Something my father always used to say. Some Shakespeare thing."

"Is your dad an English major?"

"No. Not at all. He just really likes Shakespeare."

"I think the actual quote is, 'Lay on, Macduff, and damned be him who first cries, "Hold, enough!"'"

Esme looked impressed. "Now who's the English major?"

Carson nodded. "I liked English. I also like Shakespeare."

They started walking up the gravel path to the easiest hiking trail. One that wrapped around the lake and took the path of least resistance. It was littered with lots of benches and scenic lookouts. Lots of opportunities to stop for a picnic and take in the glorious sight of Crater Lake.

Not that many people knew about it. Crater Lake barely made a Montana map. Of course that was all going to change with this grand hotel and spa, set to open Valentine's Day.

Soon Mrs. Murphy's dog Tiny was going to have a lot more people to slobber on and it concerned him about the fragility of the ecosystem around here.

Now I sound like Luke.

They didn't really talk too much as they took the first half a mile together. There wasn't really a need to talk. It was just nice.

When they came to the first scenic lookout Esme stopped and took in the sight.

"Wow, it's much bluer up close."

"The sun is overhead." Carson set down his rucksack on a bench to stretch his back.

"How long is the trail?"

"Two miles."

Esme nodded. "It's beautiful and peaceful here. Though I suspect that won't be for too much longer."

"Very true." He pointed to the far ridge, which you could see from this vantage point. "See that clear cut up there where all the dust from the road is kicking up? That's where they're going to build his hotel and spa."

Esme looked worried.

"Is something wrong?" he asked in concern.

"No, why?"

"You looked like you were going to be sick there for a moment."

"No, I'm fine. Not sick." Then she sighed. "It's just such a waste. Such a waste of trees and beauty. I guess it's a good thing we're out here enjoying the quiet solitude of this place before the parking lot is jam-packed with city folks and more dogs like Mrs. Murphy's."

"Yeah, but it's good for the town. It'll be good for our practice. Well, that's until Silas Draven brings in his own doctor for his hotel."

"He's bringing in a new doctor?"

"Yeah. A private doctor to deal with his clientele. I heard that the timeshare community that's already up and running will be bringing in their own on-staff doctor, too, but then again that's just a rumor."

Esme crossed her arms and looked a bit shaken. "I hope it's a rumor."

"Me, too."

"You just said Mr. Draven's venture would be good for the town. I thought you rebuffed change."

"Certain changes I do, but I'm realizing the benefits."

"You don't sound too convinced."

"It'll be good."

Change had brought Esme here. Maybe, just maybe, change wasn't all that bad. Carson picked up his rucksack; he needed to start moving again. If he kept thinking this way he'd kiss her. "Let's keep going," he suggested.

The sun was shining, it was warm and it was Sunday. He was going to make the most of his day off. "You ready to make it to the other side of the lake?"

She nodded. "Let's go. I'll lead the way, try to keep up."

Carson laughed under his breath. She was teasing him and he liked it. There were so many things he liked about her.

He liked the fact that even though she had lost her

mother, she didn't resent it. She didn't use it as an emotional crutch and she didn't seem dark and twisted inside. He liked her willingness to try new things. She was bright and shiny, but there was still something beneath the surface she was hiding.

Something she didn't want to share with him.

Something he shouldn't care about knowing because she wasn't his, but the more he got to know her, the more he did care.

The more he wanted to know.

CHAPTER EIGHT

"FAVORITE HOLIDAY?"

Esme rolled her eyes, but smiled. She didn't mind the fifty questions game at this moment because she was stretched out on the grass listening to the gentle waves lap against the shore of Crater Lake. She was staring up at the blue, blue sky and white-capped mountains. Only a few puffs of white clouds dragging over the peaks.

It was like a slice of heaven. Sitting here she felt small and unseen. Hidden. It was exactly what she wanted.

Do you?

Avery would've loved this place. He always dreamed of the west. Montana, Wyoming, South Dakota. Avery had wanted to be a bush pilot and work in remote areas. It was why she'd chosen Crater Lake. It would've been just the place Avery would've chosen.

A hand waved in front of her face and she glanced over at Carson, who was lying beside her in the grass.

"Hey, you agreed to fifty questions. Actually, you were the one who suggested it. Especially in light of the fact you want us to be friends."

"Sorry." She rolled over. "So what was the question?"

"Favorite holiday?"

"Independence Day."

Carson cocked an eyebrow. "July the Fourth?"

"What's wrong with that? I love fireworks, barbecues, summer. Oh, and red, white and blue."

"Most people like Christmas and most ladies like Valentine's Day."

Esme's stomach knotted when he brought up Valentine's Day. She'd used to like February fourteenth. She liked the hearts, the chocolates and the cupids. Even though she wasn't a romance girl at heart, she liked the campy fun of Valentine's. Only Avery had died on Valentine's Day. His heart had stopped right under her hands. She'd avoided the day for as long as she could until she'd met Shane.

Shane loved Valentine's Day.

It was why she'd agreed to the wedding on that day. She'd foolishly hoped she could replace a sad memory with a happy one. That was until she'd realized she didn't want to be Shane Draven's wife. They were too different. They were from different worlds.

So then Valentine's Day had become jilting day. A day of guilt.

A day she'd broken a man's heart.

So no, she didn't like Valentine's Day.

"I don't like Valentine's Day."

"Why? Most women do. I mean, such pressure for us guys."

"Well, I don't. I don't care for it."

Esme wanted to tell him how much she hated it. How she now hated the pressure, the hearts, the flowers and the romance. How it reminded her of pain and loss, only she couldn't.

She hated Valentine's Day, but she wasn't going to tell Carson why.

No one needed to know her secret shame. No one needed to know about the ghosts of her past.

"Isn't it my turn to ask a question?" Esme asked, changing the subject.

"Right."

"Your favorite holiday."

"Such an unoriginal question," he teased.

Esme chuckled. "Shut up and answer it. What's your favorite holiday?"

Carson grinned. A devious smile. "Valentine's Day."

She sat up and punched him in the arm. "It is not!"

"It is. I swear it is."

"I don't believe you."

"Okay, fine. It isn't. I'm not a romantic. I like Thanksgiving the best. All that turkey. Does that make you happy?" Carson asked.

"Yes," she said. "As a matter of fact it does."

He snorted. "This is a dumb game."

"One question in and you're ready to give up? Pathetic."

They both laughed at that. It was easy to laugh with him. She couldn't remember the last time she'd laughed like this. Shane wasn't much of a joker. He definitely didn't do PDA in public. Shane owned a successful company. He was a public figure and public figures couldn't show much affection out in the open. When they would go out, they'd always have to dress up to the nines. She would've never spent a day with him like this, playing fifty questions in her yoga clothes. Any displays of affection had been done in the privacy of her apartment or his, because he hadn't wanted the press snapping pictures.

At the time she'd got that and respected it.

She'd understood his position, that he had an appearance to keep up. There was a facade he had when he was out in public. Shane would barely touch her.

Every step they'd taken there had been press there. Photographers, paparazzi. Shane Draven was a rich, handsome, powerful man. And he needed a woman by his side. But she wasn't that woman. She didn't want to be that woman and that was why she didn't marry him.

Esme sighed and lay back down in the grass, tucking her arms behind her head and crossing her ankles to watch the water. The mirror, blue water.

"You're pretty relaxed," Carson remarked.

"I am. Is that okay?"

"Yeah, it's nice. Since I've known you, you've been on edge. Skulking in the shadows of the town trying to stay unnoticed."

"Apparently me keeping a low profile hasn't been working very effectively, then."

"No. It hasn't." His eyes twinkled. "I see you, Esme. I see you."

Their gazes locked and her heart began to beat a bit faster as he smiled at her. A smile that sent a zing of anticipation through her and she fought the urge to kiss him.

She'd thought about it before, in passing, but she'd never had the urge to just reach over and kiss him passionately. And that was what she wanted to do right now.

Desperately.

She looked away and cleared her throat. "Maybe we should head back."

"Right. You're right." Carson stood and held out his hand. "Milady."

Esme snorted and took his hand as he helped her up. As soon as she was back on her feet she let go of his hand, so she wouldn't be tempted to hold it. To pull his body closer, to let him kiss her.

That was not what friends did.

And they were just friends.

Right?

For one moment he thought Esme was going to kiss him. And for one moment he thought he was going to reach out and kiss her himself. It was hard to not reach out and touch her, to press her against the grass and capture her lips with his own, tasting her sweetness.

And he had no doubt she tasted so, so sweet.

Don't think about it.

So he didn't try. Instead he helped her up and then they continued on their hike around Crater Lake. Not that he minded the hike; it was just his mind and body wanted to take part in other activities. Activities he hadn't thought about in a long time.

Don't think about it.

"How are you enjoying the lake?"

"It's beautiful. So how did Crater Lake get its name? I would assume maybe a meteor long ago?" Esme asked.

"Well, that's one of the theories. Though no one knows for sure. They can't find a bottom at the center of the lake."

"For real?" She sounded intrigued.

Carson nodded. "They've tried and it seems almost bottomless. A local tribe, long ago, felt the lake was the gateway to another world. Of course I believe under the lake is a dormant volcano. This whole time just waiting to erupt. There are a few volcanoes slumbering in these mountains on the west coast."

"Volcanoes? I thought earthquakes in California were bad enough."

"I've never been through an earthquake." And Carson planned to keep it that way if he could help it.

"Well, I've never been through a volcanic eruption."

"Neither have I, but we have evacuation plans in town. I mean, after Mount Saint Helen's went, most towns near dormant volcanoes implemented some sort of evacuation plan."

Esme looked toward the lake. "Can you swim in the lake?"

"You can, but it's only June. It would be cold."

"Oh, that's too bad. It would be amazing to swim in. A picture-perfect lake with mountains surrounding it… it would be amazing."

"Luke told me once a monster lived in there. In the deep part in the center."

She smiled up at him. "It sounds like you and your brother had some good times."

"Yeah. We did. He was always the headstrong one. It was his way or no way."

Luke hadn't wanted the family practice. He'd wanted to be an army medic. So, his parents had let him enlist after he'd completed his residency in surgery, while Carson had taken up the family practice, not even completing his first year as an intern, to keep the legacy alive.

When Luke had been discharged after two tours of duty he was supposed to join Carson so their father could retire early. Only Luke had wanted to live up on the mountains. So their father had put off his retirement.

Carson had taken up the slack so their father would feel confident enough to leave. So that he could retire early. He worked so many long hours, nights of charting and researching. House visits and hospital visits, too, when his patients were in there.

The only life he'd known was work. He wasn't even sure what he really wanted, except he wanted to stay in Crater Lake. That much he was certain of. He wanted to live here.

It was safe.

He knew what to expect. Day in and day out it had been the same thing, that was until Esme had walked into town.

She'd shaken things up.

Now he wasn't sure how he felt. He wasn't sure of anything.

And he found he wanted a bit more.

Of what, he didn't know, but he wanted something else and it scared him.

While he was contemplating this there was a rumble in the distance. The earth shuddered beneath his feet. Just minor, though.

"Earthquake?" he wondered out loud.

"No. Doesn't feel like one. I *hope* it's not your volcano."

"Doubt that, too." Then his cell rang. He pulled it out of his pocket and recognized Luke's number immediately.

"Luke, what's up?"

"Where are you?" Luke asked. It sounded as if he was far away and out of breath.

"Hiking around Crater Lake with Dr. Petersen. Did you feel the rumble?"

"Yeah. I was right at the epicenter."

"Epicenter?" Carson asked.

"Landslide up on the mountain near the build site of Draven's hotel."

Carson felt the bottom of his stomach drop to the soles of his feet. "Landslide? Is anyone hurt?"

"Yeah. Lots of people. Some are missing. Can you and Dr. Petersen gather as many medical supplies as you can from your clinics? And can you contact as many local search-and-rescue teams from nearby towns? Other doctors. I'm trying to contact as many people up here as I can…"

"No, don't worry. I'll handle it. Preserve your cell phone battery."

"Thanks. See you soon."

Carson hung up his phone and cursed under his breath.

"What is it? What's wrong?" Esme asked.

"Landslide. We have to get back to town, gather supplies. There's a lot injured, a lot missing. We have to help."

Esme nodded. "Okay. Let's go."

Carson glanced at her. "Thanks."

"For what?" Esme asked, falling into step beside him as they all but jogged the last half mile to the parking lot.

"For jumping into the fray. I swear, it's not usually like this in Crater Lake."

"No, it's okay. Of course I'll help. Why wouldn't I?"

Why wouldn't you, indeed?

Esme had given up an extraordinary skill. She had given up an amazing talent, walked away from the hospital setting. It was something he didn't quite understand, but right now he didn't care too much about that. About her reason for running away, because she was here now.

She was here and she was willing to help and that was all that mattered.

They didn't say much on the way back to town. There wasn't much to say. Carson was trying to keep his eyes on the road and trying to think about all the supplies that he had in his clinic. What he could pack and how he could get it up to the landslide site.

When he glanced over at Esme he could see her muttering to herself and heard the word *syringes*, so he knew she was doing the exact same thing he was.

Carson parked the car in front of his clinic.

"I'll grab what I can and meet you back here in ten minutes?" she asked.

Carson nodded. "Ten. Yeah."

Esme dashed across the road. Other people were rushing around, gathering supplies, needing to go up to the accident site. Carson glanced to the south and saw dust rising from the distance and he saw smoke. He couldn't even imagine what was going on up there.

And he didn't have time to think about it.

Not right now.

Right now he had a job to do.

People's lives were at stake.

CHAPTER NINE

"HOLY..." THE CURSE word she was thinking of at the time died on her lips before it could even form. She'd been through a couple of larger earthquakes living in California, but they hadn't been anything compared to this, she thought as she stepped out of Carson's SUV.

There was dust still rising. A brown dusty cloud against the brilliant blue sky. They were still far from the accident site, but she could see the landslide from the base-camp point.

Tarps were going up as makeshift shelters and then she saw that people were being brought in. People who looked hurt, injured, broken, and it was evident to her that it was a triage area.

That was when every bit of fear she'd been feeling about this situation melted away and the surgeon in her took over. She couldn't let people suffer. She had to help.

Carson was already running toward the triage area, toward his brother, who was directing people and assessing the injured, but he was clearly overwhelmed by the sheer volume. Esme followed Carson to the first makeshift shelter. More and more paramedics and first responders were arriving, but clearly they needed help.

Luke barely glanced at them.

"Thank God you two are here." Luke scrubbed a hand over his face. "It's bad. Really bad."

"Where do you want me?" Esme asked.

"Over there, help Carson on that group of injured. I have to head back to the site and try to get out as many people as I can." Luke jammed a bunch of colored toe tags into her hand. "Tag the emergency patients with green for go. The helicopters and ambulances will take the greens to the nearest hospital in Missoula."

"Don't worry," Esme said. "Go. We got this."

Esme headed over to Carson. He was examining a head wound on a man. He was encouraging the man, telling him that it was going to be okay. He had so much empathy and compassion. An excellent bedside manner. The compassion he showed was the sign of a good doctor.

Carson was an excellent doctor. He was gentle, good and he was devoted to helping people. Just as she was devoted to medicine.

She moved to the next patient. A woman who was lying on her side, moaning.

"Ma'am, can you tell me where it hurts?" Esme bent down and the woman rolled over. Her breath caught in her throat when she saw who the woman was.

She might have run out on Shane Draven on Valentine's Day last year, but that didn't mean he'd stayed heartbroken for very long.

Six months later she'd seen in the paper that he'd married a woman from a wealthy family. A member of the Manhattan glitterati. A bit of an "it" girl.

And that was who was lying on this tarp now, moaning in pain with scratches on her face. Manuela Draven.

Esme couldn't help but scan the immediate area for Shane, because that was definitely the last person she wanted to see. Manuela Draven didn't know her from a hole in the ground. She was a self-centered person, full of herself.

Perfect for the Draven family. She looked good on Shane's arm, but Esme seriously doubted that Manuela was a good fit for Shane. Shane might have resented her time spent in surgery, they might have come from different worlds, but he was compassionate. Kind.

He's not your concern. Assess Manuela's ABCs and move on.

"My stomach hurts," the woman moaned, not looking at her. "Do something."

"Hold on, ma'am." Esme rolled Manuela onto her back and lifted her shirt. There was visible bruising on her left side.

Crap.

Bruising that fast could be an internal bleed. Esme began to palpate the abdomen and it was rigid.

Dammit.

"Ow, you're hurting me," Manuela whimpered.

"I'm sorry, but I think you have internal bleeding. We have to get you to the hospital as soon as possible." Esme grabbed the green tag, marking Manuela as priority. Where the bruising was forming, and the fact it was happening so fast, indicated that the spleen was probably involved. She would most likely need surgery.

Esme might have been able to pull off an emergency appendectomy in the clinic, but there was no way she would be able to remove this woman's spleen if needed. Not up here. Especially not since this was Shane's wife.

She didn't want to be the surgeon responsible for operating on Shane's wife.

So, Manuela had to get down off the mountain, but it made Esme wonder if Shane was here in Crater Lake—did they have one of those timeshare villas? Was she now going to run into Shane regularly?

Dammit.

It was hard to breathe and her head pounded as if a migraine was forming. That was the last thing she needed in the middle of a medical emergency.

Why Crater Lake? Why did it have to be the one place she'd settled? Couldn't she shake off the ghosts of her past?

"What're you doing?" Manuela whined.

"You're going to the hospital." Esme waved to the paramedics who had just landed helicopters at the base camp.

Manuela opened her eyes and stared at her. Hard, and there was a faint glimmer of recognition. Esme turned away quickly and rattled off instructions to the paramedics, letting them take Manuela away so that she could get the proper help she needed.

Esme kept her back to Manuela while they transferred her to the stretcher to load her onto the helicopter. There had been that faint recognition in Manuela's eyes, which scared Esme to her core, and she couldn't let Manuela recognize her.

That was why she'd come here. So no one would recognize her.

Not even herself. She didn't recognize herself anymore.

She was angry at herself, but really what could she

expect? She had to live with herself. She'd made her bed and she had to lie in it.

Esme glanced back once to see them load Manuela on the helicopter, ready to take her to the hospital as another helicopter flew over a ridge toward the base camp. Her head hurt and her stomach was doing back-flips, as if she was going to be sick. Who was she? She didn't know. Not anymore.

Focus. You have a job to do.

She watched Carson, who was bent over patients, tri-aging them with expert care. He didn't have anything to worry about. No one would ruin his career and question his medical decisions. Esme envied him.

No one questioned him. No one would question him about his right to be here. She wanted that. She wanted to love medicine again. She wanted to feel passion about her work again. Only, she'd never have that. And she had to live with that for the rest of her life.

He glanced over his shoulder. "Dr. Petersen, can you come assist me here?"

"Sure." Esme rolled her shoulders and tried to ig-nore that panicky voice in her head and the oncoming headache. Right now she didn't have time for self-doubt. Right now she had to be a doctor. Esme knelt beside Carson.

"What do you need?"

"Could you look at the woman next to this man while I suture up his scalp wound?" Carson leaned over and whispered, "I think she has a concussion. She was fine when I first triaged her."

"Of course."

"Are you okay?" Carson asked. "You're pale and squinting."

"Fine," Esme said.

She moved over to the next patient. Examining her pupillary reaction and then examining her head and asking the woman questions, which she could not really answer clearly. It appeared to be a concussion, by the woman's confusion and the complaints of nausea. Esme pulled out a green tag and assured the woman she was going to get help as soon as possible.

She then moved on to the next patient and did another assessment.

It continued like that for the next thirty minutes as more injured people came into the tent. As more people came down off the mountain.

When the people stopped coming in, Esme counted up how many people she had seen and fifteen seemed like a lot for such a remote area. She stretched her back and made a round over her patients who were yellow. Patients who weren't seriously injured, patients who could wait.

All of her green patients had gone.

Including Manuela.

Which was a relief. Now she was exhausted. She was bone tired and it was hard to breathe.

Carson ducked back under the shelter, having assisted the last medevac with the last green patient out of base camp. He headed over to her.

"How many did you see?" he asked.

"Fifteen. Five of them were green. I've seen trauma, but I've never triaged in this kind of situation before."

Carson nodded. "We've had landslides up here before, but nothing like this."

"Any word from your brother?" Esme asked.

Carson shook his head. "He'll come back once he knows that everyone is accounted for."

"Do you know how many people were around the site?"

"No. Why?"

Esme shrugged. "Just curious."

She thought of Manuela Draven and found it really hard to believe that she would be up here without Shane. She was actually surprised that she was here. She didn't think the Dravens of Los Angeles would have anything to do with Silas Draven the developer.

Carson's cell went off. "Hello? What do you need? I'll be right there."

"What's wrong?"

"It's Luke. He found a man trapped under some rock. We need to take a team up there and try and extract him."

"Do you need me to come?" Esme asked.

"Yeah, if you don't mind. We have first responders here now to deal with the patients who are injured, but this man sounds like he's in a bad way. Luke will need all the hands he can get."

"Of course." Esme began to gather supplies to refresh the bag she had filled down in town. Once she had the equipment Carson took her hand and led her away from base camp and along the trail, up around the side of a cliff. It was a ten-minute hike and during that Carson was extra vigilant and withdrawn.

Esme couldn't help but keep her eyes trained on the mountain above her, watching and waiting to see if more rocks and mud would come raining down on them. It was tiring. One thing she had learned when she had been triaging a surveyor who was used to working in mountainous regions was that landslide sites were always dangerous, even after the landslide had happened. There was a high percentage risk of it occurring again if some of the debris had been caught up by trees or larger boulders.

There was still a chance that another landslide could happen and it terrified Esme beyond reason. She'd thought earthquakes were bad, but then mudslides and landslides had happened in California before.

As did wildfires.

She'd lived in California longer than Crater Lake and already she was seeing a lot of natural disasters. All she wanted was a quiet life.

When they rounded the corner, Esme whispered a curse under her breath when she saw the devastation the landslide had caused. She could see part of the new hotel and spa was being built and it had been so close to being destroyed.

Trees up the mountainside were snapped in half or simply gone. All she could see was rubble. And then she caught sight of Luke, kneeling near the edge of the path of destruction. He didn't call out to them. Any loud sounds could start another slide.

Carson and Esme quickly headed over.

"He's in bad shape and I didn't have enough of the proper supplies to help him." Luke moved out of the way. "Carson, we have to get him out of here. He has blunt force trauma to the chest and God knows how many other fractures or crush injuries. I hope you brought a chest tube kit, Dr. Petersen."

"I did." Esme knelt down beside Luke and then glanced at the patient. "Can you tell me...?" She couldn't even form coherent words as she stared down at the half-unconscious man buried under the rock.

At least she now had her answer as to Manuela's presence.

His face was bloodied, but she would recognize him anywhere. You couldn't forget the man you left standing at the altar. A man she'd thought she'd once loved.

Shane Draven was her patient.

Carson stepped beside Luke and started to help his brother try and remove some of the smaller rocks off the injured man. They could start small until Esme had him more stabilized, then they could move the larger rocks. Moving the larger rocks would mean that they would have to be ready to get him off the mountain, because if this man had crush injuries he was going to bleed out right here.

That much Carson knew.

He glanced over at Esme, who was staring in disbelief and horror at the man's face. As if she couldn't believe this man was in this kind of situation. Then she shook her head and started pulling out supplies.

It was odd for her, because they had been in multiple different emergency situations and she didn't seem to get this distracted when it came to patients. He'd noticed her withdraw earlier, when they'd first arrived at base camp. When she'd been getting her first green patient onto the helicopter. Esme had barely been able to make eye contact with the woman. She'd looked visibly ill.

He couldn't help but wonder what was going on with her.

"Luke, please tell me a medevac has been ordered here," Esme said in a barely audible whisper.

"No. The sound and blades of the chopper could cause another landslide. We need to get him stabilized and on a stretcher. Then we can get him away from the slide zone. Once we're around that bend, then we're home free."

"That's nothing more than a trail. There's no place for a helicopter to land," she said.

"The helicopter won't land," Carson said. "We'll have to hook him up to a hoist and fly him out off the trail."

"He could bleed out." Esme glanced back down at the patient, her face getting paler. "We can't let him die."

"I don't have any intention of letting him die, Esme," Carson said.

"My team is coming with a gurney. We'll have as many men carrying him out of here and to a safe, clear spot a helicopter can send down a hoist. Right now, you have to triage him," Luke snapped.

Esme nodded and pulled out her stethoscope, quickly going over the ABCs. Airway, breathing, consciousness. Carson watched her bend and listen to the man's chest. Or what she could get of his chest.

"There's muffled sounds in his chest. I suspect a definite crush injury. I'm going to have to insert a chest tube. Just like you said, Dr. Ralston."

Luke nodded. "Let us know when you get it in and it starts draining, then we'll start lifting these larger rocks to get him free."

"Was he conscious when you found him, Luke?" Carson asked. "Do you know who he is?"

Luke snorted. "Everyone knows who he is. He's Shane Draven. One of the richest bachelors on the West Coast."

"He's not a bachelor anymore," Esme remarked as she set up the instruments she needed to insert a chest tube.

Carson wondered why she sounded a touch bitter about it and he wasn't even sure that it was a bitter tone. It was just odd the way she said it.

It's nothing.

"I'm about to insert the chest tube. If he regains consciousness he's going to scream and scream loudly."

"I'll take care of it." Carson moved to sit by the man's head. Ready to hold him down, cover his mouth so that his screams wouldn't dislodge debris, so that they wouldn't all be buried under a metric ton of rock.

Esme worked fast and as she inserted the tube Shane Draven's eyes flew open and he screamed. In agony.

"Hold him!" Esme shouted. "He may be buried under the rocks, but half his chest is free and if he moves I'm liable to puncture a lung and kill him."

Carson lay across the man's body as Esme made one last twist and the tube was in place in the intercostal space. She taped it down so it wouldn't jar. The man was still screaming, but not as loud as Carson held him.

The moment the chest tube was in, bright red blood drained from his chest.

"We have to get him out of here now." Esme jumped up and began to help Luke and Carson as they pulled debris and rocks off the man.

"Oh, God, what the hell happened?" Shane screamed.

"You were in a landslide, sir. You're going to be okay," Carson said, trying to reassure him.

The man stared up at him and then past him, to Esme. His eyes widened for a moment, as if he recognized her, but it was only for a moment until his eyes rolled back into his head and he was unconscious again.

"God." Esme moved past Carson and checked his pupillary responses. "We have to get him down off the mountains and fast. He'll die."

"Last rock," Carson said, tossing it.

The first-responder team came around the bend with the stretcher and in the distance Carson could hear the whirring chopper blades as the medevac made its way to the rendezvous point. They worked together quickly, getting Shane Draven onto the stretcher, covering him and strapping him down.

Luke and his team ran with the patient down the path toward the helicopter. Carson and Esme followed them. Carson could see the thick cable drop down from the chopper as they hooked the stretcher up and secured him.

It wasn't too long until Shane Draven was secure and hoisted up; Luke had harnessed himself in to ride with Shane off the mountain. Carson watched them as they left. He turned back to Esme.

"We have to get away from this site. It's dangerous."

Esme nodded. She looked a bit green, but it only lasted for a moment before she ducked behind a bush and was sick.

"Esme?" Carson tried to touch her, but she slapped his hand away.

"Don't look at me," she whimpered.

He looked away for a few moments, until she finished being sick. When it was over she was leaning against a tree. Her breath shallow, as if she was working hard to breathe. She started retching again.

"Are you okay?" he asked again. He was worried the

trauma was too much for her, but then again she was a surgeon. A full-blooded surgeon. She shouldn't shy away from situations like this.

Esme nodded weakly. "Just get me off this damn mountain."

CHAPTER TEN

CARSON WAS WORRIED about Esme. She hadn't said much since he'd got her back to the triage area, where she was able to get some water into her and rest for a moment. He was wondering if she had a touch of heatstroke, or too much exposure from the sun. They had been working outside for a while and running on adrenaline. She'd been a trooper through it all, but they'd started working after a two-mile hike. They both had been out of breath sprinting that last half a mile before going up the mountain.

What if it was mountain sickness?

With Esme being from Los Angeles, he knew that she wouldn't be used to the higher altitude and, working as they had been on injured people, that could be the reason why she was ill. He didn't know if she'd been this far up the mountain before. They were higher up than his place or the mill.

After he'd got her settled another shallow quake rocked the ground and they heard a pop as more debris was carried down the side. She gripped his arm and buried her face in his chest as the second landslide hit. Carson held her close to him. Soothing her, and it felt so good.

So right.

When the shaking ended he reluctantly let her go and went to see if anyone else was injured.

At least this time no one was in the path, but it was clear to them they had to get down off the mountain, even if they were relatively safe on the lee side.

Only they couldn't leave. Not until all the injured were taken down first.

Esme refused to lie down, but at least he had her sitting down, picking at the label of an empty water bottle as the last of the injured was taken down the mountain in an ambulance. Carson headed over to her.

"Here." He held out another bottle of water.

"No, thanks. I just finished one."

Carson took the empty bottle from her. "You need to drink a lot of water. I think you have altitude sickness."

Esme sighed and took the water from him. "I don't have altitude sickness. I'm just tired and have a headache."

"Something is up with you. You were sick after we got Mr. Draven off the mountain."

Her eyes widened for a moment at the mention of Mr. Draven's name, but then she shrugged and looked away quickly. "You know what? You're right—it's altitude sickness."

Only Carson didn't really believe it was only altitude sickness suddenly. She was hiding something again.

It's not your concern. How can you trust her when she clearly hides the truth from you? You're just going to get hurt again.

The sting of Danielle's departure hurt, but somehow the idea of Esme hurting him made him ill, because if she broke his heart like Danielle he'd never recover and that scared him.

Only he couldn't walk away, because he cared about her.

She was going to be his downfall.

He sat down beside her and began to pull instruments out of his rucksack.

"What're you doing?" Esme asked.

"I'm going to examine you. You could have heat-stroke or heat exhaustion. I want to make sure you're okay. You know that acute mountain sickness can be serious and if it's that we need to get you down off this mountain."

Esme sighed. "Fine. Do your exam, but I'm perfectly okay."

"Right. A seasoned trauma surgeon throws up after inserting a chest tube." Carson snorted and then peeled off his fleece sweater, wrapping it around her shoulders to keep her warm.

Esme pulled his sweater tighter around her. Even though it was hot out and it was summer, being up on the mountain was a lot colder than being down in town and if she was suffering from acute mountain sickness she could get hypothermia quite quickly. That was something Carson didn't want for her.

Not after all the work she'd been doing.

Three traumatic events since she'd pretty much set foot in Crater Lake and each time she'd thrown herself into the fray without hesitation. He admired that about her. Danielle wasn't the kind of doctor who jumped into the fray.

Danielle wasn't a trauma surgeon. She was a neurosurgeon and, last he'd heard, was working on a big research project somewhere in the South.

The woman who didn't want to stay in Crater Lake because she wanted to be a surgeon was now working on a research project somewhere. Danielle wouldn't have gone up to the mill to save Jenkins's life. She wouldn't have operated on that surveyor and she would've come up the mountain, but only grudgingly.

Luke detested Danielle. That should've been a big clue to him. Only he'd been blinded by what he'd thought was love. He wanted a family. When his father had taken over the family practice from Carson's grandfather, he had brought Carson's mother to Crater Lake and they had started a family soon after.

Carson was following in his father's footsteps. Or maybe he tried, but didn't realize that he didn't have to follow the same footsteps as his father.

"You know, you're wrong," Esme said, shaking him from his thoughts.

"About what?" Carson asked as he pulled out his stethoscope.

"You keep calling me a trauma surgeon."

"I assumed you were. You said you were a surgeon."

"I am… I mean I was, but your first instinct was right. I was a cardio-thoracic surgeon."

Carson was stunned. "Why did you feel the need to hide that from me?"

Esme shrugged. "I honestly don't know anymore. Like the specialty of surgery I practiced makes a difference."

Carson chuckled. "I knew it was more than trauma the way you worked at the mill. Now take a deep breath."

He placed the stethoscope on her chest and then realized what he was doing, how close he was to her and that his hand was basically on her chest. He could hear her heart beating fast. She took a deep breath, inhaling and exhaling for him.

"Good." He packed his stethoscope away and tried not to think about touching her. He was performing a medical exam. Just because he was attracted to her, didn't mean he had to do anything about it.

He cleared his throat and took her hand to examine it. Her hand was so small in his. Those delicate long fingers. Talented. How many lives had she saved with those hands? How many intricate surgeries?

"What're you doing?" she asked.

"Looking to see if your nail beds are blue. It's a sign of acute mountain sickness." Then he tipped her head back to look at her lips. The last time he'd stared at her lips, all he'd wanted to do was kiss them.

Focus.

Her skin was so soft. So, so soft.

"What's the verdict, Doc?" she asked.

"You have cyanosis starting in your nail beds and I'm sorry, but your breathing sounds labored."

Her brow furrowed. "Acute mountain sickness? Are you sure?"

"Positive. I've seen it often enough in newcomers to the area. You exerted yourself on the mountain. It was too much."

Esme sighed. "So the solution is descend?"

Carson nodded and got to his feet. "Descend, descend, descend. And water. We have to get you down before it progresses. I would hate for you to end up with high-altitude cerebral edema."

"Coma?"

He helped Esme to her feet. "You got it."

"I clearly need to do more research on acute mountain sickness. I thought it only affected people out of shape."

Carson chuckled. "No, it can happen to anyone not used to the altitude. Come on, I'll drive you back down."

"Can we leave?"

"I'll let the leader of the first responders know. You head over to the car."

Esme nodded and huddled into his sweater as she slowly walked over to his SUV. Carson watched her, to make sure she didn't fall over. Since she had a bit of cyanosis, he was positive that she was experiencing some vertigo and dizziness.

His case of weak knees, however, had nothing to do with acute mountain sickness. It all had to do with Esme. Once she was safely in his SUV, he found the team leader of the first responders who were still at the base-camp site.

"Dr. Ralston, how can I help you?"

"Dr. Petersen is suffering from ACM. I have to get her down off the mountain. If you need me to come back, I'll return when I make sure she's stable and resting."

"I don't think we'll need you back, Dr. Ralston. All missing have been accounted for and all injured are being taken down off the mountain. If there are any other issues I'll contact the other Dr. Ralston."

"Well, he traveled with an emergency patient off the mountain. So if you need someone, page me."

"Will do. Thanks, Doctor."

Carson nodded and walked to his SUV. When he sat

down he could see Esme was shivering, trying to keep the fleece around her tight.

"Sorry for throwing up out there," she said through chattering teeth. "I've heard of altitude sickness. I just didn't think that it would happen to me. I thought…" She trailed off and shook her head. "Sorry."

"No one expects it to. Don't worry about it. Just don't do that in my car." He winked at her and Esme laughed.

"That was a pretty big landslide," she remarked.

"It wasn't. I've seen worse. Way worse." He drove the car slowly down the mountain road. He didn't want to descend with her too fast.

Esme shuddered. "Worse. That's a scary thought."

"It was. I was ten. My father spent the night on the mountain with Luke when a landslide hit a smaller town just west of Whitefish. It almost buried the entire town. Luke was fifteen and was able to help Dad. They searched for survivors. So many were lost. I just remember being terrified. Left at home with Mom, not knowing if Luke and Dad would come back and worrying that it would happen in Crater Lake."

"I'm sure your mom probably felt the same," Esme said.

"I'm sure she did." Carson smiled, seeing she could barely keep her eyes open. "You look exhausted."

"I am. I feel so exhausted. I haven't been sleeping well at night." Esme yawned. "It's so quiet here. I'm used to the sounds of the city outside my apartment. It's too quiet here."

"Lay your head back and sleep. It's okay. It's going to take us forty minutes to get back to town."

Esme nodded. It didn't take much convincing for her to lean back against the seat and fall fast asleep. She looked so peaceful sleeping that when he got close to town he didn't head for town. She needed rest and he wasn't going to try and find her key and wake her up so she could sleep alone in her apartment above her clinic.

It was better that he took her home, so he could watch over her while she slept.

Is it really a better idea?

From a medical standpoint it was. She had experienced the symptoms of acute mountain sickness. He couldn't leave her alone—what if she didn't improve? What if her cyanosis worsened?

It has nothing to do with acute mountain sickness.

Why was he torturing himself like this? He couldn't have her. He wasn't willing to put his heart at risk.

He wasn't a fool. She'd leave. She'd miss surgery and head far from Crater Lake and he couldn't follow. He had a family practice to run. He wouldn't disappoint his father or grandfather, who'd left him this legacy.

Carson turned off the main road, to his property.

Esme was pretty out of it. She barely even acknowledged him as he helped her out of the SUV and into his house. The closest bedroom was his on the main floor, so he scooped her up and carried her into his bedroom, setting her down on his bed. The sun was in the west and flooded his room with light, so he closed the blinds slightly, to darken the room.

He picked up her hand one more time to check her cyanosis and the pink was returning. The blue disappearing.

The cure was working.

Thank God.

She didn't deserve to suffer from acute mountain sickness. Not after helping all those people today. He felt bad; she was probably suffering so much the entire time they were up there on the mountain. And their hike hadn't helped much. She was probably worn right out.

At least he'd got her off the mountain.

Descend, descend, descend.

Something his father and brother always reiterated. Especially Luke during his survival classes that he taught to people so they could survive in extreme conditions if they found themselves trapped up on a mountain.

She looked so peaceful sleeping on his bed.

He wished for moment that he could join her and the second that thought crossed his mind, he knew he had to get out of the room as fast as he could or he might do something he regretted.

She could see Shane's broken face looking down the aisle at her as she stopped midway. His sad, bloodied, broken face and as she glanced down it wasn't her wedding dress that she was wearing. It was the stained clothing from the mountain, her hands were turning blue and she couldn't breathe.

Esme woke with a start. It was dark and she had no idea where she was. It was someone's bedroom, but whose? The last thing she remembered was sitting in Carson's SUV and he was telling her to go to sleep as he slowly drove down the mountain.

So she must be in Carson's house. She got up slowly, her head pounding as if she had a hangover. It must've had something to do with the acute mountain sickness. At least she didn't feel as dizzy anymore. She didn't feel as if she was going to throw up.

Oh, God.

Esme sank back down on the bed, mortified that she had been ill in front of Carson. He was a doctor, so therefore he was used to seeing stuff like that, but it was him.

It was her.

If it had been anyone else she wouldn't be so embarrassed, but it was Carson. He'd been the one to see her at her most vulnerable on that mountain and she didn't like that one bit. No one saw her vulnerable. She was a dedicated surgeon.

That's what I love about you, Esme. You don't care. You're cool as a cucumber and have a great public image.

Of course after the jilting those endearing sentiments had changed in tone.

You have no heart. You're a cold, heartless woman.

Maybe it was true, but then why had it hurt so much when Avery died? When she'd lost her nerve in that surgery? If she had no heart why did it beat so fast around Carson? She hadn't realized how numb she'd been. And he'd seen her at her most vulnerable up on the mountain.

Granted he thought it was acute mountain sickness, it made sense, but she had a feeling it was something more.

Yeah, she had been feeling exhausted, her breathing had been harder to come by, but she could work through all that. She had been working through all of that. Her stomach hadn't turned until Shane had looked at her. When their gazes had connected and she'd seen the recognition, followed by anger or hurt.

Of course, it was hard to tell if it was because she had been there. When she'd run out on him the day of their wedding he'd told her, or rather his father had told her in no uncertain terms, that he didn't want to see her ever again.

That Shane loathed her.

Hated her. *You have no heart. You're a cold, heartless woman. You could have been great, but now you're nothing. Not a surgeon. Nothing but a shadow.*

And she didn't blame him. She hated herself for it.

Of course it was hard to tell if it had been loathing or the fact she'd been shoving a chest tube in between the intercostal spaces of his ribs, saving his life. And even then she wasn't sure if she'd saved it. He was so injured. Maybe he didn't make it down off the mountain. If he died…she didn't want to think about how that would make her feel. How it would end her career here in Crater Lake. A place she was falling in love with.

She was tired of running.

She didn't want to leave.

Shake it off.

Her eyes adjusted to the dim light of the unfamiliar room. She could see from the digital clock on the nightstand it was almost 10:00 p.m., and as she padded over to the window and peered through the blinds the sun was going down finally.

Even though she'd been here since April, she still wasn't used to extended daylight hours. At least it would still be daylight out when she found her cell phone, purse and called herself a cab, because she couldn't stay here at Carson's house.

That was unacceptable.

Her purse was at the end of the bed. She grabbed it and then opened the door as quietly as she could, peering out. The main room was dark, except for the flickering of the television. Esme could see Carson in the light and he was asleep. Flat-out on his back asleep.

Good.

She would quietly leave his house and then call a cab from outside so she wouldn't disturb him; that was the last thing she wanted to do. He needed his rest. He'd given up his bed for her. The couch was long, but it couldn't be too comfortable. Especially since Carson was over six feet tall and his legs were propped up over the edge of the sofa, his arms crossed and his head at an odd angle. It didn't look at all comfortable.

Esme's heart melted. He was such a generous person. She'd seen the way he was with his patients. No matter what the Johnstone twins thought of him, he was kind, caring. A little closed off. There was a hurt buried under there, but she didn't know what.

And she couldn't believe anyone would hurt him. She never wanted to hurt him. Which was why he was off-limits. So whatever secrets he had were his. Carson had the right to his secrets, just as she had the right to hers. As she wanted to keep her hurt private, because she didn't deserve absolution. It was her private hurt to keep.

Even if she was done carrying it.

She had to fight the urge to join him on the couch, to curl up beside him and watch a movie with him. To just feel safe in his arms, but she didn't deserve that because she wasn't sure that she could give that to a man.

She'd panicked about her marriage to Shane.

That was different.

And it was.

Shane didn't understand her. Carson did, but she

wasn't sure of that. Maybe he'd resent her eventually, as Shane did.

Esme sighed. Why couldn't she have some happiness? She deserved some happiness.

No. She didn't. She had to stop having this same argument with herself over and over again. She didn't deserve Carson. She couldn't have Carson.

He was off-limits.

I broke Shane's heart. I froze in surgery. I let everyone down.

Esme let out a sigh. Maybe she should leave him a note. Thank him for taking care of her because she didn't have anyone to care for her. She didn't have anyone to sit with her or visit her, but that was par for the course.

She turned around and headed for the door. It was best that she get out of here as fast as she could. She grabbed the doorknob. A light flicked on.

"Going somewhere?"

Esme cursed under her breath and turned around. "You're awake."

Carson was sitting up, staring at her with that goofy grin on his face. One that melted her heart. Damn him.

"And you were trying to sneak out of here."

"I wasn't trying to sneak out of here. You were asleep and I was going to call a cab."

He raised an eyebrow. "You were going to call Bob?"

"Who's Bob?"

"The only cab guy in Crater Lake. You would've been standing out there all night. He's not the most reliable."

Esme groaned. "Are you kidding me?"

He chuckled. "I wish I was."

"He's going to have to up his game when that big resort opens up."

"Maybe someone else will move into town and give him a run for his money." Carson winked at her.

Esme shook her head. "Thanks for that dig."

"It wasn't meant as a dig. It was meant as a compliment." He got off the couch and walked over to her and her pulse began to race as he came closer to her. She needed to get out of here fast. She took a step back from him.

"I should go. Tomorrow is Monday. I have to open my clinic. Patients to see."

Carson planted himself in front of the door, barring her exit. "You had more than a mild case of acute mountain sickness. You need your rest."

"I had my rest. I slept for several hours on your bed. I'm fine."

He grabbed her hand and checked her nail beds. "Well, you're not cyanotic anymore. Your hypoxia is gone."

Esme tried not to gasp at his touch. He just held her hand, his thumb brushing over her knuckles causing a zing of excitement to course down her spine.

She wanted to pull her hand back, but she couldn't. So, like a fool, she just stood there and let him hold it.

Snap out of it.

"Yes. I told you, I'm fine."

"You still need to rest. You should call your nurse and reschedule your patients. Besides, after that landslide and all the press heading into town Crater Lake will be a bit overrun tomorrow." Carson let go of her hand and moved away from the door.

Which was a good thing, because if he didn't he'd feel how badly her hand was shaking.

Press? Did he just say press?

"What?" she asked, hoping that the nervousness in her voice didn't give her away. "Why would the press be coming here?"

"It was a major landslide and among the injured was some actress by the name of Manuela Draven, who happens to be married to the head of some big internet company and nephew of Silas Draven and he's currently the guy that Luke is operating on now in Missoula."

Silas Draven's nephew?

Well, that explained why Shane was on the mountain. Then it clicked in that Luke was still operating on Shane.

"Is Sha… Is our chest-tube guy okay?"

"It's touch and go, but Luke's fairly confident he'll pull through."

"Good." She tried to take a deep calming breath, but everything began to spin and Esme gripped the door handle to steady herself and for ease of access when she bolted out of here.

It was like some kind of nightmare that she just couldn't get away from. Was her jilting of Shane going to haunt her for the rest of her life?

It would be only a matter of time before someone mentioned her name and they tracked her down. Wouldn't that be a juicy story?

"Runaway Bride of Shane Draven saves his life on top of a mountain. Is a reunion in the air? Did Manuela break Shane Draven's heart like Dr. Petersen did?"

And she felt the nausea begin to rise in her again.

Without saying a word she dashed across Carson's

house and found the guest bathroom, slamming the door and locking herself inside. She knelt beside the toilet, expecting to be ill, but nothing happened.

The only thing she could hear was the pounding of her blood, like an incessant drum in her ears as her heart raced. Her stomach twisted, threatening to heave, and she could feel sweat on her palms.

She couldn't believe this was happening.

Not again.

And the only thing she could think about at that moment was to run. Run as far away and as fast as she could.

There was a gentle knock on the door. "Esme, are you okay?"

"No," she said through chattering teeth.

"Can I come in?"

"No."

He sighed on the other side of the door. "I'm worried that it's the acute mountain sickness again. If it is we have to get you to a hospital."

Esme got up and unlocked the door. He opened it as she sat on the floor. "It's not the mountain sickness. I'm breathing fine."

"All the same…"

"It's not that. It's the press and the landslide and the Dravens."

Carson looked confused. "What's wrong? Why does that scare you?"

"Oh, God," Esme moaned and buried her head in her knees, the tears threatening to come. She felt his hand on her shoulder. His strong, strong hand.

"Tell me and maybe I can help."

"You can't help me."

"Try me. What can I do?" His eyes were full of concern, his hand so warm and reassuring as he gently stroked her cheek. "Please, let me help you, Esme."

She wanted his help. She wanted much more than that, only she couldn't have what she really wanted, but she could have tonight. One night with him, lying in his arms, and he could help chase away the ghosts that were haunting her at this moment.

Esme leaned forward and then kissed him. Just as she'd pictured a thousand times before, as she'd wanted to do the moment he'd stood outside her clinic demanding that she hand over the patients she'd stolen. She kissed him the way she'd wanted to when he'd invited her over to dinner, when he'd wrapped his arm around her on the pitch-black ride up to the mill, when he'd worked side by side with her, saving lives.

It was sweeter than she'd ever expected.

It was healing, but she wanted so much more for tonight. She wanted all of him, even if it was just for now.

She could have now.

She could forget who she was for just a few dark hours.

And maybe, just for once, she'd remember the woman she used to be.

CHAPTER ELEVEN

CARSON WAS A lost man.

He hadn't been expecting that kiss to happen. He'd wanted it to happen so many times, but, of all the ways he'd fantasized about his first kiss with Esme, never once had he imagined it would happen in his guest bathroom.

It would've bothered him before, because she was off-limits. Right now he didn't care. Right now all he could think about was her hands cupping his face and the taste of her honeyed lips on his.

And then the kiss ended, leaving him wanting more.

So much more. For once he didn't care if she was going to hurt him or that she was off-limits. He just wanted her.

"Carson, I want you. Please let me in tonight." She kissed him again and there was no way he could argue with that. It had been so long since he'd connected with someone. He avoided that for a reason, because it wasn't just sex to him. Sex to him let people in. Let them see a side of him that he shared with no one.

He'd been hurt, burned, and he didn't want to let someone in, but with Esme it was different. She made him forget about what had happened to him, about when his heart had been broken so long ago.

"Please, Carson," she said, stroking his face. "Please. Just for tonight."

"Esme, when you kiss me like that...I don't want to stop. I can't stop."

"Then don't. You don't have to promise me anything. I don't need a promise of something that I can't give."

It was a way out. She was offering him a way out. He wasn't sure how he felt about it. It should be a simple matter, only with her so close to him it wasn't a simple matter. He couldn't think rationally with her so close.

It was complicated.

Why did everything have to be so complicated?

This didn't have to be. This could just be the moment.

He could have this exquisite moment with her.

For once he could have what he wanted, even if it didn't mean anything permanent. He could have this moment with her.

All he wanted was just this moment.

She tried to kiss him again, but he stopped her. "No."

"I thought you..."

"I do. It's just we're not doing this here. There's only one place we're going to do this tonight."

Esme grinned and Carson helped her to her feet, leading her out of the tiny powder room. Once they were out of the bathroom he picked her up in his arms. He'd been wanting to sweep her off her feet since he first saw her, but he'd fought against it for so long. Right now he didn't have any fight left in him.

Right now he was going to forget everything and be with her as he wanted to, even if it meant putting his heart on the line.

He just wanted to feel again.

He just wanted to be close to someone again.

Carson carried her straight to his bathroom. A much larger room, with a large shower, because he wanted to kiss every inch of her and maybe the water would wash away some of the past.

"You read my mind," she whispered against his ear, nibbling it.

"I thought after a day on the mountain that you might enjoy a nice hot shower." He sat her down on the floor. He turned on the shower; the steam felt good. "I'll have one after you."

"Or you could have one with me."

His blood heated at her suggestion. The thought of her wet and naked made him burn with desire.

"Are you sure?" he asked.

She didn't answer him; she just smiled and took off her shirt. She was wearing a pink lace bra. It was hot pink. And though he'd never really cared for that color before the fact it was on her made him hot. Then she undid her pants, slipped them down and kicked them away, revealing a matching pair of panties.

"I'm sure."

Carson couldn't have looked away if he'd wanted to. He was entranced by her. She unhooked her bra and then slipped down her panties until she was naked. Standing there, completely naked.

"So beautiful," he murmured.

She walked over to him and started to unbutton his shirt. He reached down and ran his fingers over her bare shoulders. Her skin was so soft.

Esme slid her fingers inside his open shirt and peeled it away, touching his chest. He sucked in a deep breath.

It had been so long since he'd let a woman touch him like that. He'd forgotten what a rush it was.

Only this was different than anything he'd experienced before. It scared and thrilled him all the same. He wanted Esme to continue touching him. Her hands trailed down his chest and she undid his belt, slowing, driving him wild with need.

When her fingers broached the top of his jeans, he stopped her, grabbing her wrists and holding her back.

"I think you need to get in that shower, because I'm liable to take you right here on this bathroom floor and even though our first kiss was in a bathroom I would rather our first time be in my bed."

Pink tinged her cheeks, her eyes sparkling as she stepped away from him and walked into the glass shower.

It didn't take him long to remove his jeans and underwear. He only hesitated for a moment because he didn't lie. He didn't want their first time to be in the shower. Carson didn't want to take her up against the tiled wall. When he made love to Esme for the first time he wanted it to be in his bed. Her underneath him as he thrust into her with her legs wrapped around his waist.

He wanted her to spend the night in his arms.

He didn't want a quickie in the shower. Carson wanted to explore her body, take his time and make sure that he remembered every single moment of this time together, because it could only be this one time.

The water hit him, but his body was already heated so it felt cold instead of hot. He leaned down and kissed her the best he could. She was so much shorter than him.

"I want you," she whispered, running her hands over his chest.

"I want you, too, but not here. Not against this hard surface. I want to do it properly. I want to make love to you properly."

Something flickered across her face when he said the words *make love*. As if she was changing her mind for a moment, or maybe shock, but whatever it was it was just a flicker.

So instead he kissed her as she washed his body.

When he couldn't take the touching and teasing any longer he turned off the shower and wrapped her up in the largest fuzzy towel he had.

It might have been summer, but he wasn't taking any chances of her getting cold and catching her death. Especially not after today on the mountain.

He carried her through his en suite to his room, the room where she had spent the past few hours napping, and set her down on the bed. She tried to pull him down, but he moved away.

"I have a surprise for you." He walked over to the gas fireplace and flicked it on. He rarely had it on in the summer, but tonight was special. He didn't want her shivering while he made her come.

She was grinning, lying against the bed seductively. "Gas? I thought a rugged mountain man like you would build your own fire."

He chuckled. "I'm not that rugged of a mountain man."

"I think you are."

He came back to the bed and gathered her up in his arms. "Do you now?"

"Oh, yes," she said, nuzzling his neck. This time when she pulled him down, he didn't fight her, because whatever fight he had left in him when it came to her was gone.

He was a lost man.

It felt so good to have him pressed against her. It had been a long time since she'd been with anyone. Not since Shane and even then she was never all that interested in sex. She'd rather be in the OR, elbow deep in someone's chest, than having a night of hot sex.

Now that Carson was here with her, kissing her lips, her neck, her collarbone while his hands slipped under the thick terry-cloth towel to cup her breasts, she realized what she'd been missing. It had never been like this with anyone before.

No man had fired her senses so completely.

She'd never wanted anyone as badly as she wanted Carson now.

Esme wanted him to possess her. To take her.

Hard.

This was what she'd wanted when she'd kissed him. She wanted Carson to help her remember who she was. She just wanted to escape the world for a little while, because when the press came, and found out that she was in town and was the one who'd put the chest tube in Shane, she'd never know peace again. She'd be *that* person again. The runaway bride, the runaway surgeon, and she'd sworn to herself she'd never be that person again.

She had to leave Crater Lake. She had to go somewhere new. Someplace where no one knew her name. She didn't want to leave but she had no choice.

It was for the best, but until she had to leave she was going to cling to this moment. She wanted something to remember Carson by. Just one stolen moment that she could treasure for a long time.

Something that no one had to know about.

Something that could never be exposed and ruined.

Esme sighed, she couldn't help it. His lips were tracing a path slowly down her body. She arched her back, her body tingling. Every nerve ending standing up and paying attention.

"Do you want me to stop?" he asked, his lips hovering just above her collarbone, his breath like a brand of fire on her skin.

"God. No."

"Good." He leaned over her and a shiver of anticipation coursed through her.

So good. Just so, so good.

She didn't deserve this, but right now she didn't care. All she wanted to do was feel and she wanted to feel with him. She'd been numb for so long. He opened the towel, his eyes dark and seeming to devour her. It sent a tingle of excitement through her.

He pressed another kiss against her lips, light at first and then more urgent, as if he couldn't get enough of her. She opened her legs wider, wrapping her legs around his waist, trying to pull him closer.

"Oh, God," Carson moaned. "Oh, God, I want you. I want you so bad."

"I want you, too," she whispered and then arched her back. "Feel how much I want you."

Carson kissed her again, his tongue pushed past her lips, entwining with hers, making her blood sing with need. He ran his hands over her body, his hands on her bare flesh.

"I can't resist you," Carson whispered against her neck. "I can't. I'm so weak."

"I want you, too."

She did. Badly. Right now they weren't competing doctors in town. They were just two people about to become one. Two lovely people who needed this moment of release.

"Please," she begged.

His lips captured hers in a kiss, silencing any more words between them.

"So beautiful," he murmured. His fingers found their way up to her breast, circling around her nipple, teasing.

She ran her fingers through his hair as he began to kiss her again, but just light kisses starting at the lips and trailing lower, down over her neck, lingering at her breasts. He used his tongue to tease her and she gasped as pleasure shot through her again.

His hand moved between her legs and he began to stroke her. Esme cried out. She'd never been touched there before like that and then when his hand was replaced by his mouth and tongue, it made her topple over the edge. She tried to stop herself from coming, but she couldn't. It was too much. It had been so long.

As she came down off her climax Carson moved away and pulled a condom out. "Now, where were we?"

"I think I remember," Esme teased. She took the condom packet from his hand.

"What're you doing?" he asked.

She pushed him down and straddled his legs. "I'm just helping you out."

"Oh, God…" He trailed off as she opened the wrapper and rolled the condom down over his shaft. He was mumbling incoherent words as she stroked him.

"Now you're under me. I like it when you're under me," she murmured, leaning over him and nibbling on his earlobe.

"No. You need to be under me."

"And what're you going to do about it?"

"This." Carson flipped her over, grabbing her wrists and holding her down as he entered her. It felt so good that he was filling her completely. She dug her nails into his shoulder as he stretched her.

"Make love to me," she begged.

He moaned. "I can't say no to you."

Carson moved slow at first, taking his time, but she wanted so much more of him, she urged him to go faster until he lost control and was thrusting against her hard and fast. Soon another coil of heat unfurled deep within her. Pleasure overtaking her as he brought her to another climax.

She wrapped her legs around him, holding him tight against her, urging him on as he reached his own climax. She wanted Carson. She wanted him to make her forget about all her mistakes. Of how she'd run from surgery.

She wanted to feel again. To remember who she was.

She wished they could stay like this forever, but they couldn't. Right now she just wanted to savor the moment of being with him. That she was lying in his arms as she'd wanted, as she'd dreamed.

Carson kissed her gently on the lips, his fingers stroking her face as she ran her hands down over his back. He rolled away from her and propped himself up on one elbow, his eyes twinkling with tenderness.

"I don't want to go home," she whispered. She didn't mean to say that thought out loud. It just came out, because she didn't want to leave the safe, happy, warm bubble. She didn't want to go home to the empty apartment above her clinic and think about packing it all up and leaving.

A sly smile played on his lips. "You don't have to leave if you don't want to. I wouldn't mind you staying here for the night."

"Are you sure about that?"

"Positive. Stay. I want you to stay here." He leaned over and kissed her again. "You taste so good."

"I'll stay."

"Good." He got up to leave.

"Where are you going?"

He leaned back over and kissed her again. "I'll be right back. Just get under the duvet and relax."

Carson took the discarded towel and wrapped it around his waist. He opened the blinds and finally the sun had gone down. The inky black sky was lit by a full moon and a thousand stars.

She'd never seen so many stars.

"Amazing," she whispered.

Carson nodded and then climbed into bed beside her. "You can see it through the skylight, as well."

Esme leaned back against the pillow and stared up at the sky thick with stars. "It's like we're under the Milky Way."

"Almost."

"What would make this perfect is the aurora borealis."

Carson chuckled. "Don't push your luck. Fall is a better time to see them. You'll see one then for sure."

Will I?

Esme rolled over on her side and touched his face.

She didn't want to leave, but she couldn't stay. A man like Carson deserved so much more than her.

"I want you again, Carson." She couldn't believe she was uttering those words, but she did. She wanted him again.

He grinned lazily. "I'm happy to oblige."

She cocked an eyebrow. "Oh, yes?"

"Yes, because I'm not done with you yet. We have all night."

A zing coursed through her. Oh, yes. This was going to be her undoing.

It was going to kill her to leave Crater Lake.

It was going to kill her to leave him.

CHAPTER TWELVE

CARSON REACHED OUT the next morning, but she was gone. The spot on her side of the bed was empty and cold.

Her spot.

He'd never thought of it as anyone's spot before. It was just his bed, somewhere he slept. Now he missed her and she'd only been in his bed one night.

One night and he was hooked on her as if she were a drug. This was exactly why he couldn't be with someone.

The morning light flooded into his bedroom. It was blinding and he realized that he'd slept through his alarm.

Dammit.

At least he didn't have a patient until the afternoon. Besides, if he had a patient in the morning Louise would've called him by now, berating him for being late.

He glanced over to where Esme had been, to the spot where he'd made love to her under a sky of stars, but now she was gone. His bed felt empty.

Only your bed?

Why had he thought it was going to be any different? Why had he expected her to stay with him?

They always left.

Danielle had left and now Esme. Even though he knew logically it was just for a night, that they hadn't made promises to each other, it still was like a knife to the gut. He'd wanted to wake up next to her. He wanted to make love to her again, in the morning light. Only she was gone.

His bed was empty.

It had never felt empty before.

Not even when Danielle had left. He didn't like the way Esme affected him. He was fine before she'd come to town, but now that he'd had her, he wanted her all the more.

Dammit.

His cell phone went off and he reached over and grabbed it. It was Luke's cell.

"Hello?" Carson answered.

"I called the office but Louise said you hadn't shown up for work yet."

"I overslept."

"I haven't slept yet," Luke remarked.

"Where are you?" Carson asked.

"I'm still in Missoula. The guy we pulled off the mountain is in bad shape."

"It looked like he was."

"I had a bit of a fight with a surgeon here," Luke said and then snorted. "I won out in the end. I always do."

"Did he survive?" Luke asked.

"Of course he did. Didn't you hear me say I always win out in the end?"

Carson rolled his eyes. "Do you need me to cancel my afternoon appointments and come get you in Missoula or are you catching a flight back?"

"Can you come get me? I have to get back up on the mountain and assess the damage. Plus Eli Draven is demanding a personal status update on his son."

"You mean the surgeon Dr. Eli Draven, the cardio-thoracic surgeon?"

"Yeah. That man we saved was his son."

"Why doesn't he just go to Missoula?"

"Dr. Draven was in Great Falls with his daughter-in-law. She had a splenectomy."

"They didn't fly her to Missoula?"

"No. Missoula was slammed and Great Falls had a bed. Shane Draven got in here only because it was dire."

"Why was Missoula slammed?"

Luke sighed. "Another landslide south of Whitefish."

"So how is Dr. Draven's daughter-in-law?"

"Apparently she's on the mend and he's back in Crater Lake demanding blood."

"For what?" Carson asked. "It was an act of God."

"You know that and I know that. There's no talking to these guys sometimes. He wants to speak with Dr. Petersen. I told him that Dr. Petersen is the one who probably saved his son's life. He didn't seem thrilled that it was Dr. Petersen and not you or me."

"Whatever, his son is alive thanks to Esme."

"I know that. And Esme, eh?" Luke asked, teasing. "I didn't know you were on a first-name basis."

"Mind your own business."

"Fine. So can you come and get me?"

"Okay," Carson said. "I'll shower and come get you in Missoula."

"Thanks, Carson. Oh, and bring coffee."

Luke hung up and Carson set his phone back down on his nightstand. He'd rather just spend the morning in bed where Esme's scent still lingered on the pillow, but he couldn't do that. He couldn't leave Luke stranded in Missoula.

The bubble had burst and he had to head back out into the real world, as much as he hated to do so.

"Who called?"

Carson nearly jumped out of his skin as Esme padded into his bedroom with a tray that had what looked like breakfast on it. Though he wasn't sure.

"What?" Esme asked, confused. "You look like you've seen a ghost or something."

"I thought you left." He sat up and scrubbed a hand over his face.

"I almost did, but then realized that probably Bob's taxi service wouldn't be up and running at six in the morning when I woke up."

Carson chuckled. "You're probably right, but it's ten in the morning."

"Do you want me to leave?"

"No, it's not that…"

Esme grinned. "Good, 'cause now you can get your coffee."

He moved over and she sat down on the bed next to him, placing the tray on the bed. "I didn't know I had one of those."

"What?" she asked, glancing around.

"This tray thing." He took the mug and sipped the coffee. It was good, but as he eyed the black and yellow stuff on the tray he wasn't so sure. "So, what do we have here?"

"Eggs," she said as if he should've known what the burnt gelatinous mess was.

"Ah, can I pass? I have to get up and drive to Missoula today."

"Missoula?"

"Luke needs a ride back to Crater Lake. He has to get back on the mountain. He was in Missoula operating on Shane Draven all night, the guy we pulled out from under the landslide. Did you know he's Dr. Eli Draven's son? His father is a surgical legend."

The moment he said the name Shane Draven again her demeanor changed completely. She set down her almost-empty mug on the tray and then picked the tray up. She wasn't making eye contact with him. And then things started to piece together. He just didn't know the connection yet.

"Well, then, you better get going."

"What's wrong?" Carson asked.

"What do you mean?"

"What is it about Shane and Eli Draven that made you tense? You totally changed and, come to think about it, it happened at the mill. As soon as they mentioned Silas Draven was a client, but then you realized it was someone else. It's Shane and Eli who make you nervous. Why?"

Esme shook her head. "I—I don't know what you're…" She trailed off and then set the tray down on his dresser to cross her arms.

Carson got out of bed and pulled on his jeans and then came around the other side. "I think you know exactly what I'm talking about. Don't you? Luke said Dr. Draven didn't seem too pleased you worked on his son."

"Is that so?" Her voice was shaking so bad. As if she was terrified. Come to think of it, he was pretty terrified, too.

He was terrified about how he was feeling about her.

Last night when he'd taken her in his arms it had changed. It had all changed. After Danielle had left him and broken his heart he'd never wanted to feel anything for anybody again. He wasn't sure what he was feeling at the moment.

All he knew was he wanted to console her.

Tell her that it was all going to be okay.

Only, he wasn't sure if it would be, because he wasn't sure if he was okay.

"Tell me. It'll be all right. Tell me."

Esme shook her head. "I can't. You wouldn't understand."

"Try me."

"Right," she snorted. "Look, you wouldn't understand. You can't understand."

"I think I might. I've seen hurt before. I've seen heartache."

"Really? You've seen heartache?" she snapped. "Well, was that heartache spread all over the national newspapers? First when you froze during a surgery that cost a patient his life and then leaving your fiancé, who happened to be your mentor and boss's son, on Valentine's Day? Did you have the press hounding you constantly, camped outside the hospital you worked at? Having patients suddenly changing their minds because they had no faith in the surgeon who froze? Your mentor turning on you? Your family disappointed in you?"

Esme's lip trembled, her eyes filling with tears. "Shane Draven was my fiancé and I ran. Dr. Eli Draven was my mentor. He taught me everything. I was his star pupil. After my reputation was shattered by the press, I gave it all up. I gave up surgery, the one thing I loved more than anything, because I didn't deserve it. I don't deserve happiness. I hurt Shane. Me. It was me. All me."

Carson took her in his arms. She tried to fight him, but he held her still. "I was engaged."

Esme stopped and looked up at him. "What?"

"I was engaged. She left me, because I wanted to stay in Crater Lake and she wanted to take a job as a surgeon across the country. It was my fault that she left. So I understand heartache. I get the pain."

Only she didn't look convinced and Carson didn't think that she believed him.

That was okay, because he hated himself for being the cause of his own heartache. Just as she was the cause of her own.

Esme sighed inwardly. She wanted to tell him that he didn't understand, because he wasn't the one that left, but she didn't. Carson wouldn't understand what she was feeling and she got that. No one would understand.

It was her pain to bear alone. She'd lost herself and her career. It was all her fault.

She didn't expect anyone to take it on, to understand it.

Carson and she had shared that one night together, but that was all it had to be. It didn't have to be anything else and it couldn't be, because she was leaving Crater Lake.

As soon as she was able to, she'd send her patients back over to Carson and find some other small town where she could disappear. Where she wouldn't get involved with anyone, because that was all she deserved.

When it came to Carson she'd been so weak. She'd let her loneliness dictate her actions. She'd been so isolated in Los Angeles; people she'd thought were friends had cut her out of their lives. Her father had been disappointed with her giving up surgery and then leaving Shane at the altar, and then her job had been taken away from her. It had taken her a long time to even pluck up the courage to pick up the remnants of her life and find somewhere to start fresh.

Only, her past had caught up with her up on that mountain. Everything she cared about. Everything she loved was taken away from her in the end. She couldn't lose Carson. She wouldn't even risk it.

She had to leave and when she started over, she wasn't going to make the same mistakes that she'd made in Crater Lake.

"I need to go home now," she said, hoping her voice didn't crack too much as she tried to control the tears threatening to spill. "Besides, you have to pick up your brother in Missoula."

"Come with me to Missoula. The drive will do you good."

She shook her head. "No, thanks. I have some patients to see this afternoon. If you could just take me back into town."

Which was a lie. She didn't have any patients.

Not today.

Carson looked disappointed. If it were to anywhere else, if the landslide hadn't happened, if he hadn't discovered her secret, she might've gone with him because she liked car rides. She'd driven to Montana, her car giving out on her when she'd rolled into Crater Lake.

But now she just needed to get back to the place she called home. Two days before the landslide she had unpacked the last box, thinking that she had found a permanent home. Now she realized that was just a myth.

There could be no permanent home for her.

There was no safe place for her.

"Okay, just let me get dressed and I'll take you back into town."

Esme picked up the tray and nodded. "Thank you."

She left him to get dressed as she headed into the kitchen. She rinsed the dishes and put them into his dishwasher for him, cleaning up the mess she'd made trying to make him breakfast. Totally oblivious for a moment that her past had caught up with her.

She'd let her guard down and she hated herself for that.

Esme wandered over to the window and looked down at Crater Lake, smiling as she remembered that short stolen moment down on the shore of the lake that she'd had with Carson. When she'd forgotten who she was.

She'd forgotten she was a disgraced doctor.

She'd forgotten that she'd broken Shane's heart.

She'd forgotten that she'd disappointed her father and she'd forgotten about why she became a surgeon.

"You ready to go?" Carson asked.

Esme turned and he was fully dressed again, which was a shame.

No. You can't think that way.

"Yeah."

They didn't say anything to each other as they went out to his truck. The trip to town was awkward, too. She wanted to tell him how much last night had meant to her, because it had, but Esme thought it would just make things worse.

It wouldn't be good for either one of them.

Carson was frowning as he drove, his hands gripping the steering wheel. It was as if he was holding back things to say to her.

Things, if her circumstances were different, she'd want to hear.

He pulled up in front of her building and sat there.

"Thanks for last night," she said, breaking the awkward silence that descended between them.

It meant so much to me.

Only she didn't say those thoughts out loud and she didn't think the other three words that she really wanted to say, because if she thought about it then it would hurt all the more when she left.

"It meant a lot to me, too," Carson said. Then he turned to look at her. "We didn't make any promises, I know that, but..."

She touched his lips. "No. We didn't and that's okay."

He took her hand. "It's not, though. It wasn't your fault. Patients die all the time and you shouldn't let that inhibit your career. You're a brilliant surgeon. We all make mistakes. You shouldn't leave that talent on a shelf, rusting away."

Only she had and that inhibition had cost her her career in the end.

She smiled and then kissed him gently on the lips. "Thanks again."

Carson nodded. "Are you sure you don't want to come to Missoula with me?"

"Positive. Go get your brother. I have patients."

He nodded. "Right. I'll call you when I get back from Missoula."

"Sure." Only she wasn't going to answer her phone and by the time he realized she was leaving she was hoping to be packed up, in the new car she'd have to buy, and be on the road. If they weren't making any promises to each other, then he shouldn't worry that she didn't answer her phone.

"Do you want to have dinner when I get back?" Carson asked.

"No. Like I said, I'll be really busy with patients this afternoon and I think I'll try to head to bed early tonight. Give me a call in a couple of days. I have a lot of stuff to get caught up on."

It was a lie. She hated lying, but it was for the best.

"Okay. I'll see you later."

Esme nodded and got out of the car. "Goodbye, Carson."

And before he could say anything else she shut the door and ran into her building. Only glancing back once to watch his SUV head off on the main road out of town. Tears stung her eyes, but she wouldn't let them out. She brushed them away, because she didn't deserve to cry for him. She didn't deserve to have him.

She was going to hurt him as his former fiancée had. She was breaking another man's heart.

Even if it was the best for him.

And the worst for her.

CHAPTER THIRTEEN

"LOUISE, MAKE SURE that my afternoon is clear. I have to go get Luke in Missoula."

"Of course, Dr. Ralston."

Carson rubbed his forehead. He'd been supposed to get Luke on Monday after the landslide, but he'd got as far as Whitefish, Montana, when he'd got a text from Luke asking Carson to call him.

Carson had pulled off the road at a rest stop and called his brother back.

Apparently Shane Draven had taken a turn for the worse and Luke had wanted to stay in Missoula to monitor Shane's progress. Dr. Eli Draven had been insisting on it as Luke was the one who had saved Shane's life and Eli had made it clear Esme was not to go near Missoula.

Ungrateful jerk.

Luke knew the chief of surgery at the hospital and was getting special privileges to stay and work there. His brother had also had a few choice words about the annoying female trauma attending who was working on Shane's case with him, which had made Carson chuckle.

So Carson had returned to Crater Lake. He'd tried to call Esme, but she hadn't answered his phone or his knocks on her door and he was worried about her. She'd probably been avoiding the press that had come to town. He didn't blame her for keeping a low profile with the media circling.

Of course now the press was leaving. There was nothing new to report in Crater Lake.

Why are you so worried?

When they'd decided to sleep together, they had both made it quite clear that nothing could happen between them. He should be relieved or happy that she was now giving him the cold shoulder.

She'd been hurt.

Just as he'd been hurt.

This was for the best. It would make it easier. No awkwardness. No expectations.

Was it really the best?

It wasn't. He didn't like it one bit. It had been three days since he'd dropped her off at her clinic. Three days since he'd seen her.

Three days since he'd last kissed her.

He wanted so much more from her. He wanted it all; he just wasn't sure if he could trust her. There was a greatness in her, something she had suppressed because she had been scared. Esme would soon discover that and she'd move on.

Carson couldn't move on.

Crater Lake was his home.

He glanced out the window at her clinic. It had been closed today, which was odd. He hadn't even seen her nurse head to work.

Is it really your concern?

It wasn't and he had to keep reminding himself that it wasn't his business at all. They were just friends, just colleagues. That was all they were. He couldn't give her more and she couldn't give him more.

Why not?

Carson cursed under his breath and tried to concentrate on the chart in his hand. He was supposed to be going over his patient's file. He was supposed to be analyzing tests so that he could tell his patient tomorrow what was going on with him. All he should focus on now was his patients and the fact he had to drive about three and a half hours to Missoula to get Luke.

He shouldn't be worrying about Esme Petersen.

Only he couldn't help himself. She'd gotten under his skin, into his blood. She was in his veins like a drug.

Dammit.

There was a knock at the door and Louise opened it. "Dr. Ralston, Mrs. Fenolio is hoping that you could fit her in tomorrow. Can I fit her in?"

Carson was confused. "Mrs. Fenolio is not my patient. She's Dr. Petersen's."

"Not anymore according to Mrs. Fenolio. Apparently Dr. Petersen is selling her practice and leaving town."

Carson's world began to spin off-kilter.

I'm leaving, Carson. I've been offered a job as Head of Neurosurgery in New York. I'm going.

Are you asking me to go?

No, Carson. I'm not. You won't leave Crater Lake and that's why I'm leaving you.

That's it? You never even gave me the chance to say yes or no.

Well?

I can't leave my father's practice.

See, what was the point of asking? Goodbye, Carson.

"Pardon?" he asked, shaking the memories away.

"Actually, Mrs. Fenolio is not the first former patient to call and ask to come back. The Johnstone twins have an appointment at the end of the week. I also have a pile of patients from that timeshare community who are looking for a new doctor now that Dr. Petersen is closing up shop. So what do I tell them?"

He didn't give Louise an answer. Instead he pushed past her and ran out of the office, crossing the street to bang on Esme's clinic door.

"Esme, open up. I know you're in there."

He continued to pound his fist against the door until she answered. There were dark circles under her eyes when she opened the door just a crack.

"Carson, I don't have time—"

"You're leaving town?" Carson cut her off.

Esme sighed. "I don't have time to talk to you about this."

"I think you can make time for me."

"Go back to your clinic." She tried to shut the door, but he stuck his foot in the gap and forced his way in. "Get out of here, Carson. Go home."

"No." He shut the door behind him and stood in front of it. "You're giving up your practice?"

She crossed her arms. "Yes."

"Why?" he demanded.

She shook her head, annoyed with him. "It's none of your concern."

"You're running away from ghosts. Aren't you? I mean, that's what you did when you left Los Angeles and that's what you're doing here."

Her eyes went positively flinty. He'd hit a nerve and he didn't care. She was running away. She was running out. Just as Danielle had and it hurt. He should've known better, but he was a fool and he was blinded by love.

He'd been blinded by her.

"It's not any of your business."

Carson shook his head. "Why? Why are you running away?"

"As I said. It's not any of your business why I'm leaving. People leave towns. They grow, they change and they forge new trails for themselves. Of course, you wouldn't know anything about that, would you? Since you refuse to leave Crater Lake. I mean, that's why your last relationship failed, wasn't it?"

It was like a slap to the face. It was the truth, but it stung all the same. He should've known better. He'd opened his heart and it was being thrown back in his face. Torn asunder again. Only this one hurt worse than when Danielle had discarded him.

"Go, then. I don't care. At least I'm not a coward. I can face what I'm afraid of. I don't run away from my problems."

A tear slid down her cheek and he knew that he'd hurt her, just as she'd hurt him.

"No, you just let your problems run away for you."

He didn't say anything as he opened the door to her clinic and slammed it behind him. It was good she was leaving.

Was it?

Carson didn't know.

He didn't know what he was feeling. Only that he

was angry at himself for opening up to someone again. For letting someone in.

For letting Esme absolutely shatter his heart.

Esme wanted to go after him, even if he had hurt her, because he was right. She was running away from the ghosts of her past again, but it was for the best. She cared for Carson. She loved Carson and she didn't want to drag him into her mess.

It was in Carson's best interests that she left. He didn't need to be associated with her; he wouldn't want to be associated with her. She was a failure.

What would that do to his practice, being associated with her? It was an old practice that had been in his family for so long. She couldn't destroy that, because she loved Carson.

It was better to get out now before she got in too deep. Before she totally destroyed Carson's career or ran out on their wedding.

Who says you'll run? a little voice inside her asked.

She didn't know that for certain, but any time any relationship in her past had gotten serious she'd run.

The only problem with running was that she was so alone.

And she was getting tired of running even if it was for the best. Even if it was mandatory. She was a coward. Carson was right. She was too afraid to love. Too afraid to lose someone she loved.

It hurt that he'd called her a coward, but it was true.

She'd run away from surgery. She'd run from Shane and now she was running away from Carson. She wasn't even giving him the choice or the chance to be with her.

You didn't run from Avery. You stayed with him.

Stayed and tried to keep him from bleeding out, even though you'd been alone, young and terrified.

Esme crumpled up in a ball and began to sob.

When had her life become such a failure?

There was a knock at her door. She wanted to ignore it. Worried that Carson had come back, because she didn't want him to see her like this. She didn't want him to see her again. She didn't deserve any kind of absolution or pity from him.

The knocking was incessant and then she heard a voice. One that she hadn't heard in a long time.

"Esme, it's your father. Can I come in?"

Dad?

She hadn't seen him since she'd disappointed him so badly, when she'd given up on surgery and run out on Shane.

She leaped up and ran to the door, flinging it open. "Dad? What're you doing here?"

Before he answered he hugged her, pulling her close into an embrace that made tears well in her eyes, but she didn't return the hug, too shocked that he was standing here.

"I can't believe you're here," she murmured as the hug ended.

"Well, I saw on the news that there was a massive landslide in Crater Lake. Your mother mentioned to me that was where you were moving to. Can I come in?"

"Sure." Esme stepped to the side and let him in her clinic. She shut the door and locked it. "I don't understand. I didn't tell Mom where I was going. I haven't talked to either of you since Valentine's Day, the day I...the day I ran from Shane."

"Not your stepmother. Your biological mother."

"Ah, yes, I did tell her." She ran her hand through her hair. "I called her for the first time in a long time when I was leaving Los Angeles. She'd lived up this way for some time and she helped me make a decision about where I was going to set up shop."

Her father glanced around the waiting room. "It looks nice, except for all the boxes. You've been here a few months—I thought you would be further along with setting up than this."

"I'm not setting up. I'm packing up." She couldn't look him in the eyes. She was worried she'd see the same disappointment. When she glanced over, when she dared to look at him, she was surprised it was concern not disappointment etched in his face.

"What? Why?"

Esme sighed. "It's complicated."

"Esme Petersen, what is going on?"

She threw her hands up in the air and collapsed in a waiting-room chair. "I don't know."

Her father gave her that look. The one that struck fear in her heart and usually terrified most criminals when he was working the beat. "I don't believe that for a second. You know, I did watch the news reports. I know that two of the victims in that landslide happen to be Shane Draven and his wife."

Esme nodded. "Yeah."

"Did you see him up there?"

She nodded. "I did. In fact, I saved his life. At least, I think I did. He was airlifted off the mountain. I put in his chest tube."

Her dad made a face, as he always did when she talked medicine, but then she noticed the worry in the lines of his face and the dark circles under his eyes.

"I was worried about you. When I heard there was a landslide… You haven't spoken to me in a long time. I wanted to see for myself that you were okay. I couldn't lose another child."

A tear slid down Esme's face. "I'm sorry."

"You should've called. I've been so worried."

"I would've called, but when I walked out on Shane you made it pretty clear that you were disappointed with me. I could tell that you saw Mom in me and that I was a disappointment to you and Sharon. I know how hard you both worked to give me an education and I let you both down."

"Esme," her father whispered and he took a seat next to her. "I might've been concerned, but disappointed in you leaving Shane? Never, but I was disappointed you walked away from surgery. You walked away from your gift."

"I froze during a surgery I knew. I froze and the patient died. I don't have a gift, not anymore."

"Yes, you do…you're a damn good surgeon. I don't know how you do it, dealing with all the blood and vein things."

Esme chuckled, her dad breaking the tension that had fallen between them. "Vein things?"

"You know what I'm talking about. Point is you ran. You should've held your ground. You're stronger than that."

She nodded. "Am I?"

"You are."

"That's kind of you to say, Dad, but I don't think my surgery career would've survived. I became a surgeon for Avery. I dedicated my life to it and then…I don't even know who I am."

"Why did you give it up, then?"

"I lost myself."

Her dad nodded, tears in his eyes. "I know, but you're strong. Brave."

Esme shook her head. Tears falling freely. "I'm not a surgeon anymore."

"Yes. You are. People make mistakes, Esme. I made a mistake on the force."

"What?" she asked, stunned.

"I shot someone. I thought it was a burglar and it turned out to be a guy who lost his keys and was just trying to get back into his own house. And I shot him. I fired. I acted before I thought."

"Did he die?"

"No. Thankfully, but for a long time I was under probation. For a long time I was known as Shooter Petersen. The cop who shot first and asked questions later. It's not something I'm proud of. It was humiliating and it took a long time to earn back my unit's trust, my chief's trust and the community's trust, but I did. There were many times I wanted to run away. Give up being a police officer even though it was the thing I loved more than anything. You gave up the thing you loved and I'm not talking about Shane because I don't think you ever really loved him."

"Surgery?"

"Yeah. You gave that up and you shouldn't have. You're a surgeon, Esme Petersen. I have the bills from your college education to prove it."

Esme laughed with her dad. "What if the town here decides to listen to the press? What if they find out about my past? What if I can't...?" Then she thought about Jenkins at the mill. Tyner's appendectomy and the chest tube. She was *still* a surgeon. And no matter how much she denied it, it was part of her. Just as Carson was.

"You put a chest tube in your ex-fiancé up on a mountain." Her father shrugged. "Who cares if your past taints their judgment of you? Then it's their loss. Prove to them that they have nothing to worry about. I think you've been doing a good job so far, helping out on that landslide, and I heard talk at the local motel that you stuck a needle in some guy's chest and did emergency surgery in town, as well. If that isn't the work of a surgeon I don't know what is."

"Yeah. I did."

"They admire you. They don't want you to leave. Do you want to leave?"

Esme shook her head. "No. I don't. I'd like to stay, even if it meant I wasn't a full-blown surgeon. I could work in this town here and be happy."

"Why can't you open a surgical clinic here?"

"Dad, I was a heart surgeon. I can't really perform procedures here, but I'm sure I could get hospital privileges in the nearest hospital."

Her dad nodded. "That's my girl. So are you going to stay?"

"Yeah." Esme smiled and looked around at her clinic. She could reform herself. She could open up a small cardio clinic here in town. There were enough communities around the town that she could get patients.

She wanted to stay in Crater Lake. She didn't want to keep running and she wasn't going to let Eli Draven drive her out of town.

She might not be Dr. Draven's protégée anymore, but she didn't have to stand in his shadow. She was a surgeon in her own right and her career would only be defined by one person.

Her.

Her dad had made her see that she was being foolish. She'd run scared too many times and she was letting people's judgments of her rule her life.

She wouldn't run from Carson. She might have run from Shane, but she understood why she had now. She hadn't loved him. Shane had wanted her to be someone she wasn't. Carson loved her for who she really was. Carson wanted her to be a surgeon.

She loved Carson.

He brought out the best in her, encouraging her when she was scared of picking up that scalpel again.

Until that day at the mill she hadn't performed a surgical procedure in so long but he'd encouraged her. He thought her skill was a gift she was squandering and he was right. It was.

Of course, she'd ruined things with Carson now, but even if she had she wasn't going to run from that pain. She was going to stay now. Hopefully in time Carson would trust her again and maybe if she was lucky he'd open his heart.

And when he did, she wasn't going to let him go.

"So?" her father said, interrupting her chain of thoughts. "Have I got through that thick, stubborn shell of yours? Are you going to stay and finish the job you started here? Because Sharon and I didn't raise a quitter."

"No, you guys didn't." She kissed her father on the cheek. "Yeah, I'm going to stay here. Even if the residents find out about my past. I'm going to stay and face it. I'm tired of running away."

"Good." Her father stood up. "Now, are you going to make me stay in that little motel until I leave tomorrow night or are you going to put up your old man?"

"I think I'll put up my old man. Of course you can stay here."

"Good. Do you want to go get some lunch and then I'll grab my stuff from the motel?" he asked.

"That sounds good, Dad, but I have to do one more thing. Can you wait?"

"Sure."

Esme gave him a quick peck on the cheek and then ran out of her clinic. She ran across the street to Carson's clinic. She needed to talk to him. She needed to tell him how she felt and she needed to apologize for the things she'd said to him. Even if he wouldn't listen to her.

She ran into his clinic.

Louise, his nurse, came to the front from the back. "Dr. Petersen? How can I help you?"

"Is Dr. Ralston in? I need to speak with him."

"No, I'm sorry. He went to Missoula to pick up his brother."

"I thought he did that three days ago?" Esme asked, confused.

"He was supposed to, but the other Dr. Ralston had to stay and monitor Mr. Draven's health. It took a turn for the worse."

Oh, God.

"Did Mr. Draven pull through?"

Louise shrugged. "I really don't know. I'm sorry. Anyways, Dr. Ralston has gone to Missoula today. I don't think he'll be back until later tonight."

"Thank you, Louise."

"Can I take a message for him?"

Tell him I love him. Tell him I'm staying. Only she didn't want to leave that message with his nurse. She wanted to tell him herself.

"No. It's okay. I'll talk to him another time." Esme left the office and headed back to her clinic, hoping that it wasn't too late for her and Carson.

She prayed it wasn't too late.

CHAPTER FOURTEEN

CARSON WAS SURPRISED that he got to Missoula in one piece. He actually didn't remember the drive to the hospital because all he could think about was Esme and that she was leaving. It was a blow. He was hurt.

His heart hurt.

He should've known better. This was why he didn't put his heart on the line. It was his fault. Everything he was feeling, it was his fault. He shouldn't have cared about her. He shouldn't have let her in.

He shouldn't have fallen in love with her, because, try not to as he might, he was absolutely in love with Esme and once again his heart was breaking. Only this time it was much, much worse.

When he got to the hospital he noticed all the press vehicles around. Not surprising as Shane Draven was president of a big corporation and son of a prominent surgeon.

Shane Draven.

That was who Esme had been engaged to. He'd read interviews about Shane and his father and he had a hard time picturing someone like Esme with Shane. Then again, Luke always said he'd had a hard time picturing Danielle and Carson together.

Still, it explained her behavior when they'd been up at the mill and when she'd jammed that chest tube into Shane Draven's chest.

If she had run away from Shane, and because she was a gentle person, she probably blamed herself. Felt as if she didn't deserve love.

Boy, do I understand that.

Maybe that was why she'd pushed him away.

Still, she's running away.

While another voice inside him said, *You could go with her.*

And it scared him to think of leaving the safety net of Crater Lake, the only home he'd known, of giving up the family practice, of changing for Esme.

Could he? Could he really pack up his whole life on the possibility that she'd still be with him in the future? How could he leave Crater Lake? It would mean that the family practice, which had been open for over a century, would close.

How could he let his family down?

How could you let yourself down?

He got out of his car and headed into the hospital. At the front desk they told him where he could find Luke, who was still on the CCU floor.

Carson couldn't even think straight. He didn't know what to think. When Danielle had left it had hurt him, but he'd got over it. The prospect of Esme leaving left a gnawing hole in him. It ticked him off that she was giving up.

Why was she giving up?

Aren't you giving up?

"Carson?"

The familiar voice dragged him out of his reverie

and he stopped in his tracks. He turned around and behind him was Danielle.

She'd changed. He barely recognized her, but it had been several years. He'd thought that he'd never forget Danielle's face. He'd thought it was so burned in his brain, reminding him of the hurt as a warning to him, but now, compared to Esme, Danielle was a dim memory.

"Danielle, how are you?" He held out his hand, but she gave him a quick awkward hug.

"Good. Luke said you were arriving today."

Carson cursed under his breath. "Did he?"

"Yeah, he hasn't left Shane Draven's side in the CCU. There were several times we weren't sure he'd pull through."

"Well, when Luke saves someone on the mountain, he likes to see a job to the end."

"Did he put in that chest tube?" Danielle asked.

"No…he didn't."

She raised her eyebrows. "Did you?"

"No. Another doctor did."

"Ah," Danielle said. "Well, whoever did did an amazing job. Dr. Ledet, the other surgeon on the case, said the chest tube probably saved Shane's life. Wish I could meet that doctor, to insert a chest tube in the emergent situation like that, in conditions like that."

"Yes, she's a brilliant doctor. We're going to miss her."

A strange look passed over Danielle's face. "She's leaving Crater Lake."

"You say that like it's inevitable."

Danielle rolled her eyes. "Come on, Carson. Even with all these new hotels and resorts going up on the outskirts of town, it's still a small town. Nothing changes. Nothing. Not even you."

It hit him hard, because it was true.

He couldn't change for Danielle, but could he change for Esme?

"Some things do change, Danielle. I'm glad you found your place. I'm happy for you."

Danielle was stunned. "Thanks."

Carson nodded and then continued on his way to CCU. He had been so angry with Danielle for so long, he hadn't realized how angry he had been and, because he'd been angry at her, he hadn't been able to move past it. He hadn't been able to forgive himself.

When he got up on the CCU floor, he found Luke at the charge station, charting and wearing... "Scrubs?" Carson teased.

Luke glanced over at him. "It's about time you showed up."

"It's a three-hour drive. I had to finish some of my own charting this morning."

Luke nodded. "You're so tied to Dad's practice."

"My practice, you mean. It could be yours, as well."

Luke shut the chart and grinned. "You know it's not for me."

"Who says it's for me?"

Luke arched his eyebrows. "Do tell."

"Never mind. You ready to go?"

He nodded, handed the chart back and grabbed his rucksack from behind the counter. "Let's go."

They walked in silence back through the hospital. Carson wasn't saying much. He was trying to process everything, process his feelings, his future. He didn't know what to think.

"So you're in a mood," Luke commented as they walked out of the hospital toward the parking lot.

"Am I?"

"I take it you saw Danielle?"

"I did, but that's not really bothering me."

"What is?" Luke asked, tossing his rucksack into the backseat.

"You are."

"What?"

"You. Why won't you take over Dad's practice? Why does it have to be me?"

Luke crossed his arms. "Who said it has to be you? I didn't force you to take the practice."

"You kind of did," Carson snapped. "You went off to the army and then decided you didn't want to work in Dad's clinic. I had to step up. Dad wanted to retire and there have been Ralstons in Crater Lake forever. What else was I supposed to do?"

"Follow your own path," Luke said. "It's obvious."

Carson cursed under his breath. "It's not obvious."

"It is." Luke scrubbed a hand over his face. "Ever since you were a kid you've had this great sense of duty. You were a good kid. I was a bit of a screwup, but you've had this sense of keeping our family's practice alive. Of not changing and it's been nothing but detrimental to you. Painful. How many dreams have you given up for the sake of family heritage?"

"You need to back off, Luke."

He snorted. "No. I think you need to realize that you're never going to have what you want unless you change. Do something for yourself for once."

Carson shook his head. "I can't."

Why not?

Why did he have to stay in Crater Lake? Another doctor would set up shop. He could sell off the practice.

"She'll walk away, she's going to walk away and you know who I'm talking about," Luke said.

It was his now. His dad had said he could do whatever he wanted with it. Even though he loved his hometown, the house he'd built, it just wasn't enough when you had no one to share it with.

As much as he loved Crater Lake, his job, he loved Esme more.

"Forgive yourself," Luke said. "And for once follow your heart. Do what *you* want to do. Live!"

Carson didn't say anything as he slid into the car to drive back home. He was kicking himself now for the way he'd left it with Esme.

She was going to leave and she was going to leave hating him.

He needed to tell her how he felt.

And he needed to tell her now.

Esme couldn't believe that she'd broken into Carson's home. She'd told her father what she had to do and he'd understood. He'd encouraged her to go with a promise that they would catch up later. She wasn't even sure if he'd be happy to see her. The way they'd left things, the way she'd broken his heart, it might be too late. The person she once was screamed in her head to run away, to not face the hurt, but she couldn't run away.

Not now.

Even if he rejected her. Even if he couldn't forgive or care for her, that was okay. She deserved it, but she wasn't running. She wasn't leaving Crater Lake.

She had plans. She was going to set down roots again

and the prospect of setting down roots and not running away was something she'd always wanted.

Even if the press came pounding at her door about Shane, she didn't care. She wasn't going anywhere. She deserved the life she wanted and she was going to do everything in her power to keep that.

She was going to be a surgeon again. She was going to make her father proud, but, more importantly, she was going to be proud of herself. No more hiding in shadows, keeping her head down.

Esme wandered over to the window. It was dark out and the stars were out again. It made her think of Carson. Of being in his arms, in his bed.

And as she watched the celestial display the aurora borealis erupted across the sky. Beautiful greens, just dancing above the lake. It made her catch her breath in the beauty of it all.

Yeah, she was doing the right thing.

If Carson didn't want her anymore, then that was something she could live with, but she couldn't live with herself if she didn't tell him how she felt.

The sound of his key in the door made her heart skip a beat and she turned around, waiting for him.

He came in and flicked on the lights. He startled to see her standing there.

"Esme?" he asked in confusion. "What're you doing here? I thought you were leaving?"

"I was, but I've changed my mind."

Carson dragged his hand through his hair and then shut his door, dropping his keys on the side table by the door.

"You've changed your mind?"

"Yes."

"Why?" he asked. "You were pretty clear today about your reasons for leaving."

"I know. My reasons have changed." She sighed. "Look, I'm not a girl who ever believed in romance. I thought I wasn't the girl for you. I mean, I ruined the most romantic holiday in the world by jilting my former fiancé. Romance and love have never been my priority."

"So what is?" he asked, crossing his arms and taking a step toward her.

"Surgery." She took a deep breath. "When my brother died I dedicated my life to surgery and when I got together with Shane I forgot who I was. I thought love complicated things and I lost focus."

Carson looked confused. "Why?"

"I don't know."

His expression softened. "I'm sorry. How did your brother die? You never told me."

"I was ten and he was twenty-two. We were in an accident on Valentine's Day. I had to put my hands in his chest to stop the bleeding. His heart stopped under my hands. When he died my mother left. I was scared to love. Scared to lose. It hurt too much, but I swore I would be a surgeon. To save lives so no one had to hurt the way I did."

"So that's why you chose cardio thoracic as your specialty and why you hate Valentine's Day. Why did you choose to almost marry Shane on Valentine's Day?"

"He insisted."

"And you agreed because you thought it might make you forget that day?"

She nodded. "Yes. I did it to please him. It's what Shane wanted. I ran from that wedding because I was tired of not being me. I lost myself. Still, I hurt him. I had closed myself off for too long."

"And now?"

She nodded. "I came here to find myself. To forget surgery, because I didn't deserve happiness, but…"

"But?" he asked.

"Then you walked into my life and my priorities have changed because I didn't take into account something that's very important."

"I love you," he said, surprising her.

"What?"

Carson grinned. "I love you. I figured that's what you were going to say, too."

Esme grinned. "Y-yes, I was."

Carson smiled. "Say it, then."

"I love you." Esme took a step toward him. "I used to run. Afraid of facing my inner demons, afraid of facing rejection, pain. Afraid of facing my own failures, but you changed all that. You changed it the moment you asked me to go up that mountain during that mill accident. No one has ever been able to change my mind once it's set. A drawback of being a cardio-thoracic surgeon."

"I thought you weren't a surgeon?" he asked.

"I'm a surgeon and I'm going to stay here. I'm going to keep practicing as a surgeon."

Carson nodded. "Well, I guess I'm not selling my practice after all."

Esme cocked an eyebrow. "What?"

Carson closed the gap between them. "I was going to sell my practice and go with you. I had been so afraid of forging my own path for so long. So unbending. I couldn't change for anyone. It's cost me in more ways than I care to admit. I used different excuses to keep me here, but when you said you were leaving it…I couldn't bear to live without you. I will change for you. I'd give up anything to be with you. Without you, this isn't my home. You're my home."

Esme couldn't hold back the tears. No apologies were needed. Nothing further needed to be said. She wrapped her arms around him and he held her, but only for a moment until he picked her up, kissing her. Kissing away the tears that were not tears of sadness, but joy.

"I love you, Esme. I love you and I can't live without you. You're my everything." Carson brushed away a tear with his thumb.

"I love you, too. I'm tired of running. I don't want to run. I'm in this for the long haul."

Carson kissed her again, making her weak in the knees, making her melt into his arms. He scooped her up in his arms and carried her into his bedroom.

And she was never going to let him go.

She was done running. She was done hiding.

This was her home.

She was home.

EPILOGUE

February 13th

"THIS BETTER NOT be a Valentine's Day thing," Esme said as Carson covered her eyes and led her into the house. "I don't like Valentine's Day."

"I know. I know, but it's not Valentine's Day. It's the thirteenth and it's a Friday. Does Friday the thirteenth hold any kind of dark secrets for you?" Carson asked.

"Well, this one time at this summer camp…" she teased.

"Ha-ha. Don't tease about that. That movie scared the living daylights out of me."

"Hey, you're the one who is leading a surprise on a Friday the thirteenth. Not me. And how did I not know that you didn't like horror movies? I'm shocked."

"You do?" Carson asked.

"I do. Does that change things?" She tried to suppress the laughing.

"Well." He removed his hands and Esme gasped when she saw the spread laid out for them. They were at home and there was a new dining-room table set up, overlooking the floor-to-ceiling windows at the back of the house.

The fire was snapping and crackling in the large central fireplace, and there were candles and roses everywhere.

"Oh, my gosh," she gasped.

"So, you see, the love of horror movies might just change my mind." There was a twinkle in his eyes.

Esme laughed. "Oh, come on. It's just a minor thing."

"Well, maybe this will change your mind with associating February thirteenth as an unlucky day or a day that has to do with axe-wielding, hockey-mask-wearing monsters."

"A nice dinner? For sure." Then she gasped as he dropped to one knee. "What're you doing?"

"Giving you a good memory, I hope." He pulled out a ring. "Will you marry me, Esme?"

Tears filled her eyes. She'd never expected to get engaged again. She hadn't planned on it, but that had all changed the moment she'd met Dr. Carson Ralston. And since the summer, she'd been patiently waiting for him to ask her.

Actually, she'd planned to ask him tomorrow. On Valentine's Day. Only this time she wasn't trying to bury a painful memory with something that *could* be happy. She knew that Carson was the one. She knew that their lifetime together *would* be happy.

Esme had only been certain about surgery in her life, never in matters of the heart, but when she'd foolishly almost walked away from Carson last summer, she'd known that he held her heart. He was meant for her.

She'd found herself and her place was in his arms. The thought of losing him was more than she could bear. She wanted to be his wife more than anything, to share her life with him and only him.

She'd just thought that she would have to do the proposing. And she was okay with that, but this was so much better.

This was almost too much for her heart to handle and she thought she was going to burst. She wiped away the tears and didn't care if they smudged her mascara. She wanted a clearer look at Carson, down on one knee holding out a diamond ring, which sparkled in the firelight.

How could she ever have contemplated leaving Crater Lake? Leaving him?

"Well? Your silence is kind of worrying me." His brow furrowed. "Was this too much?"

"Yes," she whispered.

"Yes, too much, or yes…?"

Esme sobbed happily, dropping to her knees to kiss him. "Yes. I'll marry you."

He cupped her face in his hands and kissed her. "You had me worried there."

"I'm sorry. I couldn't believe you were actually asking me there for a moment."

"Can't you?"

Esme laughed. "I'm sorry, but I have to say you've ruined Valentine's Day for me."

"What?" he asked. "How could I have ruined Valentine's Day for you? This isn't even Valentine's Day. I didn't even buy a single rose."

"I was planning to propose to you at the Valentine's gala tomorrow night. I even had a dress and everything."

Carson threw his head back and laughed. "For real?"

She nodded. "Your brother was in on it."

"What? How did you manage to pull that off? He's not one for romance either."

Esme shrugged. "I have my ways."

"So what did the dress look like?" he asked huskily.

"Would you like me to model it later for you?" Her pulse began to race and she wrapped her arms around his neck, nibbling on that sensitive spot by his earlobe that she had discovered soon after they'd moved in together.

"You can model for me later, but not the dress. I couldn't care less about the dress."

She laughed. "Can I have my ring now?"

"Hmm, I don't know. Maybe I do want you to get down on one knee and propose to me," he said, teasing her.

"Do you want me to slug you?" She kissed him quickly on the lips. "Will you marry me, Dr. Ralston?"

"Let me think…" Esme punched him on the arm and he laughed. "Of course, you foolish girl."

"You had me worried there for a fraction of a second." She winked.

"Well, I want to make you work for it." Carson slipped the ring on her finger and kissed her, a kiss that melted her down to her very core. "I love you, Esme Petersen. With all my heart. There isn't anyone else in this world that's meant for me. It's you I want. Only you."

"Even if I spend countless hours in an OR a couple hours from home?"

"Even then. I love you."

"And I love you, too, Carson." She kissed him again and then whispered against his neck, "With all my heart, too."

And she did. Absolutely and completely love him. Only him.

* * * * *

FOREVER WITH YOU

KIANNA ALEXANDER

In loving memory of my sweet,
funny and fashionable aunt.
Gwendolyn Denise Mckinnon
1957–2017

Chapter 1

Jazmin Boyd sidestepped between the clothes-laden circular racks inside of Driven to Distraction, her eyes scanning the selections for just the right piece. The interior of the boutique reflected the exterior; the rose-gold paint job on the facade continued inside, where the plush pink Victorian-inspired furniture, crystal chandeliers and polished teak floors accented the space. The boutique, easily the most exclusive apparel store on the small island of Sapphire Shores, North Carolina, was the obvious choice for finding the right dress for the social event of the spring season.

She reached into a section of metallic cocktail dresses and was still rifling through it when Sierra Dandridge-Monroe, her closest friend, appeared beside her. Holding up a teal, sequined halter dress, Sierra released a squeal of excitement. "Girl, isn't this cute? I think this is it. I need to try it on."

Jazmin gave her friend a sidelong glance. "Isn't that dress a little short for a fortieth anniversary party? I'm thinking this crowd is going to skew a little older."

Sierra shrugged. "I'm already married to Cam. I'm not trying to impress anybody but him." She held the dress against herself and twirled. "Besides, older doesn't necessarily mean more conservative. Cam's parents certainly aren't, and it's their party."

"Okay, I'll give you that." She returned her attention to the rack, moving each hanger aside and inspecting each individual piece.

Behind her, Sierra quietly asked, "Still trying to cover it up, huh?"

Her hand went to her neck, her fingertips grazing over the hardened skin beneath her top. She nodded.

"You know, I've noticed a change in you since you've been here on the island, working on the show." Sierra's hand came to rest on her shoulder. "You're a lot calmer and happier here."

"That's true." Sierra was as insightful as ever, and Jazmin would be the first to admit that she'd been far more relaxed since her arrival on the island. *But I'm still not ready to let people see my scar.*

"You know, it's already getting pretty hot and humid around these parts. And as the summer wears on, it's gonna become pretty hard to cover up, the way you have been doing." Sierra gave her shoulder a squeeze before letting her hand drop. "I don't want you bursting into flames, Jaz."

She giggled, loving the way her friend could infuse

a bit of humor into an uncomfortable moment. "I appreciate your concern, Sierra. But I'm just not there yet." She slid another outfit to the left and stopped, looking at the dress she'd just uncovered. Picking the hanger off the rack, she raised the garment in front of her. The lavender dress, woven through with shimmery silver threads, had long, sheer sleeves. The high, regal neckline appealed to her, since she'd come to favor this style over the last few years for both elegance and coverage. "This looks very promising."

"Wow, Jaz. It's gorgeous." Sierra reached out and stroked her fingertips over the soft fabric. "Let's try these on. Remember, we still have to get accessories. And I want to get back to my husband before it gets dark out."

She shook her head as they headed toward the back of the store to make use of the fitting rooms.

Inside the quiet cocoon of the changing room, Jazmin slipped out of her jeans and T-shirt and into the dress. Looking in the full-length mirror, she smiled. The color of the dress made her skin tone pop, and she loved the fit—close, but not too tight. She unlocked the door, stepped out and waited in the mirrored common area for Sierra to appear in her dress.

When Sierra finally emerged in the hot little teal number, Jazmin instantly remarked, "Yeah. That's the one."

Sierra grinned, revolving and checking all the angles in the mirrors. "Yeah, you're right." She paused then, looking her over. "And you have got to buy that one, Jaz. It's perfect for you."

Regarding her reflection, she had to agree. It covered everything she wanted to be hidden from sight, but didn't obscure the figure she worked so hard to maintain. "I agree. Looks like we're ready to move on to the accessorizing phase."

Still dressed in their new finds, the two women circled the boutique, trying on jewelry and more. Sierra bought a pair of gold hoop earrings encrusted with crystals, as well as a pair of pumps nearly the same shade as her dress.

"I've got a pair of silver shoes that will work with this dress." Jazmin selected a pair of dangling crystal-chandelier earrings, a few sterling silver bangles and a silver clip for her hair. After they'd gotten back into their street clothes, they piled their purchases on the counter and pulled out their wallets.

Carrie, the boutique's owner, smiled as she rang them up. "It's so great to have you shopping with us again, Mrs. Monroe. My daughters and I are really looking forward to season two. It's starting to film again soon, isn't it?"

"In the next week or so," Sierra answered as she handed over her credit card.

Watching the exchange, Jazmin was once again thankful for her behind-the-scenes role on *The Shores*. As time passed, and the show became more popular, she watched Sierra go through more and more of these fan encounters. Sierra was a natural at this, so she was always gracious and poised while being pelted with questions and comments from eager viewers. Jazmin knew that if she had to deal with that level of attention, it would quickly start to grate on her nerves.

"You know, it's really my girl Jazmin you should

thank," Sierra commented, gesturing toward her. "She's in charge of postproduction, so the finished product you see on television is the result of her hard work."

Jazmin smiled as Carrie's attention swung her way. "Well, when your rough material is already so high-quality, it's not so hard to do." She gave Sierra a playful jab in the shoulder, then stepped up for her turn to pay for her items.

Carrie handed Sierra her bag. "Well, I appreciate both of you for your hard work. My daughters are seventeen and twenty, and we rarely agree on anything these days. But we can all sit and watch *The Shores* together." She used her price gun to scan the tags. "And it's nice to know that you're actually friends and not just coworkers."

"What can I say? I'm a lucky girl." Jazmin winked in Sierra's direction.

By the time the two of them left with their purchases, it was well past six. The sun was moving toward the horizon, but there would be another good hour of sunlight before darkness settled over the island. The cool, refreshing breeze coming off the Atlantic wafted by, lifting the loose ends of Jazmin's hair and making her sigh with delight.

"Do you wanna go for dinner? Or are you rushing home to your man?" Gripping the handle of her bag in one hand, she used her other one to gently pinch Sierra's shoulder.

"Ow!" She twisted her lips in a mock frown. "See, that type of abuse is why I'm taking my butt home."

Jazmin rolled her eyes. "As if there was any doubt. I'm gonna hit Della's on the way in. I'm starved."

"Okay. See you at the party, boo." Sierra reached out and pulled her into a hug. "Text me when you get home, Jaz."

"Sure thing." She gave Sierra a squeeze, then her friend waved and walked to her car, got in and drove away.

After she left, Jazmin tucked her bag into her trunk, then strolled down the sidewalk toward the deli.

Savion Monroe eased into the chair behind his desk with a sigh. Being able to shut himself in his office and decompress, after what had been a very long day, gave him immense relief.

He'd spent the better part of the day in meetings with the rest of the staff of Monroe Holdings, Incorporated. As the chief executive officer, he was responsible for final approval for all MHI's projects. The day-to-day management of all the existing properties held by the company, which owned 63 percent of the land and buildings on the island, would be enough to keep him busy. However, MHI was in the final stages of planning the most important project they had ever tackled: the Mary Ellen Monroe Memory Park. The green space, meant to memorialize Savion's paternal grandmother, had finally gotten all the necessary approvals and permits to move forward. His father, Carver, was overseeing a memory garden containing a bust of his mother that would serve as the centerpiece of the grounds.

I'm going to do this right. Not just to honor Grandma, but to make my father proud. He worked hard to keep the business successful, just as his father had done before retiring. Savion understood that even as the eldest Monroe child, he wasn't necessarily entitled to the CEO role. He'd earned it by showing his father a strong work ethic and a commitment to the family real-estate empire. Working side by side with his two younger siblings could be stressful at times, but he loved knowing that he was an integral part of the family legacy.

He grabbed his leather-bound daybook, opened it and placed it on the desk in front of him. The book measured five-by-eight inches, and the brown leather had started to crack around the edges, showing how aged and well-loved it was. It was his single most valued possession, and he never went anywhere without it. At night, he laid it on his nightstand while he slept, in case he awakened in the wee hours and needed to make note of something. When he drove, it rested in the center console of his SUV. Wherever he went, it was either in his hand or tucked beneath his arm. Because of its size, most people assumed it was a planner, a place where he kept track of his appointments and responsibilities. He'd migrated his schedule to a cloud-based app ages ago, along with the rest of tech-savvy society, but he'd kept the book, knowing that people's perception of it as an ordinary planner would work in his favor.

And no one, under any circumstances, was allowed to touch it. His brother and sister often teased him about his "unnatural attachment" to the book, but they knew better than to try him, so they left it alone. He made sure that every new employee knew never to mess with it, should he ever mistakenly leave it lying around. While he couldn't imagine ever being careless with the book, he considered his hands-off decree an extra insurance policy for keeping his writings private. He wouldn't know what he'd do if someone were to open it and peruse the contents.

Picking up the pencil resting in an elastic loop on the inside of the leather cover, he flipped to a blank page and started jotting down his thoughts.

He'd written three and a half lines when he heard someone knocking on his office door. With a groan, he tucked the pencil back into the loop, then closed the notebook and the cover. "Come in."

The door swung open and Hadley strolled in. Dressed in a dark skirt and white blouse with the blue-and-green MHI logo on the front, she carried a small stack of folders. Looking at his desk, she said, "Sorry. I didn't mean to interrupt your planning period. I can come back later if you want."

He shook his head. "It's already after five. I'm going home soon, so go ahead and say what you need to say."

She chuckled while stifling a yawn. "We both know you'll be here a while, but okay." She came to the desk, taking the seat across from him, and opened one of the folders. "I came to let you in on the last-minute preparations for Mom and Dad's party."

He frowned. "I thought everything was taken care of."

"It is, for the most part. But one of the interns screwed up two of the payments, and I've gotta get that straightened out." She blew out a breath, as if exasperated. "They paid the caterer the money due to the deejay, and vice versa. Now the deejay owes us a refund and we still have a balance with the caterer. It's a bit of a mess." She yawned again, her eyes closing briefly then popping open again.

"Sheesh." He leaned back in his chair. "The party's in two days. Do you have enough time to straighten it out?"

"Yes, if you let me have tomorrow off. That way I can go do this in person."

His brow hitched. "You're telling me you need the whole day off to do those two things?"

"It's not just that." She glanced down at a page in her folder. "Remember, the company is coming over to set up the tent tomorrow, too, and I'm also overseeing the decorations, the people installing the dance floor, making sure we have enough fans and that the electrical hookups are in place—"

He put up his hand. "Okay, okay. Stop rattling off items on the list. Considering all that, yes, you can take the day off."

"Great. Oh, and you know Cam's off tomorrow, too, right?"

He rolled his eyes. "Damn it. I forgot." He watched his sister close the folder and stand. "What is he doing? Because I know he's not helping with the party. He hates planning things like that."

"You're right, he's not helping me. He's taking Sierra to Wilmington to see the battleship. Apparently, after all this time here, she's never been on it."

"Fantastic," he groused. The USS *North Carolina*, a World War II–era battleship docked on the seaport in downtown Wilmington, was one of the most popular tourist destinations in the area. The most decorated American battleship of the Second World War, the old

BB-55 had seen combat in every significant American naval offensive in the Pacific theater. "I'm gonna guess he booked a special VIP tour, right?"

She nodded. "Of course. You know Cam. He never does anything by half measures." She walked over to the door, leaned against it and yawned again.

Feeling his brow furrow, he asked, "Sis, are you okay? You seem tired." Studying her face, he noted that she also looked a little pale.

She waved him off. "I'm fine, just a little wiped. Guess I should have had that second cup of coffee."

He wasn't sure if he believed that, but he wasn't about to rile up his baby sister. *I'm too tired to deal with her if she gets snappy.* "You know, you're hardly ever here since you married Devon. And it's more of the same with Cam since he and Sierra got hitched. Am I the only one around here who cares about keeping MHI in the black?"

She rolled her eyes. "Savion, you already know we care about the family business just as much as you do. The only reason you're here all the time is that you insist on avoiding romantic involvement."

"You two already fell into the 'love trap.' I can't be falling in, too. Somebody has to be the responsible one."

"Whatever. You can do both, you know." She stood in the door frame, poised to walk out. "And let me assure you, it's no trap. It's the best, most enriching part of my life." With that said, she and her folder disappeared.

Left alone in his office, Savion contemplated his sister's words for a moment, then pushed aside his thoughts and faced down the work still to be done.

Chapter 2

Jazmin reclined in the plush padded folding chair, a filled flute of champagne in her hand. The atmosphere beneath the big white tent set up on the Monroes' sprawling property was as festive as tonight's occasion called for. Sitting next to her, Sierra drank from her own glass of prosecco. "Can you believe Carver and Viola have been married forty years?"

She shook her head. "It's really something. Especially since Mrs. Monroe only looks about forty-five herself." She looked over to the head table and saw the happy couple seated at the center. While they were surrounded by their children and close family members, it was obvious that Viola and Carver only had eyes for one another. *Maybe it's the glow of love that keeps her looking so young.*

Sierra's voice broke into her thoughts. "Campbell

can be a handful sometimes. But we're in it for the long haul. One day, you'll be coming to our fortieth anniversary party."

"I'll be sure to put it in my datebook," Jazmin chided, elbowing Sierra playfully. The sound of a fork striking glass caught Jazmin's attention. Her gaze swung back to the head table, just in time to see Savion, the eldest Monroe child, climb to his feet. Conversation died down, and the hired disc jockey stopped spinning records as everyone present looked toward the front table. Savion's tall, solid frame, draped in an expensive-looking tailored tuxedo, commanded attention. The tux, a deep shade of blue, was complemented by his crisp jet-black shirt and blue-and-gold striped tie. The dark pools of his eyes shimmered in the candlelit glow inside the tent. His strong jaw and goateed chin made him look like the perfect combination of refinement and ruggedness. His deep voice filled the tent. "I'd like to thank you all for coming out tonight, to celebrate my parents' milestone anniversary. Forty years of love and commitment is no small feat, especially in today's world. It seems marriage has fallen out of fashion, and folks change spouses as carelessly as they change clothes. I'm grateful to my mother and father for the example they have shown my siblings and me, and for the stable, loving upbringing they gave us."

Jazmin felt a tear slip down her cheek as the profundity of his words struck her.

Savion lifted his glass into the air, and everyone followed suit. "I'd like to raise a toast. To my father and mother, who have shown us all how beautiful love can be. Congratulations."

"Salud." Jazmin took a sip from her glass, then set it on the table to join in the rousing applause that went up as Carver leaned over and tenderly kissed his wife of four decades. A sigh escaped Jazmin as she watched the exchange. As everyone took their seats, the band began to play the classic jazz standard "In a Sentimental Mood." Carver stood, gallantly offering his hand to Viola, then led her to the dance floor set up between the head table and the rest of the tables.

Jazmin pressed her hand to her chest, watching as the couple of the hour swirled around the dance floor, their bodies pressed close together. Mrs. Monroe looked resplendent in her floor-grazing gold charmeuse gown, and her husband's dark tuxedo, gold bow tie and vest made their attire as perfectly complementary as they were to each other.

Sierra sighed. "Look at them. They're so dang sweet together it makes my teeth hurt."

Campbell appeared next to the table, wearing his signature smile. "Sierra, come dance with me, baby."

"I thought you were supposed to be sitting at the head table?" Sierra made the remark with a cocked eyebrow.

"I am. But I'm not about to miss an opportunity to dance with my beautiful wife."

Sierra stood and took his hand. Glancing Jazmin's way, she said, "I'll be back, girl."

Jazmin waved her off. "Go on, dance with your man. I'll be fine."

After the newlyweds wandered off, Jazmin settled back in her chair, nursing the remains of her champagne. She let her gaze sweep around the tent, to the couples taking the dance floor and the folks hanging around at the tables and by the buffet. This was her second time at a Monroe family shindig, the first having been Campbell and Sierra's London wedding last fall. She had to admit, they knew how to throw a classy affair.

Thinking of the wedding brought up memories of dancing with Savion. He'd been sure on his feet as he guided her around the floor, and she could clearly recall how he'd smelled of rich amber and fir, and the way he'd kept her laughing with his dry wit. He was fine. The kind of fine that made a woman want to throw both caution and her panties to the wind. She didn't want to dwell on that too long, lest the glass of champagne already in her system make her abandon her better judgment. So, she turned her mind elsewhere.

She'd been on the island of Sapphire Shores for a little over a year now, working as postproduction manager on *The Shores*, the popular television drama filmed on location here. Showrunner Devon Granger, whom she'd known for years in Los Angeles, had pulled her in on the project, and she truly enjoyed it. Working with the cast and crew had been mostly pleasant, save for a few bumps here and there. The only thing she didn't like about her gig with the show was the slow pace of life on the island. Being a city girl, born and bred in LA, made the quiet calm of the island seem a bit maddening at times. Still, because she loved the work she did here, she did her best to embrace the island, its residents and all its quirks.

When she thought about it, the call from Devon had come at just the right time. As much as she loved LA, she'd needed to get away from there, needed to get a fresh start, far away from where things had gone off the rails for her. And after she'd secured her position on the production team, the first suggestion she'd made was to let her good friend Sierra read for the lead role. Mindful of the happiness of the occasion, she pushed away those thoughts. Today wasn't about dwelling on the darkness she'd left behind in the City of Angels. Today was about celebrating a love that had lasted four decades and was still going strong.

She noticed Savion standing at one end of the head table, talking to a man she didn't recognize, but whose features bore similarities to Carver's. The way they conversed conveyed a certain familiarity, another factor that made Jazmin think the two of them might be related. Whoever the other man was, he and Savion seemed to be having a serious conversation. Jazmin also noticed that every few words, one of them would gesture in her direction. After the third time, Jazmin could feel her brow creasing. They seemed to be talking about her, but she couldn't imagine why they'd be doing that, or what they might be saying. *What's going on over there?* It appeared she would soon get her answer because, a few moments later, Savion started striding toward her, his gaze locked on her face.

After making his toast celebrating his parents' union, Savion left his seat and moved toward the end of the head table, intending to grab a dessert from the buffet. He was waylaid when his cousin Troy stepped into his path. "What's up, Savion?"

He could feel the smile stretching his lips. "If it ain't

troublemaking Troy. I haven't seen you in forever. How you been?" The two shared a quick embrace.

"I'm doing okay. And you're right, it's been way too long since I came to see my East Coast fam."

Savion gave his cousin a playful punch in the shoulder. "You're damn right. What's it been, five or six years?"

Troy shrugged. "To be honest, I don't even remember. But, of course, I wasn't gonna miss Uncle Carver and Aunt Viola's milestone anniversary."

"How's Uncle Wardell?"

"You know Pops. He's salty as ever." Troy laughed. "But as long as I make sure to keep him supplied with cigars, he does all right."

He didn't have to ask why Wardell wasn't present—he hated weddings, anniversaries and anything associated with what he referred to as the "farce known as love." His uncle's brief marriage to his aunt Frieda had been strained at best and disastrous at worst. The West Coast Monroes were known for drama, at least up until Frieda had split, finally giving Wardell grounds for divorce. "What have you been up to?"

"Ranching, mainly. Worked on a couple different spreads out west, mainly between Santa Fe and Durango." He ran a hand over his hair. "I've stayed pretty close to home because I love it out there, ya know?"

"I get it. You've always been a fan of wide-open spaces." He'd visited the area twice in the last few years, and he could see why Troy loved the plains so much. To call the area "scenic" would constitute a gross understatement.

"I'd ask what you've been up to, but I already know.

Still working in the office, doing your CEO thing. I see you, cousin. Go ahead and take over the world."

Savion shook his head, stepping back to look at Troy's black suit, white shirt and gold tie. "You clean up all right, Troy."

"Thanks." Troy made a show of tugging his lapels. "You look pretty clean yourself. So tell me, Savion. What's been happening around here?"

He chuckled. "Man, it would take all day to tell you what's happened since the last time you visited."

"Good thing I'm staying a few weeks. You, Hadley and Cam will have plenty of time to catch me up." Troy winked.

"I was headed to the dessert table. You wanna join me?"

Troy shook his head. "Watching my sugar intake. Plus, let's be honest, Savion. The only sweet thing you've got your eye on is that one over there." Troy made a sly gesture over Savion's shoulder.

Savion already knew to whom Troy was referring. He glanced in that direction, his eyes falling on Jazmin Boyd. She worked in the production department on *The Shores*, and she'd danced with him at Cam's wedding last fall.

Today, she wore a shimmery purple cocktail dress that just grazed her knees. The high neck and sheer sleeves covered her shoulders and arms, but the hem did nothing to hide the expanse of her long brown legs, which attracted his attention. Her upswept hair, light makeup and dazzling earrings completed her elegant look.

Troy snapped his fingers. "See? You've been checking her out all evening. Do you know her?"

Savion sighed, annoyed that his cousin had so easily picked up on his interest. "I know her, but just barely. Her name is Jazmin and she works on Devon's television show."

Troy elbowed him. "Go talk to her! You've been sweating her all night. Might as well go make a move, playa."

Savion rolled his eyes. His cousin was known to be a shoot-from-the-hip type of guy, so he wasn't surprised by Troy's words. "What about you, Troy? Is there anyone special in your life?"

"Nah, man. And don't be trying to change the subject." Troy gestured toward Jazmin again. "You go get your lady, and I'm about to catch up with the rest of the fam."

Savion drew a deep breath, turned and walked toward Jazmin. Their eyes met and held as he approached. She stood from her seat as he entered her space. "Savion. How are you?"

"I'm fine, Jazmin. And you?"

"Doing well." She glanced down, the dark fan of her lashes fluttering. "It's...nice to see you again."

"Believe me. The pleasure is mine." At that moment, he felt the words of a verse bloom inside his mind. She was walking inspiration for the words that flowed from his pen.

The DJ segued into a slow cut by Ro James, and Savion saw the window of opportunity opening. "Jazmin, would you honor me with a dance?"

She gave him a soft smile. "Sure."

He took her hand and eased her out onto the dance floor. Pulling her close enough to get a comfortable hold on her waist, yet leaving a respectable distance between them, he began to guide her as he swayed along with the pace of the music. She smiled, moving a little closer to him until their bodies touched. That was fine by him. Having her so near made his temperature climb a few notches. But as long as it was her decision to close the distance, he was down.

Holding her near as they danced together felt much more natural than he had expected. She seemed to fit perfectly into his arms, as if she'd been formed to be held by only him. He looked down into her eyes, and she met his gaze.

"Savion." His name left her lips with a breathy sigh.

"Yes?"

"Either I've had too much champagne, or you're having an effect on me."

Intrigued by this development, he asked, "What makes you say that?"

"I...want you to kiss me."

He cocked an eyebrow. "Do you?"

She nodded.

"And you're sure about that?"

Another nod. "Yes."

"You don't have to ask twice." So, he leaned down and placed a gentle peck on her lips. They were yielding and sweet, and she tasted of strawberries. He purposely kept the contact brief, aware of the prying eyes of his family and friends all around them. Besides, in case it really was the champagne talking, he wanted to err on the side of caution. When he drew back, he immediately missed the softness of her lips.

She smiled. "I enjoyed that. Probably a little more than I'd like to admit."

The song came to an end, and they took a step apart, giving each other space. Still, nothing could break the attraction that crackled between them like an electric current.

The sound of a loud whistle caught Savion's attention, and he turned to see his cousin Troy signaling to him, a broad grin on his face.

"Who is that?" She posed the question in a voice laced with humor and curiosity.

Rolling his eyes, he turned back to Jazmin. "That's my cousin Troy. My only cousin on my Dad's side. Ignore him."

She laughed. "If you say so."

"Savion! Come over here!" It was Hadley, wildly gesturing to him from the other side of the tent. "We're taking pictures."

"Duty calls." Savion stepped back again, taking a moment to kiss Jazmin's hand in parting. "Thank you for the dance."

She blushed. "You're welcome."

After that, he reluctantly walked away, knowing that if he didn't, his sister would only call him again, and louder.

But even as he moved away from Jazmin, he couldn't deny the pull of her presence, which lingered around him like the sweet fragrance of her perfume.

Chapter 3

With a tall cup of iced coffee in hand, Jazmin sat at the long table in the studio conference room. She knew she shouldn't be drinking coffee past 4:00 p.m., but she'd been dragging since lunch and desperately needed a boost. The caffeine flowing through her system gave her just enough of a buzz to keep her from resting her head on the table for an impromptu nap.

All around her sat the showrunners and the principle cast members. The actors were doing table reads of their scripts for the first episode, which was due to begin filming in a few days, and the showrunners were there to observe.

Aaron Tarlton, the show's director, sat silently at one end of the table, while executive producer and showrunner Devon Granger occupied the seat at the opposite end. Jazmin sat to Devon's right, along with head writers Kris and Amelia. The actors sat on the left side of the table.

Sierra, who played the main character, Karen Drake, turned to Grayson Richardson, the gray-eyed, caramel-skinned hearttthrob who played Karen's love interest, Xander Lasalle, and delivered her line with the same passion she did when on camera.

Boy, she's really selling it. What an actress. Jazmin loved to watch her friend at work, and seeing Sierra give Grayson a deep, longing look, she was once again amazed by her talent.

Grayson, known to be something of a goofball despite his reputation as a sex symbol, read his lines in the same manner. Every bit of energy Sierra gave him, he returned to her. He even clutched Sierra's hand as he spoke of his character's devotion to Karen.

Cast newcomer Zola Revere, who'd been recently placed in the role of Xander's long-lost half sister, Phaedra Lasalle, was another story. Zola, a tall, willowy twenty-two-year-old with bountiful coils of dark hair and skin the color of almonds, was the youngest person in the cast. There were a few interns still in their teens, but none of the actors on the show were near her age.

Jazmin assumed Zola's awareness of her relative youth contributed to her shyness. Having seen Zola acting in a short-lived drama from last year, *River's Edge*, she knew the young sister had talent. She'd do fine at *The Shores*, as soon as she found her voice.

As the other two actors turned toward Zola, she delivered her line in a rushed whisper.

"Hold on," Amelia said, leaning forward. "Can you run that last line again, Zola?"

Zola did as she was asked, but without raising the volume very much.

"Hold on, hold on." Aaron put up his hand. "Zola, we need to be able to hear you. Deliver your lines loudly enough so we can hear you. If you keep doing what you're doing now, even the mics won't be able to pick up what you're saying."

"Buck up, kid," quipped Grayson. "We're all rooting for you to do well here."

Around the table, everyone added their words of encouragement.

Jazmin watched Zola's face light up. They started the read again, and this time, she delivered her line with the appropriate gusto.

"Xander, you know our father would never approve of what you're doing!" Zola stabbed an accusatory finger in the air, in Grayson's direction.

Grayson smiled. "Now we're cooking with grease."

Watching as the rest of the reading progressed without any problems, Jazmin drained her iced coffee while she jotted notes in the small pink notebook on the table in front of her. Devon always asked the crew members present at the table reads to write down their thoughts on things, including the general direction of the show, character arcs and specific lines of dialogue. She liked the new direction the writers had come up with for the second season, and she thought the viewers would like it, as well. With any luck, season two would be just as popular as season one.

After the table read ended, most of the people present cleared out of the conference room. Aaron remained, along with Sierra, Devon and Jazmin. While the men talked shop, Sierra gestured to her. "Jaz. Let's go in the hallway."

Tossing her empty cup into the trash can, she followed her friend out of the room.

In the corridor, Sierra pulled out her phone. "I wanted to show you some of the snaps from London that I haven't shown you yet."

Moving closer to her friend, she looked at the screen. "Oh, are these from filming the movie?" Sierra's main reason for being in London last fall was to film her first romantic comedy, *Her London Love*. There were photos of Sierra with her leading man, in the fitted dress she'd worn for her fictional nuptials, and plenty of random images of the sets, her cast mates and the crew at work.

"Some are, and some are from the real wedding and honeymoon." She scrolled to a photo of her and Campbell, dressed in their wedding finery.

Jazmin couldn't help smiling as she viewed the image. The happy couple was locked in an embrace, their lips pressed together, with a fantastic aerial view of London as the backdrop. "You guys are so cute."

Sierra winked. "Thanks, girl. I really want to go back. Between the wedding and the filming, we never got to see Big Ben. I'm also hoping to get out of the city, take in some of the English countryside."

She leaned back against the wall. "I feel you on that. I'd really like to go to Stratford-upon-Avon one day."

"Really? I never pegged you for a Shakespeare fan."

"Yeah, I'm down with Will Shakes. He had a real way with words. You might say he was an early insult comic."

Sierra's expression conveyed her surprise.

"If you don't believe me, look up 'Shakespearean insults' on the internet someday."

Sierra chuckled. "Maybe I will, Jaz." She tucked her phone into the pocket of her black blazer.

Aaron left the conference room then, squeezing out between the two women. "Excuse me, ladies. I'll see y'all tomorrow."

"Bye, Aaron." Jazmin moved aside as the director passed, watching him disappear down the hall.

Devon came out then, his phone in hand. "Hadley just texted me some of the pictures she took when we were in Tahiti last month. She got a lot of good ones, especially of the beach and the sunsets."

Both women leaned in to see, but Jazmin knew she was the only one holding back an exasperated sigh. The images of her boss and his wife, frolicking in the azure blue water, or the beautiful sunsets over the island, were enough to turn her green with envy.

"Wow. Looks like you two had a great time." Sierra gave Devon's shoulder a squeeze.

"We really did." He put away his phone.

For whatever reason, both Sierra and Devon suddenly looked Jazmin's way.

She shrugged, then stated drily, "I could show you pictures of my potted ficus. I named her Fiona, after our dearly departed character from season one."

Sierra's lips pursed, but Devon immediately started laughing.

"Really, Jaz?" Sierra folded her arms over her chest in mock offense.

Jazmin shrugged again. "You know I love you both,

and I'm happy you're happy. But you make a girl's life seem awfully empty."

By now, Devon was headed down the hall, still chuckling. "I'll see y'all later. And Jaz, give my regards to 'Fiona.'"

Sierra stayed behind. "Jaz, are you okay?"

She laughed. "Girl, I'm fine. I was just teasing you two. You're easy targets, ya know?"

Her brow crinkled. "Jaz..."

"I'm cool, okay? You're as bad as Mama." She started walking toward her office. "I'll see you later, girl. I'm about to starve."

Savion walked into Sweet Temptations with one thing on his mind: the sugary deliciousness of one of Carmen's key lime cheesecakes. Ever since the bakery had opened four months back, he'd been coming here once or twice a week to satisfy his sweet tooth. And while he occasionally indulged in one of owner Carmen Delacroix's other treats, like double fudge cookies or maple peanut-butter blondies, the made-from-scratch key lime cheesecake was his absolute favorite way to treat himself after a stressful day.

Carmen, stationed on a stool behind the counter with an issue of *Real Simple* magazine in hand, looked up when he entered. "Hey, Savion. How are you, boo?"

He smiled back, knowing it was Carmen's way to call everyone who entered her door by some endearment. "I'll be doing a lot better once I get my cheesecake." He made a beeline for the counter, peering into the glass case and letting his gaze sweep over her offerings. Seeing the single, generous slice of cheesecake sitting there, in front of a porcelain plate heaped with cookies, broadened his grin.

"You're in luck. I've only got one slice of key lime left for the day."

"Well, box it up for me, please." He rubbed his hands together, his taste buds already anticipating the flavor of the rich dessert. "It's been hell at work and I really need this pick-me-up."

"You got it." Carmen set aside her magazine and hopped down from the stool. As she turned to grab a box from the stack she kept on a shelf in the prep area, the bell over the door tinkled, indicating the entry of another customer.

He turned in time to see Jazmin stepping over the threshold. A group of four people entered behind her, but by the time the door swung shut again, she looked his way.

Their eyes met, and they silently assessed each other for a few moments. She wore a white button-down blouse with a pair of dark slacks that hugged the curves of her shapely hips. The silver belt circling her waist matched the buckle of the low-heeled loafers on her feet. Her hair was up in a bun on top of her head, but a few tendrils had fallen to frame her beautiful brown face.

Looking at her made it hard to think. He blinked a few times, trying to restart his brain.

"Hi, Savion." Her soft-spoken words beckoned him back to reality.

"Hi, Jazmin. Nice to see you again."

"Likewise." She swallowed, her eyes darting to the display case. "Oh, good. There's one left." She moved toward the counter.

"I see you have a sweet tooth, too. Looks like we have that in common."

She gave him a small, uncertain smile. "So we do."

Carmen cleared her throat then. "I've gotta go to the back for a box. I'm out of the size I need for the cheesecake." She started toward the kitchen. "Be right back."

"Take your time." He rested his elbow on the case, leaning on it and doing his best to look casual despite the way his heart raced whenever Jazmin was near. When he looked her way again, he found her brow furrowed.

"Did she say she's boxing up a cheesecake for you?"

"Yes."

"What kind?"

"Key lime."

Her expression morphed into a full-on frown. "Let me guess. You just bought the last piece, right?"

He watched her for a moment, then spoke. "I did. And by the look on your face, that's what you came for."

She nodded. "I know it's terrible for me, being so heavy and rich. But I don't smoke, and rarely ever drink. A girl's got to have at least one vice, and mine is cheesecake."

"You've taken a fancy to Carmen's cheesecakes? I'll bet you had some really great ones out west."

She shook her head. "Nothing that came close to the ones I buy here."

Carmen returned then with the pastel yellow box, emblazoned with the store's logo—a drawing of a smiling cupcake. Placing it on the counter, she wrapped the cheesecake in parchment paper, then slipped it inside. Closing it, she said, "Come on down to the register and I'll ring you up."

Jazmin's hand shot up. "By any chance do you have

any more key lime cheesecake stashed away in the back?"

Carmen shook her head. "Sorry, honey. This is my last one. I only make four a day. Can't stand the thought of one of my creations spoiling before it's bought and enjoyed."

"Thanks, anyway, Carmen." Her face a mask of disappointment, Jazmin clutched the strap of her handbag and turned toward the door.

I can't let her leave here with that long face. "Wait." He reached out, his fingertips grazing her arm before she could walk away.

"What is it?"

"Listen, it looks like your day was just as rough as mine. And as much as I'd like to eat that entire slice by myself, it's probably not the healthiest thing to do."

She tilted her head to the side. "What are you getting at, Savion?"

"Why don't we share it? It'll be my treat."

She appeared to think it over.

One of the other ladies waiting in line huffed aloud and made a show of crossing her arms over her chest and tapping her foot.

Savion looked from the woman's tight face back to Jazmin, hoping she'd make up her mind before Miss In A Hurry's head exploded.

Finally, Jazmin asked, "Where would we eat it?" The bakery, while unmatched in service and offerings, was a small place with no seating. "I know you don't expect me to come to your place."

He chuckled. "Of course not. I'm a gentleman to the core, so I propose a neutral territory."

"Like where?"

"Are you saying yes?"

She sighed. "Yes."

"One sec." He reached for his wallet, paid Carmen for the slice of cheesecake and took the box from her. "Come with me." With his hand resting lightly on her arm, he led her outside into the cool evening breeze.

On the sidewalk in front of the bakery, she stopped and eyed him. "Okay, so where are we going to eat the cheesecake?"

He looked out toward the water. "Weather's nice. Why don't we sit on one of the benches down at Richardson Point?"

A few beats passed before she said, "Sounds good. Tell you what. I'll run down to the Bean Bonanza and grab us two coffees, then I'll meet you there."

He smiled. "Bet."

"So, what would you like?"

His lips curled into a mischievous smile.

Her cheeks colored, and she looked away. "I should rephrase that."

"If you must."

She took another deep swallow, like the one she'd taken earlier. "How do you take your coffee?"

"Tall, dark and sweet. Just like you." He winked.

She stared at him, and he thought he saw heat dancing behind her gaze.

A moment later, she mumbled, "Um, I'll see you there."

He tried to hide his amusement as he watched her scurry off but had little success.

Chapter 4

When Jazmin got out of her car at Richardson Point, she scanned the four benches near the beach access entrance. It didn't take her long to spot Savion, sitting on the farthest bench from the parking lot. She recognized the dark blue button-down he'd been wearing, and she licked her lips when she noted the way the shirt hugged his broad shoulders from behind.

Get it together, girl. Stop gawking and get over there. Her hankering for the cheesecake compelled her forward. Holding a small plastic bag and gripping the tray bearing the coffees, she walked around the edge of the lot, taking the beach access point until it led her to the sandy strip bordering the Atlantic.

As she approached, she could see him jotting in a leather-bound book spread open on his lap. When she reached him, he looked up and snapped the book closed. With a smile, he patted the bench next to him. "Have a seat."

His reaction to her approach made her curious about what he'd been writing in the book, but she didn't know him well enough to be prying into his personal business. Sitting down, she placed the tray holding the coffees on the bench between them. With a man as sexy as Savion, she needed the distance.

"I got the guy behind the counter at the coffee shop to hook me up with a couple plates, forks and a plastic knife." She held up the plastic bag.

"Thanks, but I was just gonna dig into the cheesecake with my hands."

She stared at him, but his face gave away nothing. "Excuse me?"

He started to laugh, a low, hearty sound originating in his diaphragm. "I'm kidding, of course. Thanks for getting the accoutrements."

She shook her head. "You're just full of shenanigans, aren't you?"

He shrugged. "Sometimes. But I'm very serious when the occasion calls for it." He held her gaze for a few long, silent moments.

She reached for her coffee and took a swig, hoping the warm liquid would wash away her nervousness. Just when she felt she might squirm under his scrutiny, he broke the silence.

"Hand over the knife." He flipped open the box holding the cheesecake and held out his hand. "Not sure how well I'll be able to cut this with a plastic knife, but I'll do my best."

She pulled out the knife and handed it to him. While

he worked the flimsy plastic through the thick filling, she took out the plates and forks.

He scooped up the two misshapen slices and served them both. Then he raised his coffee cup in her direction. "Here's to new friendship, forged over cheesecake."

She raised her cup in kind, smiling. "Hear, hear."

They ate in companionable silence, with the small paper plates resting on their laps. Unsure of what to say to her handsome companion, she kept her eyes trained on the water. The crystal blue water, rising and pushing toward the shore in a show of frothy white beauty, mesmerized her. The sound of the waves set her mind at ease, giving her a much-needed rest from worrying about the bevy of tasks she still had to complete for the show's second season.

After they'd polished off their portions of the delectable dessert, they stuffed the plates inside the plastic bag. Breaking the companionable silence, he said, "How did you come by your love of key lime cheesecake?"

She smiled. "By chance. I love cheesecake, always have. I used to always get the chocolate swirl, or the strawberry one. A few months back, Carmen suggested I try the key lime, and I've been hooked ever since."

He chuckled. "Carmen's kind of a sweets pusher, isn't she?"

"Never thought of it that way, but I guess she is." She giggled. "What about you? Why do you love it?"

A broad grin spread over his face. "I got it honest. My grandma, Mary Ellen, made the best key lime pies and cheesecakes you could ever put in your face. Nobody can make it like she did, but Carmen's is the closest approximation I could find."

"I see." She loved the way he looked when he smiled. It made his deep brown eyes sparkle, put a little dimple in his cheeks and made his goatee-accented lips look even more enticing.

"Considering my grandma passed away when I was nine, and I can still remember the taste of her baking, that should tell you how special it was." He paused. "How special *she* was."

She sensed that he wanted to share his memories, and that flattered her. "Tell me about her. What was she like?"

His smile remained but became more subdued. "She was a real pistol. Only about five feet tall, weighed maybe a hundred and ten pounds, but people knew not to cross her. She only wore pants, never dresses or skirts, and she loved to fish. But she also loved her garden—she'd plant zucchini, tomatoes, cucumber, spinach, you name it. And she had the best azalea bushes on the island, hands down. After she passed, Dad had all of them transferred onto his property."

"She sounds like quite a character."

"You'd better believe it." He leaned back against the bench. "She was the one who taught me and Cam how to fish. Hadley was too small back then, but Dad taught her when she was old enough. He promised Grandma he would, when she…" His voice trailed off. The look in his eyes said he was reliving an old, yet very real pain.

She touched his hand gently but didn't press him to go on.

He drew a deep breath, then spoke again. "You know, you're really easy to talk to."

She offered a soft smile. "I try."

"It was Gram's land that started MHI. When she passed, she left it to Dad. He bootstrapped it, hustled, gathered investors and started developing the land. Once he started turning a profit, he bought more land. Now we own more than sixty percent of land and buildings on the island."

She noticed the pride in his voice. "It's quite an impressive legacy."

"I know, and we want to honor that. That's why Dad is doing the memory park in her honor." He laced his large fingers together, then stretched his arms overhead. "It's the most important project I've ever done, and that's what has me so stressed I was ready to dive face-first into that cheesecake."

She giggled. "Is it really that bad?"

He shrugged. "I guess not. Maybe I'm blowing it out of proportion or being too hard on myself. But I can't screw up on this. We all owe our success to Gram. Plus, I can't disappoint my dad that way, you know?"

She nodded. "I get it." In a way, she felt similarly about giving her parents the grandchildren they wanted so much.

"Cam and Hadley say I'm our parents' favorite, and that's probably true. What they don't realize is how much pressure that puts on me to live up to the title." He tossed her a wry look. "Anyway, I've talked enough. What's your story, Jazmin?"

She inhaled a deep draw of the refreshing salt air. "Let's see. I was born and raised in Los Angeles.

Leimert Park, to be exact, and my parents still live there. I loved hearing about your grandmother. I never knew any of my grandparents."

"Really?"

She nodded. "My parents were older when they had me. Mom was thirty-eight and Pop was forty-one. All four of my grandparents were gone before I was two."

He looked thoughtful. "Wow."

"Anyway, my parents were pretty lax in the discipline department. They were 'free-range' parents, I guess. Gave me way too much freedom, no curfew, let me do basically whatever I wanted as long as I was open with them. Pop used to joke that they were too old and tired to chase after me and punish me, so they just let me find my own way."

"Wow. That way of parenting doesn't really fly here in the South."

"So I'm told. Hadley said the same thing."

"How do you feel about being raised that way?"

She thought about it for a moment. "I don't really know. I never felt unloved or anything like that, and they took care of my every need. I guess all that freedom forced me to develop good judgment earlier than most kids."

"Makes sense." He smiled. "How is production going on the set?"

"We're working on redoing the title sequence and the end credits. The network execs wanted something fresh for season two."

"I'm sure you'll deliver on that."

"You're pretty good company, Mr. Monroe." She

elbowed him playfully in the arm, figuring it would barely register against the firm muscle there.

"I'm glad you think so. Because I feel the same way about you, Ms. Boyd."

And as the sun touched the horizon, she moved the drink tray and scooted closer to him. In any other case, she would be rushing home to prepare for the next day. But sitting there with him, she felt more content and at peace than she had in a very long time.

Savion checked his watch as he made his way across the parking lot at Shoreside Grocery Friday evening. He'd wanted to go home after another long day at the office, but since there was nothing in his fridge but baking soda and some milk of questionable freshness, he'd swung by the store after leaving MHI.

He'd parked a good distance away from the store, choosing a space that had some shade from one of the magnolia trees planted alongside the lot. He loosened his top button, and he could swear he saw steam come out. It was an unseasonably hot and humid May day, heralding a scorching hot Carolina summer ahead.

The sky was an endless, cloudless blue, the sun a bright yellow orb radiating light and heat on the island. The air was as thick and warm as an afghan, and as he speed-walked through the lot, he anticipated the cool blast of air-conditioning that would greet him once he crossed the threshold of the store.

The promise of relief from the heat propelled him forward, until he saw Jazmin strolling down the sidewalk. Even with the large, round lenses of the sunglasses concealing most of her face, he knew it was her.

She was coming from the opposite direction, around the side of the store, as if she'd parked over there. She wore a summery beige dress that barely grazed the tops of her bronze thighs, and her hair was swept up in a ponytail atop her head.

He stopped at the edge of the walk.

As she approached, she stopped, as well. She raised her sunglasses and perched them on her head, her eyes locking with his. "Savion…hi."

"Hi, Jazmin. Good to see you again." That was a gross understatement. Seeing her was such a pleasant surprise, it almost made him forget how hot it was.

"Looks like we're both shopping today." She started walking again, headed toward the store's main entrance.

He fell into step behind her. "Yep. I hate shopping, but it was either come to buy food or eat baking soda for dinner."

She chuckled. "That bad, huh?"

"Absolutely." The automatic doors parted, and he sighed as the cold air hit him, offering respite from the oppressive heat. Still following her, he clapped his hands. "Ah. Thank God for air-conditioning."

She turned his way and opened her mouth to reply as they stepped onto the rubber mat at the door.

In the next heartbeat, a shower of confetti rained down on them. It seemed to be coming from all directions, and she covered her eyes while he blew out some of the brightly colored paper that had gone into his mouth.

"Congratulations, you two!" A man in a bright red suit, holding a microphone, stepped into their path. "You're the lucky winners of the Summer Love Sweepstakes!" Several other people joined the man, including a cameraperson from the local news station, and uniformed members of the store's staff.

"Wait a minute," Jazmin began, gesturing toward Savion. "He and I are—"

"Going on an all-expenses-paid weekend retreat to the beautiful, exclusive new Water's Edge Inn in Wilmington! This new bed-and-breakfast hasn't even opened yet, and you'll be its very first guests! Aren't you excited about your romantic getaway?"

His brow furrowing, he said, "Listen, I don't think you understand—"

"But that's not all," the man continued, looking at the camera and gesturing toward Savion and the bewildered Jazmin. "Our lucky couple will also receive VIP tickets with backstage passes to the sold-out Brian McKnight concert at Thalian Hall Center for the Performing Arts."

Her eyes widened. "Did you say Brian McKnight? As in, *the Brian McKnight*?"

Mr. Red Suit nodded. "Yes, ma'am, that's what I said. And it's all yours for being Shoreside Grocery's lucky hundredth customer today! Anything you'd like to say to the folks watching at home?"

Savion glanced her way.

She stepped closer to him. "Sidebar."

He leaned down until her lips were next to his ear. "Go ahead."

"I know this sounds crazy, but I've been trying to see Brian McKnight in concert since forever. So, is there any way you could just go along with this?"

He blinked a few times. "Are you sure about this?"

She nodded. "You heard the man. The show is sold out and this is the only way I'm getting in."

He felt his lips tilt into a smile. "If it means that much to you…"

She placed a hand on his forearm and gave it a gentle squeeze. "Believe me. It does."

"Then yes. I'm down." He tried not to read too much into the situation. After all, she was simply going along with this so she could indulge her fangirl fantasy of meeting one of the best R&B singers to ever stand in front of a mic. Wasn't she?

She smiled, then turned back to the guy in the loud suit. "I'd like to say that Savion and I feel so lucky to have won the giveaway."

"Excellent!" Mr. Red Suit grinned and patted them both on the shoulder. Gesturing to another man wearing a suit in a much more muted color, he said, "This is Nathan Wesley, owner of the Water's Edge Inn. Just head on over to the customer-service desk, and he'll go into the details."

Savion fought off his shock as she reached over and grabbed him by the hand.

"Come on, honey. Let's go find out what we need to do next." A syrupy sweet smile accompanied the remark.

He grinned back at her. "Whatever you say, baby."

Her expression changed, and for a moment, he thought she might be annoyed that he'd called her a pet name. But the look disappeared as quickly as it had shown up. He let her lead him by the hand toward the customer-service desk, wondering all the way what he'd just gotten himself into. *I hope she's not mad. After all, I was just following her lead.*

They spent the next thirty minutes signing paperwork with the owner of the inn and posing for pictures being taken by a reporter from the *Sapphire Shores Dispatch*. She seemed a bit stiff as he placed his arms around her waist for a photograph, but she smiled nonetheless. Noticing her hesitance, he put a bit of distance between them. The last thing he wanted to do was make her uncomfortable, and he made a mental note to talk to her about it once the hubbub died down.

By the time the camera crew, the inn owner and Mr. Red Suit left the store, he could feel the tension rolling off her like the heat outside reflected off the road. She made a beeline for the door, and he followed her.

Outside on the sidewalk, he caught up with her just before she rounded the corner. "Jazmin, what's wrong? Did I do or say anything that made you uncomfortable?"

She stopped. Turning back to face him, she shook her head. "I just came in for a few things. Instead, I got a camera crew. I mean, I got swept up in the moment—winning those Brian McKnight tickets. But it was all a bit much, you know?"

"I get it. This whole thing caught me off guard, too. But I just wanted to be sure it wasn't something I did that made you run off."

She shook her head again. "No. Actually, I feel pretty comfortable with you."

He watched her expression, noting the panic that crossed her face. "I'm guessing you didn't mean to say that aloud."

"Nope. But there it is."

He smiled. "I'm glad you said it." Knowing that she felt comfortable in his presence pleased him in ways he wouldn't have expected. "So, how are we going to work this thing?"

She shrugged. "I'll take next Friday off work. We'll go up to the inn, check in, go to the show, then hang out and chill. Then we'll come home on Sunday."

"And does this weekend indicate any...shall we say, evolution of our relationship?"

She folded her arms over her ample chest. "Savion, what relationship are you referring to?"

He watched her for a few silent moments before speaking again. "Are you denying the attraction between us?"

Her lovely face flushed, and she looked down as if analyzing her bejeweled sandals. "Well, no."

He reached out, touched her hand. "Jazmin, I would never, ever do anything to make you uncomfortable. This weekend excursion to the mainland will be under your control, in every aspect."

She looked up then and stared into his eyes. "Really?"

"Absolutely. Still, there's something you should know."

"What's that?"

"You may think you know what you want now." He squeezed her hand. "But that may change once we're alone together. Just know that I'll respect your wishes, whatever they may be."

Her mouth dropped open. The look in her eyes seemed to communicate a mixture of shock and...desire. A few beats passed before she blinked several times and snapped her mouth shut. Turning on her heel, she started for the lot.

He called after her. "Aren't you going to do your shopping?"

"It can wait," she called back, without looking his way.

Chuckling, he turned and went back into the soothing embrace of the air-conditioned store.

Chapter 5

The next day found Jazmin at home. Grateful for a day off amid planning season two of the show, she'd decided to use the day to catch up on some of her housework. Entering her laundry room, she eyed the pile of laundry and sighed. Her town house in The Glenn was comfortable and spacious, and the neighborhood had plenty of amenities. One of the services the staff provided was laundry, complete with fluff-and-fold, but she couldn't abide by the idea of a stranger touching her underthings. So, she bent down, taking a few moments to separate out her whites, then started a load in the front-loading washer. Padding barefoot down the stairs, she stifled a yawn.

As noon neared, she made herself a quick lunch of chicken salad, lettuce and tomato on a croissant. Pairing it with a bottle of water and a small bag of plain potato chips, she took her plate into the living room and sat down on the sofa. She grabbed the remote and flipped on the large, wall-mounted flat-screen television across from her.

The default setting meant the television was always on News 10, the local station, whenever it was turned on. The noon report was just getting started, so she set down the remote on the couch cushion beside her. *I guess I'll see what's happening on the island.* She placed the plate on her lap, then lifted her sandwich and took a bite.

The anchorwoman looked into the camera, with the trademark expression worn by newscasters all over the world that said she was "serious, yet approachable." "Welcome to News Ten's noon report, your source for everything newsworthy for the barrier islands. I'm Rory Nash. For our top story today, we take you to Sapphire Shores, where a grocery run led to a run of good luck for two local residents."

Mouth full of buttery croissant and zesty chicken salad, Jazmin paused midchew. "Oh, no."

Sure enough, footage of yesterday's confetti-filled ambush at the supermarket appeared onscreen. She'd just been dashing in for some milk and a few other essentials. She hadn't expected to run into Savion on the sidewalk, and that had thrown her a bit. She felt her pulse quicken whenever he was near. He was a well-built man, charming and handsome in a way that made it hard for her to breathe when he entered her personal space.

It would have been rude to walk into his path and not speak, and she'd been in the South long enough to know the expectation of politeness outweighed most other things. So, she'd spoken, striking up a short conversation with him. And when he'd opened his mouth, releasing that deep baritone, thick with his Carolina drawl, she'd been mesmerized. He could have been reciting the alphabet and she would have been riveted by every single letter.

Because she'd been so busy talking to and drooling over Savion, she hadn't been paying attention as she entered the store. That had left her open to be caught completely off guard by the whole sweepstakes thing. Looking at the footage now, she could see the guy with the "confetti cannon" had been standing right in the middle of the produce section. *Had I actually been paying attention, there's no way I would have missed that guy.*

She watched the rest of the brief report in dismay, shaking her head at the wide-eyed, bewildered expression on her face. *I look like I'm having a bad reaction to something, and now that crazy-eyed face is plastered all over the damn TV.* She sighed. There was nothing to be done about it now. *At least I finally get to see Brian McKnight in concert.*

She tried not to think about the rest of the prize. She'd be alone, with the fine-as-wine Savion Monroe, in a room at a romantic inn for an entire weekend. And while she knew logically that she didn't have the time or the patience for a relationship right now, logic rarely ruled in cases like this. The attraction between them was real, way more real than she'd like to admit. And because of the way he made her feel, there was really no predicting how the weekend would go.

The ringing of her cell phone snatched her out of her thoughts. Reaching to the teak coffee table in front of her, she picked up the device and answered it. "Hello?"

"Hey, honey bun. How are you?"

She smiled. "Hey, Mom. How are things going?"

Azalea Boyd laughed, the sound light and airy. "Fine, fine. Your father is out on the golf course right now, and I'm just lounging around the house. Got a whole stack of magazines here I want to catch up on reading." She yawned. "What are you up to today?"

"Catching up on chores. I've got a mountain of laundry to do, and I'm going to give the whole place a good cleaning and dusting. Once the filming of the show's second season really kicks off, I'll be working really long days, and probably some weekends, as well."

"Oh, yeah. I remember you telling me about that. What's going on in the studio?"

She gave her mother a brief, layman's-term explanation of what was happening. "Right now, we're in preparation mode. The crew is redecorating existing sets and building new ones, setting up for on-location filming, testing equipment. The writers are, well, writing, and the cast is running their lines. Other than that, it's just making sure the equipment in the production suite is in working order and training an intern."

"Sounds like you've got a lot going on at work, honey bun. Is there anything going on in your social life?"

"You mean, other than hanging out with Sierra?" She chuckled. "Mom, we both know I don't have a social life. I'm too busy with work."

Azalea's displeasure was evident in her voice. "Honey bun, we've talked about this."

"Mom, I just have so many goals and plans. There are so many accomplishments I want to make in the world of television production. I want to break down barriers for the young black women coming up behind me, you know?"

"I know, baby. But you can't cuddle up to your accomplishments and broken barriers at night." She sighed. "I'm not trying to meddle in your life, I promise. Your father and I just want the best for you."

"I know, Mom. I know. And I love you both for caring so much about me."

"Breaking down barriers is wonderful. And if that's all you want out of life, I'd say keep doing what you're doing." Azalea paused. "But we both know you want more."

"After everything that happened, I don't know what I want anymore." She didn't get specific. Her mother would know what she was referring to, without her having to dredge up that old pain. Drawing a deep breath, she made her move to change the subject. "There is one thing I want. Why don't you and Pop move closer to the East Coast? Even when *The Shores* is over, I'm probably not going to come back to California, at least not to live."

"Nice segue, honey bun." Azalea chuckled. "And let me remind you, I need some serious motivation at my age to pick up and move to the other side of the country. A grandchild would do nicely."

She rolled her eyes, grateful her mother couldn't see

her. "And on that note, I'm going to get back to cleaning. Talk to you later, Mom. I love you."

"Love you, too."

She disconnected the call, glancing at her half-eaten sandwich.

Suddenly, I'm a little short on appetite.

After covering her plate in plastic wrap, she set it in the fridge and trudged back upstairs with her cleaning caddy.

"Son, did you hear me?"

Savion snapped himself out of looking out the window at the sky. "Sorry, Dad. What did you say?"

On the other end of the phone line, Carver chuckled. "I wish you'd quit daydreaming while I'm talking to you. I said, your mother and I are on our way to the airport. Time to celebrate this anniversary properly."

"Great, Dad. You and Mom have a great time in Europe." His parents had been planning their getaway to Portugal and Spain for months now, and he thought it was a wonderful way for them to celebrate forty years of wedded bliss. "How long is it gonna take to get there?"

"Let's see. Our flight from RDU takes us to Philly, that's about ninety minutes. Then it's overnight, seven and half hours from Philly to Madrid." He blew out a breath. "Longer than I've ever been on a plane, and I can't say I'm looking forward to it. But we're going first class, so it should be comfortable."

"Hopefully."

"Even if it isn't, I couldn't deny your mother this trip. She's wanted to go for so long, and after everything she's given me, and all she's meant to me, how could I say no?"

Savion felt his heart squeeze in his chest. His parents had set quite an example for him when it came to healthy romantic love. He had deep admiration for the way they cared for each other. "Tell Mom I love her."

"Love you, too, baby!" Viola shouted her reply in the background.

"You're on speakerphone, son. I'm just making sure I have everything I need in my bag. Can't be holding the phone and doing that."

Savion laughed. "Okay, Dad. Was there something else you need? I don't want to hold you two lovebirds up from getting to the airport."

"Yes. There is one more thing. Are you going to make sure the final inspections and permits are done for the memory park?"

He inhaled deeply, touching his fingertips to his temples. "Yes, Dad. I've got it covered."

"I'm sure I don't have to tell you how important this is, Savion. It's the most important project this company has ever taken on. It's about this family's legacy."

"Trust me, Dad. I'm well aware of the significance of the memory park."

Carver cleared his throat. "I trust you, son. I just don't want you to get distracted by your upcoming 'rendezvous.'"

Shock hit him for a moment, followed by realization. He cringed. "So, you know about that, huh?"

"Sure I do. It was all over the news, son. Everybody on the island knows that you're going to the mainland for a romantic weekend with that pretty producer from the television show."

He let his forehead drop against the cool glass pane of his dining-room window. "Dad, please don't make a big deal of this. I'm just doing Jazmin a favor."

"Oh, is that what it's called nowadays?" The humor in Carver's voice was apparent.

He sighed. "Good one, Dad. But I'm telling the truth. Jazmin said she's been trying to get to a Brian McKnight show for ages, and she wasn't about to turn down tickets with VIP passes. So, I agreed to go along with this 'romantic getaway' thing so she can get her fangirl on."

"Is that so."

"Yes."

Carver made a grumbling sound deep in his throat, the sound he made whenever he thought someone was trying to sell him beachfront property in Kansas.

"Come on, Dad. Don't hit me with the untruth grumble."

"Are you going to sit there and tell me you're not attracted to Jazmin? As if I don't know any better?"

"I didn't say that." He wasn't about to lie to his father. Despite being over thirty-five, he knew his father would still go upside his head, if he felt it was necessary. But his refusal to be dishonest with his dad had less to do with fear of reprisal, and more to do with the respect he had for him. "I'm just laying out what she and I discussed."

"I'm glad you had sense enough not to deny it. I watched you dance with her at Cam's wedding, and again at the party. Heck, even the way you were looking at her in some of those photos they showed on the television gives it away."

"You've made your point, Dad." *Am I really so transparent to others?* He didn't want the whole world to know his feelings, at least not until he and Jazmin could come to some sort of understanding. "I know what you're thinking. But I don't have any plans on starting anything up with her. We're just going on this trip as friends."

"Be sure you keep it that way. Proximity can give you all kinds of ideas if you know what I'm saying."

He cringed again. *I can think of a hundred other things I'd rather talk to my father about than my sex life.* "Yes, Dad. I know what you're saying." *He's reminding me of the playboy days of my youth, as if I've forgotten.* Once upon a time, the coed dorms at North Carolina State had been like a playground for him. Now, though, he was well past that revolving-door-dating stage—time and experience had shown him the folly of that enterprise.

"Let me get out of here. Don't want to miss the flight. Keep the ship afloat while I'm gone, Savion. I'm counting on you."

"Aye, aye, Cap'n," he said in his best pirate impersonation.

"I'll message you when we get to Madrid. I love you, son."

"Love you, too, Dad."

After he disconnected the call, he stood by the window for a few moments more. If his father's statement was correct, he and Jazmin's little getaway was probably already the talk of the island. He could imagine the diners at Della's and the ladies under the dryers at the hair salon, all discussing what might happen between the two of them while they were away. He hated the feeling of being grist for the gossip mill, but such were the perils of life in a small community.

Running a hand over his hair, he went to the couch and plopped down on the soft cushion. Then he picked up his leather-bound book and flipped his notebook to a blank page. Grabbing the pencil from the loop, he began to write.

> In creation
> I discovered in discovery
> I learned in learning
> I established Me in me

As he wrote, releasing his feelings and perceptions onto the page, he felt some of the tension in his body slipping away.

> I found a light
> In this light I found her
> in her I found We
> And We give love a name—Life

Ever since he'd first laid eyes on Jazmin, she'd become a muse for him. Whenever he was around her, the words seemed to compose themselves. It was all he could do to tuck them away in a corner of his mind until he could be alone to commit them to paper. With all the inspiration she provided, he knew he'd be flush with content for weeks.

His writings were a private indulgence of his innate creativity; his notebook, a secret sanctuary from the realities of his daily life.

Once he felt he'd gotten it all out of his head, he tucked away the pencil and closed the leather cover.

Chapter 6

Sunday, Jazmin crawled out of bed just after eight. Rubbing her bleary eyes, she squinted against the sunlight as she dragged herself to the bathroom. Once she'd gotten some coffee in her system, she returned to her bedroom to get dressed for her morning workout. Donning her compression shorts, a blue workout T-shirt and her favorite walking sneakers, she pulled her hair up into a high ponytail to keep it out of her face. Once she was ready, she grabbed her water bottle, purse and keys and left her town house.

During the short drive to the Magnolia Health and Fitness Complex, she hummed along to the eighties music playing on the satellite radio in her compact sedan. It was a beautiful day on the island, with wispy white clouds accenting a sun-filled blue sky. Letting down the front windows, she enjoyed the feel of the cool morning breeze caressing her face as she drove.

After she'd parked her car in the lot, she got out and crossed the grassy field that stood between the fitness complex's main building and the outdoor walking track. She'd been coming here for a while and knew the layout of the place. There was the building that housed two workout rooms filled with modern equipment, male and female locker rooms with hot tubs and steam rooms, space for group fitness classes, and a juice bar. Outside and to the right of the building was the soccer field, which was surrounded by the walking track she used. Behind the building, there were tennis and basketball courts, two of each, as well as an area designated for sand volleyball.

There wasn't anyone else out there, at least in her line of vision, and that pleased her. That meant she could keep her own counsel and focus on her walk, without being roped into a conversation with an overly friendly local.

Solitude wasn't the only reason she came to the track so early. As she stepped onto the springy, recycled-tire surface of the track, she drew a deep breath to kick up her energy. Early morning was also the only time of day she could walk outdoors this time of year. She'd learned the hard way last summer that the combination of oppressive heat and overwhelming humidity made outdoor activities unbearable past noon.

Plugging her headphones into the audio jack on her phone, she started up her favorite classic-soul workout playlist and popped the buds into her ears. Within a few moments, she'd set her pace to the rousing beat of Curtis Mayfield's "Move On Up."

She usually aimed to do eight laps around the track, which would give her about two miles of brisk walking. Though she sometimes jogged, she wasn't a runner, so she kept her focus on even pacing rather than speed. The beat of the music kept her moving around the track in time.

Rounding the corner for her third lap, an image of Savion popped into her mind. She could see the strong lines of his handsome face, the way his cheeks dimpled when he smiled. She could hear his deep voice in her ear. She could almost smell the scent of his cologne on the breeze. He smelled of fir and bergamot—earthy and masculine.

There were so many things about him that intrigued her. The way he walked, the way he exuded such confidence. The way he took his day planner with him everywhere.

She crinkled her nose about that one. He struck her as a savvy guy, full of charm, charisma and self-assurance. So why was he still carrying around a paper planner, and guarding it so furiously? That day at the beach, he'd tucked it away the moment she'd gotten close. Who was that protective of their planner? *Unless it's not a planner.* Maybe there was something else inside that leather cover.

She laughed inwardly. *Whatever is inside that leather cover is the least of my worries right now.*

In many ways, she was still processing their upcoming trip to the mainland. She'd acted impetuously in a stressful moment, but that was understandable. Who walked into a grocery store expecting to be the center of attention? From the moment the first volley of confetti had hit her in the face, she'd been gobsmacked. She considered herself a laid-back person, and all the attention had put her in an awkward place. Even so, she wasn't going to pass up tickets to that show. Her decision to accept the prize had been driven by her desire to finally see Brian McKnight in concert.

Or were there other desires at play?

She missed a step and tripped, but managed to readjust before she went crashing down on the track's surface. Continuing her walk, she cringed, wondering if she'd been motivated by something deeper, something she didn't care to admit. Yes, her love for all things Brian McKnight was very real. But she couldn't seem to shake her growing attraction to Savion, either. Was there some part of her subconscious mind that wanted to go on the trip, just to be alone with him?

What is it about him that gets me so distracted? She shook her head, but shaking off thoughts of him was going to take more than that. So, she picked up her pace to a comfortable, but quick jog.

Running from one side of the court to the other, Savion swung his tennis racket. He managed to swat the air as the Day-Glo yellow ball sailed right past him, smacking into the fence with a metallic thud. Groaning, he jogged to retrieve it and tossed it back to Troy, who was stationed on the other side of the net.

"Wow, Savion. Your game is garbage today."

He frowned at his cousin. "Thanks for pointing that out, but I assure you, I knew it."

Troy shrugged. "You know I'm not one to clown you...too much, but I didn't come all the way from New Mexico to visit my family for this, man. Your body's here, but I don't know where the hell your head's at."

"Just serve the ball," he groused, crouching and holding his racket in the ready position.

Troy chuckled. "All right. Miss this shot and it's all over for you, cousin." He winked.

Savion rolled his eyes but said nothing.

Troy tossed the ball into the air, then delivered a smack with his racket that sent the electric-yellow sphere flying. Savion darted to the rear right corner of his side of the court, extending his arm to try to return the serve. He could see the ball getting close to the racket's surface, so he flicked his wrist.

The ball knicked off the edge of the racket and hit the ground, bouncing as it rolled past his foot.

Savion tossed his racket to the court's bright green surface. "I'm done, Troy."

"I'll say." Troy jogged past him to retrieve the ball. Entering his space, he pointed at the racket. "I'm just gonna grab a water and turn the ball basket in at the desk...if that's okay."

"Why are you even asking?"

"Because you look ready to spit fire."

Savion sighed. "Go ahead and return the equipment. I'll wait for you on the bench."

"Bet. Be back in a flash." With the ball-basket hand, Troy opened the gate and walked across the grounds to the main building of the fitness complex.

Alone on the court, Savion ran a hand over his face. *Troy was right—my game was absolute trash today.* He couldn't recall ever losing to Troy in tennis. Hell, this wasn't even Troy's best sport—he was much better at baseball. Today, though, his concentration had been shot from the beginning. That lack of focus had led to probably the lousiest game of tennis he'd ever played.

He walked off the court, exiting through the gate and heading for the benches lined up in the grassy area just beyond it. The benches sat on a slight hill, facing away from the road to allow a view of the rest of the outdoor sports area, as well as the thick line of towering pine and spruce trees that bordered the complex's property. Sitting down on the wooden slats, he kept his gaze on the tree line.

Troy returned with two bottles of water and sat down next to him. "Thought you could use this." He handed him one of the bottles.

"Thanks." He cracked it open and took a long draw. The cold liquid refreshed his parched throat.

"So, you gonna tell me why you're so distracted today?" Troy turned up his own bottle for a deep swig, draining half of the contents. "You've never let me whup you at tennis like that before."

He reached for the small towel he'd left draped over the back of the bench, wiped the sweat from his brow. "You're right. If my head was in the game, I'd have dragged you up and down the court."

"You're probably right, but it doesn't answer the question at hand, does it?" Troy fixed him with a questioning look.

He blew out a breath. "It's Jazmin, okay? I can't stop thinking about her."

"The girl from the anniversary party? Or, should I

say, the one you're going on that trip to the mainland with?"

He rolled his eyes. *Is there anyone on the island who doesn't know about that damn prize?* "You saw her, didn't you? That's no girl, that's a woman."

"Very true, cousin." He whistled. "She is fine."

A pang of jealousy clenched his gut, but he held his tongue. He had no real ties to Jazmin, and therefore no right to yell at his cousin for noticing how attractive she was.

Troy must have noticed his expression because he scooted farther down the bench. "Don't punch me, Savion. I'm not trying to get with her, I would never do you like that. But you look like you could use some advice."

"I don't know." He shrugged. "I'm going on this trip with her, but I don't really feel like I know her well enough, know what I mean?"

Troy appeared surprised. "Never thought I'd hear Savion Monroe, the international playa, say something like that."

He chuckled despite his mood. "I'm reformed, Troy. This isn't college. It's real out here, and I'm too grown to be chasing skirts and playing games." He stopped short of saying his next thought aloud. *Maybe it's time to build something real, something that will last.*

Looking thoughtful for a moment, Troy asked, "Why don't you ask her out on a date? You know, before you go to the mainland together? That way, you can get to know her a little better before the trip."

He scratched his chin, thinking back to their time on the beach, sharing the key lime cheesecake. She'd talked a little about her upbringing, and he'd revealed way more than he'd expected about his memories of Gram Mary Ellen. Still, what he'd heard from her had only increased his curiosity about her past. "I probably should do that. Might make things less awkward on the drive inland."

"Then do it." Troy finished the rest of his water, then crushed the bottle in his fist.

"I will. The next time I see her." He hadn't gotten her phone number, and though he could probably have asked Sierra, he thought that might be too invasive. *Aside from that, I'm a grown man. I don't need my sister-in-law to be the go-between for me.*

"Gimme your bottle. I'll toss it in the recycling bin." Troy stood and held out his hand.

After draining the last of the water, he handed over the bottle. Troy walked away, and he went back to watching the tree line.

A moment later, Troy called, "Hey, isn't that Jazmin over there? On the track?"

Turning to glance over his shoulder, he saw her. Even though she was rounding a curve and facing away from him, he recognized the curly mop of her hair, piled into a ponytail. He also recognized her stride; it was feminine, but purposeful. "Well, damn."

Troy chuckled as he made his way back to the bench. "Time to pay the piper, cousin."

Wiping around his hairline to make sure he'd gotten as much sweat and grime off as possible, he tossed the towel on the bench and stood. Strolling up the hill, he approached the track. Rather than going up to her, and possibly killing her workout vibe, he waited near the right side of the track for her to pass him.

When she came his way, she snatched out her ear-buds and stopped, but continued walking in place near him. "Savion. Good morning. Looks like we have all the same habits, huh? Seems we're always running into each other."

"I have no complaints." He winked.

A soft smile lifted her lips.

"Listen, I know you're exercising, and I don't want to waste your time. Would you consider going out with me? I think we should spend some time talking, you know, getting to know each other, before the trip. What do you say?"

Her smile brightened. "I say yes."

Chapter 7

Jazmin entered the doors at Burgers Galore Monday evening, taking a moment to look around. She checked every corner in her line of sight but didn't see Savion anywhere.

It had been open for a couple of months now, but this was the first time she'd been inside. She'd been wanting to try the food here for a while, so when Savion had invited her to dinner yesterday, this seemed the perfect place to suggest. It was a casual setting, ideal for what she considered to be an easygoing meal. She'd chosen her outfit to reflect the nature of the evening, donning a pair of khaki shorts, a flowing yellow top with fluttery sleeves and a pair of shimmery gold sandals. The gold, seashell-shaped studs in her ears were her only jewelry, and she'd secured her hair away from her face with a thin yellow headband.

She stopped on the giant map of the world painted on the floor, waiting her turn at the hostess desk behind an elderly couple. She looked down for a moment and saw she was standing in the middle of the Pacific Ocean. She smiled. *This is the only way I'll ever be able to do that.* When she approached the desk, she cleared her throat. "I'm here to meet Savion Monroe, but I don't think he's here yet…"

The hostess, clad in a white shirt, blue jeans and a red apron, smiled. "He's here, miss. Follow me."

Jazmin followed her around the desk, into the dining room, then through a swinging door into a smaller room, probably set aside for parties and private gatherings. There, near the front of the room, where the windows faced out on the parking lot, sat Savion. He stood and smiled, showing off his perfect teeth as she approached the table. Dressed in a light blue polo shirt and dark blue slacks with brown loafers, he appeared both attractive and comfortable. She noted the way the fit of the shirt showed off the muscles of his torso, and the way the slacks lightly gripped his powerful thighs. Swallowing, she came to stand by him.

As the hostess walked away, leaving them alone, he grasped her hand and lifted it to his lips. Brushing his mouth against the back of her hand, he said. "Hi, Jazmin. You look lovely."

"Thank you." *You don't look so bad yourself.* She could feel the heat rushing to her cheeks, and to her belly.

He walked around the table and pulled out her chair. "Please. Have a seat."

She did, and as he returned to his seat, she caught a

wonderful view of his firm-looking backside. If she'd been a more brazen woman, or at least if they'd known each other longer, she might have given it a squeeze. But, circumstances being as they were, she kept her hands to herself. *Easy, girl. Don't let yourself get carried away.*

He slid a menu across the table to her. "I'm kind of surprised you chose this place for a first date."

"Just another one of my quirks, I guess." She shrugged. "I love burgers. To me, there's nothing better than a burger, when it's done right."

"Really? Because you could have easily asked me to take you anywhere on the island, and I would have made it happen."

She watched him, feeling the impact of his charm already. "I appreciate that. But I'm perfectly content here." She picked up the menu, evaluating her choices.

"Since you're a burger lover, you picked the right place. They have a great selection here."

She glanced up then, looked at all the maps, compasses and images of world landmarks painted on the walls. "I love the theme of this place—travel the world between two buns. It's a little corny, but still inspired." Her attention went back to the menu, where she looked over the selections themed for different countries or regions. "This Italian burger with prosciutto, mozzarella and fontina is really looking good to me."

He nodded as he pored over his own menu. "I've tried that one, it's really good. I think I might try the Greek burger this time."

She read the description on her menu. "'A freshly

ground lamb patty topped with grilled zucchini, red onion, sliced kalamata olives and feta cheese.' Wow."

He chuckled. "I'll let you know how it is."

Once the waiter had come and taken their order for burgers and a shared basket of hand-cut fries, they were alone again. She noticed him watching her, and suddenly felt parched. Reaching for the filled glass of ice water on her side of the table, she took a long sip.

"So, Jazmin. Let's get into this. I'm looking forward to learning more about you, so we don't go to Wilmington as strangers."

"Where should I start?" She honestly didn't know. What did he want to know most? How much would be too much? She knew of only one topic she didn't want to discuss, and she planned on keeping that under her hat.

"Let's start small and simple. For instance, I'm guessing your favorite food is burgers. So, what's your favorite color?"

She laughed, tugging on the end of her sleeve. "Oddly enough, it's yellow. What's yours?"

He smiled.

"Don't tell me it's blue."

"Yep."

She laughed again. "Look at us." She shook her head. "Let's see. My favorite music is classic soul and R and B, and you already know Brian McKnight is my favorite artist. What do you like to listen to?"

"I like classic soul, too, but I love funk. You know, Earth, Wind and Fire. The Gap Band. Dazz. D Train. But my favorite is probably the Isley Brothers."

She smiled. "I see you've got good taste. 'Voyage to Atlantis' is a classic."

"Agreed. But Brian's had some cuts, too. 'You Should Be Mine' still jams to this day." He sat back in his chair, rubbing his fingertips over his chin. "Yeah, I can see why ladies love the brotha so much. He's definitely got the chops."

She noted how he didn't feel the need to hate on Brian, as other men in her past had. "Okay, I've got a question. What's your middle name?"

He cringed. "You go first. Mine's pretty stodgy."

"Mine is Carmen, after my parents' favorite opera." She sipped from her water glass. "So now you see why I was so quick to take a recommendation from our favorite baker."

"I see. Well, my middle name is…" He stopped speaking in midsentence, his gaze going beyond her. "Saved by the bell."

"Only temporarily." She turned and saw the waiter approaching with a tray loaded down with their food. The tantalizing aroma awakened her stomach, and it growled in anticipation.

Once they had their plates in front of them, he reached for his burger, ready to dig in.

She cleared her throat to get his attention. "Hold on. I told you my middle name, now I want to know yours."

He frowned.

"It can't be that bad."

He sighed with resignation. "It's Fitzgerald, after my mom's brother."

She tilted her head to the side. "See? It's not that

bad. True, it seems a little serious for you, at least from what I know of you so far."

He appeared surprised. "Really? What makes you say that?"

"I see you as charming, and intelligent. You're laid-back, but also intense, in your own way." She popped a fry into her mouth. "You strike me as the kind of man who approaches things calmly, but who won't rest until he gets what he wants." It wasn't until after she'd said the words aloud that she realized all the ways they could be perceived.

A smile that could only be described as mischievous crossed over his face. "Your perceptions are correct, Jazmin. I'm impressed at how insightful you are."

She stuffed another fry into her mouth before she said something else that would lead to trouble. *What is it about him that makes me want to get into trouble?*

"I'm enjoying this, getting to know you. And I have to say, the more time I spend with you, the more attractive I find you."

She offered a soft smile but said nothing.

While they ate, they continued to converse about various topics. By the time the plates were cleared away, she felt relaxed, as if she was dining with an old friend.

"So, let me put this out there." He wiped his hands on a napkin, crushed it and tossed it on the table. "I've never been serious about anyone. Not really."

She blinked several times, wondering how they'd gotten on this topic. "And why is that?"

"My parents call me 'flighty and indecisive,' and my siblings call me a player. The truth is, I'm neither. I'm just very discerning. I don't like to waste time

pursuing something that I don't see real potential in."
He locked her with an intense gaze. "You are another
matter altogether."

She felt her pulse quicken under his scrutiny.

"What about you, Jazmin? Have you ever been seriously involved?"

The comfort she'd settled into over the course of
the meal began to melt away. She closed her eyes, feeling her chest tighten under the weight of those dark
memories. "Trust me, Savion. No good will come from
dredging up my romantic past."

"It's all right, Jazmin."

Hearing his voice, she opened her eyes again and
found him still watching her. His expression had
changed, softened.

"I didn't mean to be pushy. The last thing I want to
do is make you uncomfortable." He reached across the
table, clasping hands with her. "You can tell me whenever you feel ready, and not a moment before, okay?"

Enjoying the warmth of his skin against her own,
she nodded. "Thank you." The knots of tension inside
her body loosened, and she realized his sincere concern for her feelings. Something shifted inside her at
that moment. And as much as she told herself that she
didn't have time for romantic entanglements, she wondered if there was any real way to stop what was happening between them.

Savion held on to Jazmin's hands, feeling the trembling subside. He hadn't expected her to react that way
to his question about her past. Now that he knew his
query had made her uncomfortable, he kicked himself

inwardly. *I shouldn't have asked her that. What was I thinking?* While his own past had been filled with frivolous encounters with the opposite sex, that didn't mean she'd had similar experiences.

"I'm okay, Savion. You can stop looking so concerned." A soft smile tilted her lips.

He chuckled. "Good to know. Now, what can you tell me about the exciting world of television production?"

One expertly arched eyebrow rose. "Seriously? You want to talk about work?"

He shrugged. "It might be boring to you, but remember, I don't know the first thing about what goes on behind the scenes at a TV show."

She opened her mouth, but before she could say anything, the waiter appeared again, this time with their dessert. He released her hands, and they moved to free up the tabletop.

"Here's the cheesecake with key lime ice cream you ordered, sir." The waiter placed down the two plates, as well as two gleaming silver spoons.

"Thank you." Savion picked up his spoon. "I hope you don't mind that I ordered dessert ahead. They didn't have key lime cheesecake, but I thought this would be the next best thing."

Her smile brightened. "I don't mind at all. It looks delicious." She picked up her spoon and scooped up a small piece of cheesecake and a dollop of the ice cream.

When she brought it to her lips and slid the spoon into her mouth, she made a sound indicative of pleasure. "It's just as good as it looks."

His groin tightened. *I wonder if the same is true about you, Jazmin Boyd.* "I'm glad you like it."

A few bites in, she seemed to remember their conversation. "Sorry, what was I gonna say?"

He laughed. "You were going to tell me about all the exciting parts of your job."

"I don't know if any of what I do is necessarily 'exciting,' but I'll tell you about it. Basically, my team and I are the last people to interact with and make changes to the show footage before it goes to the network to be aired. We're responsible for taking all that raw footage and turning it into something cohesive, appealing and screen-ready."

"I see. You said something about the opening and closing sequences when we were on the beach." He polished off the last of his dessert. "How's that going?"

She looked surprised. "You remember me saying that?"

"Of course. I always remember the important things."

Her cheeks darkened, and she looked away for a moment, then continued. "We've got the opening sequence done, and it's approved by the higher-ups. But we're still going back and forth over that closing sequence. It just needs a few more tweaks."

"How long do you have to get it done?"

She twirled a lock of glossy hair around her index finger. "Three weeks at most. The sooner, the better." She finished the last bite of her cheesecake and set down her spoon. "What about you? How's the project going with the park?"

He leaned back in his chair. "We're in that limbo stage between planning and execution. Everything is tied up right now until we get the last few permits from the state and the town commissioner. I can't submit the

local request until the state approval comes in, so..."
He shrugged. "For now, it's the waiting game."

"When do you hope to break ground?"

"By June first. That way we can have everything in
place and properly protected before the peak of hurricane season." He hated to even think of Gram's memory park being damaged or flooded during a storm, but
with the island being where it was, the team had been
forced to make contingency plans. "We're doing as
much as we can to keep the whole place intact should
a bad storm hit—that's all by design. Dad insisted on
it and wouldn't even entertain landscaping plans that
didn't offer that kind of protection."

She nodded. "I think that's a smart approach. It's
pretty similar to the way buildings are constructed in
California, to protect them from collapse during an
earthquake. Gotta work with what you're given."

He blew out a breath. "I don't know about you, but
I need this vacation."

She giggled. "I'm with you on that. This whole thing
came out of nowhere, but in a way, I'm glad it happened. I haven't taken any vacation days the whole time
I've been working at the studio, and I need a doggone
break!" She leaned back in her chair, fanning herself
with her hand. "Our jobs aren't physically taxing but
making decisions all the time can be exhausting."

"You're preaching to the choir, for real." He'd always
been in the position of power at MHI, but now, with his
siblings constantly distracted with their young marriages,
he'd taken on even more of the decision-making around
the office. "I hope your team is more focused than mine
is right now. Both my siblings are newly wed."

She nodded. "They're pretty amazing, actually. Hard workers, great attention to detail."

He scoffed. "Don't rub it in my face. Hadley used to be superefficient before she and Devon married. And Cam, well, he never did all that much work even when he was single."

She laughed then, a deep belly laugh. "Is it that bad?"

"Yes, unfortunately." Even through his frustration, her amusement was contagious, and he found himself smiling. "I don't know what I'm going to do with those two. They're lucky I love them so much."

When she finally stopped laughing, she commented, "I guess I should pack. Although I don't know what to wear to the concert." She tapped her chin with her index finger. "I just hope my crappy luggage will hold up for one more trip. I'm not going to have time to replace it before we leave."

He tucked away that little tidbit of information. "I don't think you'll need to pack much, it's just a weekend."

"Yes, but a woman has to travel with a lot more stuff than a man."

He cocked an eyebrow. "I think that's by choice, Jazmin."

"You say that now. But trust me, you don't wanna see me without my beauty preparations."

He disagreed but didn't say so aloud. He would be honored to see her when she first awakened in the morning, to see the sun illuminating her bare, unadorned skin.

Once the dessert plates were cleared away, he paid the check.

She yawned. "Excuse me. The bed is calling my name."

"Happens to the best of us after a meal like that." He stood and stretched before offering his hand. "Let me walk you to your car."

She grabbed her purse and slung it over her shoulder, accepting his hand.

They walked out of the restaurant and into the warm night air. Strolling slowly down the sidewalk toward where she'd parked, he watched the moonlight play over her soft features. There was no denying her physical beauty. But he sensed an even more radiant beauty inside her, and it called to him like a siren's song wooing a sailor in the night.

By the time they stopped near the front of her car, he could ignore the call no longer. With his free hand, he grazed his fingertips over her jawline. Feeling her tremble beneath his caress, he said softly, "I want to kiss you, Jazmin. Can I?"

Staring up into his eyes, she nodded. "Yes, Savion."

He lowered his lips to hers, giving a series of gentle presses. Her mouth was much sweeter than the dessert they'd enjoyed together. She pressed her body against his, and his arms instinctively wrapped around her. He swept his tongue over her bottom lip, then dipped into the cavern of her mouth. He enjoyed her for a few long moments, then pulled back, mindful of where they were.

She sighed softly. Straightening, she spoke. "Good night, Savion."

"Good night." Reluctantly, he released her.

She smiled, then fished her keys out of her purse.

He stood on the sidewalk and watched as she climbed into her car, started the engine and drove away.

Chapter 8

Jazmin slid her chair up to the workstation console, exhaling deeply. Picking up the mug of coffee she'd sat on the drop leaf to keep it away from the equipment, she took a sip as she waited for the computers to boot up. She'd been the first person to arrive at the postproduction suite today, and she'd only stayed in her office long enough to fire up her personal coffeemaker and brew her first cup. Now, as she neared the bottom of that mug and contemplated a second to fight off the midweek blahs, she thought back to her date with Savion two nights ago.

He'd been a perfect gentleman in every way, yet she'd felt passion building inside her like well-tended fire. Hearing him speak about his life so openly, along with his willingness to be frank about his romantic past, had left her even more intrigued with the charming real-estate executive. And when he'd kissed her, she'd felt enough fireworks to put any big city Fourth of July display to shame. *And here I am, on the verge of going on a romantic getaway with him.* After all this time spent carefully avoiding romantic involvement, it seemed there was no way she could avoid what was happening between them.

As she set down her empty mug, she could hear voices and footsteps in the corridor outside the suite, heralding the arrival of the rest of her team. All five video monitors were booted up and displaying the time—five minutes past eight. She smiled, loving the fact that her small but dedicated team always came in a bit before their eight-thirty work call whenever they were in a pinch. She never had to ask them to come early or stay late; they simply did what was necessary to complete the work.

The voices grew louder, and she turned her chair to face the door as her team filed into the suite. First in line, as always, was Randolph Diggs, her video producer. Tall and tan with piercing blue eyes and spiky light brown hair graying at the temples, he wore his typical uniform of a pastel polo shirt, khaki pants and brown loafers. At fifty-nine, he'd been in the television industry for more than twenty-five years and had experienced the many changes in professional production firsthand. His experience and insight were invaluable.

Trailing behind Randolph was Drea White, the youngest member of the team. Fair-skinned with wavy dark hair and brown eyes, she'd just celebrated her nineteenth birthday. Before coming to intern for the show, she'd completed an associate's degree in general studies at Coastal Carolina Community College.

Trisha Dewitt, the sound producer, entered a few steps behind Drea. Brown-skinned with hazel eyes and coiled tendrils of blond, highlighted hair framing her face, she smiled at Jazmin as she entered. The twenty-six-year-old was a no-nonsense girl from the Atlanta area. She brought a sense of balance and professionalism to the team.

"Morning, boss lady." Randolph tucked his lunch bag into the drawer of his desk. The three desks for the team members were located across from the monitors and the console and separated by fabric-covered partitions.

"Morning, everybody." Jazmin stood, stretching as she watched everyone put their things away in their designated areas. "We're going to do our best to wrap up the closing sequence today. We're on a tight deadline, and at this point, we're pushing it."

"Have the writers sent us any new treatments?" Trisha slid her chair over to her spot at the console.

She nodded. "Yes, but thankfully there are only two versions this time. We should be able to wrap this up today, barring any disastrous occurrences."

"Great." Randolph flexed his fingers as he pulled up his seat to the section of the console centered beneath the monitors. "If they've finally narrowed it down to two, one of these has got to be the winner."

"We can only hope." Drea, stationed at her desk, opened the case to the touchpad she used for minor editing tweaks. Setting it and the stylus on the desk, she said, "Let's get this party started."

Jazmin chuckled. "You all go ahead. I need a second cup of coffee. Anybody else want some?"

Trisha scoffed. "You know I never touch the stuff."

"Had mine on the way in," Randolph offered while playing his hands over the dials and switches.

Drea shook her head. "Trying to cut back on caffeine."

"Suit yourselves." Mug in hand, Jazmin strolled into her private office and fired up her single-cup coffee machine. When she returned to the suite, it was quiet save for the clicking and tapping sounds of everyone at work. Trisha had donned the headset she wore to pick up every nuance of the show's sound effects, background noise and soundtrack. The headset essentially drowned out the outside world, so no one attempted to engage Trisha in conversation when she wore it. Drea was busy sketching something on the touchpad and looked very engrossed in the task.

Randolph, however, went about his job with a different approach. Leaning back in his chair, he read over the treatments that the writers had sent over that were displayed on the center monitor. "Are we going to make both versions and let them choose?"

"That's our best bet." She sat down next to him, returning her mug to the same spot it had occupied before. "Do you think it's feasible to get it done today?"

He nodded. "Sure thing." He switched to another monitor. "You know, when I first started out in post-production, everything was done manually. We had to transfer the film to video, use an edit decision list with time stamps and codes to splice the clips together, then take everything to the color-grading room to make it look pretty for TV." He chuckled. "Now, everything's digitized. What used to take an entire team of maybe eight or ten people can now be done by a team as small as this. Even smaller, depending on the software and equipment they use."

She loved listening to Randolph's nostalgic tales of television production in the nineties. That was a world that seemed almost foreign to her but still intrigued her because of her love for the profession. "I've got a lot of respect for the folks who came before me. They had to do it the hard way." She thought for a moment. "Randolph, you've been doing this approximately forever, right?"

He grinned. "Sounds about right."

"Let me ask you something. Do you know how to program a VCR? There's an old one in storage at my parents' place, and they can't remember how to do it."

He whistled. "Sorry, Jazmin. Way above my pay grade."

She shook her head, laughing. "You were my last best hope, Randolph."

A bell tone sounded, indicating an intercom call from the front desk. "Ms. Boyd?"

"Yes, Darcy?"

"There's a package at the desk for you. Courier just left it."

She felt her brow furrow. *I wasn't expecting any deliveries.* Even though she loved to indulge in a bit of online shopping, she rarely ever had things delivered to the studio. "Thanks, Darcy. I'll send someone for it." She turned to Drea as the intercom turned off. "Can you run down and get that for me, please?"

Drea nodded. "No problem. Do you need anything else from there while I'm gone?"

Randolph stifled a yawn. "If there are any donuts

in the main break room, you can bring a few of those back. That is, if your hands aren't too full."

"Got it." Drea disappeared into the corridor.

Jazmin was standing over the console, studying the monitor as Randolph built out the footage to fit the first treatment, when Drea returned. Balancing a large cardboard box in one arm, and holding a folded paper bag in her free hand, she asked, "Where do you want this thing?"

"Dang, it looks heavy." Jazmin marveled at the size of the box.

Drea shook her head. "Not heavy, just big. Where do you want it?"

"Just set it on my desk."

Drea did, then returned to the suite and handed off the paper bag to Randolph. "No donuts, but they did have bear claws."

"Score." He unfolded the bag and looked inside. "Thanks, Drea."

Offering a crisp salute, Drea returned to her desk.

Jazmin kept working for the next couple of hours, consulting with her team as they toiled on the first treatment. By the time the lunch hour neared, her curiosity got the better of her. "I'll be back in a bit." Leaving the suite, she entered her office and closed the door. The packing label indicated that it had been shipped from a boutique in Raleigh. *I haven't even heard of this place, so I know I didn't order this.* The label gave no indication as to who had sent it. Using a pair of scissors from the cup on her desk, she cut the tape and opened the flaps on the large box. Before dealing with the paper-wrapped item inside, she took out the invoice and read it. Her eyes widened when she saw the item name and price, and widened more when she read the bottom portion, labeled Note from Purchaser.

Jazmin,
You deserve something nice to travel with. I hope you like it.
Best, Savion

Setting aside the invoice, she opened the layers of glittery gold paper to reveal an overnight bag. Lifting it out, she marveled at the fine leather craftsmanship. It was dyed a sunny shade of yellow, with the handles and shoulder strap a soft shade of light brown, and high polished brass zippers and hardware.

A smile spread over her face. *This is gorgeous! How thoughtful of him.* Savion had really been listening to her and had taken the initiative to solve a small annoyance that had been plaguing her.

Tucking the bag back into the box, she sighed contentedly and returned to the suite.

Thursday afternoon, Savion walked into MHI's conference room just after 3:00 p.m. Seated around him were the other staffers: Campbell, office assistant Lisa, and the two interns, Max and Yancey.

Taking his seat at the head of the table, he laid his notebook and a loaded manila folder across his lap. He looked to his brother at his right. Campbell was busy scrolling on his phone. "Cam, where's Hadley?"

He shrugged. "Home, I guess. She left right after lunch. Said something she ate didn't agree with her."

Awesome. This is just what I need right now. He exhaled and ran a hand over his face. "Will she be back tomorrow?"

Campbell shrugged again. "I don't know. I'll text her and ask, though."

"Let me know what she says." He laid the folder on the table and opened it. "In any case, we need to get started."

Lisa, sitting to his left with her open laptop, gave him a brief nod. She was excellent at transcription and kept very thorough meeting notes.

Campbell's phone dinged. "She says she'll probably be in late if she comes in tomorrow. Depends on how she feels."

Savion held back his sigh. "We need to tie up a few loose ends on the memory-park project so that construction can get started on time. We've finally received our state approval, so now, we're moving on to gaining approval at the local level."

Placing his phone face down on the table, Campbell asked, "What do we need to be doing?"

"I'm going to hand-deliver the state-approval paperwork myself to the council office, so we can get the ball rolling there. I'll be out of the office tomorrow and Monday—"

"We know. For your 'romantic getaway.'" Yancey made a goofy, doe-eyed face.

He sighed. Having graduated from high school at fifteen and community college at seventeen, Yancey was a prodigy. She was eighteen now, but situations like this pointed to her lack of maturity. "As I was saying,

I'll need you all to be especially vigilant and efficient in my absence."

"By doing what, exactly?" Max was known around the office for his straightforwardness.

"The inspector from the council may drop by while I'm gone. If so, give them the tour of the land. Also, make sure to follow up with the contractor on Monday. He should have gotten a copy of council approval by then, and we'll need to start finalizing the schedule, so we can set up a groundbreaking ceremony."

"I've got it, bro. Between the four of us, we've got it covered. Even if Hadley's still under the weather." Campbell stifled a yawn. "Stop worrying so much."

He stared at his brother. "I'm sure I don't have to reiterate how important the memory-park project is…"

Campbell groaned. "No, you don't. I remember Gram, Savion. I loved her, too, and I'm not going to screw this up."

Surprised, yet pleased by Campbell's promise, Savion nodded. "That's good to know, Cam. Okay everyone. Remember that the everyday operations still have to be handled. Make sure the clients in our properties have the best possible experience and handle any problems that come up promptly."

Everyone around the table answered affirmatively.

Satisfied, he stood. "You're released. I'm going to be leaving early today to drop off the paperwork. If you have any problems, Cam's your man." He slapped his brother on the shoulder as Cam and the others left.

Lingering in the empty conference room for a few moments, he opened his leather-covered book and started to write.

If you would only trust me
The journey we could take
Put your hand in my hand and take this journey
with me
I understand the road we must take
Allow me to lead you, but know I understand
you travel from afar
You may have met many but not me
Allow me to explore the depths of your mind,
dive into the pools of your thoughts
Allow me to listen to your heartbeat
Share your stories, feel your pains and your
glories…

With Jazmin lingering in his mind, he closed the book and walked out into the hallway. When he passed through the lobby, headed toward his office, the main entrance door swung open. He swiveled his head and saw Jazmin standing there. She wore a pair of fitted white capri pants and a pink three-quarter-sleeve top. Her skin and the dark ringlets of her hair shimmered in the afternoon sunlight filtering through the glass. Stopping, he blinked a few times. *Is she really here? Or am I just thinking about her that hard?*

She smiled. "Hi, Savion."

Clearing his throat, he smiled back. "Jazmin. It's good to see you. I hope you're not having any problems at the town house."

She shook her head as she walked toward him. "No, everything is fine at the town house. I actually came to see you." The sweet, feminine fragrance of her perfume reached him a few beats before she entered his personal space.

A short giggle came from the direction of the reception desk. He cut his eyes briefly at Lisa, who'd returned to her post there after the meeting. Lisa had the decency to try to appear busy.

His eyes raked over her form, and for the first time, he noticed the gift bag in her hand. "I'm flattered."

She raised the bag, handing it to him. "I wanted to thank you in person for the overnight bag. It was very thoughtful of you to get it for me, and it shows you were listening to me when we went out the other night."

Knowing Lisa's prying eyes were on them, but not caring, he placed a hand on Jazmin's waist. "I always listen when there's something important being said."

"I see." She gave him a sultry wink. "So, here's a little token of my appreciation."

Taking the bag, he reached inside and pulled out a brown leather portfolio cover. It was finely made and lacked any embellishment except for his initials engraved in the cover in an Old English–style font.

"It's for your datebook. I noticed the one you have is a little ratty, so I thought you could use it." She paused. "I hope it's the right size."

He nodded, still admiring the craftsmanship. "It's perfect. Thank you, Jazmin."

"You're welcome." She leaned up and placed a soft kiss on his jawline.

Warmth radiated from the spot her lips had touched, spreading throughout his body. "I was going to call you about our travel plans. Are you okay with me driving us up to Wilmington? It's not that long of a drive, a couple of hours at most."

"Sure. What time do you want to leave?"

"I'll pick you up around noon, if that works for you."

"It does." She eased away from him. "I need to finish packing, so I'll see you tomorrow."

He nodded. "See you then." His eyes followed the tempting sway of her hips until she was out of the building and out of sight.

After she was gone, he turned to Lisa. "Entertaining enough for you?"

"Definitely, Mr. Monroe."

Shaking his head, he went to his office and closed the door behind him.

Chapter 9

Jazmin studied the contents of her overnight bag for what seemed like the hundredth time. She wanted to make sure she had everything—especially all the accessories for the outfit she'd chosen to wear to the Brian McKnight concert. *Can't be looking busted when I meet my favorite singer.*

A few days ago, she'd been nervous about what might happen between her and Savion while they were alone together. Now, though, something had changed inside of her. She genuinely looked forward to everything the weekend would bring. She was a grown woman with needs, and if she decided to let him fulfill those needs, what was the harm in that? Not every encounter had to lead to a long-term relationship. She planned on enjoying her time with him to the fullest.

I'm sure we're both mature enough to handle whatever might happen.

She checked her phone, which was lying on the bed next to the bag, for the time. *Six minutes to noon. Savion will be here any minute.* She mentally ran through a list of her essentials, while rifling through everything she'd put in her bag. Finally satisfied, she zipped it closed.

Walking to the full-length mirror on the outside of her closet door, she did a quick turn to make sure she looked presentable. She'd chosen a pair of dark blue capri leggings and a yellow tunic with long, flowing bell sleeves, choosing to balance comfort and style for the road trip. Based on Savion's estimate of their travel, she would have plenty of time to settle into the inn and change clothes before they had to be at the venue for the show.

Satisfied with her appearance, she tossed the straps of both her overnight bag and her purse over her shoulder and carried her things downstairs. As she descended the steps, she heard a knock on her front door. A smile came to her lips. *He's here.*

She walked over to the front door and opened it, and was greeted by six feet two inches of bronze masculinity. He was dressed in a pair of gray cargo shorts, a closely fitted black T-shirt and a pair of black sneakers. The shirt clung to the powerful muscles of his chest and arms, while the shorts revealed his strong, defined legs.

Her tongue darted out before she could stop it, sweeping over her lower lip. "Hi, Savion."

He winked. "Ready to go?"

She nodded. "Just let me lock up."

"Cool." He took hold of the straps of her purse and overnight bag. "I'll take these to the car."

She watched him stride toward his SUV, marveling at the way he walked. Each step exuded confidence, and she admitted to herself that he was pleasant on the eyes whether he was going or coming. Fishing her key chain out, she locked the door and returned the keys to her pocket. That done, she went to the car.

He stepped in front of her, opening the passenger-side door.

Ducking beneath his arm, she grabbed her purse off the seat, climbed in and buckled up. Before long they were underway.

As he drove, he glanced her way. "I thought you might be hungry, so I'm going to stop by Della's for some food to go. We can eat on the ferry ride to Southport."

"Sounds good."

"What would you like?" He turned onto the road where Tracemore Plaza was located.

Like most cast and crew members of *The Shores*, she'd pretty much memorized Della's menu. "Grab me a number-five lunch special with plain chips and lemonade, please." She unzipped her purse, taking out her wallet.

He shook his head. "I've got you covered, Jazmin."

She put her wallet away. "Thanks."

They pulled into the lot, and Savion went in to grab their food. He returned with two paper sacks about fifteen minutes later and handed one to her along with her drink. "Here you go."

"Thank you." She set the bag on the floorboard and settled in for the short ride to the ferry stop.

Later, as they stood on the ferry together, Savion tapped her on the shoulder. "Let's find a seat so we can eat."

Before she could answer, her stomach growled loudly. She chuckled. "I think we'd better."

She followed him around the deck, passing other passengers of all ages, until they came to an empty bench. There they sat side by side with their lunches.

"I can't believe I'm finally going to see Brian McKnight in concert." She made the comment between sips of lemonade.

He chuckled. "I'm just happy I could help you live the dream." He crunched on a chip. "How long have you been into his music?"

"Since the early nineties. The first time I heard him sing was on Vanessa Williams's album, *The Comfort Zone*. He was a guest on it for a song called 'You Gotta Go.' Been hooked on his voice ever since."

He nodded, looking thoughtful. "You've been rocking with him for a long time. Never let it be said that you aren't a loyal fan."

"What about you? You said you love the Isley Brothers. Ever seen them perform live?"

He shook his head. "Nah. I've been to a few really good shows over the years, though. Babyface, Guy and New Edition were probably the best shows I've ever seen."

"You've got good taste."

Conversation flowed easily between them, and she alternated between watching his face and watching the scenery as the ferry moved over the blue surface of the inlet. It was a beautiful blue-skied day, the warm breeze wafting over her like a whisper. Being with him like this made her feel so content, so at peace, she wondered what the rest of the weekend would bring.

By the time they drove off the ferry in Southport, she found herself stifling yawn after yawn. "Man. The good food and the warm sunshine has gotten to me."

He laughed. "We've got a good forty-five minutes or more on the road, depending on traffic. If you're sleepy, go ahead and take a nap. I won't be upset."

"I appreciate that." No sooner than the words left her lips, her heavy eyelids closed.

It wasn't until she felt tapping against her shoulder that she awakened. She looked at Savion's amused face, blinking several times against the sunlight.

"We're here." He cut the engine, taking the keys from the ignition. "I'd ask you if you had a good nap, but based on the sounds you were making, I think I already know the answer." With a wink, he slipped out of the seat.

Mortified, she clamped a hand over her mouth. She tended to talk and moan in her sleep, a fact relayed to her by her roommates and friends ever since college. Reflecting on her torrid dream made her cheeks feel like they were on fire. He probably thought she'd been dreaming of doing various naughty things to Brian McKnight. In reality, she'd been dreaming of doing naughty things to Savion. *Crap! I know better than to fall asleep around other people. Sierra's still teasing me from an incident years ago.* When he opened the passenger-side door, she stepped out with her purse in hand. "Sorry. Guess I should have had that second cup of coffee this morning."

"Don't worry about it. Cam talks in his sleep, too, and the stuff he says is way worse. Trust me." He stepped back so she could get by, then closed the door. Gesturing to his armload of luggage, he said, "I've already got your bags. Let's go check in."

During their short walk to the front door, she marveled at the beauty of Water's Edge Inn. The main building was a stately looking Victorian-style house, complete with a wide sitting porch outfitted with wooden rockers. The soft yellow siding, black shutters and white gingerbread trim gave the place a quaint, welcoming look. The grounds were gorgeous as well, with the colorful wildflowers planted around the house giving way to a rolling lawn of verdant green grass.

As they climbed the five steps to the porch, a man stepped out the front door. She recognized him as the owner of the inn—he'd been there the day she'd won the prize—but she couldn't recall his name.

"Mr. Monroe, Ms. Boyd. Welcome to the Water's Edge Inn. I'm Nathan Wesley—we met at the supermarket."

She nodded. "Yes, I remember. It's nice to see you again, Mr. Wesley."

He shook her hand. "Please, call me Nathan." He shook hands with Savion, as well. "My wife, Eartha, is waiting inside. Won't you come in?"

She entered, with Savion and Nathan following close behind. At the desk, they met Eartha Wesley. The petite brunette with a round face and kind brown eyes was chatty, as was her husband. Check-in took less than five minutes, but politely extracting themselves from the Wesleys' company took twenty minutes more.

When Jazmin thought she couldn't take another minute of pleasant chatter, Eartha smiled her way. "Nathan, look at us. We're keeping these lovebirds from going up to their room."

Usually, Jazmin would have corrected anyone referring to her and Savion as a couple, but she wanted to make sure she had time to get ready for the concert, so she didn't protest.

Nathan slapped his hands on the desk. "Dang it, Eartha, you're right." He gestured toward the stairs. "You two can go on upstairs to room two-oh-one. If you need anything at all, just give us a holler."

By the time they made it upstairs, it was after four. The room, decorated in shades of blue, green and yellow, featured a bevy of rich mahogany furniture. The centerpiece of the space was the elegant four-poster bed, dressed in a thick comforter and several fluffy throw pillows. To the left of the bed, there were two upholstered chairs sitting on either side of a round, polished table. The was also a love seat and a short-legged coffee table. Ceramic vases of fresh, vibrant flowers and paintings depicting the various seaside scenes complemented the furnishings.

That night, as Savion escorted Jazmin to their seats in the front row of the Thalian Hall Center for the Performing Arts, he could feel the excitement rolling off her body. She looked gorgeous in the fitted royal blue dress, with its high neckline and bell sleeves, and a pair of matching pumps. He didn't know why she insisted on covering her neck and shoulders, but other than that, he had no complaints about her attire.

The packed house made for a bit of difficulty reaching the front row, but after circumventing the crowd and the security guards stationed around the space, they finally claimed their seats.

"Wow." She placed her handbag beneath the chair, her gaze focused ahead. "We have an amazing view of the stage from here."

"Yeah, it's pretty sweet." He gave her shoulder a playful jab. "If Brian exhales deeply, we should be able to feel it from here."

She giggled. "You're a mess, Savion."

He winked.

"Seriously, though. Thanks for going along with this whole thing, and for bringing me here. I really appreciate it."

He shrugged. "I'd never stand between a woman like you and something she truly wants."

She smiled brightly in response to his comment, and he felt his heart squeeze in his chest. Knowing he'd made her smile like that did something to him, something he couldn't quite name. Whatever it was, it felt like getting a victory, like he scored a triple-double on the court.

Once the show got underway, he watched her reactions. The crowd was on their feet by the time Brian finished his opening number, the classic ballad "One Last Cry." As Brian moved seamlessly through his catalog of hits, holding the crowd captive with his voice, Savion had to admit he was enjoying the show. *Vocally, Brian is in top form. And what a showman. The women in here are basically eating out of his hand.* Jazmin knew every word to every song, and sang along loudly, like the true fan she was. She appeared to be on the verge of tears during "Crazy Love," and Savion could only shake his head. Her exuberance was both touching and contagious, and before he knew it, he was singing along to the songs he knew.

Listening to the lyrics, Savion felt a certain kinship with Mr. McKnight. After all, love songs were basically poems set to music, not very different from some of the writings in his own leather-bound book. Savion didn't have a singing bone in his body, but he did feel he had a romantic streak. It had been ages since he'd indulged his inner romantic, though. None of the women he'd encountered recently had seemed right.

Until now. He looked to his right, watched Jazmin singing and swaying in time with the music. She was totally caught up in the moment, with the emotions evoked by Brian's words radiating from her face. All other cares had fallen away, and she was sold out for the here and now. She glowed.

It's beautiful.

She's beautiful.

Brian closed the show with "Back at One," and when he hit the last note, the crowd erupted during several minutes of an enthusiastic standing ovation. Savion joined in, noting Jazmin alternating between clapping and dabbing at her eyes. He could tell she'd experienced something profound, and he was happy he got to be a part of it.

After the show ended and most of the crowd filed out of the venue, Savion stood with Jazmin in the VIP line. Noticing how shaky she seemed on her feet, he tapped her on the shoulder. "Are you gonna be all right? Your knees are knockin',' as my Gram used to say."

She released a nervous titter. "I'll be fine… I hope. I just can't believe I get to meet him."

"You work in television. I know this isn't your first time meeting a celebrity."

She shook her head. "Of course not. But this isn't any old famous person—this is Brian McKnight."

He smiled, finding her enthusiasm endearing.

As their turn in line approached, she hung back, so he walked up to Brian and stuck out his hand. After greeting them, the singer asked who he should make the autograph out to.

Savion gave Jazmin's name, spelling it for the singer. After Brian signed, he offered to pose for a selfie, but Savion pulled Jazmin forward. She was still hanging back, too shy to move. "Come on, Jaz. He doesn't bite…"

She edged closer to Brian, her voice trembling as she spoke. "Oh, Mr. McKnight, it's so nice to meet you. I've been listening to your music since forever and I just love you."

Savion chuckled as she gushed over her favorite singer. This was too cute.

After he gave Jazmin her signed poster, Brian reached out his arm to Jazmin to draw her closer but stopped short. He glanced Savion's way, as if seeking his approval.

Feeling his brow furrow, Savion turned the gesture over in his mind for a moment before realization hit him. *He thinks we're together.* Rather than correct the music legend, Savion simply gave a dismissive wave. "Go right ahead, man." He stood back and watched as Brian hugged Jazmin. She released a tiny squeal of delight, then posed for the selfie with the singer and Savion, whom she insisted should join them.

Later, as they walked out of the concert hall toward his SUV, she chattered nonstop about the evening. He had the poster safely rolled up and tucked beneath his arm, and as they walked, she reached out and grabbed his hand, never stopping the flow of words streaming out of her mouth.

"I can't believe he hugged me. I mean, I just can't!"

"It happened. I saw it." He shook his head but felt the smile tugging his lips.

"This was easily the best show I've ever been to. After all these years, he can still hit those notes. Amazing."

"It was impressive, I gotta admit." He stepped off the sidewalk, leading her around to the passenger side of his SUV.

"And he's just so nice. And so humble! I mean, he's a legend, and it's so nice to know he's not full of himself. If he'd have been a jerk, I would've…"

He leaned over and kissed her on the lips.

She looked up at him, her eyes wide.

Was that surprise? Or outrage? What was she thinking?

Not wanting to wait, in case he'd offended her, he took a step back. "I'm sorry, Jazmin. I shouldn't have done that without asking you. Seeing you this happy and excited just got to me, and I…"

She blinked a few times but said nothing.

He sighed. "Anyway, that's no excuse. I want you to know that you don't owe me anything. We aren't going to do anything that makes you uncomfortable."

As the last word faded, she leaned up and kissed him. Her lips parted, her tongue sliding over his lower lip, and he felt electric heat shoot through his bloodstream. She wrapped her arms around his neck as his palms came to rest on her waist. He turned her slightly, her back coming to rest against the body of his vehicle, and leaned into the kiss. Their tongues mated and mingled for several long moments.

He pulled back, knowing that if they kept this up, he'd abandon all his good sense and home training.

She blew out a breath. Her hand slipped around to caress his jaw. "Savion, you've been a perfect gentleman, and I know I don't owe you anything." She paused.

His breaths came hard and fast as he waited.

"But I want to give myself to you."

He stared into the dark pools of her eyes. "Are you sure?"

She nodded. "Very."

He moved her aside, opening the passenger-side door. "Then what the hell are we doing standing out here?"

Chapter 10

Walking hand in hand with Savion on the garden path that led to the side entrance of the inn, Jazmin glanced over at him. His features were softened by the moonlight, but the desire in his eyes was as plain as the silver orb in the night sky.

Their eyes met briefly, then she looked away. Emotions and logic were warring inside her, and neither seemed to have the upper hand. Her body craved him; the craving was unlike any she'd ever felt before. Yet as much as she yearned to feel everything he had to offer, a flicker of fear made her hesitant.

How will I explain my scar? If he sees it, he'll want to know what it is and how it got there. What if he's repulsed by the sight of it? The thoughts raced through her mind and her hand constricted around his.

"You're tense." He stated it, rather than asking.

She swallowed. He'd picked up on her feelings and there was no use in hiding them. "I'm...a little nervous, yes."

He stopped short of the doorway, turning to look at her. "You know, Jazmin, we don't have to do anything tonight, if you're not sure."

"It's not that." She looked away from his intense gaze. "I want you, Savion. Probably more than I'd care to admit."

He placed his free hand on her shoulder. "Jazmin, you can feel free to tell me whatever you think I need to know and keep the rest to yourself. I'm not here to pressure you into anything. Not talking, or kissing, and certainly not making love."

She shifted her gaze back up to meet his, seeing the sincerity in his eyes.

"I want to make love to you tonight, Jazmin. But if you're not ready, for any reason, I will wait." He gave her shoulder a gentle squeeze before dropping his hand away.

She exhaled. "Let's go inside."

They entered, then traversed the dimly lit interior of the inn until they made it upstairs to their room. There, he opened the door and stood back as she walked through, then followed her.

She kicked off her shoes, tossed her purse onto one of the upholstered armchairs. She walked to the glass doors that led out to the small balcony and stood in the circle of moonlight on the carpet. While she looked out at the night sky, she noticed Savion, sitting on the edge of the bed.

A small smile touched her lips. *He's showing respect by keeping his distance.* She admired that about him. The desire flowing between them was so thick and so electric it practically glowed, yet he was holding back until she felt comfortable enough to take things further.

"Savion." She glanced over her shoulder, calling his name softly.

He stood, silhouetted in the darkness of the room. "Yes?"

"Come here, please."

She felt him enter her space a moment later. Having him near her only made the charge in the air stronger. She closed her eyes. "Hold me."

He obliged, stepping behind her and wrapping his strong arms around her waist.

A sigh escaped her. His arms felt safe, warm. His embrace felt like home.

She turned in his arms and his lips crashed down against hers. Swept up in the magic of the kiss, she slipped her arms around his neck and leaned into him. She wanted this, wanted every inch of her body to touch every inch of his. He responded by deepening the kiss, his tongue thrusting into her mouth.

When she finally pulled back, a bit breathless, she found him watching her with glistening eyes.

"Will you let me make love to you, Jazmin?"

"Yes, Savion." She pressed herself against him. "Yes."

The kissing began again, only this time, they both knew where the road would lead. Her hands swept over his muscled shoulders and down his arms, as his large palms caressed her back, hips and thighs before coming to rest on her behind. When he gave her a little squeeze there, a yelp of pleasure left her lips.

He stepped back, stripping off his button-down shirt and the sleeveless undershirt beneath.

She drew in a sharp breath at the sight of him. His glorious body that begged to be touched. She closed the distance between them and placed her hands on his chest, moving them over the muscled hardness. When she slid the flats of her thumbs over his nipples, he emitted a low, rumbling growl.

Smiling down at her, he wove his fingers into her hair. "I will return the favor." He placed a fleeting kiss against her lips before gently turning her.

Her breathing hitched when she felt him grasp the zipper pull at the back of her dress. He dragged it down with aching slowness, and her heart raced as he spread the open halves. Bending, he placed a series of kisses on the exposed skin along the curve of her back, and her knees buckled.

He steadied her and stood, pushing the dress over her shoulders and down her arms. The garment fell away, pooling around her feet.

She held her breath, waiting.

A moment later, he grazed his fingertips over the long scar that started near the base of her neck and went over her right shoulder, extending halfway to her elbow. "What is this, Jazmin?"

Her heart stopped. It was the question she'd known was coming but hadn't wanted to hear.

Crossing one arm over her chest, she bolted for the balcony door. Throwing it open, she ignored the sound of his voice calling her name and rushed out into the balmy night. She knew there was no one else around for miles, and right now, out here felt much safer than being inside with him and his question. The tears began then, falling down her cheeks like rain. She hugged herself, wrapping her arms around her torso, and let the pain have its way.

She felt him behind her but didn't turn or acknowledge his presence.

"I'm not going to press you about this, or about anything. Curiosity got the better of me for a moment, that's all." He placed his hands on her shoulders, offering a gentle caress. "You don't have to answer me. You can tell me when you're ready, and not a moment sooner."

Drawing a deep breath, she sniffled, then used her hands to wipe her face. "I'm sorry. I didn't expect to react like this."

"Don't apologize." He used the pad of his thumb to wipe away her tears.

"I know it's ugly to look at. That's why I keep it covered."

His expression changed from sympathy to confusion. "Are you kidding? There isn't anything about you that could ever be ugly to me, Jazmin."

Having seen the scar in the mirror these past two years, she would beg to differ. Still, she gave him a teary smile. "That's really sweet of you to say."

"It's also the truth." He cupped her face with his large hand. "You don't even know how beautiful you are, do you?"

She blinked, taken aback by the earnest sincerity of his words.

"Jazmin Carmen Boyd, you are the most beautiful thing I've ever seen. And I would very much like to show you how I feel if you'll let me."

Something inside her shifted, and the change was

palpable. The tears stopped, replaced by a sense of wonder and admiration for the man standing before her.

She didn't know where this would lead, didn't know what the future held. Then again, no one knew those things. What she did know was that he'd shown himself sincere, caring and respectful. Whatever was happening between them begged to be explored fully, and she wasn't going to keep denying herself the pleasure ne promised.

She stroked his jawline. "Let's go back inside, Savion."

He grinned. "Yes, ma'am."

She screeched softly in surprise as he scooped her up, tossed her over his shoulder and carried her through the open doors.

Inside the shadowy room, Savion slowly finished undressing Jazmin. He took his time, stopping to kiss and caress each newly bared inch of her golden skin. The sounds of her soft moans and their breathing were accompanied only by the song of insects flowing in with the breeze through the open balcony doors.

He lay her down on the bed and stood back for a moment to admire her. The sight of her, naked and bathed in moonlight, made his blood race.

Words flowed through his mind, narratives pouring to describe her lush beauty. She was gorgeous enough to fuel his dreams and fill his notebook pages for years to come.

He plucked the condom from his back pocket. Stripping away his trousers and boxers, he tossed them over the armchair in the corner. He was hard and ready; the sight of her had been enough to arouse him. He covered himself, then joined her on the bed. She sat up, facing him. He rested his back against the headboard, pulling her into his lap.

They spent a few hot moments kissing and caressing each other. He wove his fingers into the dark riches of her hair while her hands gripped his shoulders. When she broke the kiss, she looked into his eyes and purred like a contented tigress.

He groaned low in his throat. He'd thought he couldn't be any more turned on, and she'd already proven him wrong. He had a feeling that trend would continue well into the night.

She kneeled up, straddling his hips. He pulled her close, so he could sample the dark tips of her breasts. Drawing one nipple, and then the other, between his lips, he enjoyed the soft cries she gave as he suckled her. His hands on her waist held her in place, giving her no means of escape from his hungry mouth.

Her hips began to rock, and he could feel himself getting closer and closer to the place he most wanted to be. He let her take the lead and kept up his attention to her breasts while she moved on top of him. Suddenly she shifted back, and he felt the tip of his dick at her opening. She shifted forward again, and as he slid inside her, he saw her bite her lip.

Her body wrapped around him with a warmth and tightness that threatened to push him over the edge. He held fast, determined to enjoy this ride with her for as long as possible. So he took his focus off the hot pleasure she generated in his lower regions, and instead concentrated on touching her. He caressed her face, her shoulders, her breasts and her stomach, then eased his hands around to give her ass a gentle squeeze.

She purred again, increasing her pace a bit. With each rise and fall of her body, a moan slipped from her lips. The sights, the sounds and the feel of her were threatening his very sanity but he held on to what little control he had left.

She changed her ride then, grinding her hips, working her body against him in sensuous circles, and he growled. Gripping her hips, he thrust up and met her movements with motions of his own. Fire shot through his blood, his insides felt molten-hot and fluid, as if he was melting, too.

"Savion!" She shouted his name in the darkness, her body flexing and contracting around his.

That did it. Moments later, he trembled as his release shot through him.

In the aftermath, he held her close to him, listening to the sounds of their heavy breathing. The still open doors allowed the night breezes in, and he felt the cool air moving over his sweat-dampened skin. "Jazmin, you're incredible."

She rested her head against his shoulder. "You're not so bad yourself."

He chuckled, reveling in the feeling of holding her. What she didn't know was that he hadn't just been talking about her lovemaking. It was so much more than that. Everything about her seemed to call to him. It was as if he'd been missing a piece all his life, without even knowing it, until he'd found her. She filled a void in him he hadn't known he possessed.

And now that he'd found her, he never wanted to be without her again.

Chapter 11

Jazmin tried to open her eyes but couldn't because her face was smashed into the soft feather pillow. Turning her head slightly, she managed to squint against the sunlight filtering into the room. Shifting around until she was on her back, she sat up, stifled a yawn and looked around the room.

Her gaze landed on Savion. Wearing a pair of blue striped pajama bottoms, he was seated at the table a few feet away, scrolling through his phone. In front of him was a covered tray.

She yawned again, then smiled as memories of his lovemaking rose to the surface of her mind. *What a night.*

He looked up from his phone, his expression conveying his contentment. "Good morning, sleepyhead."

The sheet fell away, revealing her nudity as she

reached up and stretched her arms above her head. "Morning."

He winked. "The view from here is amazing." He looked pointedly at her chest.

Feeling the familiar warmth creeping into her face, she grabbed the sheets and wrapped them around her torso. "I see you're chipper this morning."

"After what we did last night, how else would I be?"

She giggled. *He's got a point there.* "What time is it?"

"A little after ten."

"I must have really been tired. I don't usually sleep this late."

He gave her a knowing look. "I kind of figured. That's why I tried to be quiet, I didn't want to disturb you."

Her stomach grumbled. Hoping he hadn't heard it, she gestured to the tray. "What's in there?"

He lifted the lid and showed her. "Continental breakfast. There are some croissants, fresh fruit and coffee. I didn't know how long you'd be asleep, or what you'd want."

She crawled out of bed, and while he watched, she picked up the button-down he'd been wearing the day before and slipped into it. Closing the buttons, she walked toward the bathroom. "Just let me wash my hands." Moments later she came to the table.

"We can always order a hot breakfast if you prefer. We're the only ones here, so the service is pretty fast."

"This is a good start. I don't want anything heavy just yet." She sat in the chair across from him.

"How do you take your coffee?" He grabbed the handle of the white ceramic carafe and retrieved a matching mug from the tray.

"It's complicated. If you pour it for me, I'll dress it up."

"Whatever the lady wants." He filled the mug and passed it to her.

Dipping into the small, covered containers on the tray, she added a little cream and sugar to her coffee. Once it passed the color and taste test, she took a long sip. "Mmm. Good coffee."

"I'm glad you approve." He grabbed a plate and passed it to her, then took one for himself. "Let's eat."

They filled their plates with the offerings. She chose two croissants, green grapes and bright red strawberries. While they ate, they bantered.

"What a show, huh? I gotta say, I can see why you were so excited to see Brian in concert."

She nodded, swallowing a mouthful of tangy fruit. "All my girls who had seen him raved about his performances. My expectations were high, and he definitely delivered."

"What about me?"

She paused, confused by his question. "What do you mean?"

"I mean, I don't know what you expected of me for our first night together. But did I deliver?"

His forwardness caught her off guard. She coughed, then took a sip of her coffee to ease the tightness in her throat. "You shoot from the hip, I see."

He shrugged. "That's me."

Setting aside her mug, she reached for his hand. "To be honest, I never thought we would even reach a physical level, so I didn't have any expectations. But I will say you were very, very impressive, Savion." She gave his hand a gentle squeeze before releasing it.

"That's good to know." The self-satisfied smile on his face spoke louder than his words.

When they'd finished eating, he gathered all the dishes onto the tray and set it in the hallway outside their room. She watched him walk, captivated by the muscles working beneath his burnished skin. Returning to the table, he sat down and gestured for her to sit on his lap.

Her brow hitched.

He patted his legs. "I promise not to bite unless you request it."

Shaking her head, she stood. "What are you up to, Savion?"

He smiled. "Right now, I just want to hold you."

Slowly, she padded over to his chair and let him draw her onto his lap. The thin fabric of the pajama bottoms wasn't much of a barrier between her bottom and the luscious thickness of his manhood. So she shifted around a bit to get comfortable, or as close to it as she could manage.

When she stilled, he undid the top button of the shirt, baring part of her neck.

She stiffened. "What are you doing?"

"Shh." He opened the second button, pushing the shirt away to bare her right shoulder.

Knowing the scar was visible, and probably looked even less attractive in the daylight, she wriggled. "Savion..."

He stilled her by placing his large hand on her stomach. "Jazmin, listen to me, baby. I don't know where or how you got this." He traced his index finger along the part of the scar that peeked above the garment. "It doesn't matter to me, because I know you'll tell me when you're ready. But there's something I need you to understand."

She closed her eyes as he retraced the scar. His touch made her feel both peaceful and exhilarated. "What's that?"

"You are absolutely gorgeous... Wonderful... Perfect...in every way." He punctuated each descriptor with a warm kiss along the column of her neck. "I don't ever want to hear you say the word *ugly* when you're talking about yourself again, understood?"

"Yes," she replied breathlessly.

"Do you promise?" He flicked his tongue over her earlobe, then dragged it down the sensitive skin at the edge of her jawline.

She bit her lip to keep the moan from spilling out.

Another lick followed this time, down the side of her throat. Reaching the base, he suckled the area where her throat met her shoulder. "Well?"

"No... I mean yes..." She felt confused and aroused, but arousal won out. "Whatever you want me to say, so you'll make love to me."

Before she could draw another breath, he was on his feet, with her still in his arms. He carried her back to the bed, put her down and stripped away his shirt to reveal her nudity. His hands caressed and teased her sensitive skin, his lips kissed and nibbled each peak and valley of her body. Soon her entire being burned with ecstasy, and she could do nothing to stop the flood of soft moans escaping her lips.

He left her for a moment, to discard his pants and sheathe himself with protection. When he returned, the mattress gave as he climbed into bed with her.

He hovered above her, centering his hardness between her thighs. And as he slipped inside, joining their bodies, he growled into her ear.

Even in the haze of passion, she heard his words as clear as day.

"I love you, Jazmin."

Before she could respond, the first orgasm swept her away.

Savion sat on the balcony Sunday morning, with an open copy of *USA TODAY* in his hands. Wearing only a white terry robe and his shorts, he'd come out to enjoy the mild weather. The day had dawned gray and overcast, and the temperature hovered in the low seventies. The breeze rustling the pages of his paper felt good against his skin.

On the other side of the small wrought-iron table from him, Jazmin reclined in the second chair. She also wore one of the inn's fluffy robes over her lush nudity. She flipped through the pages of a fashion magazine, occasionally reaching for the bottle of water she'd placed on the table.

He couldn't remember the last time he'd felt such contentment. The rolling green lawn of the inn, punctuated by three large gardens bursting with colorful blooms and a man-made lake, provided a beautiful, relaxing feast for the eyes. The inn was located so far off the beaten path that traffic noise and city commotion couldn't be heard. Only the wind and the sound of the birds and insects encroached on the near silence.

A sudden, insistent buzzing sound drew his attention.

He looked to his left and saw Jazmin pluck her phone from the hip pocket of her robe. She looked at the screen, and from what he could tell, she was reading a message from someone. After a few moments of studying the display, she used her thumbs to tap out what he assumed to be a reply, then pocketed the device again.

She glanced his way, offering a quick smile before turning her attention back to the magazine.

He mirrored her expression, then went back to reading the world news section of the paper.

The buzzing started again.

This time, he kept his eyes on the news, but in his periphery, he could see her silently reading and responding. He drew in a breath. *I wonder who she's talking to.* She hadn't exactly been open about her past, at least not in terms of relationships outside of her family. Doing his best to shake off his curiosity, he kept reading.

The text alerts sounded four more times over the next ten minutes, and each time the buzzing cut through the silence, he did his best to ignore it. *It's not my business. She's an adult, she can talk to whoever she wants.*

That was what the logical part of him said. But the illogical part, the part of him that had blurted out the truth of his feelings during a moment of passion the night before, said other things.

What if she's talking to another man? He wondered why his mind jumped straight to that conclusion. It seemed too early in the relationship—or whatever it was they had—to be feeling jealous.

Can I really get upset with her? Are we even in a relationship now that we've slept together, or is this just a temporary arrangement?

Holding the paper at an angle that would hide his reaction, he silently cursed as she answered the sixth text message from whoever was blowing up her phone.

Or at least he thought it was silent.

A moment later, she asked, "Savion, did you say something?"

He cringed. *Damn, I'm caught.* Lowering the paper so they could see each other, he shook his head. "Nothing important."

One of her perfectly groomed eyebrows rose an inch. "For some reason, I don't believe that."

He didn't respond. Instead, he watched her, waiting to see if she'd volunteer any information about whom she'd been conversing with.

She took a deep breath, setting aside her magazine. "I hope you don't think it's rude of me to be texting when we're spending time together, because my work will force me to do that from time to time."

He shook his head. "No. Is work texting you now, while you're on vacation?"

"No. It's my mom." She sighed. "If I don't respond immediately to her messages, she starts coming up with scenarios involving me lying in a ditch somewhere."

"Your mom does that, too, huh?" He chuckled. "If Viola Monroe hasn't heard from one of her children in seventy-two hours, she's calling the sheriff and forming a search party."

She giggled, a light tinkling sound that melted away some of the tension in his body. "Well, anyway, she wanted to know how the concert was."

Surprise made him lean forward in his chair. "So she knows where we are?"

She made a funny face. "Not exactly."

"Now, I'm confused." What did she mean by that?

"My parents know I'm here. They know I got a ticket to see Brian McKnight, they just don't know all the details." She looked away, as if embarrassed.

He thought about what she'd said for a moment before it dawned on him. "Oh. So they don't know you're with me." He didn't know why that bothered him so much, but it irked him nonetheless.

She nodded. "Right. It was so much easier that way."

He sat back in the chair, feeling a bit deflated. She'd essentially hidden him from her parents, erasing him from their so-called "romantic getaway" in favor of letting them think she'd traveled to Wilmington alone.

As if sensing the change in his mood, she said, "Wait, Savion. I just figured out how this must sound to you, and trust me, it's not that way."

He folded his paper and set it aside. "It's fine, Jazmin. Technically, I didn't tell my parents, either—they saw it on the local news."

"In any case, I didn't tell my mom I'm here with a man because she's been harping on me for years to give her some grandchildren. I'm sure you remember me telling you that my parents are older than most of my friends' parents, so there's a sense of urgency for them."

"I can understand that." His parents were healthy and youthful and would probably live another fifty years, but that didn't stop them from leaning on their children for grandkids. He could imagine the pressure was much heavier in Jazmin's case since her parents were already over seventy. Luckily, one positive aspect of his younger siblings' recent marriages was that the pressure to produce a Monroe heir had been shifted to them.

"If I'd told her we were here together, I kid you not, she'd be naming the grandchildren right now."

He laughed. "Our moms should really meet. Sounds like they have a lot in common." Oddly enough, though, he could easily envision Jazmin as his wife, and mother to a few little darlings of their own. He'd never thought of any of his previous partners that way. But when he looked into her eyes, he could see a future far different, and far more fulfilling than any he'd ever imagined for himself.

"Good. Then you're not mad?"

He shook his head. "Nah. Could have been worse." *Crap.* He hadn't meant to say that last part out loud.

She tilted her head to one side, studying his face. "What do you mean by that?"

"Nothing." He leaned back in the wicker chair, gazing out at the lake, watching the light play over the shimmering surface.

She snapped her fingers. "Aha! You thought I was talking to a man, didn't you?"

He shook his head but didn't make eye contact. "I never said that."

"You didn't have to! Your face said it for you." She grinned. "You thought I was talking to another man, and you were jealous!"

He groaned, then crinkled his mouth into a frown. "Don't tease me about this, Jazmin."

She got up, walked over to his chair and stood in front of him. Her positioning essentially forced him to look at her.

They watched each other silently for a few beats.

Then she sat down on his lap, her expression of amusement softening into something much more affectionate. "I heard what you said last night, Savion."

He waited for what she would say next, bracing for the sting of her telling him for the millionth time that she didn't need romance in her life right now.

She draped her arms loosely around his neck. "I didn't have time to respond before my, um…" She chewed her lip. "Before pleasure got the better of me. But I just wanted you to know—" she looked deep into his eyes "—I love you, too, Savion."

Hearing those words pass her lips made his heart thud in his chest. Drawing her down to his kiss, he savored the taste of her and the feeling of holding her close to his heart.

Chapter 12

Monday afternoon, Jazmin watched the passing scenery as Savion drove them off the grounds of the Water's Edge Inn. Inside, she reflected on what had turned out to be one of the most eventful weekends of her life. She'd expected to enjoy her long-awaited meeting with Brian McKnight. What she had not expected, though, were the passionate interludes she'd shared with Savion.

She glanced over at him, admiring his profile as he kept his attention focused on the road. The line of his jaw, dotted with shadowy stubble, made him look even sexier than usual.

As if reading her mind, he reached up to run his fingertips over his chin below his goatee. "Can't believe I forgot my razor. I must be looking pretty shaggy right now."

"A little." She chuckled. "But don't worry, it looks good."

He smiled. "I'm glad you like it. I'm going to have to at least trim it before I go back to the office, though."

They lapsed into silence again, and she wondered what he was thinking. Was he analyzing the state of their relationship the way she was? *Do men even do that?* After a few long moments, her curiosity demanded satisfaction, so she asked, "What are we now, Savion?"

He shrugged. "I know we're in love. Not sure it needs a label beyond that."

She turned over his words in her mind and could see the truth in them. Still, it nagged at her that she hadn't been completely forthcoming with him about her past. Drawing a deep breath, she braced herself for all the possible reactions to what she had to say. "I want to tell you how I got my scar."

"I'm listening."

"Five years ago, I met a man named Dresden. He was handsome, charismatic and something of a bad boy. Played drums in a funk band, and we met at a show. He just had this presence that really grabbed my attention. We dated about six months before I moved into his place." She paused, gauging his reaction. She'd heard how folks in the Bible Belt judged people for what they referred to as "living in sin," and she wanted to see if he was one of the judgmental ones.

His expression didn't change. After she was silent for a few minutes, he said, "Go on."

"We were together almost three years, and a lot of it was good. But when he was playing gigs, he drank. And when he drank too much—" She sighed, feeling the sadness rise until she was unable to finish the sentence.

"It's okay, Jazmin." His deep voice encouraged her, reassured her.

"Dres came home one night, drunker than I'd ever seen him. I don't know, maybe he'd had more than just alcohol. Anyway, he accused me of cheating, and he started screaming at me. I told him repeatedly that I'd been faithful, but he didn't believe me." She could see the tightness in Savion's jaw, an indication that he didn't like where this story was going. Neither did she, but she felt she had to get it off her chest. "He chased me into his music room and grabbed a letter opener off his desk." Tears filled her eyes. "I was terrified. He pinned me to the wall and used the tip of the letter opener to cut me. Told me no man would want me once I was scarred."

"How did you get away from him?" His tone held a quiet urgency.

"There was a plaque he'd gotten from the lead singer of the band on the wall. It was really big, so I got one arm free, snatched it off the wall and smacked him over the head with it. When he passed out, I took my purse and keys and left." She wiped away the tears spilling down her face. "I went to the police to press charges, then to the hospital. I never went back there. I left clothes, personal items, but I've never set foot in that place again."

"And what happened to this asshole?"

She sniffled, buoyed by the knowledge of his protectiveness. "He did six months in county jail for misdemeanor assault. Right around the time he was due to get out, I got the call from Devon to work on the show. I came to North Carolina and haven't looked back."

"That was quite an ordeal you just described. And I'm happy you felt comfortable enough to tell me about it."

She took a deep breath, finally feeling the tears subside. "You're very easy to talk to."

"It just burns me up that this jerk is roaming free. He'd better hope we never cross paths."

She smiled. "I can't say I hate the idea of you giving Dres a swift kick in the rear end."

He frowned. "Did he ever hit you before that? Ever make you feel unsafe?"

She shrugged. "He'd never taken it that far."

"He was definitely a monster for behaving like that. Do you know why you stayed with him for so long?"

She narrowed her eyes, because his tone was a bit accusatory. "I've thought that plenty of times. But I can't go back and change my actions." She wanted to say more but kept quiet. If she went down this path with him, her emotions would get the better of her, and she'd end up cursing him out.

"I'm sorry, I didn't mean to say it that way." He sounded contrite. "You know I would never treat you that way, don't you?"

She nodded, because she trusted him in a way she'd never trusted another man. Though his statement about her staying too long had been hurtful, it wasn't enough to erase her feelings for him. She couldn't really explain it; a gut feeling told her that her body and her heart were safe with him.

"If I ever pulled some mess like that, Cam and Pop would take me out on the fishing boat just to throw me overboard." He shook his head. "As they should, because no man has any right to treat a woman that way."

She smiled but didn't say anything in response. Now that she'd told him the story behind her scar, relief washed through her. Being honest with him had felt good, at least up until he'd decided to question her good sense. Had his opinion of her changed? And did she really want to be involved with someone who was so quick to lay the blame at her feet?

At least he'd apologized. She shifted her gaze back to the passing scenery, resolved not to dwell on the matter.

By the time the lunch hour rolled around on Tuesday, Savion was ready to call it quits for the day. He'd arrived to work that morning to find the office in the midst of a crisis, one he'd been trying to rectify for the last few hours.

At a quarter past noon, he sat behind his desk, on the phone with the representative from the council. "Ma'am, can you repeat what you just said?"

"Yes, sir. I said, when you brought in your paperwork last week for the permit you requested, the signature page was missing. The form was turned in toward the end of the business day, so no one noticed the error until Friday. A clerk reached out to your office but was told you were unavailable."

"I was on vacation, but the signature page was here on my desk."

"Well, our clerk spoke to someone named Max, who said he didn't have access to your office because there was no one present with a key."

He rubbed his open palm down his face. "Okay, ma'am. So, what would I need to do to get this straightened out?"

"We still have all the rest of the pages of the form, so if you can bring the signature page into the office by three o'clock, we'll get you squared away."

"Great."

"But remember, sir. The filing will still take forty-eight hours to process. That I won't be able to issue you an official permit until late Thursday afternoon, at the earliest."

"Thank you." He hung up the phone briefly and took a deep breath to calm his nerves, then picked it up again. This time he dialed Caruso and Sons, the contractor assigned to the memory-park project.

"Al Caruso speaking."

"Hey, Al, it's Savion Monroe, again."

"What did you find out, Mr. Monroe?"

"The council can issue us a permit by late Thursday. So, when could we break ground?"

There was the sound of muffled conversation and typing on the line for a few moments before Al answered. "My office manager says next Monday is the soonest we can start. Not this coming week, the next one."

Savion cursed under his breath. "That's the absolute soonest?"

"Yes. When the permit didn't come in yesterday, we knew the memory park would be delayed, so we put our workers on other jobs. A few of them went back to the mainland. Sorry, man, that's the best I can do."

He sighed. "Can y'all swing a ceremony on Friday?

You don't need the whole crew for that, just the folks from the front office."

"I don't see why not. We've already got the ribbon and the giant scissors." Al chuckled.

He realized that was the foreman's attempt at a joke, but in his current mood, the humor was lost on him. "Okay. I'll let my father know there's been a slight change of plans."

"Make sure you remind him of the project-delay fee, as well. It's one and a half percent of the final project costs, before taxes."

He stifled a groan. "Thanks, Al. I'll be sure to let him know. Have a good day." He placed the receiver in the cradle and sat back in his chair. He groaned aloud, wondering how he could have let himself make such a stupid mistake. He looked at the signature page, resting on the corner of his desk. *I must have dropped it there and not realized it.* He'd been in such a hurry to go home and get ready for his romantic getaway that he'd lost focus.

I was so busy thinking about Jazmin that I did the one thing I promised myself I wouldn't do—I let my father down. His parents were due back this week from their anniversary trip, and he knew his father wouldn't be pleased to learn that the groundbreaking had to be delayed. If they were building somewhere inland, the one-week delay probably wouldn't be that big of a deal. But since they were on an island, racing against time to prepare an outdoor site for hurricane season, that week of lost time could potentially prove disastrous.

He stared up at the ceiling for a few moments, hoping his Gram's spirit would guide him to get the job done, the right way. He pushed back from the desk. If he wanted to avoid further delays to the memory-park project, he needed to get the signature page downtown. He tucked the page into a folder, got his keys and started toward the door.

He'd crossed the lobby and stepped outside when his phone buzzed with a text from Jazmin. He slipped the phone from his pocket and read it.

Wanna come by the studio?

He smiled, despite his bad mood, and fired off a reply. Will text you when I'm done with work.

The part of him that loved her wanted to see her again.

The part of him that wanted the memory-park project to succeed wondered if there really was room in his life for a relationship.

It was happening to him, just like it had happened to his brother and sister. He'd fallen into the love trap. Despite all his efforts to avoid getting involved with anyone, he'd managed to fall in love with Jazmin. And he'd fallen hard. His feelings for her ran deep, and no matter how much he wanted to, he couldn't simply dismiss them or pretend they didn't exist.

Climbing into his car, he tucked the phone away. Right now, he needed to focus on correcting his careless mistake. He was determined to make the best of this situation, and everything else would simply have to wait.

Chapter 13

Jazmin was in the lobby of the studio that evening, leaning against the reception desk. She scrolled through her social-media feeds, occasionally looking out through the front windows of the building. Most people had cleared out of the place a couple of hours ago, including the rest of the postproduction staff. Other than the janitor and the security guard stationed at the gate, there wasn't anyone else present on studio property. She'd already let the guard know she was expecting a visitor, and to let him through once he showed his identification.

When she saw Savion's car pull up in the lot, she went to the glass door and turned the lock, so he could enter. He appeared at the door moments later, and she let him in. He wore a pair of dark denim jeans, a red polo and blue sneakers. His casual dress did nothing to detract from his good looks—at this point, she'd concluded he'd look good in a potato sack.

She noticed the leather planner tucked beneath his left arm, and it pleased her to see that he'd started using the cover she'd given him.

As they walked down the corridor toward the postproduction suite, he asked, "Are you sure it's all right for us to be prowling around here this late?"

"It's only eight thirty. Besides, we're not prowling. I'm giving you a private tour of the postprod area." She opened the door to the suite and gestured him inside. "What's going on with that memory-park project?"

"We've hit a little snag, but we'll get back on track."

She sensed there was more to that story, but he didn't elaborate, and she didn't want to pry.

He moved to the center of the room, his gaze sweeping over the space. He pointed at the consoles. "That's a complicated-looking setup."

"Lucky for me, I've got a very talented staff." She spent a few moments naming some of the instruments on the panel and giving a brief explanation of their functions. "I hope I'm not boring you or being too technical."

He shook his head, though he didn't look terribly excited, either. "Whatever happened with the closing sequence? Is it done yet?"

She shook her head. "Unfortunately, no. We were given two treatments and we completed both before I left. The showrunners chose while I was gone, but they still feel the sequence is lacking something. So, we're still tweaking."

"You'll figure it out. I have every confidence in you."

"Thanks. I feel the same way about my team. With-out postproduction and the work performed by my staff on this equipment, *The Shores* wouldn't be the great show so many people know and love."

"So, this is where the magic happens?"

She giggled. "You could say that. The footage we get from next door is pretty raw, and we have to make it look presentable for television."

His brow hitched. "Next door?"

She pointed at the frosted glass wall between her of-fice and the video-editing console. "The set is just on the other side of this wall. There's a door in my office that leads over there."

"Can I see it?"

She sensed the change in his energy, telling her that his true interest lay in touring the set. "Sure, if you want." Leading him through her office to the door she'd referred to, she flipped the switch to turn on the lights.

As light filled the cavernous space, she saw his eyes widen.

"Wow. I didn't realize how huge this place is." He started walking, stopping in the center of the set that acted as the living room of Sierra's character, Karen Drake. "It doesn't look this big from outside."

"People say that all the time." She giggled as she moved toward one of the dolly-mounted cameras. "Ready to make your television debut?" She flipped the switch on the side, and a red light indicated the camera was on.

He laughed, standing in front of Karen's coffee table. "What should I do?"

"Just play along," she teased. "Do something entertaining."

He appeared to be thinking it over. "In that case, I can only think of one thing to do." To her surprise, he grabbed the planner from beneath his arm and flipped it open.

She scoffed. "Don't tell me you're going to read your appointments out loud."

His smile was mischievous. "So that's what you think is in here? Huh." He flipped through the pages, stopping on one. "Tell me what you think of this, Jazmin."

She listened, keeping the camera trained on him.

A breath later, she realized he was reciting...a poem.

For I am the beholder, I wish you could see the
beauty I see
For I am Not the Hunter preying up his prey, for
hurt and pain I shall never bring
For I am Not your Judge, but I will honor you
For I am the King praying I met my Queen
As you stand before me your very essence intoxicates me
All I see is
The intelligence of your mind
The sincerity of your eyes
The strength in your hips
The grace in your stride
Even the lightning bolt that runs down the side
of your body
Lets me know you weathered your own share
of storms
All I want is to be your Peace

When he'd finished, she switched off the camera and slowly walked toward him. "Savion, I had no idea you had that kind of talent."

As she neared him, he grabbed her hand. "No one else knows. I've never shared my poetry with anyone, until now."

A shiver ran through her body, and her heart squeezed inside her chest. "I'm honored." She felt truly special, knowing he'd shared something so private with her. "Your poem is amazing."

"So is my muse." His gaze met hers. "I've never been so inspired as I have these past few weeks."

Heat pooled in her core as their eyes locked. *The lightning bolt that runs down the side of your body... he was talking about my scar.* He'd taken the mark that had brought her shame and described it in such a lyrical, beautiful way. In an awe-filled voice, she repeated, "Amazing..."

She leaned up for his kiss and savored the feeling of his lips and his embrace for as long as she could stand it. When she pulled away, breathless and dazed, she said, "We need to get out of here."

"What's the rush?"

She traced her fingertip along his jawline. "Well, for one thing, Karen's sofa is just a prop. If we make love on it, or any of the furniture in here, it will break."

He gave her a wicked smile. "In that case, let's go."

Hand in hand, they dashed toward her office. On the way out, she flipped the switch again, plunging the fictional world of *The Shores* into darkness.

Savion awoke to the sounds of someone shuffling around in his bedroom. Rolling over in bed, he noticed he was alone. His eyes scanned the room in the soft pre-dawn light until he saw Jazmin. She stood near the foot of the bed and he could tell she was getting dressed.

"Going somewhere?"

She stopped moving, looked his way. "Sorry, I was trying not to wake you."

He stifled a yawn. "No worries."

"Anyway, I've got to be at the studio at seven this morning for meetings, and I still need to run home for a shower and fresh clothes."

He let his head drop back against the softness of the pillow.

She sat down on the end of the bed and started putting on her shoes. Her phone rang, the sound cutting through the silence. Reaching into her pocket, she slipped it out and answered. "Hello? Oh, good morning, Sierra. Thanks for the wake-up call, but I'm up."

He shifted onto his side, knowing it would be intrusive to stare at her while she was on the phone.

"No, I'm still at home, but I'm up and getting ready. Uh-huh. Okay, I'll be there by six forty-five or so. See you then."

He cringed. *Again, with that?* She never seemed to want anyone in her life to know when she was with him. He rubbed his hand over his eyes, shifting his position again to watch her.

She'd put her phone away and gotten into her shoes, and was on her feet. She came around to his side of the bed and leaned down to peck him on the cheek. "I've gotta go."

He caught hold of her hand. "Wait, Jazmin."

She sat down on the edge of the bed. "What is it?"

He drew in a breath. "Why did you tell Sierra you were at home?"

She shrugged. "That's where I'm headed."

"Yeah, but it's not where you are right now." He gestured around. "You're in my house, in my bedroom. You've been here since last night when you willingly came here to make love to me. Remember?"

She pursed her lips. "I remember. How could I forget when you're so spectacular?"

The comment stroked his ego but didn't solve the issue at hand. "I appreciate that, but if I'm so great, why are you keeping me a secret? I thought we were past that?"

She exhaled, ran a finger through her loose, dark curls. "Savion, I love you, you know that."

"I love you, too, baby."

Her lips turned up into a soft smile before she continued. "But I'm a private person. I'm not interested in being the subject of water-cooler gossip at the studio."

He sat up, wanted to be at eye level with her. "I can understand that. But do your parents know we're seeing each other? They aren't going to contribute to that."

She nibbled her bottom lip. "No. But we already talked about that. I don't want to get them started on the grandkid thing again."

He sighed.

Her expression changed then, and she tapped the center of his chest with her index finger. "Wait a minute. You've been hounding me about not telling people about us. Have you told your siblings? Your parents? Your friends?"

He leaned back against his oak headboard. "Troy

knows." That was more due to his cousin's perceptiveness than anything else, but he didn't want to tell her that.

"One person. Your cousin from the West." She threw her hands up. "See? We're pretty much even."

He ran his open palm over his face. The sun now peeked over the horizon, changing and brightening the light flowing through the window. He gazed out at the fence separating his backyard from the wooded area bordering his property, realizing he didn't know what else to say. She was right. "I don't mean to make such a big deal about it. I just don't know what I'm doing here. Remember, I've never been serious about a woman before. I don't know the protocol."

She stood, stretching her arms above her head. "There isn't any protocol. We're supposed to just do what works for both of us." She leaned in, cupped his jaw and pressed her lips against his. "This whole thing is still new. Let's just take it one step at a time, okay?"

"Deal." He patted her behind as she walked away.

"I'll call you later." She strolled out of the room.

He listened to her footsteps as she went down the hall, through the living room and out the front door.

Alone in the quiet of his room, he thought about the exchange they'd had. Part of him thought she was right. They shouldn't rush things. Yet another part of him, the part harboring such an intense love and desire for her, wanted to tell everyone they knew that they were together.

She made a good point. *I haven't really been telling people, either.* He wanted her to acknowledge his presence in her life to the people that were close to her.

He couldn't say why, but he wanted her to do it first. Could it be because none of his previous girlfriends had ever introduced him to their family and friends? He'd never really cared about such things in his relationships before. That was yet another sign of how serious his feelings were for Jazmin.

He grabbed his phone from the nightstand and checked the time. *It's just past six.* He climbed out of bed and headed for the shower. He usually got to the MHI office around eight thirty, but with things being as they were with the memory park, he thought he could stand to go in early.

When he arrived at the office just after eight, he was surprised to find his father sitting behind his desk.

Carver's face was set in a serious expression, his tone somber as he spoke. "Morning, son."

Stepping farther into the office, Savion shut the door behind him. "Good morning, Pop. How was Europe?"

"Wonderful. Your mother and I had a great time." He reclined in the chair. "We were plumb worn-out, though, so decided to cut our trip a little short."

"Glad to hear it."

"That's not why I'm here, though."

Taking the seat across from his father, Savion had a flashback to years ago, when this had been Carver's office and he'd been a newbie, fresh out of college. Back then, his father had seemed so impressive and imposing. Now, he seemed much more of the latter. "I know why you're here, Pop. And I'm sorry things didn't go as planned."

His father chuckled. "I can see you're appropriately

contrite. You do know the project-delay fee is coming out of your salary, right?"

He nodded. "That's fair."

Carver leaned forward over the desk. "Anyway, I didn't come here to lecture you about that, either."

Savion felt his brow furrow. "I'm confused, Pop."

He chuckled again. "I know you are. That's why you made such a silly mistake."

Though he hadn't seen his siblings yet, Savion knew it was a safe guess that Cam had been the one to spill the beans on what he'd done. "Cam never did get over that middle-child syndrome, did he?"

"No, but that's not important. What's important is that if you were so distracted with Ms. Boyd that you flubbed this project, the most crucial one I've ever assigned you, that means something."

He drew in a breath, shifting in his seat. Here was his opportunity to tell someone how much he cared about Jazmin, and he'd be damned if he wasn't going to take it. "I love her, Pop."

"I know that." Carver rested his elbows on the desk, lacing his fingertips together. "The question is, what are you going to do about it?"

Chapter 14

"Jazmin?"

Looking up from the weekly entertainment magazine spread open on her desk, Jazmin saw Drea standing in the door between her office and the production suite. "Yes?"

"We just got some new footage from next door."

"Visual sent over another clip? How long is it?"

She shrugged. "Less than two minutes. Randolph said it just showed up on the video server, in a new file inside the closing-sequence folder."

"Maybe it was a glitch that caused it not to be included last time."

"Or maybe they made file updates?"

She scratched her chin. "Okay. Well, if they want us to add it, go ahead and let Randolph do his thing."

"I'll tell him." Drea shut the office door as she left.

Jazmin looked back down toward her magazine. She'd been trying to read the feature teasing the second season of *The Shores* for the better part of an hour, but she found it impossible to concentrate. As long as she'd been sitting there, staring at the words on the page, the only takeaway she had was from the first paragraph—the show would need to deliver in a big way to top the ratings and buzz it received during its first season. The whole team, cast and crew included, knew there was a lot riding on this season.

With a sigh, she stuck a sticky note on the edge of the page to mark her spot and shut the magazine. There was no use in torturing herself any longer when she knew her concentration was shot.

And what's bothering me? She scoffed. A man. After two and a half years of enjoying a drama-free, single existence, she'd traded that in for a man, one she hadn't heard from in the last two days. Savion hadn't bothered to call or text her since she'd left his house early Wednesday morning. She'd been giving him his space since he seemed upset that day. Now she was beginning to get annoyed.

Should I have told my parents about him? Should I have told Sierra? At this point, if she was to inform them of her involvement with Savion, she didn't even know what she would say. She knew one thing—she loved him. But what would that mean going forward? She had no idea. All the time she'd spent outside of the dating pool had left her a bit rusty in this regard.

"Knock, knock." Sierra swung open the office door.

Jazmin jumped. "Damn, girl. Why didn't you text me that you were coming over here?"

"I did. I texted you like four times. Check your phone, sis." She pointed to the phone, lying faceup on the edge of the desk.

Jazmin noted the flashing notification light and grimaced. "Sorry. You know I keep it on vibrate during the day and I guess I didn't hear it."

Shaking her head, Sierra settled onto the edge of the desk. "We both know that thing vibrates hard enough to rattle this desk, so you must be distracted." She pointed to the magazine. "Don't tell me it's *Entertainment Weekly* that's got your face cracked like that. Because if it is, you need to cancel that subscription."

She shook her head. "I was reading the article about the show, but that's not it."

Sierra studied her face for a few silent moments. Then she snapped her fingers. "It's man trouble."

Jazmin groaned.

"It's Savion!" Sierra slapped the edge of the desk. "It makes perfect sense. Cam says his brother has been impossible ever since you two got back from Wilmington. How was that, by the way?"

Her mind went back to the trip. "The concert was amazing, and Brian…"

Sierra rolled her eyes. "C'mon, Sierra, you know that's not what I meant. It's Brian McKnight, it's not like it wasn't gonna be a good show. I mean, what happened with you and Savion? Did y'all…you know?"

She looked away.

"Oh!" Sierra giggled. "So that's what happened. Cam says Savion's concentration at work is garbage."

Mine is, too. But she didn't say that aloud.

"You're in love with him, aren't you!"

Jazmin frowned. "Girl, keep your voice down. This office isn't exactly soundproof, and there's no reason my team should know my business."

Sierra giggled but complied. Her voice much softer, she said, "Have you told him how you feel?"

She nodded. "And he feels the same. I just don't know what to do with that."

Shaking her head, Sierra stood. "Love can be complex, but it doesn't have to be. You two need to have a real conversation about where this thing between you is going."

"I agree." She laced her fingers together, stretching her arms over the surface of the desk. "I'm not sure how to approach it, though."

"Why don't you just invite him to the cast party tomorrow night? The atmosphere will be super laid-back. Then after the party, you two can go grab a coffee or something and hash this out." She turned toward the door. "I've gotta get back on set. But think about what I said, girl." She disappeared out the office door, leaving it open.

Jazmin mulled over her friend's advice for a few moments. The party, celebrating the completion of filming of the show's first episode, could potentially provide a festive backdrop to break the ice between them. Grabbing her phone, she fired off a text to Savion.

Sorry for the short notice, she began.

Drea poked her head in the door again. "The footage is incorporated. Do you want to take a look at it?"

She shook her head. "I'm out of ideas. Just submit the rough cut for the party tomorrow."

"You're sure?"

"Yes. We've been at this forever. It's possible the

showrunners will love it, and if not, maybe the cast and the rest of the crew will have some helpful input."

"Okay. I'll deliver it to the executive suite."

After Drea left, she finished her text.

…but why don't you swing by the cast party tomorrow at 8?

Sending the text, she relaxed back in her chair and pocketed her phone, telling herself she wasn't going to sit and stare at the screen, waiting for him to reply.

She stood and walked out of the office, through the postproduction suite to the main corridor. "I'm going for a snack. I'll bring back some donuts or something from the lounge."

Randolph tossed up his hand. "Thanks, boss lady."

Trisha, wearing her headphones, didn't look up. Drea offered a nod.

She was walking down the corridor when her phone buzzed on her hip. She snatched it out of her pocket to check it and sighed when she saw a message from her mother.

Ethel Charles next door just had her fourth grandchild. It's a girl.

She could read the subtext, the words her mother hadn't said. Other women her age were enjoying multiple grandchildren, and Jazmin hadn't even given her one. Groaning, she tucked away the phone and headed for the lounge.

Now I really need a donut.

* * *

Seated at the dinner table in his parents' house, Savion forked up some of his mother's lemon-dill salmon and ate it, savoring the flavor. He hadn't been feeling his most social, but he couldn't turn down his parents' dinner invitation. It wasn't just the lure of his mother's cooking that had brought him, though. He wanted to hear all about their weeklong trip.

Viola and Carver occupied the ends of the table, while Hadley sat across from him. Campbell sat to his immediate right, leaving three empty seats around the large table.

"Too bad Sierra and Devon couldn't get away from the set tonight." Campbell popped a roasted potato into his mouth. "They are really missing out."

Viola smiled. "Nonsense. There's plenty of extra for you to take home when you leave."

"You're the best, Mom." Campbell threw two thumbs up in their mother's direction.

Hadley covered a yawn with her hand. "Yeah, Mom. Dinner is great."

Carver looked her way. "Hadley, have you been sleeping? You look tired."

"I am." Hadley stifled another yawn. "All I want to do is sleep lately."

Viola looked at Carver, and Savion noticed the sparkle in his mother's eyes. To his surprise, she said nothing.

"So, Mom, Dad, tell us about your trip." Hadley crunched on a forkful of salad as she watched her parents with an expression of eager anticipation. *That's the most alert she's looked all night.* Savion sipped from his glass of iced tea.

"It was wonderful," Carver began. "Three days in Madrid, three days in Lisbon—"

"And four glorious days in Barcelona." Viola finished the sentence, her gaze locked on her husband's face. "We saw such beautiful sights. The cathedrals. The Royal Palace of Madrid. Plaza Mayor."

"Remember the view from Vasco da Gama Tower in Lisbon?" Carver wiped his mouth with a napkin. "There we were, on the observation deck, five hundred feet above the city. You could see for miles around. Remind me to show you kids the pictures after dinner."

Viola snapped her fingers. "The view was amazing. But my favorite place in Lisbon was Rua Garrett. The shops, the museums, the scenery. It was breathtaking."

"As much as you love to shop, I'm not surprised that was your favorite," Carver quipped.

Cam asked, "What was your favorite part of the trip, Dad?"

Carver scratched his chin for a moment. Then he stood, walked slowly to where his wife sat and placed his hands on her shoulder. "Honestly? Being with your mother was the best part."

Savion smiled, as did his brother and sister. He could see the blush coloring his mother's cheeks.

"When we were in Barcelona, we went down to the coast, to this little place called Sitges. And I held Vi's hand and walked with her along the Mediterranean as the sun was setting. And when I looked at my bride, I realized I still feel the same passion for her I felt when

I married her forty years ago." He leaned down, and kissed Viola's cheek. "I realized how blessed I am."

Viola looked up to her husband with tear-filled eyes and an affectionate smile. "The feeling is mutual, Carver."

The room fell quiet as the children watched their parents bask in each other's love.

Savion knew that his parents had something rare and beautiful, and it made him happy to see the way they appreciated each other. He'd never thought he could have something like that for himself. Jazmin was the first woman to come into his life and make him wonder if he could have it, even long for it.

A sob broke the silence.

All eyes turned to Hadley, who dabbed at her eyes with one of Viola's cloth napkins. Realizing everyone was looking at her, Hadley said, "This is just too sweet!" Moments later, she ran from the table, still in tears.

Cam snorted. "She seems a little bit emotional."

Carver looked at his sons, then back to his wife. "Well, well, well."

Crumpling his napkin, Cam stood and stretched. "I'm stuffed. Couldn't eat another bite." He started gathering the empty plates.

"Make sure you pack up something for my daughter-in-law," Viola instructed as Cam walked past her, carrying the stack of dishes from the table to the kitchen. "Who knows if she's eating well, working all those long hours at the studio."

Carver sat down in the empty seat next to his wife.

Viola said, "I'm really looking forward to this party

tomorrow. I can't wait to see what they've got in store for the second season." She'd been watching the show since the first episode, and since Cam and Sierra had married, she loved being able to brag to her friends about her famous daughter-in-law.

Carver nodded. "It should be fun. But at ten, we're leaving." He chuckled. "I'm old, and I need my sleep."

So, they're both going to the party. He knew his brother and sister would be there, due to their spouses' involvement with the show. Savion thought about the text he'd gotten from Jazmin, the one inviting him to the party. The one he still hadn't answered. If he stayed home, he'd literally be the only Monroe missing from the gathering.

Viola asked, "You're going, aren't you, Savion?"

He shrugged. "Haven't decided yet."

Carver frowned. "Are you avoiding Jazmin?"

"Wow, Pop. Just ask him flat out then." Campbell returned to the room at that moment with a foil-wrapped plate, retaking his seat. He set the packet on the table in front of him. "You gotta be delicate with Savion, you know he's uptight."

Savion rolled his eyes. "Shut up, Cam."

"I'm not wrong, though." Cam leaned back in his chair, crossing his arms over his chest. "Just come to the party, man. Don't be the odd one out."

"Your brother's right. Whatever's going on between you and Jazmin, that's even more reason you should be there."

"I know she invited you."

Savion cut his eyes at Campbell.

"Don't be looking at me like that. You know my wife is her closest friend here, so she told me."

Viola interjected. "Don't be rude, Savion. If she invited you and you don't have any good excuse not to go, then you should go."

Savion sighed. "Fine."

"I hope you'll show up at the party with a little more enthusiasm than that," Carver remarked. "After all, if she's already got your heart in her handbag, there's nothing you can do but give in, son."

He shook his head. His father was probably right, but that didn't mean he had to like it.

Chapter 15

Saturday night, Jazmin stood by the drink station set up inside the main studio space, her glass of punch in hand. It was a little after eight and the celebration had just gotten started. The crew had put in an entire day's work, breaking down and moving the sets off the floor of the studio and storing them away.

Looking around now, she noted how different the studio space appeared in its current configuration. Ten round tables, all set with six chairs each, had been brought in, along with two long rectangular tables that served as the buffet. Della's had catered the event, and as Jazmin looked over the assortment of sandwiches, finger foods and desserts, she knew this would be the night for cheating on her usually healthful eating. The drink station next to her was a large square table, staffed by an intern responsible for serving champagne from several bottles, and the bright red punch from two large crystal bowls.

Glancing around, she searched the assemblage for Savion. He'd finally accepted her invitation to come to the party this morning, but she wondered if he'd changed his mind. She drew a couple of deep, cleansing breaths as she headed for the buffet table. *It's still early. Chill out, girl.*

Della, stationed between the tables stuffed with food, smiled as she approached. "What's the matter, honey? You look like you lost your kitten."

She plastered on a smile. "Just nervous about the season. We put in a lot of work and we want it to be well-received, you know what I mean?"

"I know that's not what's got you looking like that, but okay." She reached over, grabbing a plate. "Listen, honey. You like chicken salad?"

She nodded.

"Good." Della placed a split croissant on the plate and layered one side with chicken salad, lettuce and tomato before assembling it. "Here. A little bit of my famous chicken salad will turn that frown upside down." She handed over the plate. "That and dealing with whatever man who's got your face screwed up." She winked.

She could only chuckle in response as she accepted the plate. "Thanks, Della." She moved on down the table, adding a few fresh strawberries, a mini quiche and a delectable-looking slice of Carmen's double-chocolate cake. Her plate filled, she wandered over to an empty table and sat down.

While she ate, she watched the scene around her.

Her colleagues were mingling, eating, having a great time. Under any other circumstances, she'd be doing the same. This thing with Savion had her so off-kilter, she didn't know what to do with herself. Sierra was right about one thing—they needed to come to an understanding about this relationship. She was ready to commit and be exclusive, but could a playboy like Savion ever be persuaded to get off the dating merry-go-round and get serious with her? His declarations of love were very sweet, and she trusted that his feelings were real. But would that be enough?

As she finished up her food and walked over to toss her trash, Savion walked in. She nearly dropped everything when she saw him. He was dressed in all black—button-down shirt, slacks and loafers with a gold-chain accent at the toe. He stood in the doorway, one large hand in his hip pocket, surveying the room.

Prickles danced down her spine. *He's looking for me.* She quickly dumped her trash and made a beeline in his direction.

His eyes met hers as she approached. "Jazmin. I was looking for you."

She smiled "Hi. I'm glad you could make it. Sorry for the short notice."

"No biggie." He gestured toward the crowd. "Did I miss anything?"

She shook her head. "Devon's going to make a speech, and so is a network exec who flew down from New York, but that hasn't happened yet."

"Cool." He moved closer to her. "When this party is over…"

"I know. We need to talk."

He nodded, then walked over to the drink station.

"Aren't you going to eat something?"

He shook his head. "Not yet. Had a big dinner—Mom's leftovers."

Once they each had a glass of champagne, they returned to the table she'd been sitting at.

The sound of someone tapping a glass with a fork echoed through the space. She turned to see Devon standing in the center of the tables.

"Time for the speeches," Savion remarked.

"I want to thank everyone for coming out tonight." Devon glanced around the room as he spoke. "We have so much to celebrate here at *The Shores*. There's our talented cast, including the newest member, Ms. Zola Revere." He gestured toward Zola, who stood from her seat and graciously accepted the applause that followed. "I want to thank Zola and all our cast members for sharing their gifts with us, and with our audience. Stand up, y'all."

Jazmin looked around and saw Sierra, Grayson and the other actors stand, and she joined in applauding them.

Devon continued once the clapping died down. "We also have our amazing crew, whose hard work makes our show the best it can be. Writers, producers, visuals, tech, equipment operators—everyone who works here is so valuable to what we do. So, if you work on the show, in any capacity, stand up so we can applaud you."

Doing as her boss demanded, Jazmin stood along with her coworkers. Savion looked directly at her as he clapped, and she felt another tingle shoot down her spine.

"So, again, thank you for coming out to help us kick this season off right." Devon raised his glass. "Here's to a brilliant season." Everyone raised their glasses in a toast, and as Jazmin sipped from hers, she noticed Savion watching her silently. *What is he thinking right now?*

Before she could ask, Devon introduced the network executive who was to speak next. She did her level best to listen to the man as he droned on about advertising revenue from the show, ratings numbers and all manner of boring corporate speak. With Savion sitting across from her, regarding her as if he was undressing her in his mind, it was near impossible to focus. She settled for just keeping her gaze on the speaker, though that didn't lessen the impact of Savion's attention.

The man from the network finally wrapped up his speech, and she clapped along with everyone else, mostly out of relief that he was done talking.

"Okay, now it's time to see the end result of all this collective effort." Devon walked over to the projection screen that took up most of the south wall. "Here's the first episode of season two of *The Shores*." He made a hand gesture, signaling the boy in the visuals booth to start the projector, then took his seat.

Jazmin looked at the screen as the opening sequence she and her team created started to play. *It looks great onscreen. I hope the closing sequence looks just as good.*

Sipping from his glass of champagne, Savion watched the episode playing before them. Sierra, being a principle character, got a lot of screen time. He found himself amused and impressed with the antics of his sister-in-law's onscreen persona.

He kept his focus on the screen, occasionally glancing toward Jazmin. She sat across from him at the small table, wearing an expression that conveyed her interest in the show. He assumed it was her first time viewing the episode as well, and he could understand her wanting to see how it had turned out.

I guess they finally got those sequences right. He thought the opening sequence had definitely improved over the season-one version. He considered telling her that, but seeing how into the show she was, he decided it could wait until later. After the party ended, he could give his opinion on the closing sequence, as well.

The plot of the episode revolved around tying up the departure of Fiona Lasalle and introducing her long-lost half sister, Phaedra, in her place. As a resident of the island and someone who knew so many people at the studio, Savion knew that Mia Hopkins, the actress who portrayed Fiona, had been fired for her off-screen bad behavior. On the show, however, the writers had come up with an ingenious explanation for her absence. He watched the scene unfold, almost wishing he'd grabbed some popcorn from the food table.

"Who are you?" Xander demanded of the woman on his doorstep.

"Your other half sister, Phaedra." She pushed past him into the house. "Another child of our playboy father, Terrence LaSalle."

"That I can believe. I see you inherited Dad's boldness." Xander closed the door behind her. "But why are you here?"

"To tell you of the sad demise of our sister, Fiona."
Phaedra's lips trembled. "I'm afraid she won't be back."

Xander made a fist. "I tried to stop her from going
on that trek to climb Mount Everest, but she wouldn't
listen."

Phaedra walked over and touched his shoulder. "I
hear she made it to the top. But she couldn't make it
back down."

Somber, dramatic music queued up as the scene
changed, and Savion could only shake his head. During the first season, Fiona, an enthusiastic outdoorswoman, had casually mentioned such an excursion. If
only Mia had known that line would be used to kill
off her character. He also loved that the writers had
decided to keep the subtle, yet campy humor that had
made the show such a hit.

The drama continued as the episode explored the
lives of the other residents of the fictional world of *The
Shores*, and he felt drawn into the various storylines in
a way he hadn't during the first season. He could tell
the writers had put forth extra effort with the script
and storyline, and the actors were delivering stellar
performances. All in all, he thought Devon should be
very proud of the hard work of everyone involved and
planned to tell him that later.

As the episode continued, he got up to get popcorn
and returned to his seat with the paper bag. Offering
some to Jazmin, he watched as she scooted her chair
closer to his. They shared the snack as they watched
the show together, and he mused on what life would
be like with her as his one and only. Would they spend
nights like this together at his place, curled up on the

sofa watching a movie and trading war stories about the crazy things that happened at their jobs? Or would she even open up enough for them to enjoy things like that?

He understood that she'd been hurt by some jerk who didn't value her. Obviously, the asshole didn't realize what he had. Jazmin was beautiful, intelligent and capable. He wanted something more with her, something special. But he also didn't want to end up paying for another man's mistakes.

He looked over at the table where his parents were sitting with Cam and Sierra. Hadley and Devon were at a table up front. Even Troy had come and was leaning against a wall by the door, enjoying the show while he sipped from a glass of punch. Troy's jeans and cowboy boots stood out among the party wear of the others in attendance, but that was typical of his Western-raised cousin. With the whole Monroe family present, he felt even more compelled to figure things out with Jazmin.

As if reading his thoughts, his father looked in his direction. Meeting his eyes, Carver gave his son a curt nod.

Savion sighed. *The episode is almost over. We'll go somewhere and deal with this as soon as it's done.*

The last scene of the episode was at a memorial service for Fiona. The characters, standing around a large portrait of Fiona, each tossed a rose into a small wooden box. As the box was shut, the image froze and the credits began to roll.

Enthusiastic applause filled the room, and he joined in but kept watching so he could see the entire closing sequence. Since Jazmin and her team had gone through so much trouble pulling it together, he was curious about the result.

Still images of the cast members flipped by, providing a backdrop for the credits. Near the end, though, a video appeared as the name of the production company rolled by.

Savion's mouth dropped open when he realized what was onscreen.

That's me.

As he watched in shock, he saw himself delivering the lines of the poem he'd recited to Jazmin that night in the studio.

I didn't even know she was recording me!

He swiveled to look at her and found her mouth agape, as well. "I… What… How did that get into the sequence?"

He stood. He had no intention of listening to whatever lame excuse she had for this betrayal. "I'm not buying that for a second. You recorded me and didn't even tell me."

"I didn't mean to save the footage and…"

He was already moving toward the exit.

Chapter 16

Jazmin trailed a few steps behind Savion as he strode out of the main studio and into the corridor. "Savion, wait a minute."

He ignored her.

She called his name again, inwardly cursing the high-heeled shoes that were now slowing her down.

He didn't stop, didn't look back. "No. I don't want to hear it."

"Please!" She picked up her pace and caught up to him, grabbing the back of his shirt.

He stopped then, turning blazing eyes on her. "Fine. Say what you have to say, and when you finish, I'm out."

"I don't know how the footage got into the sequence, but I'll make sure they take it out."

"Oh, really." He folded his arms over his chest. "You

don't know how it got included, but you didn't think it was necessary to tell me you were filming me."

"You're right, I shouldn't have done that."

"You're damn straight. Now everyone has seen me reciting my work, and now you want to say what you shouldn't have done. How could you expose me like this?"

She blew out a breath. "You can't think I did this on purpose."

"I can, and I do." His expression remained serious.

"Savion. Listen to me. Yes, I recorded you. I thought you knew the camera was on that night. But I never saved the footage, and I never intended for it to be used."

"Obviously you didn't delete it."

"Don't you remember what happened that night?" She tried to get closer to him, but he took a step back. "We left to make love and I was distracted. We were both distracted."

"Sure, we were. But only one of us did something dishonest."

She looked down at her shoes, her entire being racked with guilt.

He shook his head. "How can I believe you, Jazmin? You told me yourself that you and your team couldn't come up with a good end sequence. That something was missing. I guess you finally figured out what it was."

Tears gathered in her eyes. "I'm so sorry, Savion. Please believe me."

He turned away from her. "I've never shared my poetry with anyone. Never. I wanted to protect my art from the outside world. After all these years, I finally felt safe enough to share it with someone. And you turn around and expose my entire private world to everyone I know, just like that." He started walking once more. "I don't ever want to see you again."

She started walking, too, but when he looked back at her, with the hurt burning in his eyes, she halted her steps.

"I trusted you, Jazmin. Now I see what a terrible mistake that was." He shook his head, then turned and left. Moments later, she heard the heavy metal door that led to the parking lot creak open, then slam shut.

Leaning her back against the wall, she put her face in her hands and let the tears flow.

Motoring down Shoreside Boulevard, Savion cursed aloud.

How could I have trusted her? I should never have told her about my poetry.

He'd gone more than twenty years keeping his writing a secret from everyone, and that had worked out just fine. Now, when he'd finally felt safe enough with someone to share his work, it had backfired spectacularly. He couldn't even articulate the betrayal, the embarrassment he'd felt when he saw himself spread across that huge screen, reading his private thoughts in front of a very public gathering.

He sighed. Anger and hurt warred inside him, and he needed to get somewhere he could clear his mind. He knew of only one place to go, but he'd need to stop by his house first.

When he pulled into his driveway a short time later,

he climbed out of his SUV and went inside. In the bedroom, he changed into a pair of cargo shorts and a brush cotton T-shirt, along with a pair of sturdy sneakers. Tucking his phone into a pocket of the shorts, he searched through his closet for a duffel bag. Then, he tossed a few sets of comfortable clothes and a few other essentials into the bag. As he zipped it up and went into his den to grab his other supplies, his phone vibrated against his hip.

She'd better not be calling me. Slipping the device out of his pocket, he checked the screen. Swiping, he answered the call. "What's up, Troy?"

"What's going on with you, man? I saw you storm out of the party a little while ago."

"It's complicated."

"I bet. I don't know how much you know about the acoustics at the studio, but we could hear you two arguing in the hallway."

He sighed, pressing his fingertips to his temple. "Is there a reason you called, Troy?"

"I just wanted to make sure you were all right."

"I appreciate that."

"I never would have pegged you as a poetic soul, Savion. But I'm impressed with your work."

He gritted his teeth at yet another reminder of the way Jazmin had violated his trust. "That's good to know, but I don't want to talk about that."

"So, what are you going to do, now that the secret is out?"

He sighed. "Nothing. I mean, what can I do? As of right now, I'm getting my rods and supplies together to go out on my boat and leave all this foolishness behind."

"For real? Care for some company?"

His brow hitched. "You want to go out on the water with me?"

"I'm not about to let you go out there alone, not in such a foul mood."

"Troy, are you serious? You don't even like going to the beach." He couldn't imagine a scenario where his cousin would enjoy spending time on the open water.

"True. But that should tell you how much I love ya, fam." He chuckled. "I'm willing to suffer through it, just so you won't be out there, staring at the water and looking sad, all by your lonesome."

Despite his aforementioned "foul mood," Savion could feel his tension lessening a bit. "I hate to admit it, but I could probably use the company." He pulled his favorite rod from the rack in his den closet, setting it next to his tackle box. "Listen. Can you meet me at Sanderson Point Pier in thirty minutes?"

"Yeah. I'm already at your parents' house. All I have to do is change."

"You need to pack a couple of clean outfits. None of that boots-and-jeans stuff, either. I'm talking sweats and shorts, comfortable, nonslip footwear. And bring a jacket and a hat—it gets cool out there."

"Aye, aye, Captain."

He groaned at his cousin's corny joke. "Do you want to fish with me? If so, I'll bring an extra rod for you."

"If I'm going out on the boat with you, I might as well give it a shot. Don't know if I'll be any good at it, though."

He reached into the closet to grab another rod, slipping it into the long vinyl zippered case with his. "Don't worry about it. I'll give you a quick lesson once we're out on the water."

"Sounds like a plan. See you at the pier." Troy disconnected the call.

Pocketing his phone, Savion gathered his duffel, the tackle box and the rod case. Hauling everything outside to the car, he tucked it into the back of his SUV and shut the hatch. His passion for fishing was the main reason he owned such a large sport utility vehicle—it allowed him the space to transport his rods and gear back and forth to the pier.

He returned to the house once more, to fill his softsided cooler with drinks, snacks and sandwich fixings. He typically spent two, at most three days out on the water, since he had comfortable sleeping quarters in the hold. His boat, a gift he'd purchased himself on his thirty-fifth birthday, was named the *Queen of Zamunda*, a reference to his favorite film.

He'd been working so hard lately, it had been months since he'd taken out the *Queen*. Tonight, he planned to rectify that.

He tossed the cooler into the passenger seat along with his journal, then started the engine. He backed out of the driveway, and drove off toward the pier.

Chapter 17

Seated in a pedicure chair at Crowned by Curls Monday afternoon, Jazmin eased her head back against the leather upholstery. The droning of hair dryers and a dozen unrelated conversations going on around her were mere background noise to the soundtrack of guilt playing in her head.

I really screwed things up with Savion. She wished her feelings for him were something she could turn off as easily as Izzy, the nail tech, flipped the switch that controlled the massage function of her chair.

"Jazmin?"

She snapped back to reality at the sound of her name being called. "Huh?"

Izzy chuckled. "I said, lift your foot, honey. I can't get at your heel."

"Oh, sorry." She moved her foot.

"Girl, you are super pitiful right now."

Jazmin swiveled her head to her right, to where Sierra sat in the next pedicure chair. "You know, you could have left me at home, instead of dragging me out here. You knew I'd be terrible company."

Sierra pursed her lips. "And that's exactly why I did drag you out. What kind of friend would I be to just leave you there alone, looking all miserable?"

She shrugged. "A bad one, I guess."

"A terrible one. And how in the world do you zone out like that when somebody's touching your feet? I'm way too ticklish for that." She snorted as the nail tech worked a pumice stone over the outer edge of her right foot. "See?"

"Normally I wouldn't have zoned out. But I have so much on my mind."

"I know, Jaz. And trust me, I understand that you're in pain. But there's no reason you have to look as crappy as you feel."

"She's right," Izzy interjected while filing Jazmin's toenails. "My grandmother had a saying. 'Thank the Lord I don't look like what I've been through.'"

Sierra snapped and nodded in Izzy's direction. "Thank you, Izzy. See, Jaz? Izzy gets it." She leaned toward Jazmin's chair. "That's why we're getting pedicures, manicures and fresh hairdos. It's all on me and I'm not taking no for an answer."

Jazmin couldn't help smiling at her friend's generosity, despite her sadness. "Thanks, Sierra. I really appreciate you doing this for me, even if I am bad company."

"I'm here for you, girl."

She sighed, shifting around in the chair to get into

the ideal position to enjoy the vibrating massage function. "Good. Tell me what to do about Savion."

"Well, let's see. From what I overheard when you two were arguing in the hallway…"

Jazmin's eyes widened. "You heard all that?"

Sierra nodded. "I think everybody did. When y'all rushed out, the room got really quiet. You didn't close the door behind you, and the next thing we heard was you two arguing. Now I see why the boom operators are such sticklers for keeping the doors closed when we're filming."

She sank down in the chair, wishing the buttery leather would swallow her up. "Damn. That makes this whole mess even more embarrassing."

"Anyway, he trusted you enough to share his poetry with you, and now that the footage was shown to everybody at the party, he feels betrayed. Does that sound about right?"

"Yes, that's basically it."

"Meanwhile, let's talk about that poem." Sierra took a sip from the bottle of water next to her chair. "It was beautiful. He wrote that about you?"

A familiar warmth filled her cheeks, and she nodded.

"Honey, if he's got that kind of romantic soul, you've got to make things right with him." Sierra tapped her chin with the tip of her index finger. "First of all, tell me how this all happened."

She briefly recounted the night she'd given Savion a tour of the postproduction suite and the main studio floor. "It's true, I didn't tell him I was filming him. I thought he knew. But I never saved the footage, so I didn't think it would be a big deal."

"Help me out here. Remember, I'm an actress, and I don't really know the technical side of things. Why is it important that you didn't save the footage?"

She thought for a moment on how to explain the situation in the simplest fashion. "Everything is digital now, so video files and still images are saved to the camera's memory during filming. In the past, the visuals department manually uploaded files to the studio server to be processed by postproduction. Any file left on the camera after twenty-four hours that hadn't been uploaded by the team would be deleted automatically."

"Okay, so, if I'm following you, you assumed the footage would be deleted, right?" Sierra watched her intently, awaiting an answer.

"Right. So, I was just as shocked as everybody else to see the footage on the screen." She blew out a breath. "I wanted to get to the bottom of how this happened in the first place. So, I called Devon. He's the showrunner and the studio head, so he knows everything that happens around there."

"What did Devon say?"

"He said they just got a software upgrade for the cameras. Now, instead of manual uploads, all footage taken by the cameras is uploaded automatically to the studio's server, in real time. Then it shows up in the postproduction's department server." She wrung her hands. "Basically, the footage was being uploaded as I filmed it, only I didn't know it."

Sierra's eyes widened. "Well, damn."

"You're telling me. What makes it so bad is, Drea

came to my office and told me new footage had been sent over, but I was too distracted to check it. I just told my team to send in the rough cut of the closing sequence, hoping it would either be just right, or the cast and crew would submit ideas on how to improve it." She shook her head. "Instead, I got myself into a huge mess."

Sierra appeared sympathetic. "It was an honest mistake, Jaz. There was no way you could have known about the upgrade."

"I know. But that doesn't make me feel any better about things."

"Are you still taking feedback on the sequence?"

She shrugged. "Sure. What did you think of it?"

"I loved it. It's perfect." Sierra smiled. "And there's no way you could have known this, but everybody else loved it, too."

"Really?" Jazmin wanted to believe her, as it was the only bit of good news she'd gotten in the last couple of days.

"Yes, really. People were raving about it. And I'm not the only one who thinks Savion is a gifted poet." Sierra touched her arm. "Once you get things straight with him, you should really encourage him to publish his work."

She laughed bitterly. "You mean *if* I can get things straight with him."

Sierra waved her off. "Look, let me give you some advice. You need to make things right with him, and you are fully capable of doing so."

"How? He doesn't even want to talk to me after this royal screwup."

"Have you tried calling him?"

She nodded. "And texting him. And emailing him. I've done everything except send up smoke signals."

"What, no telegraph wire?"

Jazmin rolled her eyes. "Been watching *Dr. Quinn, Medicine Woman* again, Sierra?"

She giggled. "All jokes aside, though, I can find out where he is. Remember, he is my brother-in-law."

"Fine. You locate him, and I'll talk to him."

Pulling out her phone, Sierra tapped the screen a few times, then started thumb typing. "I'm gonna hold you to that."

"Who are you texting?"

"Don't worry about it. Just know I'm gonna find out where he is."

She sighed. "All right. Let's say you can find him and he'll see me. What am I supposed to say to him?"

"You owe him an honest apology and an honest conversation. Lay it all out on the table, just like you explained it to me. Let him decide if he can trust you again."

"What if he can't? Or won't?"

She held her hands up. "At least you will have tried. Accept his decision."

Drawing a deep breath, Jazmin nodded. Sierra hadn't told her what she wanted to hear, but she had given her the sage advice she needed.

If she got the opportunity to speak with Savion, she would do her level best to make him understand what had happened.

Around sunset Monday evening, Savion had the *Queen of Zamunda* anchored about thirty miles offshore. Standing by the port bow, he held the handle of his rod, waiting for a bite. He and Troy had been on the water about thirty-six hours now, and his onboard cooler held the eight fish they'd caught in that time.

The *Queen*, a Yellowfin 42 Offshore model boat, was a showpiece as well as a functional fishing vessel. It boasted a powerful quad outboard motor that helped her glide over the water as smoothly as a hot knife through butter. She was forty feet long, aristo blue thanks to her custom paint job and had a fully lined lower berth featuring two six-foot-six-inch bunks, and a shower and bathroom facilities. He'd purchased the boat because it allowed for both short fishing trips and longer overnight excursions in total comfort.

Troy appeared at the top of the steps then, having just returned from the berth. "How's it going up here?"

"Okay. Haven't had any bites in the last little while, so I might just reel it in." He glanced back at his cousin, who flopped down on the upholstered bench behind him. "Did you figure out how to flush the head yet?"

Troy rolled his eyes. "You mean the toilet? Yeah, I got it." He rubbed his palms up and down his bare arms. "Damn, it's cold!"

"I told you to bring a jacket." He chuckled. "Land-lubber."

"Whatever, man. I gotta say, though. Your boat is pretty friggin' sweet. I know it had to set you back a pretty penny."

He nodded, his gaze still on the rolling surface of the water. "Yes, she was costly. But totally worth it, as you can see."

"Yeah. Never thought I'd be able to take a shower on a damn boat."

"You should come to visit us here on the East Coast more often, Troy. You'll learn a thing or two."

"Word." Troy shifted on the seat. "You know we're running out of food, right? I just drank the last beer."

Savion shrugged. "We'll be good for another night, I think."

"Nah, man." Troy shook his head. "It's like you said. I'm a 'landlubber.' You've had me out here plenty long enough and I'm not staying out here another night."

"Why not? You got a pressing engagement on shore?"

He frowned. "Savion, stop tripping. If you wanna stay out here another night, you gonna have to run me to the pier so I can drive myself back to Aunt Vi and Uncle Carver's house."

"Really? I thought you said I shouldn't be out here alone?" Savion gave up on catching anything else and started turning his reel to bring his line in. "How are you gonna abandon me like that?"

"Oh, please. We both know the catch you really want is on the island. So, when are we going back?"

"I don't know." Savion stared out over the water, as he'd been doing since they'd left shore, but seeing only Jazmin's face. His heart ached at the thought of her, but he couldn't just toss his feelings for her out with the trash. Still, he didn't want to see her, not yet. It was times like this that he resented how small and close-knit the island's community was. *I don't want to risk running into her, because that will only remind me of her betrayal.*

Troy asked, "Why did we even come out here? Are you hiding from her?"

"No." He was absolutely hiding from her. But he wasn't about to tell Troy that.

"Then why fishing? You could have gone anywhere you wanted. Hell, you could have gotten on a plane, you're grown."

Savion shrugged. "Dad brought us fishing a lot as kids. Cam and Hadley don't really do it very often anymore. But when Cam's upset, he still watches *Bassmasters*. I'm a man of action. So instead of watching other folks fish, I do it."

"Okay, then let's go back, Mr. Action." Troy stood, pacing the deck. "I'm a cowboy, not a sailor. Get me back on dry land or it's gonna be a problem, cousin."

Savion shook his head. "All right, all right. Anything to stop your complaining." Moving to the console, he raised the anchor and turned the boat back toward land.

As he guided his vessel over the sparkling surface of the water, he wondered what awaited him when he returned to shore. He'd taken a personal day off work to allow him some extra time on the water. He'd have four days to prepare for the ribbon-cutting ceremony at the memory park, which was thankfully back on track now. No one had called the satellite phone on the boat since he'd been gone, which meant there hadn't been any serious emergencies. Once they got closer to shore and cell-phone signals got stronger, he'd probably get a whole heap of text messages and email alerts, but he'd deal with those once he was back home.

Troy came to stand behind him, giving him a playful slap on the shoulder. "Buck up, Captain. You'll get your damsel back."

Shaking his head, Savion focused on getting his goofy cousin back to his beloved dry ground.

Chapter 18

Early Tuesday morning, Jazmin pulled her car into a parking space at the health complex and cut the engine. She got out of the car and walked toward the track, looking around to see where her walking partners were.

She spotted Hadley and Sierra sitting on a bench by the track. Heading over, she planned to say good morning. But when she got closer to them, she could tell something was wrong. "Hey, what's going on?"

Sierra, who had her arm draped around Hadley's shoulders, said, "Girl, I don't know. But Hadley's a mess."

Hadley, her face pale and drawn, looked up at Jazmin. "I'm so nauseous. And my head is pounding."

Jazmin cringed, taking a giant step back. "When did this happen?"

Sierra shrugged. "A few minutes ago, when we got

out of the car. She rode with me, and she was fine when we were driving over."

"It's that smell," Hadley whined. "Don't y'all smell it? It's awful!"

Confused, Jazmin sniffed the air. "I don't smell anything."

"I don't, either." Sierra followed suit and took a deep breath. "Except…freshly cut grass."

Jazmin looked down at her shoes, saw the clippings clinging to the pink suede. The grass had recently been cut, but what did that have to do with how Hadley felt? "Allergies, maybe?"

Sierra shrugged. "I don't know. Anyway, I'm taking her to urgent care. Whatever's going on with her, she needs to get checked out."

Jazmin nodded. "I'll follow you over there."

They helped the ailing Hadley into the passenger seat of Sierra's car, then she climbed in and drove off, with Jazmin following close behind. The two cars made it to Stinger Urgent Care in less than fifteen minutes. As they walked to the lobby, Jazmin put in a quick call to the studio and asked to be put through to the suite. "Postproduction department, Randolph speaking."

"Hey, Randolph, it's Jazmin."

"What's going on, boss lady?"

"I'm going to be in late this morning. I'm at the urgent care with a friend. Can you all hold things down until I can get there?"

"Sure thing."

She ended the call with him as she and Sierra took seats in the empty lobby. While Hadley walked over to the reception desk, Jazmin asked, "Did you let Devon know we're here?"

Sierra nodded. "Yes. I also told him we'd take care of her. He was about to leave the studio and drive over here."

"He's a good husband." Knowing Devon was so concerned about his wife made her smile.

"Shouldn't take long for her to get seen. After all, there's nobody else here."

Sure enough, a nurse escorted Hadley through the door to the interior of the clinic a few minutes later.

Sierra turned her attention back to Jazmin. "So, any progress with Savion?"

She shook her head. "No."

"Come on, now." Sierra frowned. "Didn't I get the intel for you on where he was, just like I promised I would?"

"Yes, yes, I know. He took his fishing boat out for a few days."

"And that's why he wasn't answering your calls and texts. There's no real signal out on the open water."

She looked at her hands in her lap, not wanting to look at her friend's perturbed face.

"He's back on land now, Jazmin. So, you really don't have any excuse for not reaching out to him again."

"Sierra, I told you. I don't know what to say to him."

She rolled her eyes. "Girl, are you really sitting here in public, wearing a tank top and telling me you don't know what to say to him? Really?"

Bewildered, she asked, "What does this have to do with my workout clothes?"

"You don't even realize it, do you?"

Still confused, she tilted her head to the right. "Apparently not, Sierra."

"Look, you've been covering up your scar for two whole years. You were never seen in public with the scar visible. Remember when we were out, buying dresses for my in-laws' anniversary party? You passed up at least half a dozen gorgeous dresses because they would have shown that damn scar." She tapped her index finger against the center of Jazmin's forehead. "Hello. Girl, look at you now. Showing it without any shame whatsoever."

Jazmin glanced down at her shoulder. She hadn't really thought about it, but now that Sierra had pointed it out... "You're right. I wasn't even thinking about it when I got dressed this morning."

"It's not just today. The dress you wore to the cast party was a halter. As a matter of fact, you've changed the way you dress ever since..." She stared up at the ceiling as if thinking about it.

"Ever since I got back from that trip I took with Savion."

She snapped her fingers. "Bingo. Now, what does that tell you?"

Thinking back to that night at the inn, she recalled the way he'd kissed along her scar, all while telling her how beautiful and perfect she was. Then he'd made love to her, with the breeze blowing and the moonlight shining on the bed. That night, he'd laid claim to her soul as well as her body.

"I'm not gonna ask for the play-by-play, not while we're in public, anyway. But whatever happened between you two was profound." She touched her shoulder. "He helped you break through your shame. Shame you shouldn't have carried. No woman should carry."

Jazmin opened her mouth to say something but stopped when she saw Hadley being escorted back to the lobby by a nurse. Hadley's eyes were wide, and she looked a bit shaky on her feet as she held a small square of paper in one hand.

She and Sierra got up and walked over to Hadley.

Sierra grabbed her free hand. "Girl, are you okay? You look like they gave you shock therapy or something."

Hadley shook her head.

Jazmin asked, "Did they say what's wrong with you? What's that in your hand?"

Still wide-eyed, Hadley held up the paper. "It's…a prescription for…vitamins."

"Okay, I'll take you to get it filled," Sierra offered. "But if you don't tell us what's wrong I'm gonna burst."

Hadley stammered, "I'm—I'm…pregnant."

Stunned silence fell among the three women for a moment.

Then Sierra squealed, "I'm gonna be an auntie!"

"Wow." Jazmin giggled. "Congratulations, Hadley."

The two women hugged their poor shocked friend, then escorted her out to the car, laughing and talking the whole way.

"What's on your mind, son?"

Savion glanced at his father for a moment, before returning his gaze to the rolling green lawn behind his parents' home. "Nothing, Pop."

Shifting on his lounge chair, Carver gave him a censuring look. "Savion Fitzgerald Monroe. You're my old-est child, so you've been with me and Vi the longest. And I know you know better than to sit on my patio and tell me a lie."

He blew out a breath. "How about this? Tell me what you think about the memory-park project, then I'll tell you what I'm thinking about."

Carver shrugged. "Fair enough. You know, despite your little mistake, things are settling out with the park. Everything is in place for the ribbon-cutting ceremony in a few days."

"That's good to know. And, again, Pop, I'm sorry I was so careless."

Carver waved him off. "It's not a big deal. Actually, this worked out better than I intended."

He looked his father's way. "How?"

"If we stick to the plan from here on out, the park should open on a very special date. August sixteenth."

For the first time this week, Savion felt a genuine smile tugging at his lips. "Gram's birthday."

"Right. I was so focused on getting it open in June before hurricane season kicked off, I didn't even think of holding off until her birthday. Sure, we'll miss some of the summer tourist crowd, but there's always next summer, isn't there?"

"Certainly. The Mary Ellen Monroe Memory Park will be around for a long, long time." He sat back in his own lounger, reclining against the cushioned backrest.

"Now, tell me what's bothering you. You still haven't spoken to Jazmin, I'm guessing."

He shook his head. "No. She tried to contact me

over the weekend while I was out on the boat, but she hasn't reached out recently."

"And what's stopping you from reaching out to her?"

"Pop, I don't want to deal with her right now."

Carver frowned. "Why? Because you love her, and you're scared of where that could lead?"

He stared at his father, amazed at his keen perception. "Pop, I can't do this with her right now."

"What is it, exactly, that you can't do?"

"Be with her. Don't you see?" He sat up again, suddenly feeling antsy. "My workload at the office has tripled since Cam and Hadley got married. I'm the last one in the office who can fully focus on keeping MHI in the black. If I pursue this thing with Jazmin, then what happens to the family business? You worked so hard to build it, Pop."

Carver cleared his throat. "We."

"Huh?"

"*We* worked so hard to build MHI. We, as in, your mother and I." He leaned forward. "Stop using work as an excuse to avoid relationships, boy."

"But, Pop, I—"

"No, listen, son. Here's what you need to understand. MHI would not be the successful business it is today without your mother. It's not just about having her by my side, acting as my partner in the business. It's about having her as my partner in *life*."

Savion scratched his chin. "I've never thought about that. But you and Mom are different."

"How? You can't go through life pushing people away in some misguided quest for success." Carver stood, walked over to his son and sat down next to him. "The family company is one of my proudest accomplishments. But do you know the greatest thing I've ever done?"

"What is it?"

"Marry your mother. Without her, none of what I have would be possible. She supported me in business, and her love gave me the drive and motivation to work hard. She made our house a home and protected my heart from a cruel world. And she gave me you, Campbell and Hadley." He touched Savion's shoulder. "You may think MHI is my legacy. My true legacy lies in you and your siblings."

Savion watched his father quietly, not knowing what to say.

"Do you love her, Savion?"

He nodded. "Yes. I do, Pop." Regardless of the fight they'd had, his love for her was his truth. It had settled deep down in his soul and there was no going back.

"The love of a good woman, the right woman, can push you to levels of greatness you never thought possible." He squeezed his shoulder. "I'm not telling you what to do, son, because you're an adult. But you'd better think twice before you throw this opportunity away."

Carver got up then and headed for the back door. "I'm going in. It's getting too hot out here for an old man." He opened the sliding door, but paused. "Are you coming?"

Savion shook his head. "Not just yet."

With a nod, Carver disappeared into the house, sliding the door shut behind him.

Lying back on the lounger, he stared up at the endless blue sky. In less than two hours, it would turn to darkness. But for now, the puffy clouds moved by, passing over the island and momentarily dimming the sunlight.

His father's words replayed in his head. *The love of a good woman, the right woman, can push you to levels of greatness you never thought possible.* Could Jazmin be the one? They were each bringing their own separate issues to this relationship. Could they overcome those things and build a life together? And most of all, could he trust her? He had far more questions than answers.

Still, what they shared deserved at least a fighting chance. He resolved to hear her out if she reached out to him again. The least he could do was try, and they could see where things ended up.

Chapter 19

Don't chicken out.
   You can do this.

Drawing a deep breath, Jazmin raised her hand, folded her fingers and knocked on Savion's door. It was Wednesday evening, and she knew he was home since she'd just parked in the driveway behind his SUV.

I've cut off his escape route. Now he'll have to listen to me. She giggled at her own little joke, even as her frayed nerves threatened to make her cry. Mindful of the conversation she'd had with Sierra, she'd chosen her outfit carefully. Cutoff denim shorts, jeweled sandals and a fuchsia tube top. The top, a relic from the recesses of her closet, was the perfect thing to wear tonight.

She knocked again, this time with a little more force. Just in case he hadn't heard the first time.

Legs shaking, palms sweating, she waited.

Finally, she heard his deep voice call out from the other side of the door. "Who is it?"

"Jazmin."

There was a shuffling sound, then a few clicks as he unlocked the door.

When he swung it open, all the air left her body in a whoosh. He was dressed in a pair of light gray sweatpants but was barefoot and shirtless. He had a small white towel draped over his left shoulder. The rippling muscles of his upper body were slick with moisture. A strong, masculine scent emanated from him, a mixture of citrus, pine and something subtly smoky.

Is that sweat? She licked her lips, then swallowed. "Hi."

His expression flat, he responded in kind.

Her mind started to play through several scenarios of what he might have been doing, but she shook off those thoughts as best she could. "Am I…interrupting?"

He shook his head. "Not really. Just finished working out."

She could imagine him, lying on his back on a weight bench, his powerful arms flexing as he lifted and lowered a heavy barbell. "Oh, okay." She shifted her weight nervously from left to right. "Listen, would you mind if I come in? I really think we need to talk."

His expression softened. It wasn't quite a smile, but it was a definite improvement. "Come on in." He moved aside, allowing her entry.

Once she'd stepped onto the gleaming hardwood floor and into his living room, he shut the door behind her.

She glanced around his home, taking in the African-inspired art, deep blue walls and minimalist decor. The last time she'd been here, she'd not been looking at the furnishings. "Your home is lovely."

"Thanks." He gestured to the bright white contemporary sofa. "Have a seat."

She did, never taking her eyes off him.

He toweled himself off, then tossed the cloth back over his shoulder before sitting in the matching armchair across from her. "So, you wanted to talk. I'm listening."

She drew a deep breath, choosing her words carefully. "Savion, I can't begin to tell you how sorry I am about what happened. I swear to you, I never intended for your poetry to be inserted into the show."

He nodded but said nothing.

She continued her explanation by giving him the basics, just as she'd told it to Sierra. "So, at the time I was filming you, I didn't know the footage was being uploaded." She laced her fingers together, placed her hands on her lap. "Regardless of that, I should never have filmed you without your explicit permission. It was a stupid whim, and I'm so sorry for doing that."

He stroked his chin yet remained silent.

"Look at me, Savion. Look at what I'm wearing." She gestured to the tube top. "I've been hiding my scar for so long because it reminded me of what I endured. It made me feel unattractive and ashamed. Then you came along. You saw my biggest flaw and called it beauty. Hell, you even wrote about it. And I realized, I don't have to be ashamed anymore. Because *I* have nothing to be ashamed of."

"You got all that from me?"

She nodded. "Yes, Savion, I did. And not only am I done hiding my scar, I'm ready to do something proactive. No more running from my past. I'm going to start a foundation for battered women, do some speaking engagements." She shrugged. "I have no idea how to go about any of this, but I'm willing to do the work of finding out. Maybe my story can help someone else find their healing."

A ghost of a smile crossed his face. "That's great to hear. I applaud you for getting to that place of positivity, Jazmin. And I can forgive you for your mistakes." His tone was calm, even. "I just need to know you understand how this has affected me."

She placed her hand over her heart. "I don't, but I'm willing to listen. What I do know is that I underestimated the intimacy of the situation. At first, I didn't know you were about to recite a poem. But I should have shut the camera off the minute I knew."

His expression changed then, as if he was impressed by something she'd said. "Intimacy. Now you're starting to see where I'm coming from." He stood, started to pace as he spoke. "The reason I never shared my poetry with anyone is that I consider my writing to be extremely personal. My poems contain so many of my innermost thoughts, dreams…" He paused, locked eyes with her. "Even my fantasies."

She inhaled sharply, feeling the weight of his gaze as if he'd touched her.

He started pacing again. "That's why it hurt me so much to have my writing put on public display. For me, reading my work to you was an act of complete intimacy. I was sharing my mind and soul with you, just like we shared our bodies when we made love."

She felt tears gathering in her eyes. "Savion, your words were so potent, so beautiful. I was moved. And knowing that you wrote about me makes me feel beyond special."

He came to the sofa, sat down next to her. "You've been a muse to me since the first time I saw you, Jazmin. It was a little over a year ago when the studio first opened. I was running on the beach early one morning, down by Richardson Point. Some of the crew had gathered on the beach, I guess to talk about filming. You were all standing by the pier. When I ran past and saw you talking to Devon, I was so distracted by you, I missed a step and nearly busted my ass."

She laughed as the tears streamed down her face. "Did you write about that incident?"

He nodded. "I sure did. If you're good, I might let you read it someday."

Hope glimmered inside her. "Does this mean you forgive me, Savion?"

He used his thumbs to brush away her tears. "Yes, Jazmin. I love you too much to let you go. It's taken me some time, and some lecturing from my father, but I've finally realized how much I need you in my life."

She released a sob, but this one was fueled by joy instead of sadness.

He pulled her against him, holding her tight against his chest.

When the tears subsided enough for her to speak, she whispered, "I love you, too. So, so much."

After spending a few long moments savoring the feeling of having her in his arms again, Savion released Jazmin and sat back a bit.

She looked at him with smiling, damp eyes. "What is it, Savion?"

He scratched his chin, feeling the desire rise within him. "You know, before you showed up, I was on my way to take a shower."

Passion gleaming in her eyes, she took the bait. "Care for some company?"

He brushed his fingertips over her jawline. "Hell yes."

He stood, and moments later, she squealed as he tossed her over his shoulder and carried her down the hallway toward his master suite. Inside his bedroom, he took his time kissing and caressing her out of her clothing. By the time she was naked, she was trembling.

"Are you cold?"

She shook her head. "No. But I'm very, very hot for you, Savion Monroe."

He grinned. "That's just what I wanted to hear, baby." He stripped off his sweatpants and boxers.

Her gaze shifted down, then back up to meet his eyes as her tongue darted out and slid over her lower lip.

Taking her hand, he led her into his bathroom. The shower stall, enclosed in glass on three sides, had been custom-built after he purchased the house. It was large enough for several people; even though he showered alone, his height meant he needed space. There were three showerheads—one on the left, one on the right and a huge rainfall one mounted above the shower stall.

After opening the door, he stepped inside and started the flow of water from the two lower heads. He beckoned her with his curled finger, holding the door open. "Come here and test the water."

She stepped inside the stall with him and he let the door close. Running her hand under the water, she nodded. "It's perfect."

He turned on the rainfall head, stepped beneath the rush of water and pulled her close to him. With the steam swirling around them, he kissed her. She slipped her arms around his neck while he wove his fingers into her soaked curls. Water cascaded down his face and body, and as the kiss deepened, his desire for her only grew.

Stepping aside from the flow, he watched her. She stood before him trembling, still partially beneath the center showerhead. For the moment, he simply enjoyed the sight of the water cascading down her body, flowing over all the parts of her he wanted to please.

He leaned down, working the tip of his tongue over her nipples. She twisted and purred as he held on to her waist, keeping her near, so he could savor the dark points. Moving lower, he placed soft kisses on the plane of her belly, continuing his journey down her body until he kneeled on the tiled floor.

He moved his hand over her bottom, then beneath her thigh. Using his other hand to steady her, he lifted her leg and placed it over his shoulder. A growl left his lips as he leaned into her and buried his face between her thighs.

Her legs buckled, but he kept her stable as he worked his tongue over her most sensitive flesh. She was sweet and fragrant with desire, and as he moved his fingertips to her opening, he could feel the warm, slippery evidence of her need. Her hips undulated in tiny circular motions that expressed her ecstasy, and her soft cries rose above the sound of the water, reverberating off the walls of the shower. He kissed her there, over and over, before swirling his tongue around her hard little clit.

She came then, her hips thrusting forward as her back arched, and he held on to her wet, slick hips to make sure she wouldn't slip to the floor as she rode out her climax.

He stood again, and she fell into his arms, leaning up for his kiss. As their lips touched, their hands toured each other's bodies. While he caressed her skin, the water aiding his exploration, he knew he could never get enough of her, not even if they made love for an eternity.

She drew back from him, looking up to him with passion-hooded eyes. "Now, Savion. Please."

He knew what she was begging for and he wouldn't deny her any longer. He lifted her up, and she wrapped her legs around his waist as he pressed her back against the shower wall. Adjusting his hips between her open thighs, he probed her with his hardness, eliciting a sharp inhale. Tilting his hips back, then forward, he pushed the tip of his dick inside her.

Her tightness made him growl, and after lingering a few seconds, he eased himself deeper, deeper still until he was fully engulfed in her feminine warmth. A long, low moan escaped her lips as he filled her. And when he began to stroke her, his hands squeezing her ass as he moved inside her, she evaporated into a series of high-pitched cries.

Steam enveloped the entire stall as he made love to her. His body begged for release and he kept a tenuous hold on his crisis, wanting to see her climb the heights of passion first.

"Mine," he groaned, thrusting deeper.

"Yes" was her strangled reply.

He kept going, picking up the pace, hoping to brand his name across her very soul. Her cries rose an octave as he moved her away from the wall. Still gripping her hips, he pounded into her, raising and lowering her to meet his thrusts.

She screamed, the sound splitting the silence, and he felt her body pulsing around him moments before his orgasm tore through him. His legs buckled, and he barely managed to snatch one hand from beneath her in time to slap his palm against the wall for balance.

She clung to him in the ensuing silence, her slick body pressed against his. He savored the moment, feeling his heart swell with a love so strong, he could barely breathe.

Chapter 20

As Thursday dawned, Jazmin opened her sleepy eyes in the dim light. Blinking a few times, she came to full awareness of the heavy, muscular arm draped over her naked hips. The realization of what had happened made her smile. She was in Savion's bed, and best of all, in his heart.

She didn't dare roll over, because she didn't want to wake him. His soft snores ruffled the silence, and she snuggled down in the sheets, content to enjoy the feeling of his embrace.

The practical side of her intruded on her contentment as she wondered what time it was. Filming of the rest of season two was happening at the studio, which left little work for her in postproduction. Still, there was the matter of correcting the closing sequence, and of doing research into starting her nonprofit foundation.

She yawned, smothering it with her hand. *Maybe I'll just go in late today.*

He stirred then, groaning as he came awake. "Good morning."

"Good morning." She leaned in for his kiss. "How'd you sleep?"

"Pretty good, considering how little sleep I actually got." He reached around her, slapped her ass playfully.

"We've gotta get up, you know. Got to work, be adults and all that."

"Oh, I have some very adult things I want to do to you, right here in this bed." A wicked gleam sparkled in his dark eyes.

She teased, "Didn't you get enough last night?" He'd made love to her four times before they'd finally fallen asleep.

He shook his head. "Never. I can never get enough of you, baby." He shifted, moving his body against her until she could feel the hard evidence of his sentiment pressing into her stomach.

She licked her lips, unable to resist the lure of him. She rolled over onto her back, then slipped her hands beneath the sheets to draw him on top of her.

Later, after yet another satisfying session of love-making, she rolled away from him and grabbed her phone from his nightstand. "Okay. We really have to get up now. It's after eight."

He sighed. "I guess you're right. I would take a day off, but with the ribbon cutting being tomorrow, I'll be needed around the office."

She sat up, then swung her legs over the side of the bed and stood up. "I never know what's going to happen in the production suite. So, I should probably go in, too."

"Since we're both late, at least let me make you a little something to eat."

"Sounds nice."

They both took quick, separate showers, then dressed and met in the kitchen. Savion, in his uniform of dark blue button-down and black slacks, made a pot of coffee while he scrambled a few eggs. Adding toast and a handful of strawberries, he set the two plates down on the table. "Voilà."

"Thank you. It looks great."

"What time are you going in?"

"Ten. That's about as early as I can manage, considering…" She gave him a look.

"I know. I told Cam I'd be in by ten thirty."

She forked up some of the eggs. "About your poetry, Savion."

"What about it?" He watched her over his steaming mug of coffee.

"Have you ever thought about getting it published?"

He looked thoughtful for a moment, then shook his head. "I never thought about that. To me, my writing is more of a hobby."

"I heard that people at the party were really impressed with your poem."

His brow hitched. "Who told you that?"

"Sierra. She said everyone was talking about it, and one person even cried."

He scratched his chin. "You know, Troy went out on the boat with me, and he said essentially the same thing."

"See? Your words have the power to move people, Savion. Why wouldn't you want to share that gift with the world?"

He was quiet for a little while. "I'll think about it."

"That's all I ask." She finished her food. "Well, that, and for you to help me out with this nonprofit I want to start."

He set down his mug. "What would you want me to do?"

"I'm not sure yet. I'd definitely want you to travel with me when I go places to speak, though."

He nodded. "Whatever you need, baby. We'll make it work."

She smiled, coming around to his side of the table. Easing into his lap, she put her arms around his neck. "So, we're really going to do this thing, huh?"

He squeezed her close. "We sure as hell are. And we're gonna rock it 'til the wheels fall off, as they say."

"I love you, Savion."

He brushed his lips against hers. "I love you more."

At the ribbon-cutting the next day, Savion couldn't wait until the ceremony was over. He'd seen Jazmin arrive right before the event began, dressed in a bare-shouldered yellow sundress that showed off her sweet curves and bronze shoulders. He nodded to her, a smile pulling up his face.

"I see you took my advice," his father said from the chair next to him on the dais set up before a ribboned entrance to the work site and a small tent for refreshments. "Everything all right now?"

"Right as rain," Savion said, then stood and went to the podium for opening remarks.

The short but moving ceremony went off without a hitch, and after the speeches, the ribbon cutting itself and the handshakes with dignitaries, Savion rushed to find Jazmin. She was sipping a glass of punch when he approached, and she put it down on the table to greet him.

But he did more than say hello. He swept her into an intense hug, planting a kiss on her lips that she eagerly returned.

"Nice to see you, too," she teased.

"No more hiding in the shadows. I want everyone to know we're together."

"So do I," she said, and he noticed her winking at Sierra, who stood nearby. "In fact, I've told my parents I want to FaceTime with them in an hour, to share some great news." She looked him in the eye. "You available?"

He grinned, the warmth of his love cascading through his body.

"For you, baby, I'm available...forever."

Midsummer

The cool breeze flowing over the Appalachian Mountains touched Savion's face, and he inhaled deeply. Up here, the air was so fresh and invigorating, he wondered how he even functioned closer to sea level.

He stood on the balcony of his cabin high above the rest of the world, draped in a thick cotton robe. Looking out over the tops of the towering green pines, he felt a sense of peace wash over him.

Jazmin appeared behind him then, slipping her arms around his waist and leaning her head against his back. "I can't believe we just ran off and eloped. Your parents are going to freak out, big-time."

He shrugged. "They were so wrapped up in planning Hadley's baby shower and getting ready for a grandchild, it was easy to slip away." He chuckled. "Hell, they might not even have noticed we're gone yet. It's only been a day and a half."

"Still. I would never have expected I'd do something like this."

He turned around to face her. She wore a robe just like his, and he knew she had nothing on beneath it. Drawing her into his arms, he teased a fingertip over her full lips. "That's why I'm in your life. Adventure."

She laughed. "If you say so."

"You say my parents are going to be mad. What about yours?"

"Are you kidding me? You met my parents. They're so desperate for a grandchild, this won't even register for them. When I call them up and tell them we got married, they'll just start asking when the baby is coming."

He leaned down, placing a kiss against the fragrant hollow of her neck. "In that case, we'd better get busy making that baby. Can't keep them waiting."

She sighed, melting against him. "Savion."

He kneeled and placed a soft kiss against her knee.

Her lips formed an O shape, but only a tiny squeaking sound came out.

"Hmm?" He continued to nibble on her knee as he worked the belt of her robe free and slipped it down her shoulders.

She caught it. "What are you doing? We can't do… that…out here!"

He chuckled. "Baby, there aren't any other cabins for miles. There's no one out here to see you naked… or hear you scream."

She released her grip on the robe, letting it pool on the balcony's wooden floor. Admiring her gorgeous nudity in the sunlight, he ran his palms over her hardened nipples and savored the moan she gave in response.

"I know we're on the mountaintop," he said softly. "But let's see if we can't get you a little bit higher, baby."

And soon, her cries of pleasure were echoing in the silence of the forest.

* * * * *

MILLS & BOON
Desire

Indulge in secrets and scandal, intense drama and plenty of sizzling hot action with powerful and passionate heroes who have it all: wealth, status, good looks… everything but the right woman.

Six Desire stories published every month, find them all at:

millsandboon.co.uk

LET'S TALK
Romance

For exclusive extracts, competitions
and special offers, find us online:

f facebook.com/millsandboon

🐦 @MillsandBoon

⬜ @MillsandBoonUK

Get in touch on 01413 063232

For all the latest titles coming soon, visit
millsandboon.co.uk/nextmonth

MILLS & BOON
True Love
Romance from the Heart

Celebrate true love with tender stories of heartfelt romance, from the rush of falling in love to the joy a new baby can bring, and a focus on the emotional heart of a relationship.

MILLS & BOON
MODERN
Power and Passion

Prepare to be swept off your feet by sophisticated, sexy and seductive heroes, in some of the world's most glamourous and romantic locations, where power and passion collide.